SENTINELS OF CREATION

Dear Rick –

To the world's best
Healer & even better

Friend.

XXX OOO

Dear Rick —

To the world's best
Healer & even better
Friend.

ooo XXX

SENTINELS OF CREATION

A Power Renewed

ROBERT W. ROSS

ISBN-13: 9781523842506
ISBN-10: 1523842504

For my family: Mom who read me Narnia and cried with me through Charlotte's Web; Rachel who is my best friend and the love of my life, Tumnal-Kitty who inspired my Juliet, The Bendamin who taught me to be kind, My Little-Boy whose peaceful outlook I try to emulate, and his lovely new bride who has brought much joy by joining our motley crew.

Chapter 1

PROLOGUE

Mist rolled lazily across a placid lake as the horizon colored with the coming dawn. Two figures sat quietly, shoulders touching, their posture conveying both contemplation and intimacy.

"But Michael, why speak to Him at all? I cannot fathom it."

Michael gazed at his brother who sat stoically, great white wings folded tightly down his back. "Your challenge, Raphael, lies in learning to accept God's will rather than fathoming it."

Raphael sighed. "Michael, please, let us not begin another endless debate. I love you and hate that we see things so differently. You know the endless suffering He will cause if left unfettered."

"Do not assume to know God's mind, my brother. He sees to the finish; we do not. Your assumptions are...prideful."

Raphael flinched as though he'd been struck. He closed his eyes against the horror of it and Michael immediately regretted his words. At times, Raphael seemed so fragile - so like the mortals who were his divine charge. Michael could see the tears slowly seep from beneath the luxurious lashes. A single tear from each eye slipped silently down Raphael's cheeks and gathered by his lips. As had happened so many times before, Michael was struck by his beauty, his tenderness, his empathy. Truly, Raphael represented all that was fine.

"I am prideful," whispered Raphael, "I am no better than He who is fallen; I share his sin, Michael. Oh, Michael, I feel it within me."

"Hush Raphael. You are not as He! Your pride is such a little thing; speak no more of it."

"No, you are wrong. There can be no gradations, my brother. Truly, I am guilty."

"Fine, then be guilty. But know that the fount of your pride lies in your love for the task with which God has charged you. You seek not to raise yourself above Him. Rather you desire only to exalt Him further by your accomplishments. I know your heart Raphael and it is pure. I will not suffer you to compare yourself to Luc-"

"No!! Do not say His name. Especially when He is so near."

"Lucifer! Raphael, let the name ring out. The battle is won. He is fallen. Hallelujah!! The time for fear is past. We must be strong. Perhaps you above all others. Lucifer has lost his battle to usurp the throne of heaven. Now he seeks to destroy that which God loves. You, Raphael, stand between God and his mortal children. Of us all, you will most directly help thwart Lucifer's designs on creation."

"He will not harm them!" Raphael shouted, standing up. His eyes blazed a bright green as though stars burned about the pupil. The aura about him likewise grew bright and from the ether came attendants to see what aid they could offer him. Michael stood and embraced his brother, silently dismissing the attendants.

"Shhhhhh. Such passion, my beautiful brother. You will be their protector, their confidant, perhaps even their friend. They will feel your love and know your protection."

Raphael pulled back slightly and as Michael closed his eyes, Raphael placed a soft kiss on each. "Your words bring me such comfort. I hope I will be allowed to protect them. Yet, I fear that God and Lucifer will decide otherwise."

"The decision is God's alone, Raphael. Do not forget this. As always, Lucifer will try to influence Him. You know God's love for Lucifer had no bounds; His words may yet have some impact. However, we must believe and trust in God's wisdom. He is all that is good."

"I wish I could learn your easy detachment, my brother. You seem at such peace with all that transpires."

"And I, Raphael, pray you never learn it. Your passion brings you close enough to the mortals to serve our Father. Where I am His right hand that grips the sword of wrath, you are His arms that reach out to embrace the world with love. You are his perfect instrument in this."

Again the tears welled up within Raphael. How he loved his brother. "Oh Michael, I pray this instrument is allowed to play. How I do pray it."

The heat came in waves, lapping at him like some celestial ocean. Lucifer closed his eyes-feeling it wash over him, through him. He loved the sensation. He almost felt pity for those who would never know the feeling. Fallen as he was, Lucifer remained an Angel of the Presence. He could stand before the blinding glory of God and not be consumed. No lost battle or exile from heaven could take that away from him. He remained Lucifer. Second only to God and He knew pride.

The voice sounded sad, steeped with regret. "Your pride, Lucifer. That pride you retain even now was your undoing."

The Angel opened his eyes and smiled as he reclined. Though fallen, he still retained the beauty bestowed by the very God whose power rippled through the air. Streamers of light and energy played about Lucifer's body, growing ever brighter as his smile broadened. His eyes, which had beheld part of creation itself, glittered with flecks of red, blazing with life.

"Yes. Yes. I am prideful. And yet, I don't feel undone. I have stormed the fortress of heaven itself. True, the battle was lost, but here I remain. My strength is undiminished. My Angels and I live. I wonder why that is. Could it be that even you have limits? Could it be that I and those whom I protect are beyond the grasp of your wrath?"

A voice resounded within the Angel's mind, "Such satisfaction. You are content in your new realm, Lucifer?"

"It serves me...for now," he replied. "I am more content to rule there, than serve here. And it is not forever. I assure you. Now, what would you have of me? Why summon your fallen Angel to once again stand in your presence?"

"We must speak of those whom I have created. The ones whose lives are measured."

"Oh, the mortals. Yes, when I look forward, I see much potential in them. They will serve me well."

The waves of heat increased. Lucifer found himself buffeted by them as if in a storm. He did not flinch, but rose to face God's growing wrath. Then, the warmth faded as did their heavenly surroundings. Lucifer found himself standing atop a stoney mountain overlooking lush valleys and grasslands. He turned and beheld God walking toward him with long flowing brown hair and eyes of deep violet. Lucifer saw all of creation within those eyes. He saw all stars and planets, comets and nebulae-all within the eyes of the Creator. For a moment, so overcome with love, Lucifer wanted nothing more than to prostrate himself before God and beg to be received back into heaven, but the pride rose within him and he felt restrained.

Lucifer smiled, "I shall miss seeing you, my beloved Father. I wanted so to be like you in all things. I wanted to create beauty as you have-to bring Order from Chaos. Now, to my utter sadness, I must strive for the opposite. Do you see what you have wrought? Did you not know?"

God glanced down and several stones moved, forming an acceptable bench. He sat looking once again at Lucifer. "Yes I knew. But you did not want to be as me, Lucifer. You wanted to BE me. Your pride misled you to believe it was possible. I created you; you can create nothing." No malice touched His words, and yet they stung the fallen Angel, who motioned and from the stone a rough hewn throne emerged. God shook His head sadly as Lucifer settled onto the throne and glared at Him.

"I do not believe you created me. If you did, then why not destroy me now?"

"Things are in motion that I choose not to stop. Time has begun and must flow to the finish. You are a part of that finish, Lucifer. You have a role to play, as do we all."

"Oh yes, I know about how far you see. I know my sight does not extend as far, but I have more breadth. I see into the dark and evil side of mortals. I see in those places you would not suffer yourself to go. I see plans born in dark hearts that have millennia before their fruition. I see the chaos of freewill! From that chaos will I build my strength, and with that strength I will unseat you from your heavenly throne." God stared at Lucifer, his face displaying all too clearly the feelings of loss and sadness. Lucifer tilted his head back and laughed. "Do not weep for me, Father. Weep for yourself. Weep for your Angels whom I will cast out. Weep for your mortals whom I will control."

A single tear stood on God's cheek. "I DO weep for myself, Lucifer. And I weep for all that you were and are no more." God paused, stared at Lucifer, and composed Himself. His aura brightened, eyes glowing their brilliant violet. "You will not control the mortals, Lucifer. You will influence them. You will try to corrupt them and turn them from Me, but you will not control them. I have seen to that."

The perpetual smile Lucifer had worn since arriving on the mountain disappeared. For a moment, he feared he had miscalculated. Lucifer said, "You may not interfere with their freewill. Your law. To break your law would be to lie. Lying is a sin, Father...you know that." Lucifer's mocking smile returned, but God could see the hesitancy behind it.

"Do not presume to lecture me on laws and holiness, Lucifer. As one who broke them with such abandon, you are hardly qualified to raise the issue. You too are bound by that law but, somehow, I do not believe you plan on honoring that promise." Lucifer smiled, but said nothing. "Yes," God continued, "well, your position is, at least, consistent. Consequently, I have decided to permit another to intercede on the mortals' behalf."

"No. You cannot," Lucifer shouted, "Appointing another to intercede is no different than You interfering. Their freewill remains compromised."

God sighed, "Fortunately, Lucifer, I do not see it that way. And, your opinion in this matter, is really quite irrelevant."

Lucifer fumed. "I will destroy any you send to aid the mortals. I will rend them limb from limb. They will not survive my wrath. I assure you."

God smiled slightly and said, "Raphael sits between the mortals and the kingdom of heaven. He will guide the efforts of my Angels as they aid the mortals in what manner they are able. Do not feign surprise, Lucifer. You have already appointed Asmodeus to perform the same function for you. To my way of thinking this situation only enhances freewill. My mortal children are able to choose between the Angels of light and those of darkness. No one loves the mortals more than Raphael; I think Asmodeus will find him a worthy adversary."

"Raphael is weak. He is an Archangel only. He cannot even stand in my presence, let alone yours."

"You confuse love for weakness. Oh, and you'll find that Raphael can stand in your presence without much difficulty. Do not mistake yourself for an Angel of high heaven, Lucifer. You are fallen and all may gaze upon you. As for me, Raphael and I have met even as you and I now meet. He does not have your pride and does not need to stand in my untempered presence. He does not covet power; he knows only love. You, however, may perceive him differently when meddling with his beloved mortals. Once again, I think you will find him formidable."

"Now there is the issue of the mortal protector."

Lucifer's attention had wandered off, thinking of Raphael and his Angels thwarting well laid plans. God's statement snapped him back. "What mortal protector? Anything like that clearly violates freewill."

"Not so," God replied, "Such a mortal will have the freedom to choose the role or decline. Those that choose to protect their mortal brothers will be granted extended life, insights into the celestial realm, and the ability to manipulate the laws of creation."

"And I suppose these protectors will be instructed to oppose anything I might orchestrate. If all my plans are blocked how are the mortals permitted the freedom of choosing between Order and Chaos? Again, I say freewill is compromised."

"There will be only one protector. When his mortal life ends, the power will be renewed in another. He always has freewill. At anytime he may choose to turn his back on heaven and follow you."

"You see to the finish, remember. You already know that no such protector will turn his back on you to follow me. Empty words. Where is the symmetry, the balance? If there is to be a protector for Order, there should be one for Chaos. You told me yourself that creation was based upon balance. How can there be balance without two protectors?"

God did not look at Lucifer, but the fallen Angel knew that he had won a victory. God glanced at him as if reading the inner glee, then silently reached down and picked up a handful of soil. From his mouth, God added moisture and shaped the soil. Holding it carefully, he breathed on the form and it began to move. He opened his hand and the thing spread beautiful white wings and stepped in circles on his palm. Lucifer looked on in awe. God whispered something and the creature leaped into the air and flew off. Both watched until it had disappeared from view.

"What was that?" asked Lucifer.

"A dove. It will come to represent peace, love, tranquility, and many such things. I felt it right to create such a thing here, in the shadow of our enmity. Do not long for it Lucifer. For all your posturing, you will never be able to create. You can only alter that which has already been created. From me and me alone springs all creation. But for this balance you speak of, I will allow you one creative act. You may ask one mortal to serve your purposes. He will have the same strengths as the other. You may NOT compel him to accept the role. He must do so of his own accord."

"One thing further. I cannot see what actions these two beings will take. Neither will you be able to see. I am placing them outside our sight to eliminate any possibility of our influencing them directly."

Lucifer smirked, "You mean any possibility of My influencing them. You must not trust me, Father."

God only looked to the sky, as if watching the long disappeared dove. "Your words, Lucifer. Even now, Raphael goes with my acquiescence and blessing to bring his protector into the world."

"I know. Asmodeus does likewise. I told you, I see far as well."

God stood and moved close to Lucifer on his throne. "This meeting I allowed for what once had been. It is finished. We will not soon speak again. Send no queries to me, Satan. I will not hear them." Having finished, God turned and slowly walked away.

Not wanting to show his sorrow, but feeling he must say something, Lucifer stood. "So, these beings. These protectors; by what name will they be known?"

God had returned to his natural form and Lucifer felt the heat. From the center of the blazing light came His answer. "Choose what name you wish. Raphael calls him a Sentinel of Creation."

The words seemed to hang in the air a moment. As they faded, so did God's presence. Lucifer felt the chill of his absence. "Sen-ti-nel..." he said the word aloud. "Yes, I like the sound of that."

Chapter 2

KELLAN

"Mr...Thorny...did you know..."

"Thorne"

"What?"

"Thorne...like on a beautiful Rose stem; the "e" is silent."

The police officer shifted his weight a little and flicked the diver's license back and forth, making a clicking sound that Kellan took as the universal sign of annoyance-which was just fine with Kellan. He already knew there was no way out of this ticket.

"Ok, Mr. Thorne, did you know that this is the HOV lane?"

"I did."

"Do you know what HOV stands for?"

"I do."

The cop glanced back and forth, taking in the whole of the black sedan.

"Is yours a High Occupancy Vehicle, sir?"

"Sometimes..."

The rain was coming down harder and Kellan heard it pattering against the police officer's hat. He almost felt bad about being this obnoxious. After all, the cop was just doing his job. Still, there was a principle at work here.

The cop looked at him again with what can only be described as "cop eyes". Assessing. He took in Kellan's appearance: the two days of stubble, wavy dark brown hair, and a smile that held the promise of mischief. Then he just stared at Kellan, burrowing into his ice blue eyes. "You're not military, right?"

"Nope, but my father was-career Marine."

The cop shook his head, "That's not gonna help you. You are definitely getting a ticket."

"I figured."

"Just out of curiosity, would you mind sharing why you decided to drive in a lane you clearly weren't qualified to use, knowing you would likely get a citation?"

"Sure, I'd be glad to. You see, there are two on-ramps to the highway - One HOV and one regular. The regular ramp is always completely backed up and it takes damn near 20 minutes just to get on the road. People are beeping, cutting in front of each other, and doing all manner of obnoxious things. I've seen half a dozen fender benders and two actual fist fights."

The cop interrupted, "I assume one of those was the assault charge I saw on your record."

Kellan smiled. "First, that charge was dropped so I don't even know why you'd have a record of it and, second, the guy hit me first. Anyway, you are distracting me. The point is that the regular lane is a nightmare of accidents and violence. Not only that, but it accomplishes absolutely nothing. I totally get why you want an HOV lane on an actual highway, but putting one on the entrance ramp is just stupid. I've written to the city. I've called the city. I've thought about renting a sky writing plane and leaving a message for the city. Then, I thought, 'Hey...I'll just start using the HOV lane and eventually I'll get a ticket from one of Atlanta's finest and take it to court.'" He winked at the police officer and squinted at his name badge. "That's where you come in...'officer N. Bradley.' What's the 'N' stand for?"

The cop had been writing on his ticket pad and glanced up. "The N? It stands for 'Not going to win in court.' Enjoy paying that fine." With that, he handed Kellan the pad and said, "Please sign, sir."

Kellan stared at the ticket a moment and contemplated asking officer Bradley to read the entire citation standing in the rain based on a fictitious learning disability Kellan thought he might have just developed. Instead, he just shook his head slightly, scrawled his standard signature that faintly resembled "R.M.Nixon," and handed the pad back while flashing his most winning smile.

"Oh, Nathan, I'm an optimist and you should have more faith. See you in court."

Officer Nathan Bradley accepted the pad, tore off the receipt, and handed it to Kellan. He paused before releasing it, his face registering confusion, "How did you..."

"Elementary, my dear Bradley. You just didn't strike me as a Nathaniel and you certainly aren't a Nate. Cheerio!"

With that, Kellan accelerated into traffic and rewarded himself with a glance in the side view mirror to see a clearly bemused Officer Nathaniel Bradley still standing in the rain.

"A hero cannot be a hero unless in a heroic world." The words hung in the air after Kellan whispered them aloud. That's an interesting quote and an even more interesting tattoo. The image of the words inked on Officer Bradley's right forearm snapped into Kellan's mind like a high resolution photo.

He sighed, wondering again what useful bit of information his mind was incapable of processing because of his eidetic memory. He'd never forget that forearm just like he'd never forget seeing the quote attributed to Nathaniel Hawthorne, the 19th century american novelist.

"Interesting that Hawthorne was born on July 4th, but I guess someone had to be. Then again, he was born on America's independence day and died in 1864, just before the end of the civil war that would secure that very Union. I mean, heck, life expectancy then was only 40 years and Hawthorne lived to almost 60. That's like 50% over the average. Seems he could have managed another year and seen the end of the war. I wonder what the life expectancy will be in 2064. Probably around, shit, shit. Damn it to hell I missed my exit."

"Navigation and situational awareness, Kellan, that's what suffers for you being a flipping genius," he said while smiling to himself in the rear view mirror. "Of course, you wouldn't have it any other way would you? Nope," he answered himself aloud, winked at his reflection and started looking for the next exit."

The bells tinkled merrily as Kellan opened the door with his shoulder, hands full with two large cups of hot coffee.

The girl at the counter looked up, peering over her Ray Ban eyeglasses. She tried to scowl, but her face just wasn't built for it. She scooted the glasses back on a cute button nose whose bridge was dotted with faint freckles.

"Do you know what time it is?" she asked with annoyance that Kellan could tell was for show - mostly.

"Well," Kellan began, "judging from the twenty odd clocks tick-tocking away in my field of view, I'd hazard to say 11:00 - give or take."

"Very good, and what time do we open?"

"Why, 10:00 sharp, Miss Herrick, just like the sign says. "Beloved' Books, open daily 10:00 − 9:00"

"Kind of hard to be open if there's nobody here to open up," she said.

Kellan held up the cup in his left hand, tilted it slightly in the her direction, and flashed a smile. "But, Juliet, there is someone to open up. There's you."

"I don't work until 11:00, Kellan."

"Right, and it's 11:00 now. Congratulations on being so punctual."

Juliet reached for the cup as Kellan approached. "I've been here since 10:00 because Hamish called me on my mobile to tell me the store wasn't open."

"Pffft…Hamish hasn't bought a book in three years and just comes here to read and annoy paying customers with his endless stories featuring the stalwart McLeod family who are saving us all from vampires, werwolves, and assorted boogiemen.

Kellan wiggled the cup of coffee and taunted Juliet. "Now let's see those beautiful blue eyes look less dangerous. Tell me I'm forgiven, and you can have your coffee."

She sighed. "What kind is it?"

"Hazelnut with enough cream to give you a coronary in about three years"

"Damn," she said, her face splitting in to a fierce grin. "Damn and no fair! You are forgiven, sir. Now gimme!"

He did and she immediately popped the little plastic top off the cup, inhaled deeply, and took a long sip.

Kellan walked behind the counter and patted Juliet gently on the head, which she pointedly ignored. "From your reaction, I'm assuming your parents have, once again, restricted your coffee consumption," he said.

"Yes, despite my protestations."

"Did you try my suggestion?" Kellan asked as he flipped idly through yesterday's mail.

"Cruel and unusual didn't fly, but Dad did at least blame you for putting the idea in my head."

"Of course he did. He's been blaming me for ideas in your head for seventeen years now and I expect that won't be changing until someday you have a husband he can blame."

"Probably. Hey, you didn't mention my new glasses."

Kellan glanced up. "Yeah, pretty cool. Ray-Bans, right? I remember them from *Risky Business*."

Juliet gave him a blank stare.

Kellan sighed. "Tom Cruise. Risky Business. Dancing wearing nothing but Ray-Bans and his underwear."

She wrinkled her nose. "Gross! Tom Cruise is old and now I have an image of him in is underwear rolling around my head. Thanks Kel."

"Well, his were sunglasses and they were black, if that makes you feel any better."

"Mine are TARDIS blue so they are nothing like what was in *Frisky Business*."

Kellan laughed and felt the coffee start to burn up his nose. "Risky, not Frisky. *Frisky Business* was an entirely different thing altogether and not one that we'll be talking about."

"Ok, whatever. UPS came early today. It was a giant box so I had them move it back to your office.

"Alrighty then. I'll go check it out. You hold down the fort." Kellan headed toward the back of the store, weaving between several massive hand made shelves stacked floor to ceiling with books of every imaginable size and thickness. As he passed through the center of the store, Kellan did his best to ignore the old burly red haired man sitting in one of the many overstuffed leather chairs.

"Hey Boyoh!"

Kellan cringed slightly. "Sorry, Hamish. Can't talk now. Got a shipment of vintage books in and I have to get them sorted out. Give my regards to the VanHelsings and we can chat later."

"Someday you are going to regret making..."

Hamish's words faded as Kellan slipped into his back office and closed the door. There was a large cardboard box resting on the round side table which stood in one corner of the room. It was open.

Kellan pulled out the first book, an early printing of *The Federalist Papers,* and admired the hand tooled leather and binding. He held it up to his nose and took a deep breath.

"God, I love books," he said to no one and closed his eyes as the words which comprised the early American political work flashed through his consciousness. Kellan had only read the book once, of course, and that was when he was younger than Juliet. He never had to read books a second time - doing so tended to confuse him. *The Federalist Papers* wouldn't be that bad, but books based on translations, were a different matter entirely. He shuddered a bit at all the Biblical translations he carried around in his head. Reading all those had definitely been a mistake.

He was reaching back into the box when his mobile phone pulsed. Kellan pulled it out from his back jeans pocket and glanced at it. **Juliet Herrick**: *Customer wants you...he looks creepy.*"

Kellan sighed and headed back to the front of the store where he found Juliet nervously shuffling papers on the counter.

Standing in front of her was a man wearing a suit, a long woolen coat that went to his calves, and dark glasses that obscured his eyes completely. As Kellan passed in front of the counter, he glanced back to Juliet who mouthed, "Creeeepyyyy," and turned back to the man.

"What can I do for you?" asked Kellan with a smile as he extended his hand. The man extended his own gloved hand and accepted Kellan's gesture while affecting a smile that looked far more like a grimace. "*Super creepy,*" thought Kellan, "*and what's with a long coat and gloves.*" It was a mild spring for Atlanta, but those clothes couldn't possible by comfortable.

When the man spoke, his voice was rough and halting. Kellan saw Juliet give a little shudder in his peripheral vision.

"You are Kellan Thorne?" the man asked.

"That's me. Are you looking for something in particular?"

"I am Mr. Landry. I have books for sale," said the man in his strange halting voice.

"Well, that's great, but I actually just received a pretty substantial shipment and unless you have something really special, I'm not really in the market right now."

"Yes. Special. Rare books - very old first editions."

"OhhhKayy," said Kellan drawing out the words a bit. "Which books do you have?"

"Dickens, Verne, Burroughs"

"Um, Charles Dickens, Jules Verne, and Edgar Rice Burroughs? First Editions? Which ones?"

"All."

"All? As in you have their complete works. All in first edition?"

"Yes. All."

Kellan squinted at the man. "Ok. You got my attention, but I warn you I can pick out a fake in two seconds flat. Bring 'em on in, let's take a look."

"They are heavy and there is no place to park."

"No worries, just drive around back. I'll meet you there to help carry them into my office."

The man nodded and quietly left the store.

Kellan stared after him a second and heard Juliet let out her breath behind him.

He turned to find her doing a little wiggle dance with her shoulders and hips. "Mr. Creep. Creep Creep Creepety Creep-face from Creep-town, Creepania..."

Kellan laughed as he headed towards the back calling over his shoulder, "... and so's your dad. *Doctor Who*, 2006, "Girl in the Fireplace." I love Doctor Who references. keep it up, kid, and you'll get a raise."

Kellan unlocked the back door and stepped on the the first step of the brick stoop leading into the alley and felt it shift as his weight hit it, pitching him forward, arms outstretched to break his fall.

As he fell, Kellan felt something breeze over his head and heard a clang behind him.

He rolled over to see Landry, struggling to pull what looked like a three foot long, wickedly curved blade from where it had embedded itself in the bricks - right where Kellan's neck would have been were it not for his fall.

"What the fuck!" Kellan yelled as Landry pulled the blade free and rounded on him. Kellan quickly looked up and down the alley as he scrambled to his feet. Six more men, dressed exactly like Landry advanced from either end of the alley, all carrying the same curved blades.

Kellan looked back at Landry in time to see the blade arcing towards him impossibly fast and instinctually closed his eyes against the attack.

Through closed eyelids, Kellan saw a flash of light, heard a tremendous clash, and was struck so hard in the chest that he flew backwards against the far wall of the alley with a "woof" as the air left his chest.

As he opened his eyes and tried to catch is breath, Kellan saw another man standing in the alley. His left arm was still pointed at Kellan, palm up, clearly having pushed him out of harms way. In his other hand, he held a long sword crossways, having parried Landry's blow. The sword glowed so brightly that Kellan had to avert his eyes.

Landry screamed and moved with impossible speed trying to circle around Kellan's unknown defender. He almost succeeded. His curved blade came within inches of Kellan when the other man restrained him with each hand grasping a shoulder. The glowing sword, Kellan noted, simply hung suspended in the air. Meanwhile a little voice inside his head whispered that he was clearly having some kind of a psychotic break.

Landry struggled but could not break free from what appeared to be an iron grip as the man leaned in toward Landry's left ear and said, "He is not yours to kill. Return to your hole, skin-walker." Then Kellan watched in horror as Landry's coat, suit, and skin was literally ripped off his body and thrown to the alley floor.

What stood before him had the general shape of a man - of Landry, but pulsed and throbbed in a gelatinous fashion for several heartbeats before collapsing and showering Kellan in putrid slime.

The man was incredibly tall - nearly seven feet. He bent down slightly, eyes glowing with an internal green fire that a small rational voice inside Kellan told him was completely impossible.

"Do. Not. Move," the man said as he retrieved his sword from where it had been levitating and used the tip to carve a circle in the cement around Kellan. "I will defend you in this battle. Do not move outside this circle or you will die. Do you understand me?"

Kellan found with an odd sense of detachment that he could not remember how to speak, so he just nodded and crouched down while trying to appear as small as possible.

Then the man smiled. Not a warm or friendly smile, but a smile that was decidedly neither. Kellan immediately realized that the look was directed towards the long coats who where were advancing toward them at a run from either end of the Alley.

"Come!" the man yelled in a voice that Kellan swore to himself sounded like thunder. Then the man laughed and said, "Come and meet the very incarnation of wrath! This one is protected from your snares. I will cast you down."

"He didn't just say that did he?" whispered that tiny internal voice that was what remained of rational Kellan.

The glowing sword met curved blades as the man whirled and fought in a macabre dance at blurring speed. After what looked like one extended and fluid motion, only six gelatinous puddles remained.

As the man turned and began walking back, Kellan's rational mind began to assert itself by making observations, posing questions, and running through the vast amount of perfectly stored information that it had at its disposal. *Fact One: "Defend you in battle."*

"Do not turn around, Kellan Thorne," the man yelled as he raced toward him.

Kellan turned around and stared numbly as six long coats were wildly swinging their curved swords at him, striking sparks off of some unseen barrier that rose up from the circle surrounding him.

Fact Two: "Protection from Snares"

Kellan saw a shadow fall over him and a moment later the man landed beyond the six long coats. He was smiling again, with fierce joy - eyes still ablaze. This time the long coats didn't even have time to react before they too had been reduced to puddles.

Fact Three: "I will cast you down"

"You are safe for now," the man said, "but more will likely come. The circle will protect you until my Brother arrives."

Kellan's rational mind regained full control as he stared at the seven foot tall man with eyes of molten emerald, covered head to toe in shining armor, and who Kellan knew was the most beautiful man he had ever seen in his entire life.

"I don't believe in Angels," whispered Kellan.

Fact Four: "Big Glowing Sword," his mind answered in retort.

"Holy shit, you are Michael the Archangel"

Michael sheathed his sword and stared intently into Kellan's eyes.

"You may not believe in me, but my Brother believes in you. It is because I love him that I am here. I do not believe in you. I think you are dangerous. I am seldom wrong."

"Do not leave the circle. Raphael will be here soon."

With those words Michael gestured and a oval split open in the alley before him; he stepped through and vanished.

"I don't believe in Angels!" Kellan yelled angrily at the now empty alley and crouched down with his arms around his knees.

Chapter 3

SCOTLAND 1275

M icah brought the axe down, splitting the log in a single stroke. The three children sitting around him all clapped enthusiastically and then scurried to pick up the pieces to stack them alongside the small house.

"Father Micah! Father Micah! Are you done now? Is it time for stories?" one of the children asked hopefully.

"Stories! Stories!" the two youngest said in unison.

Micah smiled. "Of course it's time for stories. What other time would it be?"

"Now, Liam, Donal, and Shannon, why don't you make us all some lunch while I go down to the stream and wash up for a minute or two."

The children leapt up and ran into the house. Micah heard the clatter of plates and cups as he made the short walk down to the stream.

Once there he stripped off the soiled clothes and crouched down at the water's edge. He looked deeply at the man in the watery reflection.

"So old," he whispered. He wasn't referring to his face and body which surely were lined and wrinkled with age, yet appeared to retain surprising strength. It was his eyes. As he gazed at his steel gray eyes in the water, Micah wondered if others saw what he saw in them.

"Do they see that these eyes have seen the passing of millennia? Do they have any idea who lives in their midst, who watches over them in the darkness, and who reads stories to their children?"

Micah shook his head and disturbed his reflection by scooping water out of the stream to splash across his face.

Then he stood up and looked around carefully, reaching out with all his senses. Everything about him slowed and he took it all in. The fish in the stream, insects and birds in the air, the children bustling about the house. No one was near. No one could see.

Micah reached out his right hand toward the clothes, gestured, and whispered a word, *fiero*, then gripped the open air in a fist and twisted his hand slightly. A runic symbol appeared on his forearm as his eyes went from their normal slate gray to a brilliant green for a moment then the clothes were consumed in a burst of fire.

Micah then opened his arms, more runes running down their length, his eyes glowing once more and a mist gathering around his naked form, coalescing into gleaming mail that armored him from head to toe. Finally, he slowly passed his hand downward along his body and the mail seemed to morph into normal homespun clothing.

The whole process took perhaps a minute. It had the easy, instinctual, grace of a task that had been performed hundreds of times. Micah sighed softly and walked back towards the sound of children laughing.

When he arrived plates and cups had been set on the outside table along with some bread, fruit, and cheese the children had found in his pantry. They all sat around the table and were regarding a man who sat with them, his back to Micah.

Micah tensed and felt an unseen sword form across his back cloaked by the same illusion that hid his armor from view.

The children did not seem alarmed and Shannon waved to him. "Father Micah! Come quickly, your friend is here and he says he wants to hear stories too."

The man stood slowly, still with his back to Micah. He was so tall. Micah was very tall himself and this man was a full head taller still. He radiated strength and power. Micah glanced at the smiling children and his blood ran cold.

With a slow blink, Micah reached inward and found the raging river of power that coursed throughout him like molten emeralds. In that split second of frozen time, he wrapped his arms around the power and channeled it to his purpose. In his mind's eye he saw unseen shields snap into place around each child and prepared to reach for the pulsing sword on his back, dropping the glamour that hid his armor.

He knew he would have to leave this place afterward, but it had ever been so.

"Peace be with you, Micah Ben Judah," the man said turning.

Micah froze. He found he couldn't breathe properly. This must be a trick. He drew further on the power within him and it fought for release, but now the man was facing him.

"Peace be with you," he said again.

Micah stared at the man, releasing the torrent of power and letting it wink out.

The man cocked his head expectantly.

Micah's mouth felt dry and his pulse raced. "Peace be with you, Raphael."

Raphael took several long strides to close the gap between them and embraced Micah, adjusting the hidden armor and sword slightly with a knowing smile.

Liam ran up from the table. "Raphael says you and he are old friends, Father Micah! How old of friends are you? Have you known him older than me? I'm eight."

When Micah said nothing, Raphael smiled and mussed the boy's hair a bit. "Yes, Liam, we've known each other even older than you."

Liam grinned and Shannon shouted, "Stories, Father Micah!"

"Yes, *Father* Micah," Raphael said with a smile in his voice. I have heard wonderful things about these stories of yours. I look forward to hearing one."

For his part, Micah had recovered enough to respond. "Children, it has been a very long time since I have seen my friend, Raphael. Perhaps we could have story time another day."

There was a chorus of disagreement from the children and Raphael sat down at the table smiling, while gesturing for Micah to take the larger seat at its head. "Fear not, children. Never let it be said that I stand in the way of a good story. Micah, please, indulge the children and yourself in this simple pleasure."

His smile faded a bit and he added, "Remember, we are only given today and such things should not be put off to a day that may never come."

Micah stared at him a moment and took his seat, relaxing a bit. *A day that may never come,* he thought to himself then asked.

"Raphael, is it time? Really time?"

"For stories!" Donal shouted.

Raphael smiled at Micah, locking him in his gaze and said, "Yes," A heartbeat later he turned toward Donal and added, "- for stories," but Raphael's message to Micah had been clear.

Micah glanced upward as if in silent prayer as a subtle smile played across his face. "Well, now, what story will it be then? Dragons? Demons? Fairies or Goblins?"

The children all looked stunned. "You mean we get to pick?" asked Shannon.

"We never get to pick. You always pick," said Liam.

"Well, today is special. Today, you get to pick."

There was quite a commotion as the children discussed which story they should choose, but when they could not agree, Raphael tapped the table quietly and said, "I have an idea, if you are all willing. I know a very old story that Micah can tell. If you trust me, I can promise it will be the best story you have ever heard."

There was a moment of silence as his words sunk in, then Donal and Liam and started yelling, "Yes! Yes! Yes! The best story ever, Father Micah. Tell us the best story ever!"

Shannon just looked at her brothers and shrugged.

"Seems it is settled then," said Raphael, smiling.

"And which, pray tell, is the best story ever?" Micah asked.

"You know."

"Indulge me with the obvious answer."

Raphael inclined his head slightly. "Of course," he said to Micah. Then, lowering his voice conspiratorially, he looked over each child in turn and said, "The best story ever is the one where God asked His Angel to find Him a Sentinel"

The children had all been leaning in as Raphael spoke and, when he finished, silence hung in the air for a heartbeat.

"What's a Sentinel?" asked Liam.

"That doesn't sound like the best story ever," said Donal.

"I think we should have a story about Fairies," said Shannon - just to annoy Donal and Liam.

"Wait...wait...you have to trust me," said Raphael, "I promised you that this would be the best story ever. I always keep my promises and I never lie."

The children looked dubious.

"Never?" asked Donal, "You've never lied, even once?"

"Never," said Raphael, "Honestly, I am not capable of it."

"It's true," Micah interjected before Donal continued. "I can vouch for Raphael in this regard. If he says something, it's the truth, or..." Micah paused while looking at the Angel, "at least he believes it to be the truth."

"But, be that as it may, I don't think I can tell this story very well. I'm not even sure how it ends."

Raphael reached out and placed his hand on Micah's arm. "We will tell it together, my old friend, for I do know how it ends...and it is a wonderful ending."

"Well, I certainly do enjoy stories with wonderful endings," said Micah, smiling again, "But since you will be telling part of the story, I assume you have been properly introduced to our audience, yes?"

Raphael displayed mock chagrin. "Alas, Micah, the children have not introduced themselves so, in fact, I know absolutely nothing about my audience."

"Children - is this true? Were you so rude as to not greet our guest properly?"

Donal and Liam both looked down and began fidgeting.

"Father Micah, stop doing that," said Shannon.

"Stop what? Ensuring that I instill some manners during your visits with me?"

Shannon stood up and put her hands on her hips, trying her best to affect the stance of her mother. "No, stop pretending that you are cross with us. There has been no time for introductions, as you well know. Your friend only arrived moments ago and did so with no warning whatsoever." She then tilted her head and glared at both men with a fierce expression that was completely ruined when a breeze caught one of her fiery tresses and blew it across her face. She peered out through the curls for a moment, then brushed them aside in frustration and sat down looking sullen. "Stupid wind."

Liam and Donal gave each other a look which clearly conveyed their sense of "there she goes again," as they did their best to turn invisible.

"Quite right and my apologies, Miss McLeod. It was completely inappropriate for me to embarrass you like that in front of Raphael. I hope you can forgive me."

Shannon stared at him for a long moment, holding his gaze and trying to determine if she was being mocked. Finally, she said, "It's alright Father Micah, I know you were just making fun and truth be told, there might have been enough time for introductions." She added a moment later, "barely,' then flashed a mischievous smile.

She stood up again and deliberately walked over to Raphael with hand extended. "Hello, sir. I am Shannon McLeod and these are my two brothers, Donal and Liam. My father is the miller here in Glenferry and my mom, well, Mom passed away six years ago. Maybe you knew her. Father Micah knew her. That's why he came for her funeral. Remember, Father Micah, you said you'd promised to keep a watch over us so you ended up just staying here. Did you know her, Margaret McLeod?"

Raphael shook his head sadly, "No, Shannon, I am afraid I never had the joy of meeting your mother, but I do recall Micah talking about her, and the three of you."

"Skin Walkers got her," Donal said, and Liam covered his face with his hands - trying to hide.

"Donal! Be quiet, you are scaring Liam."

"I will not be quiet, Shan. He needs to know. She saved all of us. Papa says so. Without her we would all be in the ground. She's a hero and Liam needs to know it."

Shannon sank down beside Liam and put her arm around him, whispering into his ear. He lifted his face, but still looked frightened.

"Mother is a hero. I'm just afraid they will come back."

"Don't worry, Liam. If they come back, I can handle them. Papa says I'm already almost as good with Mother's bow as she was, and better with her throwing knives."

Micah had been watching the exchange, grinding his teeth silently. "Children, you have nothing to fear from them. Trust me, they will never be coming back. Not ever. I promise you that."

Raphael stood up and walked over to the three children, extending his hand first to Donal and then to Liam. "You are all very brave and strong and it is my sincere pleasure to have been introduced. As you already know, I am Raphael and Micah is one of my oldest and dearest friends. While nothing can replace the loss of a mother, if Micah says that the creatures who perpetrated this evil met justice and will never return, you can trust that as if an Angel came down and told you that himself."

All three nodded at this and Raphael flashed a smile, doing his best to lighten their spirits. "I believe now that we have those formal introductions out of the way, there is a story to be had, is that right?"

His efforts were rewarded with grins around the table as everyone settled back down and stared at Micah expectantly.

With that, Micah sighed, took a long drink from his cup, and began to weave together the tale of his life...

Raphael laughed suddenly and slapped the table with a loud thud.

"Really, Micah, I do not think you remember this quite right. Maybe you fell asleep during this part of the tale's original telling."

Micah's brow furrowed a bit. "No, I think I have it right. The Angel appeared to the young man, Tholem, who was to become this great Sentinel when he was away from home breaking horses to help provide for his family."

"...and," interrupted Raphael, "this Angel simply walked up to Tholem and said, 'Behold, I am an Angel of the Lord. Do you want to be His Sentinel?' How well do you think this young horse trainer would have reacted to that? These things require planning...finesse. Allow me to elaborate."

"Now, children, once this Angel went to carry out God's command-" began Raphael.

"Which Angel?" asked Shannon.

"I bet it was Michael," said Liam.

"No, it was not Michael," said Raphael. "Michael would not be good for this sort of thing. He is much more of a, *Here is a job for you; do it or I will cut you in half*, kind of Angel."

"How do you know?" asked Shannon.

Raphael opened his mouth as if to respond, then closed it.

"Well?" pressed Shannon.

Raphael turned to look at Micah, who pretended not to see the earnest stare. Finally, Micah said, "Raphael reads a lot and has studied all about Angels."

"Oh, that makes sense," said Liam

"Yes, so then it must have been Gabriel," said Donal, "He's probably the best Angel anyway. Was it Gabriel? Did he have his horn with him?"

"It wasn't Gabriel either, " said Micah. "The storyteller never mentioned the Angel's name. Some Angels don't even have names. It could be because they don't need them or maybe they were just too busy to take a name. Angels are evidently very busy; they disappear for centuries without a word and do not come when asked. Maybe that's because they don't all have names. What do you think, Raphael? Since this Angel wasn't Michael, the strongest and bravest, nor was he Gabriel, who, I think we all agree, is the best Angel, who was he? Do you think he had a name? Who was this not strongest, not bravest, and not best, Angel?"

Micah smirked at Raphael, who simply stared at him with a flat expression.

"The Angel doesn't matter in this story. That is why he doesn't have a name. I'm sure he is quite remarkable in his own right, but this story is about the Sentinel - not the Angel."

"What is important," Raphael continued, "is how he chose Tholem and how Tholem agreed to take up the power and responsibility of being God's Sentinel. Remember, Tholem would not be alone in his role. As you already heard, the fallen Angel Asmodeus had also gone into the world as well. Time works differently for Angels, but I can tell you that he spent what would have been many years looking for someone he thought would be perfect for the task. He talked to kings and paupers. He met with the strong and the weak, the brilliant and the average.

"In the end the Angel settled on Tholem, the horse trainer. He was a good and honest man, but most importantly he had an indomitable spirit. In him, the Angel saw someone who would stand the test of time, never give up, always be true, and never give in to pride."

"So, he made the perfect choice," said Shannon.

"No, he made the right choice. There is a difference and you will see that as the story unfolds. It seems that no one, not even Angels, can make the perfect choice."

"But you get ahead of me. So, the Angel spent many weeks with Tholem in various guises. One day it was a shopkeeper and another day a fellow traveler on the road. You can never be sure that the stranger you meet is not an Angel. Keep that in mind, children." Raphael said, smiling.

"In the end, there really was not much drama in how the Angel made his offer nor in how Tholem chose to accept. The young horse trainer was on his way home from a neighboring village where he had been breaking horses. The hour was late and it was mid fall so the night was cold. Tholem should have camped many hours earlier, but wanted to get home to his family, to see that they were well, and show them how much he had earned by training the horses. It was a little past midnight with a clear sky and full moon overhead when Tholem spied a small cook fire built a bit off the road he was traveling. He had been walking for hours and was quite cold and hungry, so he decided to see who was tending the fire and if he could share it."

"As I am sure you have already figured out, it was the Angel who made this camp and tended the fire. When Tholem introduced himself, the Angel welcomed him warmly and offered him food, drink, and the warmth of the fire. But there was a price."

"He had to become the Sentinel to get the food, right?" asked Liam.

"No, I do not think you were listening as carefully as you should have been at the beginning. The Angel could not compel Tholem to take up this burden; he had to do so of his own accord. The price was simply that Tholem listen to a story and answer a question. Well, things then were much as they are now. People love stories and Tholem was no exception. He readily agreed to the price, thinking himself twice lucky for getting both food and story.

"As Tholem ate, the Angel recounted the story of Lucifer's war on heaven. He told the young man of the betrayal and how it felt to those who remained loyal. He shared the loss endured by Angels as they warred brother against brother. He wept openly as he described the loss of life and Lucifer's final fall from grace. Then he shared the story of their final meeting - God and Satan, and of the agreement struck that day. By this time, Tholem had long since given up on finishing his meal, so struck was he by the story and the intensity with which it was told. The two sat in silence for a long time and finally Tholem reached out and touched the Angel's hand, asking him how he could possibly have crafted a tale of such sorrow and detail. Well, as we all know, Angels do not lie. So, in response the Angel simply said, 'I could craft such a tale, because I was there.' With those words, the Angel let vanish the disguise that cloaked his true nature. In that moment, Tholem saw all those who he had so recently met: the shop-keeper, beggar, and traveler. Finally all that remained was the Angel.

"What did he look like?" asked Shannon.

"Beautiful," answered Micah. "He was the most beautiful thing that... Tholem had ever seen. He was tall. Taller than me and, at first, he looked like a man, but his eyes were a brilliant green as if cut from emeralds with a candle behind each giving them light. Then he spoke, and his voice was deep and strong, like if the wind could speak."

"Did he have wings?" asked Liam

"He did," answered Micah. "They weren't visible at first, but when the Angel spoke they unfurled. They were big, beautiful and brilliant white. As you might expect, Tholem was desperately afraid at this point staring up at a large, glowing, greened eyed Angel with flowing wings. But the Angel spoke softly, telling him not to be afraid and that it was his honor to meet the young man. Then he reminded Tholem that he had not yet fully paid for his meal and fire."

"The question?" asked Shannon.

"The question," answered Micah.

"The Angel asked if he would be the Sentinel, didn't he?"

Micah paused and looked at Raphael, then back to Shannon. "You are quite the clever one - very insightful. Yes, Shannon, that is exactly what the Angel asked of Tholem."

"And he obviously said yes," said Donal.

"Actually," began Raphael, "he said, 'no.' Or, more precisely, he said 'not yet.'"

"Wow," said Donal.

"Yes, so the Angel asked what more Tholem needed to know in order to make his decision. The young man wanted to know what would happen if the wrong person were chosen and how might that occur. Well, that gave the Angel pause and then after a long moment he answered. He told Tholem that the wrong person would allow power to corrupt him, to make him prideful, and to allow him to think that he could be as God simply because he had a portion of God's power. If that happened, the Angel warned, then the Sentinel could turn his back on God, choose to ally with His adversary, and upend the very throne of heaven."

"Wow," said Donal again.

"That was a good question to ask," said Shannon.

"Yes, it was the perfect question to ask," said Raphael, "and it made the Angel all the more certain that Tholem was the right choice."

"And," began Micah, "It was a good answer, because that answer would shape all the future decisions Tholem would make. He knew he had to avoid the temptations brought on by power and live as purely as possible. If he had a piece of God's power within him, he would need to honor that by living a life that was always pleasing to God."

"No, Micah," said Raphael causing the old man to turn and stare. "As you said, you have not heard how the story ends and since I have, I can tell you with complete certainty that the answer given by this Angel was gravely wrong."

A long moment passed with only the sounds of birds and insects to be heard. Then Micah said very slowly, "*Gravely wrong?* What exactly do you mean by, *gravely wrong?*"

Raphael looked pained as he stared at the older man. "Angels are not perfect and while they cannot lie, they can make mistakes. This Angel was living with the pain of betrayal and his hands were awash with the blood of his brothers from a war that had, as its core, pride and power. But Tholem was not an Angel; he was a man. Angels are either light or dark; there are no gradations, but it is not so with man. Man is a complex weave of light and dark constantly warring for dominion. By giving the answer he did, the Angel thought of Tholem as if he were an Angel and not a man. A man must be free to struggle against his inner demons to reach his full potential. He must risk destruction in order to grow strong enough to choose its avoidance. This Angel set Tholem on a path that would forever avoid such temptations and thus stole from him the ability to overcome them. This Angel, with his answer, not only was gravely wrong, but also did a grave disservice to Tholem. God never intended his Sentinel to be a priest like Micah or a perfectly obedient servant like the Angel. God needed his Sentinel to see into the dark places and risk all to bring His light to them. This Angel, for all his good intentions, failed to properly prepare his Sentinel for the tasks ahead and compounded that failure by not recognizing the need to correct an error he did not know he had made.

Micah felt chilled to his very soul as he stared at Raphael. "What are you saying, Raphael? Was this experiment all for naught? Was this Sentinel's life lived throughout the ages without purpose or effect?"

Raphael reached out to place a hand on Mica's shoulder. "Peace my friend. No, that is not the lesson of this story. Children, as you must know by now, Tholem was satisfied with the Angel's answer and accepted the burden he offered. Tholem did great honor to the task before him, never once straying from a path that would have been pleasing to God. He served as a stalwart defender of the light and thwarted numerous attempts by the Adversary to exact untold hardships on the world. He ended wars, avoided others, changed the course of plagues, and fearlessly entered the very bowels of the earth to extract righteous justice on demons who had harried the mortal world. No, this Sentinel was all that is good and fine in the world. And, without Tholem having lived the life he did, the Angel would never have recognized the error of his initial instruction. This first Sentinel lived his entire life outside the sight of God, but when his task was finished and all his deeds laid out, I am completely certain he was welcomed home as a good and faithful servant.

"Wait," said Shannon, "You said 'this first Sentinel,'" and talked about Tholem as if he were gone.

"Of course," said Micah, "You have heard the saying, 'for everything there is a season.'"

"A time to be born and a time to die?" asked Shannon.

Raphael nodded. "How cruel would it be to ask someone to shoulder a burden, live outside the site of his creator, and do so for all time? Yes, there came a time for Tholem to set down his burden without betraying his responsibility. As with all things, it was his choice to lay it down. This Sentinel could have held tight to his power, allowing it to grow within him as he continued to live. His adversary made that choice; he refused to give up his power to another. In our story, though, Tholem made a different choice: he set out on one last journey that took him far from all he had known. You see, the Angel had learned his lesson and knew he could not be trusted with choosing Tholem's successor. The Sentinel had all the strengths and weaknesses of man and thus must be chosen by man."

"So, Tholem found his successor and passed on his power?" asked Liam.

"I think," said Micah softly, "that is probably another story entirely. And one that will certainly take us past when your father will be expecting you home."

"When can we come back to hear that part of the story?" asked Liam.

"Yes, will Raphael be staying with you a while so we can come back next week and hear?" asked Donal.

Shannon looked first at Micah and then to Raphael. "I believe Father Mica and Raphael are going to be traveling for a bit. I'll try and convince them to let me know more about the story while I clean up the mess you've both made. Go home now, and please tell papa I'll be home by sundown."

Shannon had employed her "mother" voice. The two boys reacted by instinct - gathering their things and giving hugs to Micah and firm handshakes to Raphael. Moments later they were gone and Shannon quietly gathered up an armful of cups and headed into the cottage.

Micah looked to Raphael. "What just happened?"

"I am not exactly sure. I have a sense that..." he cut off as the girl emerged from the cottage to complete her cleaning off of the table. She gave an innocuous smile to each of them as she disappeared back into the cottage.

"You have a sense of what?"

"I said I was not sure...just an odd feeling. How old is she?"

"I don't know; she's a girl. Do you remember how old I am, Raphael? I haven't been able to judge peoples' ages in centuries. Wait, no, I do remember something. Her father mentioned it the other day. She's 14; she just turned 14. Why?"

Raphael thought a moment. "Where were you 14 years ago? What were you doing?"

"What? I don't know. Why do you...What are you implying?"

Raphael had been staring off into the distance thinking, when Micah rounded on him. "Hmm? Oh. No...no, Micah I was not implying that. It is just that the girl seems to have an impression of things." Raphael's brow furrowed as he sought to find the right words and then just shook his head sighing slightly. "From the very beginning she asked questions and had insights that I found a bit...unique. These things happen from time to time, generally it is because the child was conceived at the same time as some unifying event. So, for example, if you had saved some village from destruction by turning floodwaters to ice at the moment of her conception, she might feel cold when around you. Sometimes these things are subtle and sometimes not."

"Well, let me think," began Micah absently running his hand through the tangle of his beard. "I've been living here about eight years now. Four years before that was the situation down south with those demonic insect creatures. Did you even know about that? I called to you about that too. You, of course, didn't answer."

"Micah, please, concentrate now, castigate me later. She will be coming out soon and we need to figure this out; this could put her in danger."

"Fine. Two years before that? Nothing really. Nothing out of the ordinary for me anyway - which does leave a fair bit for space for strange things. Well, there was something odd with my ring, but that wasn't very..."

Raphael grabbed Micah's wrist. "Your ring. The ring I gave you when you accepted the power? What happened to it?"

"Yes, that ring. It's the only ring I have, Raphael. Well, you know how it glows when certain things are going on - use of power, danger nearby, all sorts of things. By the way, figuring all that out was none too easy either. It would have been helpful if you-"

"Micah!"

"Fine. Well, it had been getting consistently dimmer over the years, and really noticeably over the past hundred."

"Yes, that was an indication that the time was coming for you to decide if you wanted to set aside this power."

Micah narrowed his eyes at Raphael. "Again...would have been good to know. Anyway, one night, and I'm sure it was almost thirteen years ago, that ring grew warm to the touch and went bright as your eyes the night you gave it to me. It stayed that way for several solid minutes and then went back to normal."

Raphael got up and started pacing, ran his hand down his face and crouched down before Micah. "This is important! What were you doing when it glowed like that? What exactly were you doing and what were you thinking?"

"I was sleeping. I wasn't doing anything. Dreaming, I guess."

"Do you remember what you were dreaming about?"

Micah didn't answer.

"Micah?"

"Yes, it hadn't happened in a long long time. I was dreaming of my family. The family I never had. The wife I never had. The daughter I never had. I woke up in tears and then the ring started glowing."

"Merciful God!" Raphael shouted his countenance growing dark, "That is it. This is not good at all. They are going to try to use her - to kill her."

"What? Wait. What are you talking about?"

"It is complicated and I do not even fully understand it. I am guessing some of it. You are the first, Micah. I do not have all the answers. I clearly have made mistakes and I am sorry for that. But as this cycle came around and you drew closer to the point where you could set aside the power, you became...I am not sure how to put it...closer to your original humanity. Those very human wants combined with your approaching mortality and current power left an imprint."

Micah shook his head and waved upraised hands toward Raphael. "Wait. What? I might have understood half of that. An imprint of what...on what"

"Not on what - on who. On *her*. Your deep want and deep love for the daughter you never had reached out through your power. You were not fully in control. While you were asleep, it reached out into the guff and imprinted itself on the soul that left to become Shannon at the moment of her conception. She is your daughter."

Micah barked a mirthless laugh. "I'm pretty sure her father would disagree on that point."

"Not your physical daughter - on a spiritual level. She is connected to you and she will be connected to *him*, through you. Which is why they will want to use her."

"Him who?"

"Your successor, if you chose to make it so. She will be connected to *him* through you. So, through her, they can get to your successor when he first accepts the power and is at his most vulnerable."

"For God's sake, Raphael, you know who the man is! I thought you were saying I was supposed to find him."

"It is your choice, Micah. I found someone who I think is right, but I do not trust myself to decide and I am certainly not the right person to ask him. You will need to do both."

"This is a lot to take in. Even for me."

"I am sorry."

"You've been saying that a lot today."

Raphael looked down and said nothing. Micah looked at him and tapped him softly on the head, causing the Angel to look up.

"I love you, Raphael. I know that even when you didn't come, you heard me. I felt you with me even when I could not see you. We are a team, you and I. We always were."

Raphael looked at Micah. "I wanted to come, but you were not sure if I should. You were conflicted that if I came, it would upset some balance some-where and cause worse problems. Your concerns became mine and I stayed away. I'm sor-"

"Don't say it again, please. You're right. You were right about everything. Maybe I was the best person for the task when I took it up, but I'm not anymore. You need someone who is not afraid of what they might become. You need someone more aggressive than I have ever been with you. Someone who, when they call you, the sound of their voice is still echoing off the mountains by the time your heavenly self is standing in front of him. And I'm tired, Raphael. I'm so tired."

Raphael embraced Micah and whispered, "I know. I feel it. One last task my Sentinel and you will be free."

Micah gave a humorless laugh. "One? What about my daughter in there? She seems like quite the task as well. I can't have my darker reflection coming after an innocent who is only in danger because I dreamed a dream that could not be."

"You dreamed a dream that is, my friend. She will be safe. We will make sure she is safe. I will watch over her as long as she lives." Raphael stared at Micah with eyes blazing as they had that night so many centuries ago. "I promise you."

Micah nodded. "Ok, let's go in and see what she knows."

⌒⁊⫙⭤

Shannon felt the pressure change in the room as the door to the cottage opened. The two men entered without making a sound. She gave no sign that she knew they were there, just continued to wipe down the cups and plates, putting them away without a backwards glance.

She pictured where they stood behind her: first together then, walking a couple paces away on either side of the small table.

Silence. She continued to wipe the plate in her hands.

One of them, Micah she thought, slid a chair rather loudly. She raised an eyebrow at the clumsy attempt to get her attention. She ignored it.

Moments passed. She continued to wipe and was down to her last plate.

Another chair, even more loudly.

"I hear you and I hate being lied to. You know how much I hate it, Micah. I hated it when my father lied to me about Mother and I like it no better when you do it."

Silence.

"I assume you both are simply staring at each other."

Finally, Micah spoke. "Shannon, I really have no idea-"

"Lies!" She whirled and there was a flash of silver extending from her outstretched hand.

"Shannon! What has gotten into you, child?"

She simply stared at Micah, flaming red hair all tousled about her face. A look of anger and determination set there, and her light brown eyes focused on his.

"Why don't you ask what's gotten into your friend?"

Micah turned to find Raphael standing just as he had been by the second chair, but with a throwing knife buried to its hilt in the center of his chest. Micah stared at the Angel and turned to Shannon, speechless.

"I want that back," said Shannon flatly.

"An impressive throw under normal circumstances, but with your back fully towards me," Raphael shook his head as he grasped the knife hilt and removed it from his chest. The blade glowed brightly for a moment as if it were awash in starlight then faded to its normal metallic hue. There was no blood. "Really, quite remarkable," said Raphael smiling.

"Thank you. I still want it back."

"You want it back?"

"Yes, it was my mothers." Shannon paused and her voice pitched lower as she stared into the Angel's impassive eyes and growled, "I want it back, now!"

Raphael's eyes flashed as he the twirled the knife and, to Micah's utter horror, flipped it in a blur toward the young girl.

Instinctually, Micah reached inward and grasped the torrent of power even as his armor shone through its disguise. He groaned with effort as he bent time, slowing it, but Raphael was so fast. The knife was half-way across the room, moving in slow motion. He moved toward it but knew he would be too late.

He screamed. This could not be happening. This had to be a nightmare, but then he saw her start to shift her weight. First, she turned her face sideways, red hair slowly flying, as she kept her left eye on the blade. Then, the slightest movement of foot and chest. Micah couldn't breathe, but even as he realized the knife would pass her by, Shannon's right hand swooped up in a blur. It was impossible to move that fast with time bent as it was.

He released the power and time snapped back. Shannon deftly scooped the knife out of the air twirled it three times about her fingers, and slipped it back up her sleeve.

"Thank you," she said, and walked toward the table.

"Oh my God!" shouted Micah. "Are you both completely out of your minds? Shannon, what were you thinking? You would have killed him!"

"And you!" he rounded on Raphael, "What the hell was that? After all you just told me about her, you throw a knife at her with all the strength of an ang-" He cut off.

"Angel?" finished Shannon. "I assumed my little knife wouldn't be able to kill the Archangel Raphael. I did give you both the chance to be honest with me. And I thought Angels didn't lie."

Raphael smiled. "I did not lie." He pointed at Micah. "He lied. I just stayed quiet."

Raphael turned to Micah shaking his head in clear amazement. "She is definitely a special one, Micah. Strongest imprint I have ever seen and that is saying something."

Shannon slapped the table with an open palm causing both Micah and Raphael to jump. "Don't talk like I'm not here. I am right here. I am standing right here."

"Please don't throw anything else - either of you. Sit down. Forget it, I'm sitting down."

Raphael walked around the table and pulled out the chair. "Miss McLeod would you please sit? I am afraid we have some explanations to provide."

She looked at him a moment and smiled. "Thank you, I am looking forward to hearing them. Will there be any more lies today, from anyone?"

"Not from me," Raphael said with a chuckle.

Micah had laid his head down on the table, but raised one hand and waved it slightly in a vaguely negative fashion.

"Wonderful, then I'll get us all something to drink before we talk."

With that, Shannon spun on her heel and picked up the three mugs that she had prepared long before either Micah or Raphael had entered the cottage. She handed one to each of them and Micah took a long and quick draught. For her part, Shannon sat down in the offered chair, sipping daintily.

"So, you are an Archangel," she said to Raphael, then turned to Micah, "And you are the Sentinel *Tholem*. Now, what is this imprinting that you were talking about?"

"No, he is really Micah, but you are right. He is God's Sentinel. I made Tholem up."

"Sounds like a lie to me."

"I was telling a story; it was storyteller's license."

Shannon did not look convinced, but turned her gaze to Micah. "And you are dying. You certainly look old, but you seem quite healthy to me."

"Apparently," began Micah, "I am, and a few moments ago I thought it might have been today."

Shannon ignored his jest. "You don't seem too upset about it. You want to die?"

Micah sighed. "It's not that easy, child."

Shannon raised a finger. "Please, I think we are well passed that."

"Indeed," Said Raphael.

Micah glared at him. "Not helping. I'm serious, Shannon. It is complicated. I have lived a long long time and seen many terrible things. It feels right. It feels time."

She looked at him. "Many terrible things? Like my mother dying?"

Micah winced. "Like that, yes. I should have been able to save her. But I was already too slow - too weak. I had been chasing them for months and might never have stopped them were it not for Margaret."

Micah smiled sadly. "You are just like her. Same face and the same hair - touched by fire." He sighed. "I found her fighting three of them. She shouldn't have even been able to fight one. A blade in each hand - she was a blur of elegance and motion. I stepped out of what must have looked to her like a glowing hole in the air, with eyes sparking green, covered in armor, and holding a sword."

Micah looked first at Raphael and then to Shannon. "Do you know what she said to me? Do you know what she said to this glowing god-like being that stepped out of the air?" Micah didn't wait for a response. "She said, 'can you get one of these off my back; I'll take the other two.' So I did."

"That's why I could tell Liam those monsters weren't coming back. Your mother killed them; I helped a little."

Shannon's eyes were bright. "If you killed them, why isn't she here?"

"It was him?" asked Raphael.

Micah looked over and nodded silently. "Yes, it was him. Maurius, my opposite. Once the skin walkers were dead, your mother ran toward your house to make sure you were all safe. I followed but was quite a ways back when she ran through the door. I heard the conflict and thought one of the skin walkers might have been in the house. I started to run. I was almost there when the door opened and I saw him there with Margaret."

"What happened?" Shannon asked through clenched teeth.

"Shannon, it is enough to say...'

"What. Happened. To. My. Mother."

Micah shivered. "He held her in front of him. His sword was through her back, impaling her. He was gloating, spewing nonsense about how he'd won. He went on about how he'd waited patiently, that he'd searched for her. He said she was the first soul-born and that he'd killed her Without her, darkness would grow and that I could not prevail. Then he pushed her forward tore open a portal and stepped through. I was going to leap through after him but your mother called to me. She was still alive and as I drew near she grabbed me. Her voice was like iron. She made me promise, Shannon. She made me swear to watch over you and your brothers, so I did. In those last moments, that's all I could give her. A promise. That's why I stayed. That's why I'm always underfoot. Because I let your mother die and I wasn't going to fail at keeping the promise I made to her."

Shannon's eyes were wet with tears as she stared into the ancient eyes of God's first Sentinel. She reached up and cupped his face with her hands wiping away his tears as well.

Raphael took in the scene. Looking first to the young woman who seemed so much older than her years and then to his friend, the Sentinel who had fought across the ages at his bequest. Angels didn't doubt; it wasn't in their nature, but as he reflected on the story he wondered at how it could be. In that moment of contemplation, he saw it on Shannon's outstretched wrist and he smiled a smile of the Angels.

"Maurius did not win. Maurius did not kill the soul-born."

Shannon and Micah turned toward the Angel.

"Did your mother have a tattoo, Shannon?"

She paused. "Yes, how did you know that?"

"It was on her wrist and it was in the form of a Dove." Raphael did not ask this, he stated it as fact.

"She told you she had it made to keep you safe."

Shannon's tears were flowing freely now. "Yes. She said it was our secret and that I should never speak of it."

Raphael reached over and gently raised the sleeve from Shannon's left arm and Micah let out a gasp. There was a perfectly formed dove on her arm.

"That," said the Angel, "is no mark made by man."

Micah looked, stunned, at the dove shaped birth mark. He touched it and the stone in his ring blazed brightly, just as it did that night 14 years ago. He stared into her eyes and saw tiny flecks of green that each glowed like small emerald stars.

Raphael placed a hand on Micah's and Shannon's shoulders. He looked at the Sentinel. "Behold, my friend. Behold your soul-born and rejoice."

Micah exerted a fair amount of will in order to keep silent. Shannon stared intently at the Angel, flipping her dagger absently across her knuckles. Each time it reached her little finger, she'd grasp it and bury into the table right between the fingers of her other hand as it rested there.

The old Sentinel watched as the dagger thunked between each finger in turn.

"Four hundred," she sighed, turning her eyes to Micah.

"Hmmm?"

"Four hundred. I have been rolling this dagger since I was younger than Liam. I can do it with my eyes closed, and I have placed it perfectly between each finger four hundred times while you've been waiting for me to slice something off."

"I assume four hundred is something special?" Micah asked, exasperated.

"Not really. I just like going through the whole hand a hundred times. It's a nice, round number."

"Seems you still have five fingers until you finally manage to cut one off. Wouldn't that be five hundred little thunks I should have heard rather than four hundred, if you wanted to attempt self amputation four hundred times?"

She narrowed her eyes a bit. "You aren't very good with numbers are you?"

"No, he is not," answered Raphael. "I gave up trying, millennia ago." The Angel held up a hand and nodded to Shannon. The girl placed her own finger between those of Raphael, each in turn. As she did so, he counted off, "One, two, three, and, four. Five fingers, but only four spaces between them. Thus, four hundred thunks."

"Four fingers and a thumb," she corrected.

"True enough, four and a thumb," Raphael accepted graciously.

"I'm glad you two didn't know each other before today," Micah grumbled and got up to look for some of the cheese they had eaten earlier.

"As I was saying," began Raphael, "I don't know why your mother recognized your birthmark as something special or had the foresight to understand that having it would place you in danger. Sometimes, Mothers just know things. You grew within her for nine months and, under normal circumstances, that creates a bond that borders on the magical. In your case, at the moment of conception, your very soul became imprinted with a sliver of something very special, unique in fact. Perhaps, in that moment she saw something, or felt something, that gave her insight into your destiny."

Shannon felt the air stir as something flew past her ear.

Raphael casually reached up and caught the wooden cup a scant second before it would have hit him full on the nose. Without taking his eyes off of Shannon, he said, "Micah, has a real problem with destiny. Makes him angry to think he does not have a choice in things. I find it one of the most confusing aspects of humanity, really. I just accept what I am and that I have a planned role to play."

"Freewill, Raphael. You have a hard time understanding freewill."

The Angel shrugged.

Micah returned to the table and set his plate and cup down with a bang. "Destiny means nothing for those who have freewill." He looked at Shannon. "You are free to do whatever you like. Do not let him take that away from you. Every choice I made across more years than I can count, I made freely and with full understanding that those decisions would have ramifications."

"I don't know, Micah. Raphael makes a pretty good case for destiny. He serves God, who exists outside of time. He sees the beginning, middle, and end, all at once like a tapestry laid out on a table. Just because we have to live our lives in one direction, following the thread from one end of the tapestry to the other, doesn't mean that the pattern hasn't already been woven."

Raphael looked smug. "That is the very thing I have been trying to explain to him for, well, forever."

"No, wait." said Micah, "You are looking at this wrong and also discounting something very important. First, let's just say you both are right. You aren't. But just for a moment let's just assume that you aren't horribly wrong - which you are. If only God sees this unfolded tapestry and none of the threads are the wiser to its overall weave, then how would each thread know the difference whether each decision were to affect a different weave or not?"

Shannon looked thoughtful and Micah continued, "Beyond that, Raphael always leaves out a critical aspect of my existence. I exist outside God's sight. He doesn't know what I will do or what effect it will have on the weave of His creation. If destiny is just the direction one's life will take because God has foreknowledge of it, then I cannot have a destiny, because God has no idea what I'm going to do next."

Micah popped a piece of cheese into his mouth as both he and Shannon turned to Raphael.

"I do not know why I always forget that part," Raphael said - his brow furrowed. "When I try to concentrate on that aspect of Micah's character, it is as if my mind slips off of it and cannot hold on to the thought." He turned to

Shannon and stared so intently at her that the girl began to fidget. The Angel gave an exasperated breath. "You too. It is the same with you. This is really quite remarkable. With everyone else, if I concentrate, I can see hints at their futures - at what they will do or what might be done to them. With you two, it's like a starburst of shadows reflecting back into facing mirrors. There are infinite possibilities." He shook his head, clearly uncomfortable.

"Don't worry, Raphael," said Micah, "By tomorrow, you won't even remember us having this conversation."

The Angel looked startled.

Micah turned to Shannon. "We've had this conversation at least a dozen times over the years, he and I. Usually it's because he notices something odd about a person who is close to me, something that unsettles him and he looks closer. That's when he usually finds it, but most times he just passes along without noticing."

Raphael grumbled. "Do I always hate being referred to in the third person as if I were not here?"

Micah brightened, "I don't know, actually. This is the first time I've actually been able to share it with anyone."

"Wonderful," said the Angel, "I hope you two enjoy the conversation that I am likely to forget."

"Oh, it's more than likely. You are *destined* to forget it."

"Now, that was just mean," said Shannon and she placed her hand on Raphael's.

"Wait, how did I become the villain in this story?" asked Micah.

"You are making fun of his disability," she said protectively patting his hand. Raphael smiled at her warmly.

"Says the two people critiquing my skill with numbers," shot back Micah, "Keep this in mind, my young soul-born lady, you have known him for a bit less then three hours. I've been putting up with his 'I'm a nigh omniscient Angel' speeches for nearly three. Thousand. Years. All I was trying to say was that you do not have a destiny that is outside your control. You have freewill."

"I never claimed to be anything close to omniscient, Micah. I can just see the pattern of people's lives."

"Not mine you can't. And, evidently not hers either. We are outside His sight," Micah said while making a vague upward gesture, "and thus way, way outside yours. So much outside yours, in fact, that just trying to pay too much attention to our futures makes you all wobbly at the knees. Tell me I'm wrong."

Raphael looked first to Micah and then to Shannon. He said nothing for a solid minute, then whispered, "You are *not* wrong."

"But, what does it mean?" asked Shannon, "This is all just a jumble in my head. My birthmark, my mother, you, Raphael. I can't make sense of any of it."

Micah chuckled warmly, "Not surprising given that much of it is confusing even to me. Raphael over there gets the angelic equivalent of nausea if he thinks about it too much. Let's try and break it down into smaller parts."

"First, you understand my task and how I came to be - at least conceptually." She nodded and Micah continued, "As I understand it, for me to be effective in this role, I had to be free of celestial interference as it were. I'm free to act without any fears of godly smiting, but any prayerful requests for aid and succor go unanswered as well. Raphael can hear me when I call him, but most times he stays away too, which is probably my fault because I usually just ask him *if* he should come rather than telling him that he *should* come. But that's a bit beside the point."

"That seems lonely."

"It is," said Micah with a sigh, "You have no idea how lonely it has become, and I hope you never do."

"But I don't see how any of that has to do with me or my mother. I don't see what caused me to be what you say I am. This soul-born, whatever that is."

Micah, lifted his hands, palms upward, in an expression of both regret and impotence. "All, I know is that one night, 14 years ago, my sleeping mind lashed out in both loneliness and sorrow. It used my power to fuel my wish for a family and a daughter. That wish imprinted itself on your soul as it was conceived. Truth be told, I don't even *know* that; it's really just a theory that Raphael advanced only hours ago. That said, given your birthmark and its reaction to my touch, I'd say it's a pretty good theory. As for why you were gifted or cursed with this connection to me, I cannot say. It seems a cruel joke for me to finally have such a connection with another person only to lose it"

"I remember. I think I remember?" The Angel looked imploringly at Micah. "Quickly, ground me to this moment. Shield me from my own nature and help me to remember."

Micah reached out to grasp the Angel's offered hands and held them tightly. Shannon gasped as both their eyes came alight blazing green and the air sparked with energy. "Shield me Micah. Shield me from myself."

The Sentinel clearly strained with the effort. "It's very hard, Raphael. There is so much connecting you to the heavens. I don't know if I can block it."

"You must or I will forget it all and you will never know."

Micah nodded and redoubled his efforts. The air crackled with the energy playing about both men and Shannon saw the Sentinel give a great heave as he formed his hands into fists around those of of Raphael. She felt a popping sensation. Around them formed a glowing green orb through which she could see the room, but it distorted as if viewing it from beneath the water. Shannon looked at Raphael. The Angel met her gaze but his eyes had lost their glow.

"I don't know how long I can hold this," Micah said, "It's like I'm being crushed by tons of rock."

"Understandable," began Raphael, "You're doing something that was not supposed to be done. You've abducted and subdued an Angel, removed from him all his power and all his constraints. It's remarkable."

Beads of sweat had broken out on Micah's forehead as he trembled from the strain and growled through clenched teeth, "Marvel later…explain now. Really heavy rocks crushing me."

Raphael pulled his hands free from Micah and turned to Shannon. She instinctively reached out and accepted the offered embrace. "Forgive me, child. I've done you a grave injustice. I've placed a burden on you without your knowledge and without your leave to do so. Micah rightly points out the nature of Angels is to obey, perfectly, and without question. I'm not to interfere with Micah's decisions regardless of whether they serve the light or darkness and I've held true to that charge throughout the centuries.

I've seen this man live a life of sacrifice, trial, and tribulation. It's my responsibility to ensure that the Sentinel's power endures and I saw that it could not without a dramatic change. Micah endured this lonely existence cut off from both earthly and spiritual love, but by enduring it, he limited his ability to transcend my original expectations. So, I used the freedom I was given in the narrowest of areas, the succession of power. Only there, where I was charged to ensure continuity regardless of cost, was I free to interfere as deeply and directly as was needed. I had seen Micah's need for family and love wax and wane over the years. I saw it manifest in many forms, but the strongest of these was when he lived his wish in the world of dreams. That night, 14 years ago when those dreams fused with his Sentinel powers and were given form, I was there waiting. While he sleeps, Micah's power does likewise, lest dreams and nightmares result in dramatic impacts upon the waking world. I removed that protective mantle at just the moment when he called his daughter into being within the dream. I knew that creative act would seek out the only acceptable vessel for such love and want. Only the human soul can contain both in such abundance. I watched as his desire and need gave form to the power and saw it lance upward and pierce the guff where souls are conceived of human parents. There, your parent's love brought you into being and at that moment, so too was your soul infused with a splinter of Micah's power.

I knew you would be needed for Micah's successor to prosper and exceed what Micah had been able to achieve absent the support of one such as you. I went to your mother and told her she had conceived a daughter and that you would be born with a mark that she could use to confirm my words. I told her that agents of darkness would seek to destroy the one who bore that mark because such a person would give the new Sentinel strength and support that was withheld from Micah. Withheld not from malice, but from yet another erroneous angelic act made by one too ignorant of human nature to realize the need for companionship and mortal love.

That is why your mother bade you keep your birthmark secret and why she took that same mark upon herself. She made herself the willing target - the sacrifice for those who would do you harm. She epitomized the agape love a mother has for her child. A love born of sacrifice."

Raphael turned from Shannon to look at Micah as he struggled to maintain the shield. "She is not for you, my old friend," Raphael said softly as tears gathered in his eyes. "I orchestrated her birth not for you, but so that he who comes after you would not have to suffer as you have. She carries a sliver of you within her and with that she can do things that none could do for you. She can, if she wills it, support and defend the man who takes up the burden you are so near to setting aside."

The shield collapsed and Micah slumped forward, eyes reverting to their normal color. Raphael stood, eyes now ablaze, looking quickly about the room, alarmed."

"Are you two alright?" He asked, "Some great energy was just released. I can feel its residual effect and it seems I have lost time. Why are you both staring at me like that? What has happened?"

"Raphael," Shannon began, clearly flustered, "You were just telling me that I-"

Micah reached over and placed his hand on hers. "Raphael, don't you remember my old friend? You were just telling her your age old views on destiny and freewill."

The Angel paused a moment looking at Micah. "Oh, well, that explains why you look so upset then. You never agree with me on that subject. He sat down again. I always have a hard time recalling it when we discuss that; I wonder why that is…"

Shannon looked from one to the other, wondering at all that must have transpired throughout their centuries together. She leaned down, gently placing a kiss on Micah's hand as it held her own. She gave him a sad smile, stood, and walked out of the cottage.

Shannon continued to sit on the large rock, eyes closed, mind open to the world around her. Micah had taught her how to do it. Meditating, he called it. She didn't do it very often because the feeling was so disconcerting. She only did it when very upset and the world felt like it was closing in around her.

The world was large when seen through her mind's eye. So large, so peaceful, yet so very odd. She could see herself sitting cross-legged on the rock at the edge of the river, as if she were hovering from above. Micah had told her that she wasn't really seeing herself, but that her mind created the images to give order to all she sensed around her. She called it her mindscape, this place to which she now retreated. Everything around her was crisp and clear. The river rushed by as fish darted within, animals moved about in the woods nearby, and birds flew into her field of awareness. The mindscape only extended a few hundred feet around her, but within it, she had almost complete knowledge. Beyond those three hundred feet things became indistinct, as if the world was being covered in a thick mist. If she concentrated, she could detect faint movement within this area but doing so for any length of time usually gave her a splitting headache so she avoided it. Beyond this misty area, all was blackness and no amount of concentration gave any inkling into what might be happening within or beyond. She had learned to simply ignore the blackness and pay very little attention to the mist. Nothing out there was her concern. Her world was her mindscape and within it there was peace. Even violent things seemed peaceful to her when viewed from that vantage. She remembered one time when a stag had raced into her field of awareness followed immediately by a small pack of wolves. She felt the stag's desperation and the wolves' determination at the same moment. She watched as predator and prey danced their deadly dance. When the wolves had cornered the exhausted creature and their alpha went for its neck, Shannon looked on with peace and understanding. The world depended on this harmony between predator and prey, just like it depended on so many other opposing forces. Had Shannon seen this outside the mindscape, she would have been horrified at the violence, and in desperate fear from the wolves. Not so within the mindscape. All was as it should be.

Movement within the mist. Deliberative movement in a direct line towards her. Shannon's full attention snapped to the misty point and remained focused and waiting. She was not alarmed. She was never alarmed within the mindscape. She just waited.

Micah stepped out of the mist and into the fullness of her awareness. He looked very different. The old man was wreathed head to toe with ribbons of green energy that played about his body. Interesting that she had never seen that before when he approached her within the mindscape. Something had changed.

She noticed how old he looked. Strong, yes, but so old as if the years were weights laid across his shoulders, making it hard for him to stand. Yet he stood straight despite the weight of those years. Shannon felt his emotions. That was new as well. They were a torrent of conflict; no harmony. He was sad and hopeful; angry and compassionate. He gave off regret and resolve in equal measures. Micah was still a good ways off, walking through the steeply wooded hill from his cottage to the river where Shannon sat. She knew he couldn't see her yet, she knew that, but his thoughts were preoccupied with her.

Shannon watched as Micah took the last few steps between the trees that obscured his view of the river. He stopped just outside the tree line, staring at her as she sat motionless upon her rock.

She shuddered within the mindscape as she felt his emotions shift abruptly. The conflict vanished and she felt her entire world shudder again as his focused attention rested upon her. She felt tears form in her closed eyes as his emotions poured out to her. Love. Protect. The emotions pierced her mindscape and the entire construct threatened to collapse around her. She knew it would be impossible to block his waves of emotion so, on instinct, she incorporated them into the mindscape itself, releasing her own equanimity and feeding her newly embraced emotions back into it as well. The mindscape grew still and strong once again and she saw Micah's eyes grow wide as he felt the now two-way emotional connection.

Micah began walking toward her again and Shannon turned her attentions back to the entirety of the mindscape, enjoying the new sensation brought about by fusing the peace that was inherent to the construct with the newly incorporated emotions fueled by both Micah and herself.

Shannon always found time to be quite tricky within the mindscape. She once thought she'd been meditating for hours, then discovered only minutes had passed. There was also one time, early on, where she had begun her morning by constructing a mindscape, intending just to hold it a few moments, only to realize that those moments had encompassed the entire day.

Micah sat down beside her on the rock. How long he'd been sitting there, she could not say. It felt like a long time and his posture suggested the same, but she knew such things were not to be trusted. Shannon made to speak, forgetting for a moment that she had no form within the mindscape. Her body remained still and silent, eyes closed facing out over the water.

"I will not enter," Micah said softly, "Truth be told, I'm not sure I could if I wanted to, but doing so would carry risks that are best left untaken."

Shannon remembered him telling her that before. Never invite another mind to share this place, he told her. Should you ever find another mind within, collapse the mindscape immediately. The mind is a solitary place and is not meant for others. The lessons skipped and skittered through her consciousness. When she directed her attention back to Micah, he was no longer on her rock.

He had made a small fire just behind her and was idly adding small twigs and sticks to the flames. That was curious. The day was warm and he wasn't cooking anything - why the fire?

Within the mindscape she took a long, formless, breath. She knew it wasn't a real breath, but it was what she had been taught. As she released it, she closed formless eyes, collapsed the mindscape, and opened her physical eyes on the world about her.

Sensation flooded her body - mostly pain. She was very stiff and one of her feet had fallen asleep. She looked up. The deep dark of a moonless night made the starlight sparkle all the brighter.

"How? How long?" she asked.

"Dawn is about two hours off. You've been in there quite some time. I'm not surprised, no doubt you had much to consider."

She felt a stab of panic and missed the peace of the mindscape immediately. "Oh no, Father..."

"It's alright. It's alright, Shannon" Micah said quickly, "I've spoken with him. I told him I was leaving tomorrow and asked if he would give you leave to help prepare the cottage for my lengthy absence."

Shannon felt her breathing steady and she stiffly swiveled herself around to face the Sentinel, extending her legs and rubbing blood back into her sleeping foot, grimacing at the tiny pinpricks of feeling.

"Lengthy absence," she said, "Permanent absence you mean, right?"

He nodded. "So it seems."

Neither said anything more for a long moment and Shannon slid off her rock, tentatively putting weight on her now wakeful foot. She walked a few paces away, looking out over the water.

"What happened to Raphael? Why didn't you let me ask him about what he did to me...to us?"

Even without the awareness granted by her mindscape, Shannon could feel the frown in Micah's voice. He sighed, "He wouldn't have understood, Shannon. What I did, cutting him off from all creation like that. It created a trauma so great that he suppressed even asking me to do it. I don't know what would have happened if your question had brought that reality back to him, but I suspect it would have been all kinds of bad."

Shannon spun, turning away from the river, voice rising. "He had no right to do what he did!" she shouted. "It's a violation! I don't even know what I am now. He said I have a sliver of you inside me. What the hell does that even mean?"

Micah flinched at her curse and spoke so softly that she could barely hear. "He had no right and it was an invasion." She saw the firelight sparkle in his moist eyes as he continued, "He invaded my dreams and used them to give form and substance to a plan he thought necessary even though that plan violated your very soul."

He stared at her. "I'm sorry."

"You did nothing wrong, Micah. You have nothing to apologize for."

He laughed softly. "No, you don't understand. I'm sorry that I can't bring myself to wish he had done otherwise. This intrusion into freewill - this violation. This horrible act resulted in the most amazing and beautiful gift I have ever seen. It resulted in you, Shannon. For the first time in my long life, I just wish I had more time."

Shannon walked back and sat down with Micah before the fire, taking his wizened hands in hers. "What am I?" she asked again, this time softly and without her previous rancor.

Micah turned to look at her and smiled, leaning over to place a kiss on her forehead. "You are as you always were. Strong, beautiful, brilliant, and fierce. You are my flame haired little wolf, and I love you like the daughter I never had.

Part of me lives in you and I pray that, in time, you come to accept that as a good thing despite how it came about."

"I can't believe you are just going to leave me with all..." she motioned to herself, "this. It's not like I can talk to Father about it."

"No!" Micah said quickly, "No, you are right about that. You must never speak about any of this. Not with your father, or Donal, or Liam. No one. Your mother gave her life so that you would be hidden from those who want you dead. The best way to honor that sacrifice is with your silence."

"So, I just sit with this magical sliver in me? To what end?" She snorted.

"I wish I knew, Shannon. More than anything, I wish I knew the answer to that. I can only assume that it's something that will unfold when you meet... him."

"Him? Him who?"

"My successor. The one to whom the Sentinel's mantel will go."

"So he's near?"

Micah shook his head, "No, according to Raphael, he's just about as far away as a person can get. In fact, as I understand it, he hasn't even been born."

"Oh, that's wonderful. This just keeps getting better. Shall I look for a star to lead me on to where the magical baby Sentinel is going to born?"

Micah smirked - his aged face cracking with lines. "Apparently, you will be long dead before he is born."

She stared at him, expression completely flat. "What?"

"Yes, that was my reaction as well. This is one of the many things today has revealed to me. Do you recall my telling you of how I could rip open a portal and travel quickly from here to there? How I used that to find your mother when she fought the skin walkers?"

Shannon nodded silently.

"Well, and this is the really special part, evidently I can do that through time as well."

Shannon took a deep, calming breath. "You can travel through time and place?"

"Apparently."

"But you don't know how to do this?"

"Not the slightest idea how to do it, no."

"But you are going to do it anyway?"

"Well, Raphael is going to do it. He knows how. He was there when God set all these rules up, so he has a better idea how to take things apart or bend the rules. I don't understand it, Shannon, but it seems I would have to in order to use my abilities. Look, I understand fire. I understand how to make it, how it acts, how it doesn't act. Because I understand it, I can do really remarkable things with it. I thought I understood time; it flows forward. The day starts, it continues, and it ends. That understanding allows me to affect it, make it flow a bit faster or a bit slower. Evidently, time is a bit more complex than that. According to Raphael it can be folded and ripped in addition to bent, but I have no earthly idea how. Doesn't really matter, though. As I said, Raphael knows how and he's going to bend, fold, rip or do whatever he thinks needs doing to get him and me to the same place as my potential successor."

Shannon gave Micah a sly grin. "The one who will be born after I'm dead?"

"Long dead...six hundred years from now - give or take."

Shannon threw a twig in the fire. "I'm pretty sure being dead six hundred years is going to reduce my effectiveness."

"Unless..." began Micah, "he can rip time and come here."

Shannon's eyes widened. "Why would he be able to do something that you've been unable to do for the couple thousand years you've been doing whatever it is you've been doing?"

Micah laughed. "Raphael says he's smarter than me."

"Raphael needs to develop some tact. Are all Angels so incredibly inept?"

"No idea. He's the only one I've ever met. But, according to Raphael, he's the epitome of human connectedness, at least from the vantage of the heavenly hosts."

Shannon whistled softly, "Wow...that's hard to believe."

"Yes, well, be that as it may, supposedly my successor has a better grasp on the rules that hold creation together and thus will be better able to take them apart. Science is quite advanced in his time and he is one of the smarter people of his generation. All that comes together in a package that results in a Sentinel that could rip time and come to you."

"Great, well, something to look forward to. Why would he even think to do that."

"I'm going to tell him to do it, Shannon. I will extract his promise. I told Raphael this. I will not pass on the power unless that man assures me he will come for you, explain what happened to me, and protect you as needed."

"I can take care of myself, Micah. Besides, according to your Angel, I'm supposed to be supporting *him*."

"You are supposed to support each other, and I'm going to make sure he lives up to his end. That's all."

Micah stirred the fire as he glanced up, noticing the first hints of a lightening sky.

"Wait a minute," said Shannon, "If Raphael is going to rip a hole in time and take you both six hundred years into the future, why doesn't he just do it ten years from now and just go five hundred and ninety years. Why do you have to go now?"

Micah looked at her, "You know, that is a really good question, maybe we can-"

"No, we must leave tonight. Before dawn in fact."

Both Shannon and Micah jumped and turned toward the voice.

"Raphael! How many times have I asked you not to do that?"

The Angel looked at Micah considering, "Many. In fact, many times many."

"And yet…"

The Angel shrugged and the act seemed awkward, "It is in my nature to travel thusly. I am sorry."

"Well, that answer just isn't good enough," said Shannon, standing to face the Angel, "You drop all this information on me and also tell Micah that he has the closest thing to a daughter he will get, but has to leave her the same night he finds out. Fine, but then you say the reason he has to leave is because he can't be late for something that won't occur for six hundred years."

The young woman put her hands on her hips and glared at the Angel. "Start making sense, or he's not going anywhere."

Raphael cocked his head slightly. "I do not see how you could stop us."

"How about if I swear on my mother's soul to never give your precious new Sentinel the time of day? How about if I swear on her soul to simply ignore any request he ever makes even if it means his life?"

"I don't see you making or keeping such an oath, child."

"Oh, yes I would."

"But, why would you do that?"

"Because I can be spiteful - really spiteful."

Micah was nodding. "I've seen it, Raphael. And if she makes such an oath, you can trust it will be kept."

The Angel sighed. "Very well, but you will not understand my explanation."

Shannon narrowed her eyes further and Raphael hurried on.

"Some points in time are fixed while others are related to each other. Those that are relative can be moved around and manipulated. Those that are fixed cannot. The time for Micah to release his power to another is one of those fixed points in time because its only other relation is to the fixed point of creation itself. I have worked backwards to this moment from the point at which the new Sentinel will, or will not, accept the mantel of power. The only way this occurs at the appointed time is if we leave - now."

Shannon looked down at Micah.

"I told you that you would not understand it," said Raphael.

She snapped her gaze back to him. "Try not being so arrogant around people who you are asking to help save the world, especially those whose souls-"

"-Are committed to helping this new Sentinel achieve his goals," interrupted Micah as he stood and gave Shannon a curt shake of the head.

Raphael looked perplexed. "I am sorry. I did not intend to insult you. Micah does not understand this any better than you."

Shannon ground her teeth as Micah put his hand on Raphael's shoulder. "I know you didn't mean to insult her. Shannon just hasn't had as much time to get to know you as I have. You gave a fine explanation. Even I understood it."

Micah gave Shannon a little wink and she found herself smiling despite herself.

"Excellent," said the Angel as his eyes sparked to life and energy gathered about him, then let us be off Micah.

"Wait!" shouted Shannon and she felt the gathered energy dissipate. "You have to give us time to-" her voice faltered, "- say goodbye."

She turned to Micah and took him in trying to sear the entirety of him into her memory. The thick, wavy salt and peppered hair and beard. The lines of his face and about his eyes. His tall, lean form, and finally the eyes. Those eyes she looked into ever since she was a child, deep and gray, and full of love. She felt the tears come, filling her own, as she quickly covered the few paces that separated the two of them. She wrapped her arms about Micah and buried her head into his chest, squeezing him, holding him tight. After long minutes, she felt his finger under her chin lifting her face towards his.

"I have to go, little fire wolf."

"I don't want you to. I don't want you to," she cried all bravado gone, "You've been like a second father and I don't want you to leave."

Micah stared down at her through his own tear filled eyes. "Oh, child, that was the best gift you could ever have given me. I have always loved you like the daughter I never thought I had, but that you truly are. Remember," he said tapping her softly above the heart, "part of me lives in you, now and forever. Trust me that someday we will see each other again. Not in this life, but someday."

Shannon was crying harder now and turned angrily toward Raphael, "Is that true, Angel? Angel's cannot lie. Is it true?"

Raphael looked at down at her, "Yes, it is true."

"Then say it. Say it plain and say it to me now."

"I say to you now, Shannon McLeod, I, Raphael, Archangel and guardian of humanity promise in sight of God and creation, you will meet Micah again unless the stars fall from the sky and creation ceases."

Micah felt her slump in his grasp and she stepped back, wiping away the tears. She kept her gaze locked on Micah but felt the power gather and crackle as Raphael did something beside her. The Angel shouted a word she did not recognize and behind Micah, the air rippled and tore open revealing a glowing oval through which she could see what looked like a narrow road with bricked walls to either side and, in the distance, strange houses of enormous size that rose against a midday sky.

She watched as Micah faced the portal and stepped through. She could see him look around and turn back to her and to Raphael. As the Angel followed Micah through, Shannon yelled after him, "His name - do you know the name of this man I will be waiting to meet?"

Now they were both standing on the other side of the portal facing her. Raphael's voice was distorted as it passed through the portal and the centuries it bridged. For his part, Micah simply raised fingers to lips, kissed them, and pointed to her.

"Kellan Thorne," the Angel answered.

The portal closed and they were gone.

Chapter 4

A POWER RENEWED

"S eriously?" Juliet asked as she stood in the alley, hands on hips. "'Would I lie to you?' is the best you could come up with? You lie all the time. Remember the moon incident?"

Kellan cringed a little.

"Oh yeah, let's revisit that little 6th grade gem for a moment. I maintained against all logic and proof that my "Uncle" Kellan had, indeed, been on the moon because *he* wouldn't lie to me. Middle school is a nightmare under the best of circumstances and, trust me, being the idiot girl whose bigger idiot pseudo-uncle wasn't EVER on the moon does not make for the best of circumstances. Now, it's not cool leaving me in the store by myself; there's a customer looking for a first edition Heinlein, and Hamish is being more annoying than usual."

Kellan looked up and down the alley for what must have been the hundredth time since Michael left him. "Look, Juliet, it's been years since I've been able to pull anything like that on you. I'm not kidding you. I'm not messing around. Go inside, now. It's not safe to be near me."

She stared at him appraisingly, taking everything in. Something was definitely wrong here. Kellan's normally unflappable demeanor was all akilter, with some gelatinous slime covering his face and clothes. He was bleeding from several small cuts to his hands and arms and his jeans were torn at both knees. His eyes held a wildness she had never seen before and reminded her of the frantic look on George Bailey's face when he realized Uncle Billy had lost all the bank's money.

"Monsters? What did you call them? Slimewalkers?"

Kellan shook his head violently. "Skin-walkers! Go inside, Juliet. Now!"

Juliet looked down where something had carved a thin circle into the cement and then looked directly into Kellan's eyes. "Make me."

Outside the alley someone slammed a car door and Kellan jumped turning quickly toward the sound and then whipped around looking to the other end of the alley.

Juliet took a hesitant step backwards towards the still open door to the shop. "Kellan, you look really really freaked out and that's scaring me. If you are messing with me again, now would be a very good time to stop."

"I am not messing with you and I cannot make you go inside. The guy said don't leave the circle and after what just happened, I'm not leaving the circle." Kellan paused a moment before continuing. "Unless you don't go in. If you don't go inside right now, so help me, I will make you, but I'm pretty sure if I step outside this circle those nightmares will show up in short order and shred me."

They locked eyes again and Juliet stood with one foot on the stoop, unmoving.

"Fine!" yelled Kellan. Juliet saw him tense about to move forward.

"Stop! Stop! Stop! I'm going," she said scrambling up the stairs and into the shop. There, she turned around, closed the door halfway, and looked back at Kellan. "I'm just going to stay right here. If you see any monsters let me know and I'll close the door immediately. How about I call 911?"

Kellan laughed. It sounded as wild as his eyes looked. "Yeah, sure, call 911 and tell them a dozen homicidal Skin-walkers, whatever they are, just slimed up an alley in Roswell and were sliced and diced by Michael the Archangel." He laughed again. "I'm sure they'll race right over. Juliet, I am completely aware of how bloody crazy this sounds, but apparently that's where I live at the moment - Crazytown."

Juliet felt a chill run down her. Kellan was absolutely one for mercilessly pranking someone, but he always went for the quick laugh. This was something different entirely.

"I'm closing the shop and getting your gun."

"What? No! Just go inside and..."

She slammed the door and was gone leaving Kellan to impotently shift his weight within the circle while softly cursing himself for ever hiring the girl.

Kellan's peripheral vision caught movement to his left at the end of the alley. Rather than whip his attention towards it, he stood transfixed, musing internally about how he must look like every victim in a slasher movie.

With what felt like an extreme effort of will, Kellan finally turned to fully face the closed end of the alley.

He swallowed hard and blinked several times.

Two men stood with their backs to him. Beyond them glowed an open portal - a twin to the one used by Michael earlier. Both men appeared tall, with the one to the left being a head taller than the man to his right. The taller one wore what appeared to be robes of some kind while the other wore armor similar to that of Michael. The armored man raised his right hand as if in greeting to someone but who was obscured by the two men. Around them and through the portal, Kellan could make out a night sky full of stars which glowed down upon a wooded scene.

Kellan thought he heard something coming from the portal, but couldn't be sure, then the taller man responded crisply, "Kellan Thorne," and the portal winked out.

"Oh shit," Kellan said. The two men turned toward the sound of his voice.

Micah and Raphael closed the space between Kellan and themselves, stopping a few feet from him.

Micah regarded several of the puddles surrounding Kellan and raised an eyebrow to Raphael.

"Apparently," began the Angel, "Someone knew of my previous visit to see Kellan Thorne."

"So it appears," responded Micah who then turned his attention to Kellan.

"Impressive. Really quite impressive. I am Micah Ben Judah and I am very pleased to meet you," said Micah offering his hand.

Kellan backed away slightly and paled as Micah's hand passed over and through the circle's barrier, disrupting the energy and collapsing its protection.

Micah lowered his hand turning to Raphael. "What is going on? This man has no idea who I am and clearly didn't destroy these skin-walkers or erect a defensive circle."

The Angel looked perplexed. "Of course not; he has never met me and how could he possibly have defeated half a dozen skin walkers?"

Micah sighed, "Of course he hasn't. Well then who created the circle and dispatched the walkers."

"Michael." Kellan answered causing both Micah and Raphael to turn to him. "Your brother, Michael, gives his regards. Raphael is it?"

Raphael nodded. "Michael was here?"

"Oh yes, he was here. Blazing sword and all. And guess what? He doesn't like me. He thinks I'm dangerous and seemed pretty cool with the idea of those skin walker monsters having their way with me. He sliced them up into tiny Jell-O pieces against his own better judgement and did so only because he evidently loves you a lot. So, you have that going for you, Raphael, which I'm sure is quite nice. Of course that leaves me, nearly killed, covered in monster slime, and having talked to three Angels who I didn't believe existed an hour ago."

Raphael gestured to Micah. "He is not an Angel."

Micah shook his head. "That's what you took away from his statement? Kellan, I sincerely apologize for the way you have been treated." He offered his hand.

This time Kellan slowly extended his own, accepting the older man's grasp.

"Ohhkay," said Kellan as he released Micah's hand, "I've pretty much figured out that you guys aren't here to kill me. So, how's about we all three go inside, I fill the biggest glass I can find chocablock full of Scotch, and we sort all this out."

Micah smiled, "I love Scotch."

There was a clang and all three turned as the shop's backdoor opened and slammed against the wall. "Kellan, I closed the shop, and brought your—"

Juliet broke off as her eyes found those of Raphael glowing brightly with alarm at the sound she had made. She raised the Smith and Wesson .45 and pointed it directly at the Angel, "Get the fuck away from him!"

He took a step toward the girl. Kellan saw Juliet's face darken and tried to call out to her but it was already too late. The alley was split with the barking report of the .45 as Juliet emptied every round of the clip into a very startled Raphael.

"I'm going to need to find a support group, that's for sure. Hello, I'm Juliet Herrick, and I killed an Angel."

"He's not dead," said Micah for the third time. "He's just…a little stunned is all. You can't kill an Archangel with a gun, even a really big gun, like yours."

"It's Kellan's gun. I just borrow it from time to time—to kill Angels."

Micah realized he was getting nowhere and opened the door of the little office. Juliet moved past him and slammed the door shut again.

"Kellan said stay in the office, so that's what we are going to do."

Micah glanced past her at Raphael slumped limply in the overstuffed chair. "Ahh. Look, he's back."

Juliet turned to see Raphael's eyes snap open and he stood up as they blazed to life.

"Stop, Raphael," said Micah reassuringly. "There was a little accident. You are fine now. Everything is fine."

Raphael nodded and sat back down, looking over at Juliet. "You cursed at me."

"I shot you thirteen times and you are critiquing my language?"

"He really hates foul language," Micah said. "It's one of his quirks."

"Well then, Mr. Angel, I hope you don't plan on spending much time around Kellan, because he can weave a tapestry of profanity that'll make your ears bleed. Of course he never does it when he thinks I can hear, but I hear things he doesn't know I hear."

The office door opened and Kellan walked in.

"Ok, the cops are gone. Holy shit, I almost thought they were going to search the place."

Raphael flinched.

"See," said Juliet as Micah smiled, "that's just an appetizer. Wait for the full course."

"Huh?" said Kellan.

"Nothing, boss, so what did you tell the cops?"

"Oh, I told them that some kids were setting off firecrackers in the alley and I went out to tell them to stop."

"And they beat the crap out of you?"

"No, and I tripped on that stupid loose brick, but rather than stay to help me, the kids ran off. I'll tell you one thing, it's good you hit Clarence there with every round because those cops were looking for bullets in the alley."

"Who's Clarence?" asked Raphael

"You are." answered Kellan and Juliet at the same time.

"So, it appears that Micah here was correct, bullets don't kill Angels. How are you feeling, Raphael?"

"Actually, I am in quite a bit of pain. That weapon is surprisingly powerful and it caught me completely unaware. I never imagined the girl would attack me that way."

"*The girl*," began Juliet, "asked you to move away nicely."

"Ok, whatever," said Kellan. "The Angel is back from the dead, and you two have a whole bunch of explaining to do. Starting with, how come monsters tried to kill me earlier today."

"I am perfectly prepared to answer all your questions, Kellan. In fact, I've been looking forward to having that very conversation although I admit this is not how I expected it to start," Micah said with a smile. "Now, you did mention the possibility of Scotch earlier and I saw some very nice chairs elsewhere in your establishment. Might we go there?"

"Uh, yeah, sure," said Kellan, going behind his desk, opening the lower drawer and removing a half full bottle of Scotch. He smiled, "25 year old Macallan. Juliet, would you mind grabbing a few glasses and bringing them to the reading room? Get yourself a Coke while your at it, I have a feeling this explanation is going to leave us pretty parched."

"You got it," Juliet said as she turned to open the door and leave.

"Shouldn't the girl head home to her parents? I am not sure if she should be exposed to what we have to discuss."

Juliet gently closed the door again, smiling at Micah.

"Uh oh," said Kellan.

"*The girl,*" said Juliet, "has a name. Her name is Juliet and she hates being talked about like she's some potted plant. In addition, *the girl*, still has a .45 caliber handgun and now that she knows it won't kill you, isn't afraid to use it again."

Micah raised his hands in surrender, "I apologize and, for the record, I could most certainly be killed by that weapon. Really, I just didn't want to expose you to—"

"What? Skin-walkers that tried to kill my friend. Archangels that rip their stolen skin from their bodies or decapitate them?"

Micah turned accusingly toward Kellan.

"Don't you dare look at me that way! I thought I was going insane and Juliet asked me why I wouldn't leave a little scraped circle in the cement. So, you can just put away that look of disdain, Sontaran. If you had done your job right, I wouldn't have had monster assassins on my ass before you arrived."

Micah sighed, "Sentinel..."

"What?"

"Sentinel, not Sontaran. You said Sontaran"

"Oh," Kellan laughed. "Sorry about that; you don't look anything like a Sontaran."

Juliet shook her head. "He's from the 13th century, boss, they don't have TV—let alone Doctor Who. He's not going to get your clever Sontaran reference. I'll get the glasses and meet you guys in the reading room."

"Is she always like that," asked Raphael?

"Yeah, pretty much."

"I like her," said Micah. "She reminds me of someone from back home."

"Really?" said Kellan walking past them and out the door, "If that's so, I'd like to meet her."

"You will."

"What?"

"Let's wait for the glasses," said Micah as Kellan led them to the chairs.

"No, I have not had enough," Kellan said wiggling the empty Scotch bottle at Juliet.

She frowned, turning to the old Sentinel for support, "Micah, talk sense to him."

He shrugged. "Actually, I'd like some more too. It's likely the last time I'll ever have it and the last time it will affect Kellan the way it is now."

"Hold your horses right there. I haven't agreed to anything—not one damn thing. Well, except to drinking more Scotch. Juliet, if you please."

The young woman gave an exasperated sigh. "Fine." She headed back toward Kellan's office.

He raised his hand to stop her. "No, would you get the bottle from the front case?"

"Uh, Kellan, you want me to get the 1943 Single Malt?"

"Yep, that's the one. You're gonna love this Micah. It's to die for." He laughed. "Quite literally in your case, eh?"

Juliet hadn't moved. "Kellan, I thought you were saving that for—"

"—For today, Juliet. Now please fetch it."

Kellan watched her head towards the front of the store, one hand pressed against her stomach as if she felt ill. *Well, that made sense. The only thing keeping me from doing the same was the four glasses of Scotch I've just drunk.*

Kellan turned back to Micah and gestured to the dozens of books scattered amongst the chairs.

"Your stories?"

The old man spread his hands, "So it would appear."

"Let's recap, shall we," said Kellan, picking a large leather bound book up from the floor.

"The Bible. Evidently a pretty big chapter is missing where the Devil and God hang out and play let's make a deal while Angel McWeepy there cries to the Flaming-Sword-Angel who, it just so happens, hates me."

"He does not hate you," interjected Raphael, "He just does not—"

"Bup. Bup. Bup," Kellan said, silencing Raphael with his hand. "You weren't there. He looked at me and trust me…the dude doesn't like me."

"That is probably true, but dislike is not hate."

"Whatever." Kellan set the Bible down on a side table and tapped it while staring at both men.

"Jericho—and the walls came tumbling down, 1400 BC. Joshua's priests spoke of a young man with eyes of emerald who could command the earth and did so at the last blowing of their horns."

"Micah is not in the Bible," said Raphael.

"No, probably because he smacks too much of magic," said Kellan, "but I read an apocryphal account once years ago and dismissed it at the time. That was you they were referring to Micah. Nice job killing everyone in a city, well except Rhab. A bit excessive don't you think?"

Raphael glared at Kellan. "You are not one to judge what is or is not excessive. That city was a—"

Micah saw the look on Kellan's face and tried to intervene. "Raphael, it is perfectly reasonable for Kellan to ask whether—"

"I'm not one to judge?" Kellan yelled rounding on Raphael. "That's some bullshit right there. I am exactly the one to judge, because I'm not going to be a puppet on some celestial string, Raphael. I was perfectly happy with my little mundane life before you brought all kinds of hell into it. So, yeah, I'm going to ask all sorts of uncomfortable questions, and you two are going to answer every bloody one of them. Or you can make with your fancy glowing portals and get the hell out."

Raphael stared, clearly shocked by the outburst and then rose, turning to Micah. "This may have been a mistake; this is what Michael warned me about, but I wouldn't listen."

Kellan closed the distance between them and said very softly, "Always good to recognize mistakes early. Don't let the door hit you in the ass."

"Stop. Both of you, just stop," said Micah. "Now sit down!"

Neither of them moved.

"Sit. Down."

Raphael sat down.

"Fine," said Kellan taking, the other chair. "Juliet! What are you doing? I asked you to bring me the Scotch not distill it and smoke it over peat."

He noticed her standing between two bookshelves holding the bottle with two hands and looking more frightened than she had while blasting away at Raphael earlier.

Kellan's voice immediately softened. "Juliet? What is it? Are you ok? Come here. Please, sit down."

She did as he asked, passing the bottle to him as she sat and looked from Micah to Raphael, then finally back to Kellan.

"Really? What is it? Am I *ok*? You think this guy was knocking down city walls and murdering people almost thirty five hundred years ago, and that's what you ask me?"

Kellan actually smiled at the absurdity of it all. "Well, when you put it *that* way, it makes me seem like an idiot."

Juliet arched an eyebrow clearly communicating an "if the shoe fits—" message.

"I can't believe you are actually considering this," Juliet said.

"Considering what? There's nothing to consider," replied Kellan as he first filled Micah's glass, then his own.

Kellan swirled the amber liquid around in the glass and lifted it to his nose, inhaling. He closed his eyes and took a long pull from the glass, feeling the liquor glide smoothly over his tongue.

"Oh man. That is just heaven in a glass. Where have you been all my life?"

"In a bottle waiting to be opened the day your book got published, that's where it's been. Since I don't think that miraculously happened in the last twelve hours, I'd definitely say you were considering something. I was done with my Coke an hour ago. Give me a glass of that."

"What? No. You're a kid."

"Shut up. I'm almost nineteen, sitting in a room with a 3,500 year old guy and an Archangel, who I shot thirteen times in the chest and face. Do you really think I'm going to do a whole lot more growing up in the next two years than I did in the last two hours?"

"She has a point," said Micah smiling behind his glass. I told you that you should have sent her home.

"Fine," said Kellan, "If there's still Coke sloshing around in that glass go get another one; I'm not going to have 70 year old Scotch mixing with sugar water."

Juliet held out her glass defiantly. "It's been bone dry for an hour and, given the trauma of the day, I'll let your blasphemy against Coca-Cola go—this time."

Kellan gave an exasperated sigh and poured a short finger of Scotch into her glass.

"More."

"No. You aren't even going to like it."

Juliet pulled the glass back and drained it in a swallow. "You're right—that's horrible. More."

"What the hell, Juliet? That's not Jaegermeister. You don't shoot it. God's sake you shouldn't be shooting anything."

"Except Angels," she said toasting Raphael with her empty glass. "Now give me an adult portion and I'll sip it like a lady."

Raphael was watching the entire exchange silently and turned to Micah. "I really don't understand any of this."

Micah lowered his voice to give the illusion of privacy, "I know, but it's alright. They are just worried about each other. Let them be."

Kellan and Juliet ignored the exchange as she settled back in her chair, snuggling deep into the overstuffed leather with her now half full glass of Scotch.

"Ok, gentlemen, you may continue."

Kellan laughed, gifting her with a seated bow complete with a flourish. "Why thank you, m'lady."

"Micah," he began, "Let's talk Homer 700 BC. He wrote a poem entitled *Sentalus*."

"Wait," interrupted the Sentinel, "I want to linger on your last example for just a moment. You mentioned my killing a city full of people. That's not what happened."

"OK, well, maybe you didn't kill them directly but blowing down their walls for someone else to kill them is pretty much the same thing. I get it, war is hell or some other cliche'. I don't have all the facts. There were mitigating circumstances, but aren't there always?

"No," said Micah firmly. "When I said it didn't happen that way, I mean all those people didn't die. Yes, I was there. Yes, I was the one referred to in the account you referenced. Yes, I was the tool used to bring down the walls."

"I'll never be anyone's tool," growled Kellan, but Micah ignored him.

"War histories are written by the victors and to the victors' ends. There were deaths in that conflict to be sure, but not wholesale slaughter although rumors of it prevented future conflicts for centuries."

"Not to mention the atrocities that were taking place behind those walls; no one wrote of those either," said Raphael.

"True," replied Micah "but I don't think Kellan is interested in hearing justifications for past actions."

"Quite right" Kellan said, "now back to Homer."

"Kellan," Juliet interjected, "Micah just gave you a darn good explanation despite you pretty much calling him a mass murderer. Don't you think that's worth some kind of acknowledgment?"

Kellan looked over at Juliet, now sitting cross legged in the leather club chair holding her glass in both hands and peering over its rim.

He sighed. "You know I hate it when you use your 'Mother' voice on me. I'm almost twice your age"

"And a man so almost half as smart." She made a pointed glance in Micah's direction.

"Fine. Micah, assuming what you say is true, I'm sorry I implied you supported mass homicide almost four thousand years ago."

He looked back to Juliet. "Happy?"

"That was pathetic," she said, dismissing him with a wave.

"For the love of all that's holy, I'm trying to get through half a dozen pretty serious questions here. Can we all just stay focused? Damn it, Homer 700 BC. The poem *Sentalus* that described—"

"Me," interrupted Micah. "Next question."

Kellan opened his mouth to respond, but then just shrugged and set the small volume of Homeric poetry on the side table. He picked up another book from the floor.

"Plague of Justinian, 541 AD, nearly half of Constantinople wiped out until the initiation of what was then described as a blood-grasp spread throughout the city. Seems someone meeting your general description: out of place garments, glowing eyes, the whole schtick, started the practice because he was immune to the plague. He cut a gash along his palm and had the infected person do likewise and then they'd grasp hands, mingling the blood. The infected person got better and could then heal others the same way."

Micah nodded, his expression distant. "So many dead. Young, old, men, women, children. Stacked up like cordwood burned outside the city. Raphael told me my blood was special and that I could not get sick so I figured if I could give it to someone else, it might help. It did."

"You're immune to the Bubonic Plague?" Kellan asked incredulously.

Micah shrugged, "I don't know what that is? But I didn't get sick. I never get sick."

"The Sentinel is immune to all pestilence," Raphael stated matter of factly.

"Really? Bacterial and viral?"

"Of course. Metabolic too."

"No cancer," murmured Juliet thinking of her own mother's successful struggle against the disease. "That's a handy ability to have."

Micah shrugged again, "I'm feeling the full weight of my being displaced in time. I don't understand what you three are saying. As I stated. I have not gotten sick since the day I accepted Raphael's request and became the Sentinel. My blood can help some things but not others and I don't know why."

"You know why, don't you Raphael?"

The Angel nodded.

"Then why didn't you tell him?"

"It is not my place."

"That's bullshit too. I hope you realize if I end up doing this thing, I'm going stick my blood in a petri dish and start figuring out what the hell's up with it."

Raphael smiled for the first time in hours. "Yes. I suspect you will and much more. That is one of the positive aspects of my gambit in selecting you. The negative aspects are much more apparent."

Kellan gave Raphael a flat stare. "Impressive back hand there. Moving on." He dropped the last book atop the other two and picked up a fourth.

"Mayan civilization had a bit of a problem between 1020 and 1100. You know anything about that, Micah?"

The Sentinel's eyes widened. "How in heavens name could you have known about that?"

Kellan tapped his temple. "I'm brilliant, remember? I remember everything."

"He's not kidding," interjected Juliet, "He really does, quite literally, remember everything he reads or sees. The brilliant part is open for considerable debate though." She flashed her teeth at Kellan.

He squinted at her glass, which was still mostly full, and turned back to Micah. "I pieced some things together from a few hundred disparate accounts I've run across over the years but this engraving of Ajaw Yaxun B'alam is the clincher. Ajaw is, of course, their word for king. So this engraving has the king meeting with, hey, someone that looks like you. Beams shooting out of the eyes and everything."

Kellan turned the page around and showed it to Micah then to Raphael.

Juliet reached over and grabbed the book. "Holy crap, that actually does look like you, Micah."

"They were sacrificing people. Continually and in great numbers. I was there for other reasons and," he paused, "I found myself in a rather difficult predicament. A young woman saved my life and I asked her how I could repay her. She asked me to stop the sacrifices. So I did"

"Woah," said Kellan, "that is one packed statement you just made."

"She saved your life? What happened to the whole immortal Sentinel thing."

"He is not immortal," said Raphael.

"Yeah, I just picked that up, so what happened?"

Micah waved his hand. "It really is a long story and, in all honesty, not a particularly interesting one. The important thing is that, yes, I can be killed and, yes, I did something rather dramatic to repay that woman."

"Which you should not have done," Raphael said sourly.

"Well, now we are getting somewhere," exclaimed Kellan. "So, you trashed an entire civilization by creating an 80 year long drought. And apparently pissed off Raphael in the process. Well done."

"I'm not proud of it, Kellan. It was a mistake and Raphael didn't speak to me for nearly 100 years."

"That seems a bit excessive and petulant," Kellan said—giving Raphael a pointed look. "You are going to have to be a bit more chill about things, or we won't be talking very much."

The Angel nodded, "Another of the aforementioned negatives."

Kellan smiled, "See, we are starting to understand each other already." He drained what little Scotch remained in his glass and filled it again, this time only half way.

Juliet glared at him.

"Last one, I promise."

"And speaking of last one. This is my last reference and, I have to admit it's my favorite. It refers to Vlad Tepes who was killed in 1447 and his head sent on to Constantinople"

Kellan stopped. "You sure have a thing for Constantinople don't you?"

"Anyway, the dominator of the principality of Walachia wrote a very interesting account of Vlad's death."

"Wait," said Juliet, "We're talking Vlad the Impaler—as in Stoker's Dracula?"

"Yeah, isn't it cool? Now you see why I saved the best for last."

"You were doing them in chronological order, Kellan."

"I was? Oh, wow, I was."

"Yeah, you're brilliant. Just not observant," she said with a smirk. "Dish on the Dracula story."

"Ok, well, according to Basarab Laiota, Vlad had bathed in so much blood that he had become a real live, well, undead, monster. Now, everyone figured that Basarab was completely full of it, because, after all, he was Vlad's rival. But, maybe he was on to something. What do you think, Micah?"

"He was a vampire. He made lots of other vampires and I killed them all."

Kellan took a sip from his glass, looked at Juliet and then back to Micah. "You really don't have a flair for storytelling do you?"

He shrugged.

"So wait," said Juliet, "Stoker was right. No way. Absolutely no way. Vlad Dracula was the first vampire?"

Micah shook his head. "I don't know what a Stoker is, but Vlad Tepes was far from being the first vampire. He was a ruthless tyrant who, in his mind, defended Europe from muslim encroachment. The vast blood he shed attracted vampires to his land and, eventually, one turned him into the Undead as well. It's really as simple as that."

"Yeah, Juliet, it's as simple as that—vampires. Too bad you couldn't start a war between werwolves and vampires, that might have kept the numbers down."

Micah looked perplexed. "Werewolves and Vampires have natural antipathy for each other as it is. They don't need my help to be at each other's throats."

"Uh, I was trying to lighten the mood a bit. So there are werewolves too. Dear God, Hamish was right. " Kellan said, taking a longer drink.

"Of course there are werewolves, but werewolves can be cured. I have never found a way to help a fully turned vampire, save by granting them a true death."

"So, are they beautiful?" asked Juliet

Micah looked perplexed. "Are who beautiful?"

"The vampires."

Micah shuddered. "Far from it. They can appear human after they have fed, and can enthrall the unwary, but, beautiful, no."

She sighed, "So much for team Edward."

Micah looked even more puzzled and Kellan waved a hand. "Don't pay any attention to her. In this century, vampires can day-walk, are all sparkly and beautiful, and everyone wants to be one."

"That is...very disturbing," said Raphael slowly with Micah nodding in agreement.

Kellan placed the last book on the stack of others and all four sat silently for a long moment. Only the ticking of the many clocks filled the silence.

Finally, Kellan said, "So, now what?"

"Now you must choose," said Raphael.

"Wait," said Micah. "Just wait." He got up and crouched down before Kellan, taking the younger man's hands in his.

"Before you brought out all your research and asked all these questions, I told you what I was and what it was like to be me. Remember, I told you it is a life of vast contrasts. It is beautiful and ugly. It is transcendent joy and horrible sadness. It is power and weakness. I told you of how much I wanted a family but never did. There are countless sacrifices you will have to make and, yet, you will have the power to do tremendous good. You will trod through dark places and bring the light of creation with you. It will bend to your will and dispel those who inflict pain on the world. Kellan, you will be God's unchecked hand on the world. How does that make you feel?"

Kellan closed his eyes a long moment and then stared deeply into the aged face before him. "It makes me feel very small, and scared, and not nearly up to the challenge."

Micah reached up and held Kellan's face in his hands, eyes filling. "Yes. Yes! I know exactly how you feel. Never forget this moment. Hold on to it and put it someplace safe in your mind, locked away. Then go forth and do what you believe to be right. If you ever feel yourself getting lost or heading too far down a dark path, unlock this moment, and experience it again, but not for too long. Never for too long. Gaze too often or too long at this moment and it will leave a residue of timidity and doubt. That was my mistake, Kellan. Do not make the same mistake I did. Be bold and, when warranted, be irreverent and a bit reckless."

The old man stood up and, as he did so, placed a kiss on Kellan's forehead, then turned to Raphael. "I believe you did better this second time around. He's going to make you think otherwise, and often, but he'll be able to do what I never could. He will be able to accept, embrace, and control the darker aspects of his nature, rather than simply avoiding them. That will make him stronger and that is what's needed. You have done so very well Raphael. I know this choice could not have been easy."

The Angel looked up, "No, it was not easy, but the right things seldom are."

Raphael's eyes locked on Kellan. "Again, I say to you, Kellan Thorne," you must choose, but not in your current condition."

"My current—what?"

Raphael stood up and placed his hand on Kellan's shoulder, eyes flaring bright green. Kellan felt power course into him, causing his heart to race and his blood to feel hot. It only lasted a moment and was gone."

"Oh, damn," Kellan said.

"What? What is it, Kellan," asked Juliet, alarmed.

"He burned all the Scotch out of me. I'm stone cold sober."

"Damn it, Kellan, you scared the crap out of me."

Raphael ignored the exchange. "Your full faculties are restored; now you may choose."

Kellan looked again at Juliet and he saw the worry and tears in her eyes. She nodded to him. "You are the best, Kel. You've been like the big brother I never had and a second father all rolled into one. Your moral compass is dented, rusted, and more than a little cracked, but it always points true north. This grubby planet would be lucky to have you watching over it."

"Aw, shit, Juliet," now you've gone and made me cry too.

"Kellan, your language will need to improve," said Raphael.

"Fuck off, Clarence," he replied which brought a snort of laughter from Micah.

"Ok. I will choose, but I have a condition first."

Raphael raised an eyebrow. "A condition? What kind of condition?"

"I need something from you, Raphael. I need you need to tell me your name. Your whole, true, name."

The Angel froze.

"My name? You know my name."

"Bullshit. Raphael is *a name*, but it isn't *your* name."

"What's the name Michael calls you? What's the name God calls you. I want your real name. Real names given freely have power; you know that."

The silence stretched for long moments.

"You couldn't pronounce it."

"Try me."

"You won't remember it."

"I remember everything."

The Angel looked truly distressed. "I cannot."

"Ok, then we are done here," said Kellan getting up.

"You would truly decline?"

"Damn straight. If you can't trust me with your name, then you certainly can't trust me to be 'God's unchecked hand on the world.'"

"Even Micah doesn't know my name."

"And it is inexcusable that he does not, Raphael, but as you will learn, I am not he. Your name. Offer it freely now, or leave."

Raphael looked helplessly to Micah, who simply shook his head sadly.

Finally, Raphael spoke, voice barely a whisper, "Very well, Kellan Thorne, I will speak my name, but will do so to you alone."

The Angel stood very straight, eyes blazing to life, and stared directly at Kellan. A glowing shield snapped around them. "I am Raphael, Archangel of High Heaven, and this is my one true name. I give it freely and without regret."

Kellan felt the air charge as Raphael spoke the words that were not words. The sound flowed out and through him as his mind drank in the many aspects of the Name, locking each permanently and perfectly into place.

Tears flowed down his cheeks at the pure beauty of the name given to this being at the moment of creation and then it was over.

The shield vanished. The Archangel stared at Kellan expectantly.

Kellan spoke, surprised at how calm he suddenly felt, "I am Kellan Caufield Thorne and of my own free will I accept the power and responsibility you now offer. I will be the successor to Micah Ben Judah. I will be the Sentinel."

⌒⁊↿⫏⤙

Nothing happened. Kellan looked to Juliet who was clearly holding her breath, hands interlaced near her chest. Next, he looked back to Raphael who, aside from seeming slightly pleased with himself, had not moved or changed in any way. Finally, he looked at Micah.

"Is that it? I gotta say, I'm a bit disappointed. I was expecting something a little more, I don't know, dramatic?" Kellan looked again to Juliet who was nodding in agreement.

"I figured the windows would blow out or something...*there can be only one!*" She said.

Kellan snorted, "Yeah, well I'd just as soon not be replacing windows, and I'm pretty sure Connor McLeod didn't have to sweep up after that pyrotechnic extravaganza."

"That wasn't it," Micah said softly as he rose from his chair to stand in front of Kellan, "This is it."

Micah reached for his left ring finger as his eyes sparked to life, glowing brightly, and slowly drew the ring from his finger. Kellan watched intently and saw Juliet out of the corner of his eye craning to do likewise.

At first the ring seemed to stretch like it was made of molten silver and as Micah continued to pull, a second ring broke free of the first, and he held it out for Kellan to see.

The ring was large, but elegant, and appeared to be crafted of silver, or white gold with a dark green gem set in its center. The gem itself seemed to glow, albeit darkly while being cut in a terraced fashion that Kellan had never seen before. The bottom of the stone where it met the ring had twelve sides making it appear almost round. Higher on the stone four sides were cut, while the top of the stone showed only three sides.

Micah turned the ring between his fingers, gesturing with it toward Kellan.

The younger man chuckled nervously, "What? Are you proposing to me, Micah?"

"Well, it is legal now—even in Georgia," Juliet quipped.

"True, but I prefer younger men," replied Kellan, glancing her way with a mischievous grin.

Micah turned to Raphael who, for his part, seemed confused by the whole exchange and then back to Kellan, "No, uh, no no. This ring is part of the process. I, um, well I've known men who—but I'm not..."

The older man stopped, clearly flustered and Juliet punched Kellan on the shoulder.

"Ow! Dammit girl, you hit like a freight truck."

"Well, you deserve it, Kellan. Now stop embarrassing Micah. For God's sake, just look at him!"

"Fine," said Kellan, reaching out to take the ring which Micah still held out for him, "I'm sorry, Micah. Just a little contemporary humor, that you'd really have had to live around here for the past few years to fully appreciate."

Kellan was about to put the ring on when Micah shook himself out of his semi-stunned silence and put his hand on Kellan's to restrain him.

"Kellan, I'm serious. This is your last chance to walk away—put on that ring and there's no turning back. Be sure."

Raphael looked frustrated and opened his mouth to speak, but Kellan simply said, "I made my decision, Micah. This, apparently, is just the final formality. It is finished."

His last three words seemed to hang in the air as Kellan slipped the ring on and three pairs of eyes focused on him as the dark green stone burst outward with a blinding light.

Kellan felt his entire body burn and crackle with what felt like a massive electrical shock. He thought he heard himself screaming, but couldn't be sure as the green light continued to brighten from green to white. He felt as if he were falling through an endless hole that seemed to have opened up beneath him. Then there was nothingness.

Chapter 5

NURIṢHA

Kellan blinked, trying to get his eyes to adjust. They didn't. The light was blinding, but he couldn't determine its source. It seemed to come from everywhere, yet nowhere. Looking left and right, Kellan found no change in the world around him. All was bright white and completely empty.

Kellan felt his pulse start to quicken as he turned around in a tight circle. The terrain was so completely absent of any markings that he could not even determine when he had turned completely around.

He crouched down and placed his hand between his feet to feel the ground that clearly was not ground. It was completely smooth and devoid of both heat and cold. In fact, he only knew it was there by the resistance it provided against his outstretched palm.

Kellan stood and tried to slow his breathing and heart rate with a conscious effort of will. As he did so, images and words from texts read long ago flashed through his mind in perfect clarity. He sighed. This, for him at least, was normal, but there was something else—something new. It felt like it was just outside his perception, barely in the peripheral vision of his mind. The more he tried to grasp The Something, the more illusive it became. Finally, he decided to ignore it and concentrate on the calming knowledge that flowed through his mind. As he did so, The Something, encroached from the edges of his reality.

He continued to ignore it. It came closer. He continued to ignore it. Finally, The Something, seemed to overlap with his knowledge stores and vanished.

Kellan cried out with a start but heard no sound. He whirled around and yelled louder but was there was only silence. The slight burning in his throat provided the only evidence he had done anything at all.

As his heart raced, he felt perspiration break out across his body and a wave of nausea wracked him, bringing him to one knee. He absently noted that his heart rate had easily passed 150 and darkly thought what a shame it would be to die of a heart attack two seconds into this new adventure.

"No!" Kellan yelled at the all encompassing silence. He reached inward grasping at the calming knowledge he had recalled moments before and felt a slight burning in his eyes as he willed the knowledge into reality. The Something returned, but did not retreat when he focused on it and fed it into the calming knowledge. "Be…at peace," he said to himself, and The Something flared in him causing his eyes to burn even hotter, but then a calm washed over him like nothing he had ever felt before.

Kellan took a deep breath as he slowly listened to his heart rate fall from it's previous drum roll to a slow steady cadence.

"Fifty beats a minute," Kellan said silently to the world around him, "I'm a bloody olympic athlete." He lifted a hand directly in front of his eye and could see a glowing green light reflecting off the fingers. Kellan closed one eye and saw the reflected light diminish on that side of his hand. He reversed the test and the results likewise reversed.

"Well, looks like I've got those green laser beam eyes going for me, which is nice," Kellan said as he tried, with an act of will, to hear the words he spoke. Still there was nothing.

He began walking in no particular direction because there was no direction to his world and almost immediately noticed something moving on the horizon.

Kellan focused on the speck, moving quickly and directly towards it, finally breaking into a run. After a few moments he began to hear his feet beating against the ground and the measured sound of his own breathing. The ground took on texture, moving from the white nothing to form familiar earth. Clouds burst into being and Kellan felt wind on his face as he closed on the figure walking slowly towards him.

Kellan stopped just in front of Micah and regarded the old man for just a moment then embraced him tightly. Moments later, Kellan stepped back and, again, looked at Micah who smiled at him broadly.

"You seem to have missed me," the old Sentinel asked with a chuckle.

"This place sucks; why didn't you warn me? I thought I was dead or something."

Micah laughed again. "Warn you about what? I have only been here once before and that was the day Raphael took me here, but it was quite different then. I suppose it was my birthday of sorts, like this day is yours."

"Well, happy birthday. I nearly had a heart attack. Why didn't you meet me here?"

"Where is here?"

"Huh?"

"Kellan, where is here?"

"I have no idea. I'm the padawan here, master Jedi. Why don't you just explain it and use small words."

Micah sat down in a large overstuffed leather chair that looked all the world like one from Kellan's shop.

"Whoa! Where did that come from?" Kellan exclaimed.

"Please sit," said Micah and motioned to an identical chair that now sat directly in front of him.

Kellan sank into the chair without a word and stared at Micah.

"This," the old Sentinel said with a flourish that encompassed the world around them, "is God's workroom."

"Um...His what?"

"His workroom. It sits outside creation, but is where creation was, well, created. It's not used for anything now because everything's been created, so Raphael repurposed it for my training and now I am doing so for you."

Kellan blinked slowly and joggled his head. "God's workroom? So, God plays an uber celestial version of Minecraft?"

Micah sighed and lilted, "Reference?"

"Oh for God's sake. Micah, it's a computer game that lets you build..." Kellan stopped. "Forget it. So, this place. It clearly has special properties, right?"

"Oh yes. All the elements of creation are here and we have the ability to bend those elements more powerfully here than in the real world. Anything you will be able to do there, can be done here with a fraction of the effort. Somethings I can do here, I have never been able to do there, but perhaps you will exceed me in that regard. In this place, you can do the miraculous if you only have the will." Micah smiled expectantly.

"Yeah, well, that sounds cool, but, um, look I'm not trying to be indelicate here, but I thought you were going to, you know..."

"Die?" Micah said with a chuckle. "How do you know I'm not dead already?"

"Oh, Come on!" Kellan yelled, "You are so annoying. Do we have to play these games; it's such a waste of time."

"We can't waste time here."

"Exactly my point, so let's save time and give me a straight answer."

"We can't save time here either."

"Oh dear God, there you go again. Do you even realize you are doing that?"

Micah laughed again, "Yes, but I'll try and tone it down a bit. As I said, we are in a unique place and it has correspondingly unique characteristics. While we are here, we exist out of time. After all, time is part of creation, and this place is not. So, to my earlier point, we have, quite literally, all the time in the world."

Kellan pondered that for a moment. "So, am I now the Sentinel?"

"You are."

"What about you? You seem the same. You brought form to this place so what are you, if I'm the Sentinel?"

"Well, for this moment of frozen time, we share that role. When we leave this place, you alone will be the Sentinel. Our time here is the final gift I can give you, assuming you want it."

Kellan stared at the old man as he sat in the big leather chair and shook his head smiling, "Ok Morpheus, are you going to ask me if I want to take the blue pill or the red pill and see how far the down the rabbit hole goes?"

Micah cocked his head questioningly.

"Sorry," said Kellan, "One of the more annoying downsides to my super powered memory is the vast amount of obscure references that pop out."

"Ahh, well, that's not the best reference given that the Morpheus I knew was a winged demon who tortured people in their sleep."

"I almost hesitate to ask, but what happened to your Morpheus."

"I killed him; well, not killed exactly, more exiled him back to where he belonged by destroying his earthly vessel and then barring his spiritual form from returning."

"How did you—"

Micah, held up a hand. "Let's start with something a bit more basic, shall we?"

Kellan shrugged and Micah continued.

"All of creation is based on certain principles, laws, or rules. The principles of creation provide guide posts, the laws are inviolate, and rules, well, some rules can be bent."

"—And some rules can be broken," intoned Kellan and then winced slightly.

"You did it again, didn't you."

"Yeah, sorry. I'll try to control myself. Seems we are both annoying. So, what's an example of an inviolate law?"

"While we have the ability to materially alter creation and bend the rules of creation, we cannot create ourselves. We cannot, for example, create life. Look around. There are mountains, streams, hills, rocks, wind, and clouds. But no grass, trees, birds, or animals. Everything you see here I formed from the creative energy in this place and everything you see here you can manipulate in the real world, but you can never create even the smallest spark of life nor reignite life's flame if it is ever extinguished.

"Let me give you a simple example from one of the three elements I use most often which are Fire, Ice, and Lightning."

"Those aren't elements."

"I'm sorry?"

"Fire, Ice, and Lightning aren't elements. You mentioned that creation is based on principles, rules, and laws, so I figured it would be important to know the foundation too. I mean fire is really just the exothermic chemical reaction of combustion. Hydrogen is an element, which happens to be combustable, and thus is a great candidate for being on fire."

Micah stared at Kellan flatly. "Do you want me to show you how to control fire or not?"

Kellan gave him a sheepish look and nodded.

Micah's eyes blazed green as he held his hand out and a moment later flames danced upon his upturned palm. Kellan watched the old man furrow his brow with concentration and the flames began to circle his palm, slowly at first and then gaining speed until they were just a blur of light giving off gentle waves of heat until Micah closed his palm into a fist and they vanished.

"That," he began, "might seem small and trivial, but it took years to master. It is more impressive and, ironically, easier to do something like this."

In a fluid motion, Micah stood, stretched out both hands and gestured as if forming a bowl with his hands and a gout of flame erupted from the ground several feet ahead of him. The heat buffeted them for a moment and then vanished as Micah lowered his hands, eyes returning to their nature color.

He turned to Kellan, "Now you do it."

"What? How? You just *did* it. You didn't show me *how* to do it."

Micah frowned. "Weren't you watching?"

"Yes, I was watching. I was watching you wave your hands around. Look, I can do that too." Kellan made the same cupped hand gesture to no effect. "See, nada."

Micah sighed. "You were not watching, Kellan." His eyes flashed brightly as he tapped near his right temple. "You have to see through different eyes to truly see. Now watch again."

"No, wait. Micah, you are trying to get me to do Thermo Dynamics and I don't even know how to add and subtract." He tapped his own right temple. "Dude, I don't even know how to turn on my—whatever they are—eye-lights."

Micah opened his mouth to respond and then just shook his head. "You are completely right. We need to start at the beginning. Let me think a moment."

"Alright, let's start with this. Close your eyes and try to clear your mind."

Kellan did.

"Now, just try to kind of feel for something that seems different than before. I wish I could be more specific, but it is so much a part of me, that I don't know what else to say."

Kellan grimaced but started taking a mental inventory of both his physical and mental attributes. He was just about to give up in frustration when he, again, sensed The Something.

"There!" he said opening his eyes. "I found it, well, almost found it. It's like something you see out of the corner of your eye but when you turn, it's gone."

Micah smiled, "Yes! That's it exactly. I don't know how I could have forgotten that. Now, Kellan, you can't chase it. You have to let it come to you and you must welcome it, not force it."

"Huh? What is *it* exactly; you make it seem like it's alive and sentient."

"Even after all these years I'm not exactly sure what *it* is. Call it a sliver of raw creation, a fragment of God, who knows. But I can assure you that by any definition that matters it most certainly is alive and sentient. Try again."

Kellan took a deep breath and let it out slowly while closing his eyes and opening his mind to the entity he has sensed before. Immediately he felt its presence and he urged it closer. It came, hesitantly pulsing close only to then back away. Finally, in frustration, Kellan mentally grappled for the power when it next drew close only to feel it buffet him and vanish.

"Arghh. This is not working, Micah. I cannot get it to come close enough to grab."

The old man shook his head. "No, Kellan, not grab, that's your problem. Force, control, domination are not things of the light. The power will be repelled by such things. Worse, that approach might attract its opposite toward you."

"What? Its…opposite? I swear, this is feeling more and more like Star Wars, Episode 0, birth of a Jedi."

"Never mind about the opposing force; I'm sorry I even brought it it up. You need to focus on what's in front of you."

"Micah, you didn't just call it "the force," did you? And you can't just bring something up like that and expect me to——"

"Yes. Yes I can. Stop dwelling on all the stories in your head. Storytellers are creative, some immensely so. Is it so hard to imagine that their inspirations might come from somewhere true even though that inspiration is a mere fragment of the truth. Now clear that library you call a mind and try again. Sit calmly and close you eyes."

"Forget this," said Kellan standing up. "That whole Zen Buddhist approach might work for you but it's not happening for me." Kellan bounced up and down a few times on the balls of his feet, shaking his arms and hands down by his side. He saw Micah looking at him quizzically. "I'm loosening up."

"It's not a wrestling match, Kellan. That's just not going to work."

Kellan ignored him and closed his eyes, questing out with his senses for the energy. Again, it immediately appeared in the periphery of his senses but kept its distance. Kellan smiled and slowly inhaled until he felt he might burst, then slowly opened his arms and eyes, breathing out while imagining his entire body become an empty vessel, less than empty, a vacuum desperately needing to be filled lest it collapse in on itself. As he held this image of his entire being, empty of all things, Kellan sensed alarm from the entity as it drew closer. He made no mental moves toward the energy, but rather increased the sense of distress and collapse he had created and flung his arms outward in a gesture of total openness and vulnerability.

Kellan felt the power rush into him, filling every fiber of his being coursing through him like fire and light. He felt it roaring though him, felt his eyes blazing with the power of it. He saw himself, standing in an empty room in which green bolts of energy continually flashed and felt as if he were watching himself from the corner of an unseen ceiling.

In what seemed like the far distance, Kellan thought he could hear Micah calling to him. No, yelling at him. Some kind of warning. Kellan didn't care. Whatever Micah had to say could wait. He relished the heat coursing though him and nothing else mattered.

Then he heard it. He heard her coming from the energy flashing throughout the room.

"You are not like he."

"What are you?" Kellan asked.

"This is creation given form and thought," came the response. "Your body is about to die, Kellan Thorne. You must release this energy. You must release it!"

Kellan's mind laughed. "Release you? I'm not holding you; I am doing the exact opposite of holding you. I am merely open to you—all of you. It is wonderful. You are so beautiful."

"You are this energy's vessel, young Sentinel. It is the purpose of this energy to fill you, by opening yourself to it as you have done; this energy has no other purpose and can do nothing else. But all vessels have their limit; yours overflows and begins to crack. Send this energy forth to do your will, or you will surely die."

"I don't want you to go. I want you to stay with me always. I have never felt this complete."

"This energy will always be here. You need but call and it will come, always and forever. Release it now, Kellan, or all will be lost"

"I don't know how."

"Listen to Micah, quickly!"

Kellan vaguely became aware that he was being shaken about the shoulders.

Micah was screaming at him. Saying something about letting the power go and turning it to fire. It didn't seem important.

"Nurisha, why does Micah want me to turn you to fire?"

Kellan sensed confusion and hesitation from the energy field but it replied, "As has been explained to you, my vessel, if you do not release this energy, your body will die and with it, the power of the Sentinel."

There was the briefest of pauses and the voice continued, "What is Nurisha?"

Kellan laughed, "Why, you are, silly. You are Nurisha."

"This energy has no name; it is but a sliver of creation."

"No, Nurisha. You are more than that. I need you to be more than that. You are Nurisha and we will walk this path together."

"Kellan, your body is already failing. Your mind is not clear. This energy is not—"

"You are Nurisha!" Kellan yelled with force but not anger. As he spoke the words, Kellan felt the world warp for the barest of moments and snap back.

Some portion of his awareness saw Micah being thrown backward by a wave of raw power that pulsed from Kellan's outstretched arms. Kellan felt his words and will fuse with the power that raged within him and take form. The bolts of energy ceased their endless pulsing and coalesced. In the darkness of his mind's eye she stood there, vague at first, but then sharpening into a perfect human shape.

Her body was made of living molten green light with trailers of energy playing about her form. Running along her limbs were runic symbols that continually appeared, then faded, then reappeared in a slow, lazy, fashion. She looked startled, holding up one hand before her face, watching the energy pulse through translucent green skin, then turned her blazing eyes on Kellan.

"This energy..." She paused, looking again at her hands as the ribbons of light played about the fingers, then spoke haltingly as if doing so for the first time, "I...I need you to release me—before you die.

"But I don't want to," replied Kellan. "I just found you."

Nurisha walked to Kellan, took his hands in hers and shook her head. "You did more than find me, young Sentinel. You gave me individuality and a sense of self. You gave a true form to what was only a purposeful force. I do not understand how you did this nor the implications. I can tell you that what you have just done is unique in all of creation. It is just remarkable. But, Kellan, this miracle you have wrought will likely not survive you, so you must listen to me. You are holding the entirety of my essence within; even Micah could not safely do so and he has had millennia to learn how to control and form this power. Release it now before it is too late. I will be here when next you call to me."

She released his hands and took a step back. "Release me now!"

Kellan's vision blurred and he was again staring across the barren landscape. Micah had just regained his feet.

Kellan could barely speak through the pain. "How do I release this energy, Micah. It's burning me to cinders from the inside out."

"Fire, Kellan. Fire is the easiest." Micah pointed to a rough stone outcropping in the near distance. "Direct it there just as you saw me do. Convert the raw energy to fire and have it well up beneath the outcropping."

Kellan followed Micah's outstretched hand and saw the rock formation. He reached out with both hands as he saw Micah do earlier and could feel the energy begin to flow down his arms. As it did so, four runes appeared on each arm glowing so brightly that he had to avert his eyes. Kellan's mind raced through an endless stream of facts he had read about all forms of combustion. With the image of a plasma fire and a complete understanding of its characteristics fixed firmly in his mind, Kellan breathed out, willing all the energy within him to be converted to that form.

He felt a vast emptying as the power he held rushed out and was converted to plasmatic fire. In the distance, a white pillar of incandescent heat rose up from the ground and engulfed the stone outcropping. Kellan continued to hold his hands outstretched as the power flowed for what seemed like an eternity. Micah stared in wonder, shielding his eyes from the blinding light. When the last of the power had been expelled, Kellan lowered his arms as the runes faded and slumped into his chair, exhausted.

Micah continued to stare. The outcropping was gone with nothing to mark its passing but dust and a charred landscape immediately around where it had stood. A moment later he regained his wits and rounded on Kellan.

"What in hell did you think you were doing?" Micah yelled, grabbing Kellan by the shoulders and lifting him up like he was a doll. He shook the younger man. "You were seconds from self immolation! What possessed you to take all that power in at once?"

Kellan pushed off from Micah and sat down once again with a sigh. "I don't know, Micah. I felt the energy and it was so good and strong that I wanted more of it. Then, I noticed it had intelligence, of a sort, and, well, you know how my mind works. I needed to know more. I needed to understand it completely, so I brought more into myself. Finally, I had the whole of it within me and I could see the potential that was there. Her potential, so I unlocked it. I couldn't have done so without the whole of her within me. I wouldn't have understood enough."

"Her? Her who, Kellan? I swear I think you burned something out inside your head."

"Nurisha," he replied with tired contentment.

"What's a Nurisha?"

"Not what, my friend. Who. Nurisha is the personification of our power."

Micah stepped back and stared at Kellan, clearly distressed. "Power is power, Kellan, it doesn't have a name and it certainly doesn't have a personality."

Kellan watched as Micah's eyes blazed to life and he felt the older man call for their shared power. "Kellan, watch, it is just power, raw energy. It does not have—"

The old man trailed off and stumbled back several steps, his eyes not fixed on anything.

Kellan smiled. "She in there? Tell her I said 'Hi.'"

Micah didn't answer and just continued to stare off but Kellan could see his lips moving almost imperceptibly and knew he was getting acquainted with Nurisha.

With an effort of will the young Sentinel called to his power, but just sought a trickle rather than the raging torrent he had previously gathered. The room formed around him and he saw Micah facing away from him and toward the glowing female form of Nurisha. Kellan watched as Micah hesitantly reached out a finger and placed it on Nurisha's lips. She kissed it lightly and opened her arms. The old Sentinel only hesitated a moment before he stepped forward and melted into her embrace. She held him tightly and looked over at Kellan smiling.

When at last they parted, Kellan walked up beside Micah and said, "So, I see you've met Nurisha."

The old man's eyes were moist. "Kellan, I met her over two thousand years ago and have walked throughout the millennia with her, but never knew *she* was there."

Nurisha smiled. "I didn't know I was there, Micah. In fact, I am quite sure I wasn't there until Kellan made me be there."

"No, you were there, Nurisha. I could feel you there. There's a reason why so many cultures have the concept of the sacred masculine and the sacred feminine. I suspect the creator of this place and, well, everything represents the masculine, but you, Nurisha, animate those acts of creation. Anyway, all those centuries being formed with Micah led you to this place where our ability to affect reality is at its strongest. I just made the scales fall away from your eyes so you could finally see yourself."

She laughed and startled herself at the sound, then recovered saying, "I'll say it again. I think you did a bit more than that."

The three stood there for a few moments in silence.

"Ok, so this is starting to just feel awkward," said Kellan finally, "Aren't we supposed to be doing something? I thought we were pressed for time."

"There is no time here," Micah and Nurisha said simultaneously.

"Oh no you don't. I will not deal with two autistic hyper-beings." Kellan concentrated and found himself resting comfortably in the chair.

Micah continued to stare off, clearly still engaged with Nurisha.

"Micah, how long are you going to be in there? Do we really have time for this?"

Kellan paused. "There is no time here," he said to the open air, "Great. Now I'm doing it to myself."

Kellan chuckled softly, "Well screw it then, I'm taking a nap." He snuggled deeper into the chair not noticing as it gently extended to accommodate his reclined position and within moments, Kellan Thorne, second Sentinel of creation, was fast asleep.

Kellan's body resisted the call to wakefulness. He grumbled and swatted away the hand shaking him, but it persisted. Moments later, he opened his eyes to find Micah continuing his attempts to gently rouse him.

Kellan yawned. "How long was I asleep?"

"There is no—"

"Stop. Please, just a general idea. Pretend you aren't annoying for a minute."

Micah smiled, "Well, I'd say that you were asleep the equivalent of a very good night's sleep."

Kellan returned the smile, "See, now was that so difficult?"

"How's our girl? You have a nice time catching up?"

Micah raised an eyebrow, "Nurisha? She's headed off to explore creation as she put it."

Kellan sat up, alarmed, and immediately opened himself up to the power. He felt his eyes warm and as the power flowed into him, but didn't sense her. He constructed a room where they had met but it was empty. He released the power and turned back to Micah.

"What the hell? Where is she and how can I still use the power without her?"

Micah had walked a few steps away during Kellan's moment of searching and the old man glanced over his shoulder.

"I suspect that if you seek her out intensely, she will come, but excepting that, she probably has better things to do than simply wait for you to need something."

"But without her, how can I still—"

"She is still raw creative energy, Kellan, just now personified and with a sense of individuality. That energy is linked to you and is not constrained by locality. It is everywhere and everywhen. The individual aspect, the Nurisha aspect, well, that's something new and it seems she can be somewhere or somewhen."

Kellan smiled. "Wow, that's pretty cool."

"And," the old man said, "pretty terrifying. There is no telling what the unintended consequences will be from what you've done here. This is the first time anything done within this space has had effect on real creation. She is not bound to this place so clearly there will be ramifications."

"Fortunately," Micah continued with a wink, "I'll be dead and you'll have to deal with it."

"Not cool, Micah. Not cool at all."

He shrugged.

"Ready for a lesson on evil and the unnatural? What did you call yourself—Padawan?"

"Yeah, Master Jedi, I'm ready," replied Kellan rising from his chair, but feeling very uneasy about the whole exchange.

"Good," said Micah, "because your eyes are open now and you will see all manner of evil and unnatural things in the world, so it will be best if you know how to deal with them."

"All manner of evil? Like what? Vampires? Werwolves?"

"Of course, but many others. Demons, Djinn, Changelings, Fairies—"

"Wait? What? Tinkerbell is evil now?"

"Tinkerbell?" Micah asked with a raised eyebrow.

"Yeah, she's a fairy."

Micah looked taken aback. "You've met fairies before; that's highly unusual for a mortal."

"Well, no. Not exactly," began Kellan, "I've read and seen movies about them. Tinkerbell is just kinda famous is all."

"Really," said Micah, his voice rising with amusement, "Famous is she, well I've never heard of her."

"Whatever," said Kellan, "continue."

"No, you raise an important point. There are evil things and unnatural things. All evil beings are unnatural but not all unnatural beings are evil. Fairies are a good example of such. Of course some fairies are evil, but not necessarily so."

Kellan looked thoughtful. "Well, what's an example of something that is just always evil then?"

Micah didn't hesitate. "Skin-Walkers, Demons, Ghouls, Wraiths—"

Kellan sat down again, "Ok, you can stop now. Do I look like one of the Winchester brothers? How the hell am I supposed to know how to kill all of those things?"

Micah's brow knitted in confusion and then he broke out in a short laugh. "Ah, I see what you're asking. Yes, there are very specific ways to defeat each of these creatures—if you were human, which you are not." Micah reached out a hand. "Come on. Walk with me. I'll explain."

Kellan accepted the hand and Micah pulled him up, then continued as they walked down the gently sloping hill toward a distant stream.

"As a Sentinel, you are infused with some portion of the power used in creation, but not all aspects. This is why we cannot create but only alter that which has been created. However, the beings I mentioned, exist outside the natural order of creation. You will sense them when they draw near and will easily be able to pick them out by their aura."

Kellan stopped. "Their aura? Really? That sounds a bit *Ms. Powers reads your future* to me."

Micah kept walking and shrugged. "You are ignorant of such things so what it *sounds* like really doesn't matter much. Everything in creation has an aura most are aligned with nature and natural things so are ignored. Those beings who exist outside of nature have auras that will be starkly different, usually visible to you are dark red pulses surrounding them."

Kellan had quickly jogged back to, again, keep pace with his teacher. "Ok, so that explains how I'll recognize them, but you said I wouldn't need any particular knowledge of how to fight them. Why?"

Micah nodded to himself. "Yes, I understand your confusion. Vampires must be killed by decapitation or wooden stakes. Werewolves and Wraiths with silver. Ghouls, well, ghouls are difficult. Not only do you need to decapitate them, but you have to destroy the head or they will just put it back on."

Kellan stopped again and this time Micah turned to him quizzically.

"Really? They just put their heads back on?"

"Unfortunately, yes. Ghouls are annoying that way. But—" Micah waved his hand in a vaguely negating way, "None of that really matters for you because you are infused with Ordered creative energy."

"Great, and what does that do for me?"

"Well, beyond making it easy for you to identify unnatural beings, any lethal blow from you destroys them."

"What do you mean? I could shoot a vampire in the face and kill him?"

Micah had picked up a smooth stone and stood examining it. He held it out to Kellan. "Look at the colors in this. It is almost iridescent."

Kellan glanced at the stone. "Great—pretty rock. Dude, stay focused will you? Vampires. Shooting them in the face?"

Micah sighed and slipped the rock into the folds of his clothes. "Honestly, I don't know about the shooting? You mean with a gun?"

"No, I mean with a sling and a rock," answered Kellan sarcastically.

"Oh, then yes, I think that would work because the sling and rock would be an extension of you so would carry your essence with it. I know the same to be true of sword and bow."

Kellan ground his teeth. "I was being sarcastic. Yes, I meant a gun. I like guns. You can hit things from far away with guns. I like the idea of being far away from ghouls when I kill them."

"Understandable," said Micah almost to himself. He turned to Kellan and smiled, "but I don't think a gun will work. It's too disconnected from you and never had life in it. A sling is made of leather or cloth. Bows of wood. Your sword, well, your sword is an extension of mind and spirit. It will always be your most powerful weapon. Although——"

"What?"

"Your ability with fire was devastating and whatever you channel is a complete manifestation of your inner power: fire, lightning, wind. All those natural effects will serve you better than ever silver or a wooden stake could."

The two men had reached the narrow stream and Kellan marveled at how clear it was. Micah knelt down, dipping cupped hands into the rushing water and brought them to his lips. He looked up, smiled at Kellan who then did the same.

"Ready?" Micah asked.

"For?"

"More lessons of course. I'd like to introduce you to lightning and earth channeling before the day is out."

Kellan stood and then bowed deeply, "I am but your humble Padawan, my Master. You command and I follow."

Micah looked up at the young Sentinel and laughed, "I find that quite hard to believe, but let us begin."

～７１\〉〉

Kellan crested the rocky hill to find Micah sitting on a stone bench staring out into the distance. He put a friendly hand on his mentor's shoulder and squeezed slightly, then turned and chuckled.

"This for me? Doesn't seem like your style. Why'd you make it?" Kellan asked as he moved to settle into the rough hewn chair. "It's a bit 'Iron Throne,' don't you think?"

"Don't sit there, Kellan." Micah's words were little more than a whisper but something in them brought Kellan up short and he stopped, looking back toward the old Sentinel questioningly.

"Let's just say the last person to sit in that chair is a bit of an," Micah paused, "asshole."

Kellan laughed. "Very good, after all this time, I'm glad to see I'm rubbing off on you."

Micah patted the bench next to him, "Come. Sit."

Kellan did and the two looked out over the expanse before them saying nothing, the silence between them spreading outward to match the distance that lay before them.

Finally, Micah shattered the silence, speaking softly but still causing Kellan to start as the quiet between them vanished.

"Time has almost caught us my friend," Micah said.

Kellan grinned, "Has it? Do you think we should go on?"

Micah glanced over, "I think we should have a party."

Kellan clapped. "Oh, bravo! An obscure Highlander reference, quoting Kastagir no less."

Micah smiled sadly, "Yes, your incessant cultural references have throughly corrupted me."

"It's a gift," Kellan replied, "but, hey, not the best quote because ol' Kastagir loses his head right after that part of the story."

Micah just stared at Kellan pointedly.

"Oh no, not yet. No, Micah."

"It's time, Kellan."

"There is no time here. You've only said that dozens of times."

Micah ignored the comment. "You know what's strange? I've been waiting so long for this moment. I've been so tired for so long. I asked Raphael to help make this happen and now that it's really here, I'm disquieted. Isn't that just the height of ridiculousness? Apparently, I'm a ridiculous man, who would have thought that? Anyway, I find myself envious of you, Kellan. You have the whole adventure spreading out before you and I've seen over our time in this place how you will proceed. You have learned in a span of what would be months out here, what it took me centuries to master."

He laughed, shaking his head.

"And that's not the half of it. You have done things that I've never been able to do and you don't even see how miraculous that is. What was the fire thing you did yesterday?"

Kellan was staring silently at his friend and mentor, eyes moist, but didn't respond.

Micah slapped his leg. "You know the stupid thing you did with fire and your voice—hydrogen was it?"

Finally, Kellan answered. "Fusion—it's fusion."

"Right, fusion. You took the hydrogen, turned it into…" He paused thinking, "helium, breathed some of that in, and then took the remaining helium and turned it into carbon. Then crushed that into a diamond"

Micah laughed again as the memory played through his head.

"And you did all that in the blink of an eye so that you could make a joke about proposing to someone while sounding like David Duck."

"Donald," Kellan said softly as he struggled with his tears.

"Huh? Oh, yes. Donald Duck."

"Fusion, Kellan. I didn't even know that existed. I didn't know that's how stars work. I didn't even know that the sun is a star, just closer."

Micah paused, shaking his head, "Raphael out did himself with you, that's for sure, but I'm so afraid for you, Kellan."

"This all comes so easily to you. You progress so quickly that I'm afraid your capabilities already exceed your wisdom."

The old man looked again at Kellan, "I don't mean this as a slight. You have a good heart, a strong moral compass, and a solid constitution. You *are* a good man, Kellan, but history is replete with good men who do unspeakable things because they lack wisdom."

"Then you shouldn't leave me, Micah. We should take this journey together."

Micah turned on the bench staring intently at Kellan. "What do you mean? That is impossible, Kellan. Even after all the lessons I provided in this place and the many times I've explained it, still you persist. We share this power for but the frozen moment while we are in the place. Once we have held the power, we cannot live without it. It is part of us and we it—inseparable."

"That may not be true. I've been thinking about this and have tried a couple things."

Micah grew very still. "What kind of things, Kellan?"

"Well, you know how the power can be splintered slightly and redirected? I tried to do that with you while you were sleeping earlier. I was able to redirect almost all of it into you, holding back just a sliver. I'm sure I could do that outside of this place as well. If I'm fast enough when we leave, I think I could keep you alive. Then it would just be a matter of maintaining that link so that you could—"

"No, Kellan."

"Yes, I think it would work. I'm almost positive."

"No!" Micah growled, standing up and walking several paces ahead before turning back toward Kellan. "This is exactly what I'm talking about. Have you thought about the ramifications of what you're suggesting? What would happen to Nurisha? Could she be splintered in such a way? What about our strength? The power is finite and balanced against its opposite. Even if you could do as you say, we would both be half as powerful as your adversary. Stop acting like a child, Kellan!"

The young Sentinel said nothing, just lowered his face into his hands, finally speaking so softly that Micah could barely hear, "I just don't want to lose you., not now. I'm not ready."

Micah seemed to immediately regret his anger, and walked over, kneeling down before the younger man, kissing his tousled hair. "You are ready, Kellan. More ready than I was, trust me on that. I just wish I could be around to tell you when you are about to do something especially stupid."

Kellan looked up, "Just when I'm about to be especially stupid?"

Micah smiled, "Well, if I had to be around when you were just being normally stupid, I'd have to be omnipresent, now wouldn't I?"

Kellan snorted, "So true."

Micah brightened further. "Wait a moment, I actually have an idea. One of your endless retellings of modern stories just popped into my head. I could create a fetish stone for you."

Kellan just looked at his friend blankly.

"It's a means to impart the semblance of one's self to an inanimate object that can interact, be questioned, and respond similarly to to how the original person would."

Micah stood up, pacing and talking to himself. "It would, of course be limited, and I'd have to try and anticipate most of the situations, but it is definitely doable and time isn't an issue if I make a pocket universe and do it there while he waits."

"Hey! I'm right here; your talking about me in the 3rd person again. What the heck are you on about?"

Micah looked back to Kellan and was about to explain all the details of what he had in mind, but then just smiled and said, "I'm going to be your Jor'el."

Kellan's eyes widened with complete understanding, "Oh. Wow!"

From Kellan's perspective, Micah had only vanished a moment before, having stepped into the glowing blue oval that was the portal to what the old Sentinel called his pocket universe. As he explained it, this was simply a way of leveraging the strange lack of time that existed in this place. By creating another instance of the workroom and closing it off from the one in which Kellan existed, Micah could, quite literally, spend an eternity building his fetish without any time passing for Kellan.

The blue oval appeared again and Micah stepped through, looking somehow older and definitely haggard. "So, how long did it take you," Kellan asked?

The older man just shook his head, "No way to know for sure, but months of normal time if not years."

Micah smiled tiredly. "But, here it is. Don't use it until," he paused, "until I'm gone. I don't want to see it." With that, he handed the fetish stone to Kellan who turned it over in his hands.

It was about a hand span in length, and appeared as a long, hexagonal white crystal that glowed slightly while being warm to the touch. After taking in its appearance for a moment, Kellan chuckled and looked up at Micah.

"Really?" he said laughing again.

Micah returned the laugh, "Well, I did say I was going to be your Jor'el so figured I'd go all the way. How did I do?"

Kellan grasped the crystal firmly so only a bit of light escaped between his fingers, his voice becoming solemn. "You did great, Micah. It's perfect. It's simply perfect."

Micah, wanting to keep the mood light, pressed on, "Great, now you can't break it and you can't lose it."

"I won't," replied Kellan seriously.

"No, no, I mean you really can't break it or lose it." With that, Micah pulled the crystal from Kellan's hand and, in a fluid motion, threw it off the hill and far into the distance.

Kellan jumped up alarmed. "Oh my god, what the hell?" he shouted as he ran to the edge of the precipice, trying to make out where the crystal had fallen.

"Relax, Kellan. Do you really think I would have spent the time I did and trust you not to lose or break something that could be lost or broken. You are so distractible, I'm sure you'll end up leaving it somewhere. Oh, and I know your magic brain will remember where you left it, but it might not be there when you get back, so, I fixed that problem before it became a problem. Call it back."

"Huh?"

"Call it back. Use a trickle of power and just call it back."

Kellan opened his palm and closed his eyes, felt the familiar warmth in them as he drew on his power willing the fetish to return. He immediately felt weight in his palm and opened his eyes to find it resting there completely unmarred and glowing softly.

"Holy shit…"

"Yes, holy shit indeed." Micah said gravely but with a grin.

The two men said nothing for a time, both content to enjoy the silence and each other's presence, neither wanting to be the one to break the moment.

Finally, Micah shuffled his feet a bit and spoke, "Seems this is it—graduation day."

Kellan's stomach wrenched and flipped at the words, but he nodded slowly, angrily wiping tears that sprang unbidden and unwanted.

The two men embraced, and Kellan felt Micah channel the power causing the blue glowing portal to spring into being. He could see the bookstore's small reading room on the other side. Kellan squeezed tighter, not wanting to let go.

"I don't know what to say," Kellan whispered.

"You don't have to say anything. I know. Time out there hasn't changed, but we have and we'll have this time forever." Micah pulled back holding Kellan firmly by the shoulders staring at him intently. "I love you as if you were my own son, and, in a way you are. You will do great things, Kellan. You will, indeed, shine light into dark places where Angels fear to tread. You will succeed, fail, fall, and rise again. Through all that remember you were chosen by those who exist outside of time and can see eternity laid out like a quilt. You are ready, and so am I."

Micah finished speaking, eyes moist and gave Kellan's shoulder's one more reassuring squeeze, then turned and walked through the portal. He didn't look back, but knew that the Sentinel followed him.

Chapter 6

THERE CAN BE ONLY ONE

The world snapped into focus with scents and sounds hitting Kellan like an assault. He had forgotten how loud the world was and how sharp the smells were of a living place. The dust, the old leather, the myriad of smells filled his nose as the sounds of life filled his ears: clocks ticking, cars moving about, an airplane overhead. He was home.

Kellan spun around and his heart caught in his throat. Micah sat in the over-stuffed leather chair, head leaning against one side of the large shoulder-back. He looked asleep, but Kellan knew.

A sob broke from his mouth as he moved toward his friend kneeling before the chair. His hand was warm but there was no life within. He held the old man's hand as the tears streamed down his cheeks and Kellan let the full sense of loss wash over and through him.

After long minutes Kellan wiped his face and started to rise when he felt a hand on his shoulder.

"Greetings, Sentinel," came the commanding voice.

Kellan stood and turned towards the voice. Raphael stood before him smiling. "You have grown much since last I saw you. How fare you?"

"My friend is dead. Leave me alone."

Raphael cocked his head, then looked to Micah's body. "That," he said, pointing, "is nothing. *Our* friend is free of the limitations of that body and the responsibilities you now bear." Raphael paused. "Perhaps you knew that. Were you weeping for yourself or for him."

"Dear God, Raphael, you are such an ass. I was weeping for my friend being gone. I can't see him. I can't hear him. I miss him already. Just go away and let me deal with this on my own."

The Angel seemed completely unaffected by the insult and simply nodded. "Very well. I will collect the husk and depart."

"The…what?"

"The husk. The body that held Micah. Like few others before him, corruption will not take this body. I will take it with me."

Raphael walked to the chair and picked Micah up, cradling the body without any discernible effort. He turned as a portal opened before him and stepped towards it.

"Wait!" called Kellan. Raphael stopped, turning back to the Sentinel. "Will you see him? Will you talk to him?"

"I do not know, Kellan Thorne. If he wishes it, then I will see and speak with him. If he does not, then I will not."

"Will you tell him something? If you see him, I mean."

Raphael stared at Kellan for a long moment eyes ablaze, "Probably not. He is done with this world and its troubles are now yours, but perhaps. What is your message?"

"Just tell him 'Thank you and that I love him, too'",

Raphael's features seemed somehow to soften, almost imperceptibly, and he smiled slightly, "He knows, but yes, that is one message I can promise to impart. Remember young Sentinel, in all you two shared there was love and words were the faintest shadow of how you communicated that during your times together."

Kellan nodded as Raphael turned again, walked through the portal, and vanished. He looked down at the end table and spied the bottle of Scotch from what felt like an eternity ago. He picked it, examining it. It was empty.

"Shit!" said the Sentinel. "I definitely need more Scotch."

Kellan heard his office door slam from the back of the shop and the sound of running feet.

"You're back!" Juliet yelled as she ran into the room, throwing herself at Kellan and hugging him tightly. A moment later, she drew back a little with a quizzical look on her face, eyes red and swollen. She placed one hand on Kellan's chest and pressed, then grabbed his upper arm and squeezed first one and then the other, eyes widening.

"Um, Juliet, what the hell are you doing? You are kinda grossing me out here."

"Dude, what in the seven hells have you been up to? You're, well, you're totally buffed up."

"Huh, I'm what?" said Kellan pulling open his shirt and reaching for the belt of his jeans.

Juliet turned around, "Stop right there mister. Now *I'm* grossed out."

"Holy crap, Juliet, I'm built like the dude from *Arrow*. This is awesome."

"Totally awesome. Get yourself back to being dressed."

No response.

"What are you doing?"

No response.

"Oh my God. Are you flexing or something."

"Uh, no."

"Ew, you were! You totally were. Can you actually be serious for one minute? I kinda thought you were burned up and dead and have been crying in your office for the better part of an hour."

"Burned up? Why on earth did you think I was burned up? Wait. What? You've been crying for an hour?"

"Yes, dammit. And I'd still have been in there blubbering for god knows how long if I hadn't heard something going on out here."

"An hour...", Kellan said again, shaking his head. "I guess that makes sense, but..."

Juliet watched him and made the connection. "How long was it for you?"

"Months, Juliet, many months, at least."

"Well, that at least explains your *Arrow*'ness. Are you fully dressed yet?"

"Yeah, I'm good"

Juliet turned around and gave Kellan another big hug, kissing his cheek as well.

"Oh, Kel, I am so glad you aren't dead. You started screaming after you put that ring on and then your whole body glowed like The Doctor regenerating, only green. Then, then you just went poof!"

"Poof?"

"Yes—fucking Poof!"

"Language..."

"Fucking! Poof! Kel!"

Kellan laughed and grabbed Juliet by the shoulders lifting her effortlessly off the floor. "Language, young lady. Kellan Smash!"

Juliet was laughing now too. "Put me down and dish on the 411."

He did and they both collapsed into reading chairs where Kellan relayed his time in the workroom with Micah.

Kellan glanced down through the rows of books at the gathering darkness exposed by the shop's front window. He knew they'd been talking for quite sometime and glanced at his phone. 6:30. Juliet needed to get home soon or her parents would be calling.

"So, he's really gone, then" said Juliet sadly. "He had such a kind face, like an old weathered sailor or something. You seem to have really taken to him, Kel. I'm so sorry."

"Huh? Yeah. I'm sure it seems weird given your frame of reference, but from my perspective, I just spent every day of the past I don't know how many months with a guy I came to love and respect. And he's dead. And I'm left with all this," he finished gesturing around himself.

The room fell into silence for several long moments when Juliet brightened.

"Well, Sentinel," she began enunciating the honorific with as much snark as she could, "Show me something."

Kellan smiled, "I'm not a carnival freak and I will not use these powers for parlor tricks."

She cocked her head and smirked at him.

"Ok, I kinda am, and I totally will," he said laughing. "What do you want to see?"

"I have no idea. You described so much." She paused. "Let's build up to something grand, but start small. Fire up those peepers."

"Good idea, but I have to have the environment right for it to work, so I'll need your help."

"Cool, what do I need to do?"

"Just get to the side of that chair and pray like you were saying your night-time prayers, but in this case just pray that I'm worthy to call forth this awesome power."

"Really?"

"Yep."

Juliet slipped out of her chair, kneeling before it, interlaced her hands, and closed her eyes. "I have to admit, Kel, I'm out of practice at this; don't tell Mom and Dad."

Kellan could see her lips start to move silently and then stop. Still with her eyes closed, Juliet said, "Umm…what happens if there's no one to do this when you need to clobber some baddy?"

"Now, that's an excellent question, Miss Herrick," he replied and she heard the laughter in his voice.

Juliet opened an eye to see Kellan smiling broadly, clearly about to break into open laughter.

"Ass! Ass! Double ass!" she yelled getting up and punching him on the arm as hard as she possibly could."

"Ow!," she yelled.

"Yes, ow indeed—didn't hurt me one bit though"

She glared at him, and then her mouth dropped open as Kellan's eyes burst to life glowing with the same brilliant green as did Raphael's.

"Let's have some fun. We've earned it."

With that he grabbed Juliet firmly about the waist, and concentrated for a moment while gesturing with his free hand. A bright blue line appeared in the shop and revolved into an oval sphere through which they could both see a rocky coast from high above.

"Here we go," Kellan said with a laugh as he jumped through the open portal, Juliet gripping him tightly.

"Kellan! Oh my god, we're falling," Juliet yelled.

"Why are we falling?" Kellan yelled back.

"Because you are an idiot and did something wrong. Fix it…fix it!"

"Relax, I got this," and Juliet instantly felt them slow, their decent becoming that of a gently falling feather.

"Oh, wow, what did you do?"

"Look carefully around us—see anything?"

She looked and could make out the barest ripple of distortion and then looked all around them.

"Are we in some kind of bubble?"

"Sort of. Watch." Kellan reached into a pocket and pulled out some change, then threw it directly in front of them. The coins seemed to tumble lazily for about a foot and then suddenly streaked down toward the ground.

She looked at him, "Gravity bubble?"

"Ding ding ding! Give the girl a cee'gar. Simple thing, really. Mass creates attraction, so I've just changed the amount of attraction that the Earth can exert on us by separating us from everything else by way of this little bubble. Pretty simple really."

"Yeah, sounds it," Juliet said as she continued to look down, feeling her feet gently touch the ground, her ears popping slightly, "Bubble gone?"

"Yep, all gone."

"But, how exactly did you make that work? Did you actually change the mass of the Earth?"

She watched as Kellan's brow furrowed, "Hmm, good question. I don't think so, that would have required a lot more energy than I used, and it probably would have done some pretty horrible things to the planet." He shook his head. "Yeah, I'm sure I couldn't have done that if I tried. Anyway, I'm not exactly sure how it worked. It's mostly like I understand what has to happen, in that the relative gravitational attraction needed to change and then it sort of just happens."

With that, Kellan turned and started walking along the grassy cliff towards its edge.

Juliet hadn't moved when he looked over his shoulder, "Come on, let's try some stuff."

"Wait, what do you mean, 'sort of just happens'?"

Kellan walked back to her. "It's like this. I have to understand at least the fundamentals of what I'm trying to do. If I understand more than the fundamentals, then I can do more or be more effective with what I'm doing. Beyond that, I'm not sure of the exact physics associated with what I'm doing, some of it seems highly improbable."

Juliet looked baffled.

"Ok, let's take an example that I haven't tried and, honestly, won't be trying because I'd likely end up dead."

"Okay," she said slowly.

"C'mon, walk with me. You know I think better walking."

She did.

"So, suppose I want to go to the moon, how do I do that?"

"Well, I suspect you would just make one of those portal thingies that opened on the moon," she said rather matter-of-factly.

"Huh," he responded, "Yeah, you're right. So, for the sake of argument, let's say I want to get there the old fashioned way: directly, non-stop from good ol' planet Earth."

"Okay," she said again.

He nodded. "There are steps between here and there. I have to escape earth's gravity, survive a vacuum, and survive really cold or hot temperatures."

"Don't forget finding the moon. Your sense of direction is crappy on Earth, I doubt you could even find the moon. You know it moves right?"

"Very funny. Let's just stipulate that I'm looking at it the whole time and just keep heading in the right direction."

"Unrealistic for you," Juliet said with a snicker, "but stipulated."

Kellan ignored her.

"Step one: escape gravity. Pretty easy—just do the opposite of what I did when we were falling. I could also change my relationship to Earth's mass relative to that of the moon, sort of making the moon, 'down,' if you will. Anchoring me to it rather than Earth, then I would sort of fall to the moon, which means I couldn't really get lost. So there, Ha!"

"Yeah, that doesn't explain *how* at all, Kel."

"Wait, you are missing the point I'm trying to make. It's not about the specific how, it's about a solid understanding of what's involved; in this case, gravity. Anyway, now about the vacuum and temperature. I'd have to insulate myself from both, right? Or alter my actual body so that it could withstand those extremes."

Kellan paused, his eyes losing focus. "Hey, that's an idea. I wonder if I could actually change something that fundamental about my own physiology. I suppose it would..."

Juliet started snapping her fingers in Kellan's face, "Hey! Stay focused. Vacuum, temperature..."

He looked at her, "Right, right, so, insulated. That would just require a simple shield that kept temperature controlled air in and everything else out. See, simple." He smiled.

"You are insane, really. That makes no sense at all and is anything but simple."

Kellan ignored her and held up a finger. "Now, what would be hard is building a campfire on the moon. I mean I could make one if it were inside the bubble, but just on the surface of the moon, no idea how to make that work. No fuel, no oxygen, no fire. You see what I'm getting at, Juliet, I apparently can manipulate some of the basic constructs that hold," he gestured in a wide arc, "all this together, but there are rules to creation and I can't simply ignore them. I have to work around them, bend them, trick them maybe."

"You are saying there are rules?" She asked.

He pointed at her, "Yes!"

"And some rules can be bent?"

"Yes!"

"And some rules can be broken?"

"Yes! Wait. Dammit, you totally just Morpheus'ed me. By the way, did you know that Morpheus was real and was a demon?"

"Um, no?"

"Yeah, apparently a serious douche-canoe; Micah killed him. Anyway, just a bit of trivia for you to sock away. C'mon."

Kellan walked toward the cliff and this time Juliet followed, shaking her head slowly. He paused leaning against one of the large rocks that dotted the cliff and pointed up smiling, "Pretty cool, huh?"

"What?"

He frowned and pointed again, "Seriously?"

Juliet walked a little closer to get a better angle at the rock Kellan kept pointing to and the profile came into view. She looked to her left and saw the other rock, too, had a human profile.

"You are such a nerd, Kellan. Of all the places you, zapped us to Easter Island?"

He grinned. "Pretty cool, huh?" he said again.

"You really are just a boy, aren't you?"

"We all are," he said as he stopped leaning against the giant head and walked to the edge of the cliff.

"We? We who?"

"Men," he said glancing over his shoulder, "Now take a look down at the surf."

She walked up beside him, staring over the cliff to the roiling ocean below as it frothed against hundreds of jagged black rocks.

"Most of Micah's understanding revolved around elemental forces, like Fire, Water, Wind, Lightning, and such"

"Those aren't elements."

"Yeah, I know. I told him that."

"Great. And now I'm telling you that."

"Right. They aren't elements, but they are elemental forces."

"Not really, no. The gravity you keep messing with, that's an elemental force. You've only told me that for years."

Kellan frowned at her. "Am I this annoying to you when you are trying to make a point?"

She nodded and he sighed.

"I'm going to be better then from now on, because I must really have been insufferable."

"Pretty much," she said.

"From Micah's perspective, he was most familiar with elemental forces so that's what he taught me. I'll have to be self taught on other things, like time travel and such."

Juliet's eyes widened, "What? You can travel in time? Seriously? Do you have a TARDIS?"

Kellan stared at her, not completely sure which of her questions were sarcastic, then shrugged, "Not yet I can't, but I think it will be similar to traveling across distances like getting here, just temporally. Not sure enough of the concepts yet to try though and, sorry, no TARDIS. My point is that I only have a few tools in my toolbox right now, but they are still pretty cool. Watch."

She did, and saw Kellan concentrate his eyes brightening as he pointed up toward the sky. Almost instantly she saw clouds condense in the otherwise clear blue, first white, then dark with dangerous looking flattened bottoms. She saw as Kellan gestured, forming a fist and quickly pulling his hand down as if he were swinging an invisible hammer. As he did so, a brilliant white blue blot of lighting streaked out of the just formed cloud striking one of the rocks below. Kellan spread out both hands wide and the lightning leaped from rock to rock each one exploding in turn. He lowered his hands and she saw the dark cloud vanish as quickly as it had appeared.

"Wow," she said softly.

Kellan slapped a closed fist against his chest twice. "I am Thor," he said, smiling.

Juliet sighed again, "You just ruined what really was an awe inspiring moment."

"Now," Kellan began. "I couldn't have done that out of a clear blue sky. Lightning doesn't work that way; it can't, so I can't. But, I could condense clouds adjust the relative charges and *then* make lightning. I understand this process more fully than Micah so my lightning control is better and stronger than his was."

"Why not just use the natural electrical charges inside your body and enhance those?" Juliet asked.

Kellan paused, staring at her, then she saw his eyes lose focus again and begin to dart back and forth. A few moments later, she saw the focus return as he look directly at her.

"Mind palace?" she asked.

He nodded, "I don't have much to draw on, just some basic stuff I read once about how we are all bioelectric machines, but it might be enough to test something."

She watched as Kellan stretched out a hand, fingers up forming a bowl and began wiggling his fingers. Nothing happened and he grunted with frustration.

"Doesn't work," he said.

"Really, one try and that's your conclusion? Try again."

He frowned but did as Juliet suggested. A moment later she saw him gasp. "Did you see that?"

"No," she said, as he continued to rotate his fingers in a slow gripping fashion and then she saw the small sparks begin to leap and play across his fingers. The sparks grew faster and larger and within moments they coalesced into a glowing ball of electricity.

Kellan laughed, smiling at her as he juggled the sparking ball of power from one hand to the other finally throwing it toward one of the rocks below. They both watched as it streaked toward its target striking the rock with a shower of sparks and stone chips.

Kellan frowned a little, "Not nearly as much umph as the cloud lightning,"

"Yeah, but that was self generated—no clouds required and, I bet with practice you could make it stronger."

He nodded brightening, "Hey, I bet I could use my body heat and do the same thing with fire."

Kellan repeated the hand motions and very quickly small tongues of fire appeared in his hand then raced together forming a ball. Juliet saw Kellan concentrating, straining, to add more energy to the fire in his hand. The ball grew in size and intensity, first glowing red, then white hot. She stepped back as it began to burn her.

"Kel? That's enough. Kellan? You don't look so good." Kellan's skin had become pallid, his lips blue, and his teeth chattered.

"Uh oh…" he said, then collapsed unconscious.

Kellan opened his eyes and shivered.

"Oh thank god," said Juliet. "You've been out cold for almost half and hour, are you ok?"

Kellan shivered again, "I f-feel really cold. Where did the fire come from?"

"From you, idiot, now crawl closer to it and warm up."

Kellan did so, embracing the warmth from what seemed like a small campfire.

"When you passed out, you dropped that fireball and it burned through the grass and turned the rock all molten. I just scooped up anything dry enough to burn from around here and threw it in the hole, then tried to keep something burning until you woke up. You realize you gave yourself a serious case of hypothermia, don't you?"

Kellan groaned a bit, "Yeah, I think I figured that out just about the time it was too late to do anything about it. You realize, this is your fault."

"What!?"

"I never thought of using my own internal reserves to generate external effects."

"I didn't tell you freeze yourself nearly to death. Good thing you didn't try to do that with the lightning, you probably would have given yourself a heart attack or fried your brain, and that's not something I could have helped with since I don't see any defibrillators around."

The color had rapidly returned to Kellan face and he sat up. "That's a fair point. I think I'll experiment some more with this concept, but will do so cautiously."

"Good thinking."

He smiled at her. "Seriously though, Juliet. That was brilliant. I might never have thought of it. Thanks!"

She beamed at him, "Twern't nuthin', boss, but…"

"What?"

"I think you need a focus of some kind as a means to unleash this stuff. It just seems to come out of nowhere with no notice."

Kellan snickered a little, feeling very much better as the warmth of the fire continued to seep into him. "What do you want me to do, yell, 'Fuego!'"

"Ha! That'd be awesome, but, seriously, you are no Harry Dresden. He'd totally kick your ass."

Kellan was about to protest when Juliet pulled out her cellphone and looked at it.

"I don't think you have service on Easter Island," Kellan said with a laugh.

"No kidding, I was just checking the time. We need to get me home. We are about 30 minutes from my folks freaking out and both our phones are going right to voice mail."

"What time is it?"

"7:30"

"Oh, crap, we are already half an hour late. Hey, I could try to figure out that rip in time variant of the distance traveling and we could get you home whenever you wanted."

"No, no, no. We are so not trying that now. You go experiment with that little process on your own and very slowly. In fact, don't experiment on your own. Wait until tomorrow and do it when I'm around so I can spot you"

"Spot me, it's not like doing bench presses."

"You know what I mean. Like maybe try to jump forward or backwards 5 minutes or something and see how that goes. Regardless, we are not doing that now and we are getting me home."

Kellan smiled as he got up. "Yes, Ma'am!"

"Good, now make with the sparkle eyes and open us a portal."

He did so and, as it opened, she saw the inside of the small shed that her family used to store gardening equipment. "Wow, curbside service, Kel, nice job. By the way, I think I am handling all this craziness with a lot of grace."

Kellan laughed. "You certainly are. Now run on through, bending space isn't as easy as it looks."

Chapter 7

SEMPER FI

Kellan watched from the driveway as soft yellow light spilled out from the open front door. Juliet turned to wave as did her mother.

"Sorry to keep her out so long, Rach," Kellan yelled as he waved his hand in greeting. "Inventory—won't happen again."

Rachel Herrick smiled as Juliet squeezed past her, disappearing into the house, "Yes it will, Kellan. Just, please make sure you guys have your cell phones on; we were getting worried."

"Yeah, yeah—sure thing. We were in the basement, no signal and all that, but I'll be more careful. Maybe run a land line down there or something.

She nodded, waved again, and closed the door leaving Kellan standing alone in the pool of orange made by the mercury streetlights.

His stomach contracted a bit and he felt the butterflies.

"What's up with that," he mumbled to himself as he turned and walked down the driveway to the street. Then it hit him. This was the first time he had been alone since all the craziness started. From this world's frame of reference, that was just this morning, but for him, it had been the better part of a year. A year of constant activity, but also with constant companionship of one kind or another.

He stopped suddenly in the street, looking back and forth, "Oh well, now this sucks. My car is at the store." Kellan again realized he had actually said the words out loud and made a mental note not to spend so much time talking to himself, at least where people could see, smiling at his own internal caveat. He started walking down the street trying to clear his head and think what to do next. He really didn't want to go home and bounce around the walls of his house, but also had no desire to really socialize with a bunch of people either.

He stopped and snapped his fingers, "Meghan. Of course, I'll go see Meghan. Oh man will she be happy to see me." Kellan cringed and looked about. "I just did it again, didn't I," he whispered. "Yes, you did—now stop it." Fortunately, Kellan remembered that he'd been having these external conversations with himself for as long as he could remember, so didn't attribute it to all the recent changes and traumas he'd endured. Still, as a somewhat innocuous bookstore owner, he could afford to stand out a bit as an eccentric. In his current situation, drawing attention was probably much less desirable.

For a moment, he considered trying to make a portal directly to Meghan's house, but immediately thought better of it. Micah had warned him not to become too reliant on his extra-normal abilities for normal activities. Apparently, this Maurius character who had it out for him, was the master of that kind of thing, using his abilities for almost everything from the mundane to the spectacular.

Kellan pulled out his iPhone, tapped the Uber icon, and input his bookstore as the destination. He'd just drive to see Meghan, like a normal person. A few minutes later, a white Subaru pulled up beside him as he walked along the street driven by a kid that looked like a cross between an emaciated member of Duck Dynasty and Where's Waldo.

"You Kellan?"

"Yep, that's me. Cool 'stache dude."

"Thank, bro. I'm Brian, hop in."

The two chatted about nothing for the few miles between Juliet's neighborhood and Kellan's shop. When they arrived, Kellan tapped his app giving Brian five stars for being strong in the Hipster Force and got out with a final wave.

As Kellan walked down the alley towards the back of the shop where he'd parked his car, his eyes were drawn to the scratched, circle in the pavement, now faded somewhat over the past months. He suddenly began to think coming back here by himself wasn't one of his brightest moves and picked up his pace, almost jogging down the alley to where it appeared to dead-end. There was a low railing to the left which Kellan grabbed onto and leaped over with practiced ease, landing softly some four feet below in the parking lot behind his and the adjacent shops.

He quickly walked up to the black, 1967 Impala, and gave it a quick pat as he slipped his key in the door lock. "Hiya, baby, miss me?"

Kellan settled into the well worn seat, turned the ignition key and smiled at the deep rumble. "Yeah, I missed you too. We're going to see Meghan!"

Meghan lived in Cabbagetown, a quasi gentrified section of downtown Atlanta where a number of old factories and mills had been converted into lofts. When Kellan arrived at the security gate, he decided he wanted to surprise her, so punched in the gate's UPS code instead of Meghan's. The large steel and chain barrier rumbled to life and slowly slid out of the way on squeaking wheels. He gunned the engine, excited to see his friend, zoomed past the now open barrier and sliding into a visitor's spot, tires protesting with a squeal at the abrupt stop.

"Sorry, baby," Kellan said sliding his hand along the steering wheel for a moment as he slipped out the door.

Moments later he was at her loft tapping on the door. He gave the door his standard "shave and a haircut—two bits," knock and waited.

Nothing.

"I know she's here. She's always here." Kellan mumbled, as he looked at his watch. "9:30, she can't possibly be asleep yet." With that thought in mind he just proceeded to play the equivalent of bongo drums on her door. He was about to begin a second round, when the door flew open and Kellan found himself staring down the barrel of a very large handgun.

What is it with the women in his life and handguns thought Kellan? Meghan stood in a practiced, sideways stance designed to minimize her vital areas to attack. She had both hands gripping a military issued service weapon as she grimly sighted down its length, eyes burrowing into Kellan's while he stood there, aghast, both hands up as he prepared to bongo the door again.

"Easy, Woody, it's just me. It's Kellan."

Meghan's eyes looked a bit wild and, for a few heartbeats Kellan really thought he might get shot in the face, then he saw her let out a breath as she lowered the weapon.

"What the heck, Kel? How did you get in here?"

"I wanted to surprise you. I just used the UPS code."

She stared at him, puzzled, waving him inside, "The UPS code? What do you mean?"

"Oh I saw the UPS guy tap in a code when he was delivering a package."

"UPS doesn't deliver packages inside anymore; they deliver them to the front office."

"Really, that seems like a pain." He paused, "Was that your idea?"

Meghan grunted something that sounded fairly affirmative and closed the door.

"You should really have that code reset then."

"It's not really a problem except when mental mutants stop by who can remember six digit random codes for over a year. You are the mental mutant in this story, if you were wondering."

"Yeah, I figured," said Kellan as his eyes washed over the small industrial loft. He could never figure why people loved these places so much with all the exposed pipes and brick. Meghan's place fell neatly into the category of being intentionally shabby, sporting a small kitchen with breakfast bar that spilled out into an even smaller living room that consisted of a couch, coffee table, and entertainment center. In between the kitchen and living room was a short hall that led to the only bedroom. Kellan, being much more an old leather and reclaimed wood kind of guy, never liked this place, but was happy to see that Meghan had finally taken his suggestion of having hardwoods put down over the previously acid etched concrete floors.

"So how are ya, Woody, it's been like a month. You don't call. You don't write. Your mother and I are worried about you."

Meghan frowned as she sat down on a stool by her breakfast bar.

"Well, maybe it's because I enjoy my solitude and communicating with you usually ends up with a visit, which I might not have wanted."

"Hmm…well that's one point of view. Got any beer? I'm really parched and have had one hell of a day."

"Sure. You know where they are. Don't expect me to play hostess for you."

Kellan walked over to the fridge and rummaged around for a second or two, "Oooo, Innis & Gunn! My favorite. It's like you knew I was coming."

"No, Kellan, If I'd known you were coming, then I wouldn't have been here."

Kellan ignored the jibe and walked over to the bottle opener Meghan had attached to the wall near the pantry. He gave the bottle a quick downward pull and watched the cap fly off only to be caught by a magnet hidden beneath the wood of the bottle opener. He smiled, "That just never gets old; I really need to get myself one of those."

He sat down on the stool next to Meghan and silently drank his beer while she continued to stare straight ahead into the living room area.

Finally, having almost finished his beer, Kellan cleared his throat garnering a sideways glance from Meghan.

"So, Woody, I need a favor."

"Please stop calling me that."

"Why? You earned it."

She snorted.

"Seriously, when a Marine Captain gets chewed out for having you flying into an FOB and goes toe-to-toe with his CO saying, now, wait, let me make sure I remember the quote properly…"

"You remember everything properly, jerk."

Kellan ignored her and continued, "Oh yes, I've got it, 'We had injured Marines and Daugherty here is tough as Woodpecker Lips.' Come on, Meghan, don't bullshit a bullshitter. Somewhere deep down you like having every seriously bad ass Marine in the area calling you 'Woody,' cause they consider you even more bad ass than themselves."

Kellan stared at Meghan's profile and saw her mouth twitch up ever so slightly. He smiled to himself as he drained the rest of his beer.

Not for the first time, Kellan's libido reminded him that Meghan Daugherty was an amazing physical specimen, even as she sat wearing an old extra-large t-shirt emblazoned with a stylized "Coca-Cola" logo and, what looked to be men's boxer shorts. Her short, dark brown hair was cut in a way that always reminded Kellan of a young Demi Moore in Ghost, and she smelled slightly of what he knew to be Ivory soap. Despite his perfect memory, Kellan never tired of taking in the sights and scents of his reluctant hostess.

She smiled at him, "You know what, I think I want one of those beers too."

Kellan heard the pop, hiss, click as two bottles were opened and their respective caps were captured by the magnet. Meghan handed him another Innis & Gunn, and he watched the muscles ripple along her arm as she slowly twirled the neck of the beer bottle between her fingers again sitting down on her stool.

"We've known each other a long time, right?" began Kellan. "I mean you were my first kiss and all."

"Yes, a long time, and I remember. We were 14 and you kissed like a dying trout." She grinned.

"Wow, a full-on Meghan Daugherty smile, I haven't see that in a long time. Perhaps we should discuss my sexual deficiencies more often."

Meghan wasn't tall by any means, perhaps around 5'6", but she bore the frame with a stature that clearly bespoke both former military and present cross-fit enthusiast. She smiled at him wolfishly, brown eyes twinkling and Kellan suddenly felt flushed.

"This a booty call, Kel?"

"Huh, no, Meg, no, nothing like that. I just have——"

"Aw, too bad," she replied using what Kellan immediately recognized as her 'come hither,' voice that had left men wrecked across 15 states and the District of Columbia, which he reminded himself absently, wasn't actually a state. She then yawned, and stretched, causing the t-shirt to ride up revealing, what Kellan believed was the most perfect stomach in human history even as the t-shirt also pulled taught against her breasts. "You, surrrree?" she said accentuating the final letters into dangerous purr.

Suddenly, Kellan was anything but sure.

Meghan walked up between Kellan's spread legs as he sat on the stool, wrapped her arms around his neck and leaned in, giving him a long, and passionate kiss that went on for years.

Finally, she broke the kiss, pulling back and giving his shoulders and arms an affectionate squeeze. "Ooh, someone has been working out too. Those arms are like iron. Come on book-boy, let's relieve some stress." Kellan felt himself being pulled gently but insistently off his stool and toward the bedroom. He was half off his stool when his frontal lobe finally engaged and got the better of his rather insistent reptilian core.

Kellan pulled his hand free from hers, "Meghan Chesterson Daugherty, I am *not* going in there with you."

"Sure you are," she replied with a grin even more predatory than before. "You totally want to." She glanced down. "I can tell."

Kellan followed her gaze, inwardly cursing that reptilian core, and waved in a general downward direction, "Mike down there has no say in the matter. I am in charge here an *you* are backsliding, mister."

She stared at him silently for a moment, appraising him, then he saw her eyes go hard, all seduction evaporating.

"Fuck you, Kel. Get out."

He sighed, "That's my girl."

She didn't smile. "I'm serious, get out. If you aren't going to give me what I need, then," she paused, "I'll use small words for you. Get. The fuck out. Before I shoot you—in the face."

"I'm not going anywhere, and you have some explaining to do. When was the last time you went to a meeting? Have you even been talking to your sponsor?"

"Fuck meetings and fuck my sponsor; she's a stupid army bitch and has no idea what I'm about. Now, I'm serious. I like you and we had some amazing nights together, but I *will* hurt you if you don't get out."

"Night, Meghan. It was one night and I still feel guilty about that."

"Whatever, that's yours to deal with, I enjoyed myself thoroughly."

"This is *not* you Meghan. This is your—your illness talking."

She hurled her beer bottle at him and Kellan deftly caught it an inch from his nose, gently setting it down on the counter.

"I don't have an illness, you pretentious prick."

"You do and clearly it's gotten out of hand."

"PTSD is bullshit. Sexual transference of trauma is bullshit. I'm a Marine god dammit. Marines don't get PTSD; they give the other poor bastards PTSD."

"It's not bullshit. You are a Marine. I've no doubt you've left permanent psychological scars to enemies across the entire middle east, but that has nothing to do with anything. What I came to talk with you about has everything to do with your condition and I think I can help."

"Ok, that's it, I've had it with you tonight," and she stalked towards him pulling both hands back, bracing herself, and smashing them, open palmed, against his chest pushing him towards the door.

Kellan absorbed the blows barely rocking backwards.

She looked up at him with a mixture of confusion and anger and he saw her countenance darken further.

"Uh oh," thought Kellan as he reached inward for just a trickle of power, not enough to be seen, just enough to give him what he needed.

Meghan raised a knee to kick towards his stomach but Kellan pivoted ever so slightly at the last moment so felt only air. She turned to deliver a kick, but found he had leaned back scant inches past her reach. Yelling now, she delivered a flurry of perfectly executed mixed martial arts attacks, any one of which would have debilitated Kellan the bookstore owner. Each came within scant inches of connecting, but none did.

Meghan stopped, breathing heavily despite her obviously impeccable conditioning. She stared into Kellan's eyes uncomprehendingly, and then he saw them well with tears.

"Oh god, oh god, oh god," she cried, crumpling to the ground. She wrapped her arms around her chest and began rocking. "Oh god, I'm really losing it." She looked up at him. "I had to have hit you. I had to have. Are you even here, or are you just another delusion like *they* where?"

Kellan was already on the floor beside her, holding her as the hot tears streamed down her cheeks; he felt her tremble. He leaned her down so her head was in his lap and he stroked her hair.

"I'm here, Meg," Kellan said softly. I'm really here and I'm not a delusion."

He felt her nod several times against his lap as he continued to rub her hair, "Ok, ok, ok, not a delusion."

"Now Meghan, I have something to tell you. Something that will be difficult for you to believe immediately, but I want you to stay with me and trust me, ok?

Kellan felt her nod.

"First, I need to ask you probably the worst question I could ask at this moment and I want you to know that it's because things are going to get better for you. Not just soon. Tonight, Meg. Things are going to get better for you tonight. You trust me, right?"

Another nod.

"Ok, here it is. I've never asked you to go into it. I've left it for others to poke, prod, or shrink you as the case warranted, but now I'm asking you to tell me what happened. What really happened in Samangan Province."

Kellan felt her stiffen and watched as she pulled her knees up to her chest curling.

"No, Kellan, no!"

"Now, wait, I told you not to freak out and give me a chance to explain."

She was trembling again, "I can't believe you are doing this. You! Of all people, I thought I could count on you to leave this alone and just be with me when we were together. To treat me as a person, not as some subject to be understood, or some broken thing to be repaired. Get out Kel." But the heat had left her voice.

Kellan didn't move. "Meg, I'm not going anywhere. I need you and, more importantly, you need me. You really do."

He paused and she said nothing. "Ok, Meghan, I can see this isn't going to work, so I'll go first. I know what happened there. I know what you say you saw. I know what you say they did to those Marines and I know that everyone told you it was PTSD generated delusions, but I know better."

Megan twisted so she was lying on her back, head in Kellan's lap looking up at him, "What? How do you know all that and what are you saying?" She started to sit up, but Kellan stroked he hair back from her forehead and whispered for her to please relax and just be still.

"I know because your parents told me. They wanted me to confront you and tell you what everyone else told you, that you didn't see what you thought you saw and that you needed to admit that as the first step to getting better."

"But, but you didn't," she said softly.

"No, I didn't, because I didn't want to be that guy. I didn't want to be that one more person to called into question your experiences there. Hell, Meghan, you are braver than me just for having been there. Who was I to step into your nightmares. But, all that said, I agreed with your parents, and your doctors, and the chaplains. I agreed with all of them."

"Of course you did," she sighed, barely above a whisper.

Kellan shook her softly and she looked back at him, "I agreed with them, and I was dead wrong, Meghan. Dead. Wrong."

"What? What do you mean? Why are you saying that?"

"Because I know better now. I know Meghan. I know werwolves are as real as those scars on your back. I know they made the scars and they killed your Marines."

She stared up at him, eyes starting to become wild again, "You *know* Kellan? How do you know?"

He bent down placing, a kiss on her forehead, "Well, Woody, that brings me to the big favor I have to ask of you."

Kellan smiled in somewhat bemused surprise at the rapid transformation in his friend. Gone were the furtive glances, false seductions, and uncertainties. As Megan paced back and forth, bare feet slapping against the aged hardwoods, he saw the Marine who served two and half tours and garnered the respect of all who met her.

She looked over at him, "Do it again."

"Which?"

"All of it."

He laughed, "Ok, Woody, but just for you."

Kellan reached out his hands and Meghan inhaled softly as she saw his eyes begin to glow with their supernaturally green light. Moments later, tongues of fire danced across the finger tips of his right hand, even as frosty mists of ice crystals performed similarly on his left. Making two fists, he softly lobbed the now flaming orb into the air followed by the ice. The two burst together in a hiss releasing a cloud of steam, which quickly wafted away.

"That's just crazy."

"Yeah, I know, right?"

"And, when I tried to pummel you earlier, you are not actually super fast, it's just that you made me slow? I still don't quite get that."

Kellan shook his head, "Not so much making *you* slow, more like making time around me flow slowly. Everything is slower except me."

Meghan sat on the sofa, folding her legs beneath her, "But couldn't you just do the opposite too. I mean make time flow faster around you?"

Kellan paused thinking, "I suppose so, but what would be the purpose of that? I mean that would just give some baddy a virtually unlimited amount of time to kick my ass."

"No, idiot, you wouldn't use it like that. I mean, take for example a 3 min egg. You put a speed bubble around all that and, poof, egg done."

"I'm pretty sure that expediting my culinary activities isn't the best use of these abilities."

Now Meghan was openly shaking her head, "So literal. No, Kellan, I was just using that as an illustration. You could use it for lots of things, like surveillance. Hang out, speed up time in your bubble, and everything looks like one of those time lapse movies. That has to be useful for something."

Kellan pondered a moment, "Hmmm, that is good point. Not sure how much surveillance I may be doing, but still—figuring out how all this works is task #1."

"So, back to the main point. Let's be clear, you haven't actually seen any supernatural bad boys, Vampires, Werwolves, One Direction?" She smiled at the last and Kellan's heart warmed at the joke.

"No, however, that last one has me the most worried. Clearly they are destroying the musical tastes of an entire generation."

They laughed and Kellan continued, "So, no to Vampires, and Werwolves, but yes to blade wielding skin-walkers that turn into Jell-O and Archangels"

"Alleged Archangels," she replied holding up a hand.

"Dude, I saw them; you didn't. They were the real deal. Angels are like porn; you may not be able completely describe it, but you know it when you see it."

"Ha! Only you would juxtapose recognition of porn with that of Angels; I really wonder at the celestial judgment of tapping you for this post."

"Trust me, I did tell them that anyone who would pick me for this isn't qualified to pick anyone, especially me. But, apparently, I'm just what's needed at this point in time."

"A sarcastic, irreverent, nerd with an eidetic memory and a love for pop culture?"

"Exactly!"

They both laughed for what seemed like an eternity, slowly settling in to a comfortable silence.

"Let's go back and save them," Meghan said.

"Huh?"

"My Marines. Let's go back, frag those bastard werewolves and save my Marines."

Kellan frowned and held up his hands. "Easy Meghan, I've still got my training wheels on and don't even have any idea how to rip open holes in time."

"So, we learn, together."

He ignored her. "And I don't have any idea about the ramifications of altering timelines, or even if they can be altered. I could create a paradox. Or I could do something that causes a worse tragedy to occur."

"Worse than an entire squad of dead Marines?" she said evenly.

"Yes, Meghan, as horrible as that was, yes it could be worse. I don't know how it could be worse, but that's the point isn't it? Screwing around with time is not something I am going to do willy nilly. Again, even if such screwage is even possible. God set up all these physical and temporal laws and didn't leave me a manual."

"Well, then, God's a dick and you can tell Him that for me."

Kellan sighed, "Noted, but weren't you listening to me? I'm completely blocked off from Him. No cards, no letters, no e-mails, no prayers. I'm persona non grata to the big guy, by design."

"Then you're a dick too. I want these monsters dead."

"Now that," Kellan began, pointing a finger at Meghan, "is a different matter entirely."

She perked up. "What do you mean?"

"What I mean, my fine one woman wrecking crew, is that I do know how to rip space and we do know where these furry bastards were last hanging out. What's to think that they aren't still roaming around the same general area?"

"What's to think they are?"

"Plenty. Micah told me that these critters tend to take on some aspects of their more bestial selves and one of those aspects is…"

"Territorial." she responded.

Kellan touched his nose, "Ding ding ding."

Meghan got up without another word and walked into her bedroom.

"Hey," Kellan yelled after her, "What are you doing?"

Minutes later she walked back into the room, already wearing desert camouflaged military pants and then peeled off her Coca-Cola shirt.

"Whoa!" shouted Kellan, almost, but not quite, turning away.

Meghan stood staring at him for a long minute, then smiled, "First, nothing you haven't seen before and second, I'm no longer the slightest bit interested in," she glanced down towards the floor, "Mike. But while I do appreciate your gallantry earlier tonight I also wanted to remind you of what you missed out on, so there." With that she quickly pulled on her military tee and returned to the bedroom.

Kellan grumbled mostly to himself, "Trust me. I remember everything."

From the bedroom he heard a lilting, "Oh, I know you do."

Kellan sighed, "Frack me."

Meghan returned to the living room holding a massive footlocker and dropped it on the coffee table, "Not a chance of fracking now, we have some monsters to kill," and she flipped open the lid to reveal nearly every manner of firearm and knife. Time to gear up."

"You gear up, Rambette, I'm good."

She eyed him. "You are far from good. You need body armor, appropriate clothes, and weapons, unless you just plan to throw fire, ice, and lightning everywhere. Just let me give you a few things that will…" She trailed off as Kellan's eyes sparked to life and his image shimmered, first revealing what appeared to her as gleaming silver mail covering him from neck to toe and then faded to be replaced by clothing that very much resembled her own.

Meghan closed her mouth, "Okaayy, Lancelot, I'm assuming that the shiny stuff you are wearing is better than ballistic Kevlar."

Kellan just smiled in return.

"And weapons?"

Kellan held out his right hand and a brilliant longsword formed in it from mist that had coalesced there.

"Kinda big," said Meghan nonplussed.

Kellan raised an eyebrow and the sword shrank in size with ornate carvings forming on the blade.

"Oh, you did not just do that, you juvenile geek."

"What?" asked Kellan innocently.

"You know very well, 'what'. That is totally Bilbo's sword."

"You said the other one was too big," said Kellan smiling, "besides this will be far more effective than your weapons. Bullets don't kill werewolves, sweetie."

Meghan popped the clip out of her Glock with practiced ease, tilting it toward Kellan, "Silver bullets do. Sweetie."

He laughed. "Holy crap, Meghan, how many of those rounds do you have?"

"About a thousand. Look around, Kel, I don't have really expensive tastes and that disability money has to go somewhere. Silver is a good investment and a hedge against inflation," she smiled, but then it faded, "I knew those werewolves were real…always knew it. And now I'm gonna kill them—all of them."

Kellan put a hand gently on her shoulder. "Listen, Meghan, I came here looking for *your* help because you are the baddest badass I know and because there are some nasty things after me. Well, I assume they are still after me. I figured having you at my back would do wonders for my survival chances even with all my nifty new abilities. You are the clearest and most focused that I've seen you since you got home and if I had any part in that, I'm glad. I just don't want to see you regress. Afghanistan is a big place and while I agree that odds are these critters are still in Samangan, that's a lot of area to cover."

"I know exactly where they are."

"Say what?"

"Yeah, you know my boys were sent in after an IED killed that Afghani Assemblyman, Samangani. That was in Samangan City. Well, when the whole op went casters-up and those furry bastards had killed my Marines and left me for dead, lying there bleeding out, I heard one of them talk about getting back to *the stupa*. There's only one old Buddhist stupa anywhere near Samagan City and I'm betting that's where they'll be. The only thing I can't grok is how I'll know who's who if they are not all wolfy and such."

Kellan stood for a moment, quietly impressed at his friend's calm, clear, command of the facts, so different than a mere few hours ago. "Um, yeah, well I can help with that." He waggled the small engraved sword. "This will let you know if there be monsters. Arg"

Meghan stared at him flatly. "I thought Sting only glowed around Orcs."

Kellan laughed, "Nope, it's been upgraded to the new, improved, All-Monster glow model. Besides, it's not always this small either. Watch." Kellan held his arm out to the side with small sword held loosely and Meghan saw his frown furrow slightly as he stared at the weapon. A scant moment later it seemed to wobble slightly as if it were made of quick silver and then extended to become a gleaming longsword that shimmered with a soft inner green glow that played off intricately engraved words. Meghan leaned in to try and read them, but the script eluded her. Seeing her confusion, Kellan brandished the sword pointed to one side and said, "Take me up," then turned the sword over, pointed again, "Cast me away."

Meghan shook her head slightly trying to take in what she was seeing, "Those words sound familiar, and I know I've seen that sword before."

"Of course you have," said Kellan looking immensely pleased with himself, "It's Excalibur. The sword is just an outward manifestation of my will for it to become—"

"What?," Meghan interrupted, "*The* Excalibur,"

"Huh, no, don't be silly. The real Excalibur wouldn't look nearly this cool; this Excalibur is from the 1981 John Boorman movie of the same name. It's totally the best Sword and Sorcery movie of all time—trust me Meghan."

Meghan's eyes misted over a bit. "I do trust you Kel. Completely." And Kellan immediately sobered knowing they were no longer talking about any movie or even the sword as she continued, "You trusted me with this secret of yours. You came and lifted this burden from my soul. You are helping me avenge my boys and you trust me to have your back when we're done." She walked around the coffee table and embraced him tightly. "You, Mr. Sentinel, are a good and trusted friend and I'll always love you for what you did today."

Then, she released him, leaned back a little and said, "Now, enough with the mush, rip a hole in space and let's go fuck up some werewolves."

"Don't let it close yet," whispered Meghan as she crouched down next to the weather worn stone wall.

"Huh? Why? This looks easier than it is and it's the third freaking portal I've opened.

"That's your own damn fault for Stargating us to the wrong bloody place—times two. Now hush." Meghan pulled out her phone and held it up to her mouth, speaking softly, "Siri, what time is it in Afghanistan?"

"Oh for god's sake, Meghan." The portal blinked out.

She held up the little phone triumphantly, "Got it! 5:47 AM here, I thought as much, sky's lightening."

"And why did I need to strain to keep a portal open for that?"

"Does your roaming plan cover Afghanistani war zones? No? I didn't think so and since we wasted so much time galavanting…"

Kellan ground his teeth. "Could you just try not being such a bitch. I get that it's 'your thing,' but do keep in mind that I'm literally tearing a hole in the fabric of creation and, yeah, I screwed it up a couple times. In case you didn't know it, there aren't any independent bookstore conventions in Afghanistan so I didn't have much of a frame of reference for getting us here. In short, STFU."

Meghan ignored him as she scanned the immediate area. "This is definitely it. I remember the layout from having done an evac here."

From their vantage next to the massive stone stacked wall Kellan looked over the ancient structure. It was roughly rectangular and reminded him a bit of terraced temples in Mexico and Central America although the stupa definitely showed its asian influences. The bottom tier was largely intact while showing signs of both weather and war. Across the side facing them there were four pillars equally spaced while the longer side had six. The pillars seemed more decorative than structural and vaguely resembled the Doric style although the pillar's top and bottom portions were a bit thicker.

The second tier of the stupa also had the decorative pillars but each wall had a large arched entrance carved into the center. Finally, the domed portion of the structure had mostly been worn away and collapsed with only the northern face remaining, given the slight impression of a tired Hogwarts's Sorting hat resting upon the middle tier.

"Griffindor!" whispered Kellan.

Meghan just stared at him, "What are you talking about? No, don't tell me. We're going to need to cover that open ground to the primary stupa wall then circle around the back where the lower tier entrance is located. From there, I have no idea. Some of these structures have subterranean levels while others just go up from ground level. Given the state of the the dome, my guess is that at least part of the second tier is impassable from the rubble, so, if they are there, I'll bet we'll find them on the main level."

She sighed, "Which will make getting in undetected a huge pain in the ass."

"I think I can help with that. It's not easy. Give me a minute."

Meghan raised a high arched eyebrow questioningly as she saw Kellan's eyes begin to glow. His brow furrowed with concentration and she saw his form waver like the ghost in every poltergeist movie, then he vanished."

"Woah," she said reaching out to where he had been crouching. As she touched what felt like his shoulder, Meghan saw her hand vanish making her arm seem to end in a stump at the wrist.

Kellan let out a breath and reappeared, eyes returning to normal.

"How?" she asked simply.

"I altered the gravitational affect on those photons which were striking me, causing them to warp, strike, and reflect off objects around me instead."

"English?"

"I bent light around me which creates the effect of you being able to see through me." Kellan smiled, "Like Harry's cloak. Griffindor!"

"You really are a child," said Meghan as she removed each of her Glock 41s in turn, checked them and returned them to their holsters. She then confirmed the placement of her extra magazines and finally removed and resheathed both short katana blades that criss-crossed her back.

"What?" she growled, as Kellan stared at her grinning.

"I was just thinking you should have worn a green tank top and shorts."

"This is serious, Kellan, stop being a dick."

"Look, Ms. Croft, I get it. Trust me. This is my freaking life now so if I'm going to remain sane for any length of time, I need to try to keep my defensive humor intact. So, let's raid the tomb."

"Fine, but you are still a dick and it's not a tomb. Now, make with the wizardry and vanish us."

Kellan concentrated and they could see the world warp and shimmer around them. "I think that does it."

"You think?"

"Well, how can I test if we're invisible. It's not like I have a toggle switch. It feels right."

"Wonderful. Ok, let's go." Meghan crouched starting to run towards the stupa only to have Kellan grab the leather used to lash the swords to her back."

"Stop," he whispered. "I can only make us both invisible if you stay really close. Don't go running off. I know it feels like we're horribly exposed, but you need to slowly walk with me."

The two then continued to head towards the closest wall of the stupa, Meghan moving slowing at a crouch.

"This is ridiculous," she said softly, "the hair is standing up on my neck and I'm waiting to be jumped any second."

"Why are you crouching?"

"Because it makes me feel better. Now shut up and—"

Kellan bumped into her back, kicking up several rocks, as Meghan stopped pointing upward. Above them she saw two men on the second tier apparently talking with one another, both whom turned suddenly at the sound from below. Two bright blue beams of LED light illuminated the ground around Meghan and Kellan, then swept directly through their position. Kellan leaned in and spoke directly in her ear, "I guess we really are invisible."

He felt her stiffen and then mouth something which was hard to see from his angle but was able to piece it together. "I'm pretty sure that's anatomically impossible and I'm definitely sure it wouldn't be enjoyable. Now move. They can't see us and I can't keep us hidden much longer—changing gravity here."

The two reached the wall and Kellan released the power as they both saw the world shimmer back into focus. The lights from above continued to waft back and forth for a minute or two and then went off leaving Kellan and Meghan pressed against the wall in the predawn darkness.

"Let's—" began Kellan

"Shhh, I hear something," she said reaching back as if to press Kellan further into the wall.

Moments later two figures resolved themselves from the gloom.

"That's two of them," Kellan whispered into her ear.

"How can you tell? They just look like men."

Kellan reached down and took Meghan's hand in his and, as he did so, her image of the men changed. About them both glowed a faint red aura that seemed to pulse as they walked.

"Werewolf aura?" she asked incredulously

He shook his head, "Just unnatural and dark energy, not specific. I got the one on the right."

She nodded and silently removed the Glock from her right hip and sighted along it's length, "You first, I'll take lefty when yours goes down."

Kellan had already poured a palmful of water from his canteen and felt his body temperature rise as he drew the ambient heat from the water into himself. Within seconds, four dangerously pointed icicles rotated silently above his closed fist. With a final burst of will, Kellan flicked open his palm and the frozen projectiles streaked towards the right figure striking him three times in the chest and once in the forehead. As the man started to crumple, Kellan heard a short puff from his left as Meghan squeezed the trigger of her silenced Glock 41, and Kellan saw the left man's head snap back as he, too, collapsed to the ground.

"Two down—unknown amount to go," Meghan said grimly then drew her hand across Kellan's moist brow and wiped the sweat on her pants. "Don't do that. What if there were more of them? Put the heat somewhere else, stupid."

Kellan stared at her, shaking his head slightly, uncomprehendingly.

"Well, you could have just shunted the heat into the guy you were about to perforate; it's not like he would have known why he suddenly had a low grade fever. Just don't be dumb, ok? That was dumb."

Kellan sighed, knowing she was right and hating it.

The two continued around the side of the stupa without incident and saw the large steps that lead into the dark gaping maw of an entrance.

"Well, that certainly looks inviting," Kellan said softly.

"Yeah, sure does, can you invis us up just long enough to get inside and find some cover? I've no idea what that interior looks like from here."

Kellan nodded, "Ready."

"Really, you are getting good at that."

"Fast learner, remember things. Let's go; stay very close." With that Kellan moved quickly up the large stone stairs and into the dark interior, turning immediately to his left seeking out a darkened corner near the entrance where he crouched down.

"We're visible again." Kellan said.

"Ok, I can see some light up above, coming down from those two stairwells." She replied.

"Yeah, I see it. Look over there," Kellan said, pointing, "a stairwell going down as well."

"Damn...this would be one that goes subterranean. No telling how many levels there might be. We should split up; I'll take the upstairs, you the down."

Kellan grabbed her arm, "Are you completely insane?" he hissed, "that is the plot to every bad ending of every bad war movie. We are not splitting up. We'll both go upstairs first."

Meghan just nodded as the two moved quietly to the leftmost stairs and started up, trying to navigate the worn and broken stone stairs. They were about halfway up when Kellan suddenly stopped and turned to Meghan, "Get ready, they've found us. Run with me!"

He started bolting up the stairs two at a time, Meghan keeping pace. Since stealth was clearly no longer an issue she yelled after him, "How did they find us?"

Kellan called back over his shoulder, "Smell. I should have thought about that; these assholes have a heightened sense of smell."

They had just crested the top of the landing with Meghan only two steps behind Kellan when she saw the first werewolf resolve from the darkness in mid-leap. It didn't really look like any werewolf she had ever seen in movies or read about. The creature stood mostly erect and, while certainly substantially muscled, still wore whatever clothing it had been wearing prior to its transformation. It's arms clearly looked longer than that of a normal person and it's fingers ended in what appeared to be long, sharp talons—black as onyx. Its face, from nose to forehead, seemed mostly normal but its mouth was inhumanly large with sharp, extremely lupine teeth showing prominently and it howled at her, clearly enraged. Most disconcerting were its eyes, which while wild with anger, were also clearly human, showing no signs of the creature's bestial nature. She instinctively reached for her katana knowing there would not be the time or the room to use her Glock. Meghan felt a powerful whoosh of wind. The werewolf before her was pushed out to the side and into the air above the main chamber, scrambling for purchase it could not find. Seconds later the entire chamber was illuminated as a white hot ball of fire engulfed the creature as it fell to the floor below.

Meghan didn't take time to appreciate her reprieve. She launched herself over the last few steps and fell in next to Kellan who stood with a glowing blue sword in one hand while dozens of frozen projectiles rotated above the other.

"I found a good place to put the heat," he said with a grin.

Meghan laughed despite herself and shook her head, filling both hands with the comforting heft of her Glock 41s.

They waited, tensing at every sound, when a voice called from the darkness. Kellan responded in a language that, to Meghan's ear, sounded vaguely like Farsi.

"So, they say they are going to kill us and eat our hearts. I told them to fuck off."

"You speak Farsi now?"

"Dari actually. At least I assume it's Dari, that's the predominant language in this region, but, yeah, I guess I do." More words came out from the darkness and Megan touched two fingers to Kellan's bare wrist, causing the words to suddenly resolve into a thickly accented English "…and let you watch while we do that to her."

Meghan concentrated, keeping her finger in contact with Kellan's wrist; "You killed my Marines, you bastards! Now I'm going to butcher every last one of you."

She heard a staccato of confusing chatter, but was able to make out two words clearly. "English. Americans."

"I guess they couldn't understand me?" Meghan asked.

"No, you called out in English. I don't think you can appropriate my language ability actively, just passively, which, I suppose makes sense since were it otherwise you could probably—"

"Forget it. Focus Kellan—lecture later."

A phalanx of at least six werewolves converged on them. Meghan let go of Kellan's wrist and unholstered her second Glock. One of the creatures said something, its language guttural. "They are making fun of your guns, Meg; they probably assume—"

"Assume this, fuckers!" She squeezed off five perfectly spaced rounds, each followed by the thud of a werewolf falling dead to the ground. The last one skittered to the side and leaped back into the darkness with a shriek. "What did it say?"

Kellan looked down at Meghan. "Nothing much—just one word," he grinned, "Silver! So I'm thinking they have more respect for your guns about now."

"Not that it's going to do them any good," she growled, advancing across the landing.

Kellan threw his swirling ice projectiles ahead of her advance, but only heard them chatter harmlessly against a distant stone wall. Grumbling, he pointed his small sword into the darkness and watched it glow more brightly cutting into the gloom.

The two walked slowly, but found no more immediate resistance, finally coming to the end of the landing and confronting a huddled ball whimpering softly in the corner. It was smaller than all the previous werewolves had been, maybe one third the size.

"Oh Jesus, Kel, it's a kid."

The small girl continued to face her body to the wall but turned to look at Meghan, her dark brown eyes catching the light given off from Kellan's sword.

"It's ok," Meghan began, lowering her pistols, "We're not here to hurt you. We just want those that are keeping you here. Where did they go?"

As if in answer, the young girl turned toward them. Kellan saw she was holding something. He saw the red blinking light and trigger too late—

Kellan's entire body thrummed as he drew deeply on the river of power within him, trying to simultaneously bend time and place a shield around Meghan and himself.

"We're too close," he thought to himself, feeling a rise of panic as he saw the blast slowly billow out, engulfing the small child while simultaneously immolating her, countless steel bearings shredding her tiny body. He saw the shield he created project outward from himself as a shimmering, faintly blue, haze creeping lazily towards Meghan. He lunged for her, unaffected by the temporal shift he had created and grabbed her about the waist just as the concussion blast and first round of projectiles slammed into them both, forcing them over the edge of the platform and into the darkness below.

With both arms around Meghan, the temporal shift vanished and Kellan desperately shifted his weight so they fell with his back toward the floor, shielding her from the inevitable impact. He saw them pass through the first floor, apparently having fallen through the entrance to the subterranean level, giving Kellan additional precious seconds to begin altering the gravity acting on them both before they came to a painful and shuddering stop some thirty feet below the surface.

White light flashed through Kellan's mind at the sudden impact and he felt his consciousness begin to ebb. He reached for the emerald torrent within him only to notice it as now more of a substantial, but slower moving river. Still, he drew from it and the energy served like a splash of ice cold water bringing his thoughts back into focus.

He lifted Meghan gently from on top of him and laid her on the ground next to him, fingers immediately questing for her neck.

There was blood everywhere. Kellan had no idea how much of it was his, hers, or those they had fought above. With relief, he found the slow thrum of a living pulse in her neck, but it seemed far too weak to be anything close to normal. Meghan's left shoulder, the one furthest from where the shield emanated, was a ruin of bone and blood. Kellan could see that several of the steel bearings had gone clean through, while some were stopped by her ballistic armor, and others were still embedded in flesh.

Her eyes fluttered open and tried to focus on him, "Kel? Kel, we should be dead. That IED was massive. She tried to move her head and take in their surroundings, wincing in pain. Where...?"

"Shhh," Kellan said, placing both hands to her cheeks and gently straightening her neck. "Please don't move. I have no idea what, or how badly, you are hurt. I also don't think we have much time before we're found down here so let me try to get you stable. You're bleeding pretty badly from that shoulder. I think your armor and my shield stopped the worst of it."

Meghan looked back at Kellan, taking in the blood that ran freely down his face and at the dozens of deep indentations that marked his chest. "Seems your body armor is better than mine," she said smiling slightly, as foamy red spittle dribbled down her chin. "Kel, I think I'm in trouble."

"No you aren't. I'm going to take care of you; just tell me how best to stop the bleeding in your arm." Meghan had begun to pale significantly. Kellan knew she would die if he could not get the blood loss under control, and quickly.

"My left shoulder...there's a tissue sealing compound. Looks like a small aerosol spray bottle—white."

Kellan quickly found it and leaned over her, spraying the entire contents into her shoulder wound. The foam expanded and seemed to seep into all the bleeding crevices as she sighed in relief from the anesthetic in the foam.

Her eyes suddenly widened in fear and she tried to speak, but Kellan was already moving. He flattened himself against Meghan and felt the air stir against his neck as something *whooshed* inches from where his head and neck had been moments before.

Looking quickly over his shoulder, Kellan saw a massive, hair covered arm continue its leftward arc, spinning the beast enough in that direction to leave it off balance. Kellan rolled right and kicked out with his feet—slamming the lycanthrope into the wall of the tunnel where they had fallen.

It bounced backward slightly and turned to face Kellan and Meghan, shaking its head to clear the effects of Kellan's kick. It charged, leaping toward Kellan as he raised both hands, palms touching, forming an outward facing bowl. A concussive force of unseen air struck the werewolf in midleap throwing him backward twenty feet into the tunnel even as Kellan scrambled to his feet, trying to ignore the many points of pain that registered throughout his body.

"Ok. It's on now, bitch," yelled Kellan as he grabbed a handful of magnesium flares that had spilled out from his pack. He dragged them all against the rough walls of the tunnel. Immediately the gloom was beaten back by the bright magenta flames from half a dozen flares. Kellan dropped two by Meghan and tossed the other four a short distance ahead.

In the reddish light, he saw at least two or three additional lycanthropes had joined the one that had been thrown back with the blast of air he had unleashed moments before.

Apparently that display had made them wary— not understanding who, or what, they were dealing with. Then one of them spoke.

"You have trespassed into our home and killed many of us, but I give you this one chance to take your wounded and leave."

"F-Fuck You! You hairy murderous bastards! You killed my Marines and—" Meghan spasmed, coughing hard, as more red foam spilled on her lips.

Not good Numerous medical texts filed past Kellan's consciousness. He addressed the row of werewolves before him. "I don't think we're going to find a peaceful way out of this, Rover," he called out as he looked inward, calling to his power and noticing it had diminished again. It was now fully half of what it had been at its height.

"Well, that's not good either," he said softly to himself, "and it clearly didn't mention any of this in the 'become a Sentinel' brochure."

"Wizard or no—you will die then," growled the werewolf as they all tensed to attack, but were suddenly engulfed in a blindingly white plasma fire that erupted from the floor. All all four magnesium flares winked out. Kellan could see the skeletal forms of the six werewolves for a frozen moment before they collapsed to dust.

"Wizard?" said Kellan quizzically, picking up and lighting his last flare and walking down the tunnel toward a faint light he could barely discern. "So, there are wizards too? If Merlin and Gandalf are real, I'm going to completely shit my pants. Stop talking to yourself. That's crazy—not intimidating."

Kellan squared his shoulders, wincing with the pain that it brought. He glanced towards his right hand as the glowing blue sword appeared, allowing him to grip it tightly. He then reached inward to check his reserves and found only a small flowing stream of power remained. What would happen when that stream ran dry? *Nothing good.* He passed into a dimly lit room that was roughly hewn from the surrounding stone. Aside from the rustic nature of the walls, the room was fully appointed with fine materials. Intricate Persian rugs lay across the floor while rich, embroidered pillows were scattered throughout. Golden braziers were placed strategically to both provide light and take the chill and damp from the subterranean air.

"Well, down to just the two of us it seems."

Kellan's eyes focused on the middle aged man seated amidst several pillows at the far end of the room. He was surrounded by several plates on which sat what appeared to be internal organs. They glistened wet with blood. The man appeared to be in his late forties, with dark black hair cut short and a meticulously trimmed, close cropped beard. He spoke with a polished British accent and motioned to Kellan. "Will you sit?"

Kellan frowned. "No."

The man sighed with feigned disappointment. "Pity. Everyone seems to be in such a rush to die these days," he said, rising.

Kellan felt his heart rate increase as his hand flexed against the sword's hilt. "I am Sargon," the man said, affecting a slight bow, "and you are?"

"Amused at the irony of your name," replied Kellan smoothly.

"Impressive. Did you study Persian history?"

"Nope, I just read a lot. 'Sargon—sun prince' also known as 'douchebag werewolf'."

Sargon's smile faded and his face grew hard. Kellan tried to appear casual as he circled closer. "You really fucked up, Sarg. Can I call you Sarg? Yeah, you killed some folks who were really close to a friend of mine and, in the process, nearly drove her nuts. So, I'm here to give her some—"

"Revenge," interrupted Sargon.

"Closure," continued Kellan with a smile.

"You have no idea with whom you are dealing."

"Likewise."

Sargon sneered. "Oh, I think I know well enough. You think I have not run across those like you before? Those who dabble in the mystical and think themselves powerful wizards."

There's that wizard reference again. I really need to dig into that—assuming I get out of here alive. Kellan broke his internal monologue with a tight shake of his head, "Well, I think you may find me a bit diff.."

Pain shot through Kellan as a massive crushing blow struck from behind sending him sprawling to the floor. He reached around to his back, feeling hot blood where large claws had raked through the circlets of his armor. He felt the metal knit itself back together just in time to receive another rending blow. Lights blossomed in his head as Kellan struggled to retain consciousness even as he knew another strike would soon be on its way. Rolling to the side, he saw the coal black fur of his attacker as it slammed two clawed fists into the stone were Kellan's head had been moments before.

Kellan felt the heat in his eyes as he drew on his waning power, willing strength into his battered muscles and focusing his mind while pulling his knees to his chest. The werewolf leaped towards him, jaw aimed at Kellan's neck. It met the young Sentinel's feet instead, which he heaved upward with a primal yell. Kellan felt bones crack as his kick reversed the lycanthrope's momentum and hurtled it in a blur toward the far wall. He was rewarded with another series of cracks as the creature slid down, twitching.

Without thinking, Kellan spun around, gaining his feet in time to see Sargon running toward him, face contorted with rage. He seemed to shimmer and was replaced with the now familiar werewolf form while not losing even a step during the transition. Kellan crouched low, planting both feet and brandishing his sword protectively crosswise from chest to shoulder, noticing absently that the sword had more than doubled in length from it's previous short blade form.

Sargon flew into Kellan, driving him back even as the glowing sword deflected one clawed blow, biting deeply in bone and sprouting dark gouts of blood. Howling, Sargon thrust his arm upward, sword embedded in bone, wrenching it from Kellan's grip where it vanished to mist while the werewolf connected hard with his other hand, sending Kellan several feet in the air. He landed painfully toward the back of the room and struggled back to his feet, dazed.

The young Sentinel again reached for his power and drained all that remained, feeling it course through him, waiting to be given form.

Sargon paused, staring deeply into Kellan's blazing green eyes. "Not wizard—Sentinel," he growled, voice slurred by his more lupine features. "I've heard of you, seen the the wreckage you've made of my kind. You look younger than I've heard described. I will not be added to your atrocities; I will end you, Micah Ben Judah."

"Yeah, good luck with that, fuzzball," said Kellan as he channeled the heat from the burning braziers into a gleaming ball which he hurled at the unprepared lycanthrope.

Sargon howled as he became engulfed in flames even as Kellan fell to one knee, exhausted with this final effort. When he again looked up, Kellan felt his stomach lurch. Sargon continued to approach, nearly all the hair burned away and skin blistered. Kellan reached inward but found nothing but a dry riverbed where once his power flowed. He felt Sargon's clawed hands around his neck, lifting him from the ground and slamming him against the back wall.

"I'm not that easy to kill," Sargon growled, "Now I'm going to end you. Then I'm going to turn that bitch of yours."

Kellan could feel darkness starting to encroach on his field of vision as Sargon continued to squeeze his throat, claws biting deep and blood flowing between them, but he managed a strangled laugh and wheezed, "Now, you've done it."

"I'm nobody's bitch, asshole! You killed my Marines and I'm sending you on an express trip to hell, fucker!"

Kellan watched as Sargon's eyes widened in surprise a moment before two gleaming katana blades sliced through his neck from behind. Blood spurted and the clawed hand convulsed, releasing Kellan who collapsed to the ground even as Sargon's corpse shimmered back into human form.

Meghan fell to her knees, blood foam flowing from her mouth, and Kellan dimly heard the clatter as her katanas hit the stone floor.

She fell over on her side, eyes lolling back in her head even as Kellan reached out for her.

"Meghan...Meghan stay with me. You're gonna be ok."

"No, I'm not," she coughed, "I'm going to see my boys. They are going to take good care of me."

"No, no, no, your boys are going to be pissed at me and I don't need that kind of bad karma. You stay right here missy."

"Raphael!!" Kellan screamed, eyes hot with tears as he cradled Meghan in his lap.

Nothing happened. "Raphael, you motherfucker, I am not Micah, get here. Now!"

"I am here Sentinel. How may I serve?"

"Do something!"

"I cannot."

"What the fuck do you mean? Let me rephrase. Do! Something!"

"She is dying and I cannot interfere. It was her choice to come to this place at this time. It was your choice to bring her here. Your combined choices created this moment. I cannot interfere with your freewill."

Kellan had stopped listening and pressed his fingers to her neck feeling the faintest thrum of a thready pulse even as he recalled Micah's words: you can never create even the smallest spark of life nor reignite life's flame if it is ever extinguished. Kellan closed his eyes, concentrating, and found himself standing in the riverbed where the emerald river of his power once flowed. He felt the liquid power begin to trickle past his feet with ever increasing rapidity and within moments it was rushing past him ankle deep.

"Nurisha!!"

"I am here."

Kellan whirled about as tears continued to stream down his face. "Nurisha, help me. Meghan is dying. What can I do? I have to be able to do something."

She smiled and walked up to Kellan as the river of power arced around her. He felt her arms around him, embracing him, holding him tight. "No, Nurisha, there is no time. She's dying. She's dying. Tell me what I can do"

"Hush, young Sentinel. There is no time here and there is yet time to help her, but I warn you such sacrifice comes at a cost you may not want to pay."

"I'll pay it, whatever it is. Tell me."

Nurisha released Kellan and stepped back; he stared at her glowing form, more fearful than he had been in the Atlanta alley that seemed like so long ago.

"Walk with me," she said, climbing the bank and turning to offer her hand to Kellan, who accepted it and joined her beside the now raging torrent of power.

"Your power," she began, "the power of which I am an incarnation, is founded on agape. Do you understand?"

Kellan nodded, "I suppose. Agape...the sacrificial form of love."

She nodded. "Yes, it was that form of love that founded all of creation. It was that form of love that allowed for freewill and that form of love which prevented Lucifer's destruction after His rebellion." Nurisha paused and turned again to Kellan, "You can heal your friend, my Sentinel, but only by taking her wounds upon yourself. That is the essence of empathy; that is the foundation of Agape."

"Great, I'll do it. Send me back."

She laughed and it sounded like silver on crystal. "Kellan, you are so impulsive and so ignorant—a dangerous combination to be sure. I cannot send you back, just like I did not draw you here. You are master of this place, your power and," she paused again, "me."

"Will yourself back to the world, and it will be so. Channel your power to heal your friend and it will be so. I only warn you that doing so can only happen by empathically linking yourself to her."

"Will she live?"

"Undoubtedly, but you, my impulsive Sentinel, may not and where will that leave the world?"

Kellan opened his eyes and felt them blazing with power as he stared down at Meghan's pale form. He began to channel the power through her and back into himself.

"Kellan? What are you doing?" Raphael asked, becoming alarmed.

Blood began to drip from Kellan's nose and he coughed, red spittle forming on his lips, but still he channeled the power through Meghan.

"Stop!" yelled Raphael. He tried to grab Kellan by the shoulder. The Angel flew backward as if shocked by some immensely powerful force.

"This is my choice. My freewill, Raphael. You may not—you cannot interfere," coughed Kellan as he felt several of his ribs crack and perforate his lungs. His vision swam and the pain made it hard to think, but through the haze he saw Meghan's eyes flutter open.

"Kel? Kel, what are you doing?"

Kellan smiled through the pain. "S—Something exceptionally stupid, I'm sure," then he let the darkness take him.

"Am I dead?"

"No, you survived, my Sentinel, but it was a near thing"

"Nurisha? Is that you?"

Laughter, again like silver on crystal. "Who else would it be?"

"I don't know, but I can't see you."

"That is because you are unconscious. Your body is channeling me to heal itself. You will wake up soon."

"I feel pretty good for being almost dead."

"All part of being unconscious I suspect, but you are waking now, so I suspect we will find out."

"Holy Shit! That hurts…take it out…take it out!"

"Stop moving, you idiot, and I'll take it out," yelled Meghan as she struggled with the small tube protruding from Kellan's side. Finally she was able to get enough of a grip to pull it free, and watched in wonder as the wound started to seal up behind it.

"Oh, dear God that's better. Now I only feel like I *want* to die, instead of feeling like I'm actually dying."

"You did die—twice. Be glad you weren't alive to feel the adrenaline needle I stuck in your heart. Then, you had a tension pneumothorax and I had to use a trach-tube to reinflate your lung. That's what I just pulled out— not that you'd know given your Wolverine-like healing abilities"

Kellan relaxed at the sound of his friend's voice, enjoying the cool stone beneath him. "Wolverine," he began, "wouldn't have gotten his ass kicked in the first place."

Meghan laughed, "True, but you did pretty good for a non X-man." She paused and Kellan opened one eye to look at her.

"What?"

"Well, there's this giant robed guy here with eyes that sparkle like yours and he looks really pissed."

Kellan sighed, "Don't worry about him. That's Raphael and he's a friend. A mostly useless friend," he added, voice rising, "but a friend nonetheless."

"That's good cause he stalking over this way."

"Kellan Thorne, that was the most irresponsible thing I have seen done in millennia. Had you died in this place, at this time, your power would have died with you and thus tipped the scales in favor of the adversary."

"Then you should have helped me when I asked, shouldn't you have?"

"What?" the Angel yelled, and Kellan could actually feel heat wafting off him, "You dare blame me for this—this folly?"

"Sure, you picked me for this gig. You said I…," Kellan changed his tone making it deeper and resonate, "would bring light to dark places that Angels feared to tread." Then, voice returning to normal, he continued, "Well, Raphael, this is what that looks like. I am not going to leave friends to die when there's something I can do about it. So deal!"

Meghan had been taking in the whole exchange and finally made the connection, then leaned forward and kissed Kellan on the forehead. "He's right Kel, you were being stupid. But thanks."

"Don't get all mushy on me, Meghan. You can always count on me."

Her lips quirked up in a sarcastic grin. "To be stupid?"

"Exactly!"

Raphael stood watching the two, shaking his head. "Micah would never have been so reckless," he said in a clearly disapproving tone.

"No, Raphael, no he wouldn't have. But as I keep telling everyone, I am not he."

Chapter 8

GLENN FERRY

K ellan opened his eyes, grudgingly acknowledging the light streaming in from his bedroom window. "Hey Siri, what time is it?"

The pleasant and comfortingly familiar female voice responded, "The time is 10:42 am."

Kellan groaned as he swung his legs over the side of the bed and sat up, running one hand through his hair. He headed to the bathroom and stumbled slightly as the last vestiges of sleep left him.

"Hello," he said to his reflection as he stared into to bathroom mirror. "You, sir, look like warmed over shit." Kellan continued giving himself his winningest smile.

"Well, thank *you*, sir, but I think I look pretty good for having been mauled, strangled, and dead twice only twelve or so hours ago. Kindly piss off."

Kellan took a couple steps back so he could see from head to waist in the large mirror and began to give himself the once over. He whistled slightly as he poked and prodded, then turned his back to the mirror, looking over his shoulder to repeat the process. All the bruises, cuts, and puncture wounds that had covered him nearly head-to-toe were gone. Even the spot where Meghan had inserted the improvised trach tube to reinflate his lung was healed, leaving only a pale scar as a reminder.

"That certainly is a bonus," he said as he reached into the shower and turned on the water. While he waited for it to warm, his phone came to life playing the familiar "Amy Pond" theme from Doctor Who as it sat on the nightstand next to his kingsized bed. He walked over and stared at the name and face illuminating the phone while the music continued—Juliet Herrick.

"Shit. She's gonna kill me," He slid his finger along the phone anyway and tapped the speaker icon.

"Kellan? Kellan are you there?"

"Hey Juliet." He heard her give a relieved sigh.

"Kellan, you're alive."

"Yeah—"he began, but she interrupted him.

"Good, cause I'm going to kill you!"

He cringed. "Look, Juliet, I'm sorry. It was a," he paused, "really weird night and I'll fill you in when I get to the shop."

"And when exactly will that be?"

"Oh, come on, don't do that."

"Do what?" came the innocent reply.

"That—that mother voice. I'm the boss, remember? I'll be there when I'm good and ready to be there."

"You better be here in an hour, mister, and bring lunch"

Kellan sighed, defeated, "Ok. I'll be there in an hour with lunch," then smiled to himself as he continued, "Now let me get going, Juliet. The shower is running and I'm standing here stark naked."

"Ew! Gross Kel. Gross. Gross. Now I have that in my head," and the phone when blank.

"Heh." Kellan said to the air, feeling somewhat victorious as he headed back to the shower now billowing with steam.

Some minutes later, Kellan had toweled off and pulled on his favorite uniform: well broken-in jeans and graphic t-shirt. Today's depicted a man wearing a long coat, broad brimmed hat, and carrying a staff that blazed with energy. Beneath the figure the shirt was emblazoned with "Don't mess with a Wizard when he's wizarding." It seemed appropriate. "God, I love a hot shower," Kellan mused as his bare feet slapped against the aged wood of the floor. He crossed to the living room and slid down in the chapped leather of his sofa to pull on his socks. The smell of wood and leather filled his nose. He paused to look around, reveling in the simplicity and familiarity of his small home.

All about him were old things made with hands rather than machines—except for the abundant technical gadgetry of televisions and Apple products. That aside, Kellan's home consisted mostly of full grain leather and reclaimed wood. He rested one foot on the old wooden chest that served as his coffee table. It was bound with iron bands, dark brown with the patina of age. He pulled on each shoe in turn, kicking against the heavy chest to drive them home, then hopped up and headed to the kitchen.

Kellan's love for natural materials was evident there too. Old, hand finished walnut cabinetry stretched across the small kitchen and down to rich forest green granite that always reminded him of a creek running hither and yon. He reached up and pulled down a mug and a coffee pod, then slipped it into the little machine and pulled down the lever.

Affecting his best British accent, Kellan said, "Tea. Earl Grey. Hot," and pressed the glowing brew button. The machine hissed and sputtered as Kellan waited impatiently for it to finish dispensing its nectar of the gods. He took the mug, now warm in his hands, inhaled deeply, and smiled as he brought it to his lips.

"That isn't tea," came a loud voice from behind him.

"Wha!" yelled Kellan, whirling about and sloshing hot coffee all over his neck and chest.

"That is coffee, not tea. You asked the machine to make tea. It must be defective."

"What the fuck, Raphael!"

The Angel winced. "Your language—"

Kellan held up a hand palm out. "Stop—just stop or I'm going to unleash a torrent of profanity that will rip a hole in space-time, and suck you away into its profanity vortex."

Raphael seemed puzzled as Kellan turned back to the sink, setting down his mug, and reaching for a sponge. "There is no such thing as a...profanity vortex."

Kellan had put down the sponge in frustration and stripped off his shirt. "Well, there should be!" he yelled over his shoulder as he went to find a clean one.

A minute later he returned, drank the quarter cup of coffee that had remained after the spill, and pushed past Raphael, bumping him out of the way as Kellan made for the door.

"I'm going to be late—again. And she's going to give me shit—again. And it's your fault—again. Why don't you make yourself useful, fly away, and get us lunch."

Kellan slammed the door as the Angel continued to stare at him from within the house. He locked the front door, turned, and jogged down the four steps of the stoop to find Raphael staring at him from the walkway that led to Kellan's small house.

"Nice trick," he said walking past the Angel and turning right onto the sidewalk.

It was warm, but not unpleasantly so and there were many people walking on both sides of Canton street. Canton street was in the old historic district of Roswell where Kellan lived. His shop was one of the few remaining that had not been renovated into a restaurant of some kind.

"Why are you even here right now?" Kellan asked while noticing the strange looks sent his way by those he passed. He stopped, staring at the Angel.

"Don't take this the wrong way, but people are staring at you because, well, because you look weird. I'll grant you that you're pretty darn handsome, but you are also freakishly tall and wearing long robes with shiny embroidery scattered over it. That may be all vogue in the celestial realm, maybe even in midtown, but here in Roswell...you just look stupid."

"They are not staring at me, Kellan Thorne? They are looking at you."

Kellan laughed. "Ha! Denial doesn't become you, Raphael. Look at me. I look normal. You don't."

The Angel cocked his head slightly, "No, you misunderstand me. They are not staring at me because they cannot stare at me. I am not visible to them."

Kellan paused. "Say what?"

Raphael smiled in what was almost a mischievous way. "Which word was difficult for you to comprehend, my young Sentinel?"

Kellan felt his stomach clench as he looked around. "So, to be clear, it looks like I am talking to—"

"Empty air, yes." Replied Raphael with a supremely satisfied look on his face.

Kellan turned stiffly and resumed his walk, talking softly out of the side of his mouth. "You know, I thought Michael was a dick, but now I'm starting to think it is a prerequisite for the whole Angel job."

Kellan turned left and stepped into the crosswalk and cars stopped as he jogged across the street, walking into the small shop with a "Roswell Provisioners" sign hanging over its door. He went up to the deli counter and greeted the clerk. "Hey Ben…how's it going?"

"Good, Kel. What can I get ya?

"Patton's sausage po-boy, loaded, and a turkey and ham panini with lettuce, tomato, mayo, and mustard.

Ben raised an eyebrow and smiled, turning away to make the sandwiches.

"What?" asked Kellan, but Ben just waved his hand, dismissing the question as he continued to work.

"We need to discuss what you did last night," said Raphael.

"Not talking to you in public," Kellan mumbled as he pulled a Mexican Coke out of the cooler and selected two bags of Zapps potato chips.

"Here you go," called Ben smiling, "I added extra pickles since you forgot to mention that. Hope it helps you get out of the dog house."

Kellan accepted the bag and tapped his phone to the register where it chimed pleasantly. "Hey, I am not in the dog house. I'm the boss, Ben. The boss."

The young man laughed, "Sure you are, Kel."

Kellan glared, first at Ben and then Raphael, but said nothing more as he stalked from the store, went two more doors down to the right, and swung open the one to his shop.

The bell jingled as he, again, closed a door in Raphael's face. Juliet looked up from her book, then glanced meaningfully at one of the many clocks. 12:32.

Kellan spread open his hands. "It wasn't my fault. It was his." he said, gesturing to Raphael who had materialized just to Kellan right in front of the counter.

Juliet, directed her gaze at the Angel. "That true, Raphael?"

"Wait, what? So she gets to see you all the time?"

"Of course. She already knows about me. Why shouldn't she be able to see?"

Kellan sighed. "Whatever. Here's your lunch."

Juliet sifted through her bag and brightened. "Mexican Coke *and* extra pickles? Ok Kel, you are forgiven."

Kellan had seated himself on a stool by the counter and was about to take a bite of his po-boy. "Forgiven, Juliet? I think you are forgetting again. I am—"

"The boss. Yes, I know, and it was very sweet of you to get me my favorite lunch as if you had nothing at all to apologize for."

Kellan nodded and took a bite.

"Raphael," Juliet began, "for reference, that was sarcasm."

The Angel nodded gravely. "I will make a note of it. Thank you, Juliet."

Kellan put the remaining half of his po-boy back in its bag and headed toward the rear of the shop. "I'm gonna eat in my office; I need to check in on Meghan and you two jerks can enjoy each other's company."

Moments later, they heard the door slam and Juliet turned to the Angel suspiciously. "Meghan Daugherty, can catch bullets with her teeth. If she needs checking up on, then something went down that I need to know about. Spill it."

"Kellan?" Juliet asked, tapping softly on the door.

"What? I'm busy."

She opened the door and peered inside to find him leaning, back swiping something on his iPad. He glanced at her. "What part of, 'I'm busy,' is confusing?"

"I just wanted to say I'm sorry."

Kellan brightened. "In that case, have a seat. Please, go on."

Juliet walked around the desk and gave Kellan an awkward hug, then punched him hard on the shoulder.

"Ow!" he yelled reflexively, then noticed Raphael's head had poked in through the partly opened door.

"The hug was because you are a freaking super hero. The punch is because you nearly died like an idiot."

"In actuality, he did die—twice," offered Raphael.

Kellan's eyes narrowed and Juliet turned to the Angel. "Not helping." Raphael nodded and moved silently to a corner of the office.

"How's Meghan?"

Kellan shook his head. "She's Meghan—all pissed off that she's too sore to do her cross-fit today, but other than that she seems no worse for wear."

"No worse for were-wolves," said Juliet, snapping her fingers and pointing at Kellan.

He snickered despite himself. "Very clever, Miss Herrick."

Her smile faded. "So, I closed the shop."

"Huh? Why?"

"Cause we have work to do."

Kellan immediately became suspicious again, looking first at Raphael and then to Juliet. "Work? What kind of work? What have you two been up to out there?"

Juliet held up a hand. "Nothing sinister. Raphael was just filling me in on your exploits and that you needed to...go meet someone."

"Why did you say it like that? You paused. Who do I need to meet?"

"A girl who apparently, needs your help because there are monsters after her."

Kellan sighed. "Of course there are. Fine. Where is she?"

"Scotland, a place called Glenn Ferry."

Kellan paused as information flashed through his mind. "Glenn Ferry Scotland—annexed in 1282 by Alexander III and became part of Berwick. Glen Ferry doesn't exist."

"Now..." added Juliet softly.

"Aw shit, really?" said Kellan, looking toward Raphael who nodded solemnly. "This isn't cool. I fought werewolves all night. Can't we just deal with this some other time, like maybe next week? I mean if I'm going back in time, it doesn't matter when I leave, right?"

"Unfortunately," began Raphael, "It does matter because the girl is rapidly approaching a fixed point in time that, once reached, cannot be altered."

"Seriously," replied Kellan, "That's mighty convenient, Doctor Who. A fixed point in time—really?"

Raphael continued, clearly confused, "It is not convenient at all. If she is killed, or even materially diverted, it will absolutely create a fixed point that no one or no thing can alter. These fixed points are a foundational aspect of creation."

Juliet placed a hand on Raphael's arm. "He was being sarcastic."

Kellan nodded.

"Oh," replied the Angel, "It is difficult to tell with him." It was Juliet's turn to nod in solidarity.

"Fine," said Kellan, setting down his iPad and standing. "Open up a portal, Raphael, and I'll jump through and save the damsel."

"I cannot."

"What? Why? Micah told me you did it for him."

"He was incapable to create such a portal and, more importantly, when I intervened it was directly related to your ascension to the position you now hold. For both those reasons, I cannot interfere with your freewill. You are free to learn how to make a time portal or to fail. Assuming you do learn how, you are then free to go back to Glenn Ferry or not. Assuming you go back, you are then free to help or—"

"Ok, ok. I get it," said Kellan, shaking his head as he shouldered past Raphael and Juliet and walked back to the reading nooks. He stared at the chairs a moment thinking back on the conversations between them all, then turned back as they joined him in the room. "So, Mr. Nonintervention, are you able to help me understand how to do this thing or are you prevented from that as well?"

Raphael smiled, "No. I am absolutely able to help, but I suggest you take a seat because it can be a bit complicated."

Kellan plopped down heavily into the overstuffed chair nearest him. "Hit me."

⌒〜|\〜⌒

The portal shimmered into being and the three of them stared through its oval opening. Waves of heat buffeted them as various acrid scents assaulted their noses. The ground, such as it was, lay cracked with glowing rivers of molten lava running throughout. In the distance volcanic plumes of smoke and ash billowed into the grey sky.

Raphael walked through the portal and stood, ankle deep in a pool of lava, slowly turned around, and walked back through to rejoin Kellan and Juliet.

"About two or three," Raphael said.

"That's not too bad Kellan," said Juliet brightly, "two or three million years ago; it's a start."

Kellan sighed. "You clearly need a geology refresher. He meant two or three *billion* years ago. Two or three *million* years ago—Jurassic World."

Juliet looked to Raphael, who nodded grimly as the portal winked out.

"Let me try explaining it again," began the Angel.

"No, Raphael, I don't need you to explain it again," replied Kellan, clearly frustrated. "I remember exactly what you said—exactly. I also understand the concept of tachyon particles and time dilation. It's mashing all that understanding together and then somehow envisioning the relativistic position of those particles as if they were seen from some distant location in space, and then translating the imagery seen from those particles in that relativistic place into the physical manifestation of a portal. It's *that* part which," he paused for a breath, "has me a bit. Fucking. Stumped."

"The portal? Have you tried turning it off and on again?" offered Juliet with a smile.

"Not helping!"

"Sorry."

Kellan waved a hand dismissively. "It's ok. Not your fault." He turned back to Raphael. "And how come my little river of power keeps running dry? It did that when I was fighting werewolves last night and it's happening even faster when making these time portals."

Raphael looked surprised at the question. "Your power is finite. You used it faster than it could replenish itself last night and thus it ran out. What you are doing now is much more difficult than that, so it causes your power to be expended that much more quickly."

"Well, that's not good," replied Kellan. "When I made that last portal, I felt the power flood out of me like someone had opened a massive spillway. I would have been bone dry if I held it open for more than a minute."

"Then you should endeavor to hold open such a portal for less than a minute."

"Thanks Rainman—very helpful. How about you help me figure out how to make that river of power deeper and wider?"

Raphael looked thoughtful for a moment and then said, "Your power will grow with use if you strain beyond what feels comfortable, like a muscle grows. However, be cautious, because too much power carries risks even as does too little."

"Well, I think I'd rather have the too much problem," Kellan said absently, his eyes glowing and brow furrowed with concentration as another portal opened up on a green landscape. Raphael was about to step through when it snapped shut, causing him to turn to Kellan questioningly.

"It was just a distance portal; I'm trying something different. Now go."

Another portal opened and Raphael went through.

"One day."

"Come back."

Another portal.

"One month."

Another.

"One year."

Juliet clapped as Kellan continued to make quick portals that went incrementally further back in time until he had worked up to one that went back several thousand years.

"I think I've got it," he said smiling, "It's really not all that difficult once you get the hang of it."

"That is what I tried to tell you before," Raphael said with a satisfied look.

"Oh no, you don't get to look smug. You are a horrible teacher."

Raphael looked pained and Juliet smacked Kellan on the shoulder. "Hey!" he complained.

"Apologize. That was mean!"

"Fine. I'm sorry, but you really could have been more helpful rather than giving me a celestial history lesson about how creation was stitched together."

"Well?" asked the Angel.

"Well, what?"

"Glenn Ferry? Are you ready?"

"Oh, well let's see." Kellan took a deep breath and felt the heat in his eyes as he channeled the power, seeing it flow as that raging green river in his mind's eye. He held his right hand out as if to grasp an invisible doorknob and the portal rotated into existence. Through it could be seen a small village.

"Um, Kel, unless they had asphalt and cars in the thirteenth century, I think you've missed the mark."

He smiled, "I find your lack of faith disturbing," and then began to slowly turn his outstretched hand leftward. The world seen through the portal began to move backward: cars, birds, and people all moved unnaturally in what appeared to be the wrong direction. As he continued to turn his hand, the image blurred but still moved backwards. Buildings vanished and were rebuilt only to vanish again. Seasons came and went. Kellan continued to turn his hand as Juliet and Raphael stared with rapt attention.

"There!" Kellan said suddenly, causing Juliet to jump.

The Angel stepped through, smiling broadly. "Perfection. Simply perfection. I could not have done better. This point in time and place is mere moments after Micah and I left."

Feeling the power continue to rush out of him, Kellan stepped through the portal to join Raphael and then turned back to smile at Juliet who waggled her fingers at him and then yelled, "Hey, who is he there to save anyway?"

"Oh," replied Raphael, as if just remembering he had never shared that bit of information, "Her name is Shannon McLeod and she is very special."

"McLeod," said Kellan in surprise, "Really?"

Juliet laughed and shouted, "There can be only one!" The portal winked out.

Raphael continued to stare at the spot where the portal had vanished. "What did she mean, 'There can be only one'?"

"Geek stuff, you wouldn't understand and it's really not important. So, she's around here somewhere? This little redhead I'm supposed to help rescue from monsters."

"Yes, we left her by the stream—that way. Just take the path leading down from here. It will lead you there and then you will find her a bit upstream from where the path drops you off."

"I assume the Babelfish in my head is going to translate Gaelic here the same way it did Dari when Meghan and I were in Afghanistan?"

"Babelfish?" Raphael asked uncomprehendingly.

"You know, the ability I apparently have to hear everything in English no matter what language people are speaking."

Raphael nodded. "Ah, I understand now, but you do not. You are not translating anything, rather, you are simply hearing all language at its most basic phonetic level. You naturally decompose the foundational phonemes and then reinterpret them as something that makes sense to you."

Kellan looked at the Angel flatly. "And exactly how is that different from translation?"

Raphael opened his mouth to answer, but Kellan held up a finger.

"Let me clarify. How exactly is the difference between what you said and what I said relevant to me in any way?"

Raphael considered a moment: "I suppose it is not relevant at all."

"Exactly. And I have lots of new things to keep track of so, next time, let's skip to the end where you just say, 'Yeah the Babelfish will let you understand the little red haired lass when she speaks Gaelic.' Now, I assume you will be off to attend other angelic duties and leave me to my own freewill devices?"

"Yes, I will leave you now."

"Wonderful, and I don't suppose you care to tell me about these monsters?"

Raphael looked puzzled. "I do not know why you and Juliet kept referring to monsters. I never indicated that Shannon was beset by monsters— just that it was imperative you meet her now, in this time and place. The 'monsters', Kellan Thorne, are in your head. Farewell."

"What? Wait!" But the Angel had already vanished.

Kellan sighed and started to walk down the path, already hearing the faint gurgle of a nearby stream.

He had been walking along its bank for only a few minutes when he spied a young flame haired woman sitting cross legged on a large rock. She appeared to be meditating or something.

Kellan called out, but she didn't acknowledge him. Finally he walked directly in front of her, his feet almost touching the large boulder on which she sat. Her eyes were closed as he looked at her, thinking she appeared for all the world like Merida from Brave. Kellan reached out and was about to tap her freckled nose when her eyes flew open and he felt the cold tip of a knife touch his neck. He froze, hand still outstretched.

"I'd advise you to keep your hands to yourself."

"Hey, hey…easy now Shannon; I'm a friend."

Her eyes narrowed and she uncoiled her legs, swinging them around the rock, all the while never letting her blade leave Kellan's neck. "How do you know my name?"

"Raphael sent me."

She slid off the rock and stood directly in front of him.

"What's your name?"

"Kellan, Kellan Thorne," said Kellan.

The knife vanished as quickly as it had appeared. Shannon walked past him and did a quick circle looking around.

"Where are they? Are they here, too?"

"Who?"

"Raphael and Micah; they just left a short while ago."

"Raphael, no. He left because he's a di-um…dispassionate Angel and had other things to do I guess."

"And Micah?"

Kellan looked down, feeling he's eyes start to moisten.

"Oh no," said Shannon. "He's—"

"Yeah, Raphael took him away after…" Kellan couldn't bring himself to say more.

Shannon leaned back against her rock, "He said it was going to happen, but hearing it makes it real." She looked back at Kellan.

"So, you are the new one?"

"Guilty as charged, ma'am."

Shannon cocked her head. "You talk very strangely. Does everyone from your time talk that way."

"Just the cool people," Kellan said with a grin.

Shannon just shook her head. "People speak differently based on their temperatures?"

"Uh, no...never mind. Forget it. Too hard to explain."

She nodded, accepting this, and then said, "Touch me."

"What?"

Shannon held out her hand. "Take my hand. Touch me."

Kellan gave her a quizzical, look but reached out and, as he took her hand in his, they both had a quick intake of breath and a jolt of power arced through them. Kellan felt his eyes burn with the heat of his power and saw tiny flecks of green flash to life in Shannon's eyes. She tried to pull away, but Kellan's grip held her firm.

"Let me go; you are hurting me," she cried.

"I...I can't. I'm trying but I can't. It is burning me as well"

Then, as quickly as it began, the jolting power vanished—leaving her hand still in his.

Shannon looked down and pulled her hand back, drawing it to her mouth. "My God, your wrist."

Kellan looked down to find the perfectly formed image of a dove burned into his right wrist. He prodded it with his other hand but there was no discomfort, then looked back up at Shannon questioningly. She held out her own wrist. "See, I have one too. Always have"

"Wow that's really—"

"Weird," she finished. "You were going to say, 'weird'"

"Yes, I was. And yes, this is. You are like a little knot in my head now. I can feel you—sort of."

She nodded. "And I you. I suppose this was what Raphael meant when he said you needed to come to me, so this could happen."

"I suppose," replied Kellan feeling, the anger rise in him, "But I don't see why he had to be so cryptic about it all. He's always so damned cryptic."

She laughed and Kellan realized it was a good and hearty laugh, "What?"

"He's an Angel, silly. I don't think anything about him can be damned."

Kellan smiled, "Yeah, I guess you're right about that. Doesn't make him any less annoying."

Shannon reached out and touched the dove mark on Kellan's wrist, but nothing happened. "Seems that was a one time thing, thank God."

"No shit," said Kellan as he joined Shannon leaning against the rock and then realized what he'd said. "Um, sorry, I've kinda got a mouth on me."

She smiled broadly. "Well that, dear sir, is another thing we apparently have in common."

Kellan smiled back and she asked, "Are you thirsty?" She held out her small skin of water.

"Actually, yes, thanks," said Kellan, taking a long pull from the skin.

"So, Kellan Thorne, are we to be married then?"

He spat half a mouthful of water right in her face. "What? No. What made you say that?" Then, seeing her wiping the water from her cheek, added, "Oh shit, sorry I didn't mean to do that."

"Am I that horrible to look at that you would, literally, spit in my face?"

"No, no you are beautiful—really beautiful." Then Kellan caught himself adding, "But you are a child and I'm a grown man, and not that kind of grown man."

"I am no child and my cousin was a full year younger than me when she was married; she has a little one now too."

Kellan held his hands up. "Look, Shannon, where I come from, you are a kid and I'd be thrown in jail for—"

She smiled mischievously and walked up to Kellan placing a hand on his chest. "For...what? What were you thinking?"

He looked panicked. "I wasn't thinking anything. You said..."

She backed away and started laughing again.

Kellan glared at her. "You are joking with me? Really? Are all the women in my life just evil?"

"So, I'm a woman now am I?"

Kellan just looked back, saying nothing. He was at a complete loss for words.

Shannon waved a hand at him. "I just asked because I thought that might have been what Micah and Raphael had in mind, given that I'm sort of Micah's step daughter or something. You are handsome enough, but I'm not in the marrying mood anyway so I'm glad that wasn't the plan."

"Hang on…hang on. I'm still trying to catch up. You are Micah's what?"

"Come up to the cottage. I'll make us some tea and we can both share what we know." With that she started walking back up the gently sloping hill toward the forest, then looked back over her shoulder, causing her flame red curls to toss as she flashed him another smile. "Come on, don't dawdle down there."

"I'm coming," Kellan said and started to follow, feeling another wave of guilt run through him as he, again, realized just how drawn he was to this beautiful young woman.

⌒⁊⋀⋏⋏

Shannon set down her empty cup and sat quietly for several minutes. Kellan didn't want to intrude on her thoughts, so said nothing. Finally she glanced up at him and shook her head. "That is quite the tale and who would have thought God had a workroom?"

Kellan chuckled softly, "Well, your story seems just as interesting as mine and I can certainly see that your mother's strength has made its way to you."

She inclined her head. "Good of you to say. Thank you." Shannon stood and continued, "I really should be getting home. Will you be staying long?"

Kellan leaned back in his chair, causing the two front legs to lift up. "I don't rightly know, Shannon. I really don't. We've shared everything the other knows and that just leads us to where we are now. The power has been renewed in me and I've come back through time to meet you. Now what?"

She shrugged. "Now, I go home, take care of my father and brothers, and go to bed. I'll stop by tomorrow and maybe you will be here. If not, I'm sure our paths will cross again."

Kellan stood. "Wait, I thought this was your home?"

Shannon laughed. "This? Have you looked at this place?"

Kellan admitted to himself that he hadn't really made note of the small cottage—not like him at all. He used to notice and catalog everything, but now he seemed more focused on things of import rather than minutia. The young Sentinel wasn't sure he liked this subtle change in his world view and made a special effort to take stock.

The front legs of his chair returned to the hardwood floor with a thud and Kellan stood, eyes washing over the small home. It was roughly shaped like an "L" that had rotated counterclockwise twice, with the one door separating the short wall in two. The walls were of weathered stacked stone, held together with a mortar that appeared made of mud and straw. Glancing up, Kellan saw rough, but sturdy, beams making up the roof and between them he could see the thatch which served to keep the cottage dry. Sparse furniture appointed the cottage with the table and chairs he now stood beside taking up the bulk of what appeared to be the primary living area. There was a wooden counter and two rows of shelves on which had been the cups Shannon had used for their tea. At the far end of the cottage lay an ample fireplace with a wrought iron arm protruding, and on which the kettle had warmed earlier. Finally, his eyes took in the strong, but simple, bed that lay in the nook crated by the "L" shaped home. There was no room for a nightstand, but Kellan could see how, placed where it was, the little bed would be amply warmed by the fireplace.

Having taken in the entirety of the place, Kellan felt all the details nestle deeply into his mind, and turned back to Shannon. "So, I've looked the place over and still don't see why you couldn't have been living here. Although I do see that it's clearly too small for a family."

Shannon just looked at him for a long moment while Kellan tried to puzzle out her expression. "A man is a man no matter the age from whence they come, I suppose."

"Huh?"

Shannon then dragged two fingers along the table and held them up for Kellan to see.

"What?" he said.

Shannon made a disgusted sound and dragged the fingers against Kellan's chest. "It's filthy and clearly only a man lives here." She paused, looking suddenly sad. "Or lived here. Had I lived here, Kellan Thorne, I assure you that the floors, let alone, the table, would have been fit to eat from." She then glowered at him with hands on hips.

Kellan just held his hands up in a placating gesture. "I meant no offense. Honest. But you seem more upset about my slight to your housekeeping skills than about the craziness that is our lives now. Apparently you are in danger and I think I'm supposed to keep you safe or something. How will I even know if you need me?"

Shannon walked around the table, demeanor shifting so abruptly that Kellan tried to take a step back, but she continued forward, standing uncomfortably close and smiled the Devil's own smile. "How do you know that I am not the one who is supposed to keep *you* safe? Regardless," she said, now flashing an innocent smile while tapping her finger to her temple, "You are nestled up here somehow as I am up there for you. I imagine that happened for a reason and if either of us needs the other, we'll know. Good night, Kellan Thorne. Rest well. And remember you do so in the home of our dear friend, Micah."

Without another word Shannon slipped out the door, closing it behind her with a soft click and leaving Kellan with his mouth agape and mind dumfounded.

"Ok, let there be no doubt, I totally hate the 13th century. I hate you," Kellan yelled to the rafters while laying supine on the small bed. It was not a comfortable bed. He wondered exactly with what it had been stuffed. Twigs and rocks competed for top spots within his mind. With a final frustrated groan, Kellan swung his feet off the bed and walked into the small common room of the cottage. Some small amount of starlight sprinkled in from two glassless windows, barely illuminating the gloom enough to see. Kellan held up a hand and rubbed his thumb rapidly against pointer and middle finger, causing them to make a soft rasping sound for a couple seconds while he channeled a trickle of power. Moments later, a small, bright flame appeared above his fingers, flickering there as if the digits were the wax of a candle. He waved his hand slightly and the flame danced away, floating towards the nearby pillar candle that rested in the middle of the rough hewn table. It paused momentarily above the wick bringing it to light and then meandered to the three other candles, slender tapers, scattered about the room. In moments all were flickering merrily. The disembodied flame returned to Kellan and slowly wavered in midair. He smiled, puffed out a short breath, and the flame vanished with a barely discernible pop.

Kellan pulled out his iPhone and tried to wake it, but the device remained dark and silent. Kellan sighed, sitting down heavily while staring at the small screen. "Note to self," Kellan said to the air, "Never travel back eight centuries without fully charging your phone. No plants vs zombies for you, mister."

He spun the phone quickly on the table and stood again, resolving to find something he liked about his current situation, then walked over to what, in Kellan's mind, passed for the kitchen. He quickly took stock of what was at hand. Within a small wooden chest he found some potatoes, carrots, and onions. Opening a cabinet door rewarded him with a rather large round of cheese that had been half eaten. He pulled that down along with the wooden plate on which it sat, then crouched down to peer at the other shelf. Reaching in, he pulled out a quarter loaf of brown bread that was wrapped in a rough spun cloth and a single apple. The bread seemed slightly stale, but not horribly so and the apple was full and fresh. Glancing to the right, Kellan spied a brown clay pitcher and hefted it to find it still half full with some liquid. He sniffed, then poured its contents into one of the cups he and Shannon had used for tea hours earlier. Kellan took a sip. Water. Gathering up his cup, cheese, apple, and the lone knife from the counter, Kellan made his way back to the table and had himself a quite passable, if somewhat unique, apple-cheese sandwich.

He was just taking the last bite when he heard a soft tap at the door. He stiffened, but didn't move, hand paused holding the final bit of sandwich. He cocked his head, wondering if it was just a tree branch scraping against the cottage or some such thing. When the sound didn't repeat, he shrugged and popped the final bite into his mouth.

Another tap—this time much clearer and insistent came from the door.

"Ok, not a branch," Kellan said, standing. He walked over and reached for the door as he channeled power, snapping a shield around himself, then paused, making note of the heat in his eyes. *Hmmm, shield myself but look like I've got Kryptonite contacts or look normal and risk getting sliced and diced—great choice.* A moment later, he released the power, felt the shield vanish, and opened the door.

"Hello?" called Kellan. The woman, who had begun to walk away from the cottage, turned back and smiled shyly.

"Can I help you?" he added, while his inner monologue took stock of her appearance with masculine glee. She looked about Kellan's age, seemed of average height, and moved lithely as she turned back toward Kellan, her long blonde hair sweeping down to her middle back. Her skin was pale, almost like porcelain in the starlight, and she had large almond shaped eyes the color of honey. She wore a long brown skirt that ended just above the ankle and a blue vest that was largely obscured by the tartan shawl draped about her shoulders.

"I saw your light."

"Heh, yeah. That's my light alright. I'm awake. Very awake." Kellan shut his mouth, cursing himself for an idiot.

She cocked her head, smiling more broadly. "Yes, I can see that. I'm very sorry to intrude so early in the morning, but I've been walking most of the night. My horse threw a shoe some miles back without my knowing it and went lame. I left her to graze while I looked for help. Might I come in to rest until first light?"

"Sure, sure; c'mon in," he said, stepping aside to allow her entry into the small room. "It's not much to look at, I'm afraid."

"It's lovely," she replied removing, her shawl and looking about for a place to hang it.

"Um, I'll take that," said Kellan, accepting the shawl and feeling a warm tingle as her hand brushed his. He turned the corner quickly and laid it gently on the bed, pausing for a moment. "What is wrong with you," he whispered to himself, "Jesus, pull it together dude." Kellan gave himself a curt nod and returned to his guest, whose face again lit up with a smile.

"I'm sorry, I didn't introduce myself. I'm Amy. Amy MacDonald of Glencoe."

"Kellan Thorne," said Kellan, holding out his hand.

She stared at his outstretched hand for several long heartbeats and then slowly reached out, uncertainly placing her hand in his.

With his inner monologue laughing uproariously while hurling a string of self-directed insults, Kellan leaned forward and placed a soft kiss on her hand. Amy accepted the gesture graciously but giggled and said, "I thank you for that, but I am no Lady."

"I try to always treat a Dame like a Lady and a Lady like a Dame," replied Kellan, while picturing his inner self rolling on the floor laughing hysterically at his anachronistic Sinatra quote.

"A…Dame?"

"Never mind, please have a seat. Can I get you something? I have," Kellan paused wincing, "Um, water and cheese."

"That would be wonderful, Mr. Thorne. Thank you."

"Oh please, it's Kellan," he said while draining the last of the water into a cup and handing it to her.

She accepted it, eyes widening slightly, and replied, "Well, then you must call me Amy." She took a small bite of cheese and smiled. "Delicious, and much appreciated. I didn't realize how hungry I was."

"I'm sorry I don't have more. I, uh, haven't been to the…market," Kellan began haltingly, "Unless you want a carrot. I have some of those."

She laughed. "No, the cheese is fine."

They settled into an uncomfortable silence with Kellan stealing a sideways glance as she nibbled the last of the cheese.

"Hey," he began, "Why don't you take me to where you left your horse and we'll get you two fixed up."

She brightened at the suggestion. "Are you a farrier then?"

"Uh, no, not exactly, but I do know a thing or two about horses and I'm sure we can get your girl fixed up enough so she'll make it to the village nearby. I have a friend who lives there and she'll be sure to know someone who can help."

"That's very kind of you to offer, but I've imposed on you enough by taking both food and sleep from you."

"Nonsense. I was awake anyway and it's not like I laid out a four course meal for you." She looked at Kellan quizzically again and he quickly moved on. "Let me get your shawl and we'll be off."

Amy rewarded him with another smile and Kellan felt himself flush, laughing slightly as he went to retrieve her shawl. "Here you go," Kellan said as he turned the corner, his right foot catching the foot of the bed, causing him to stumble.

His right shoulder suddenly felt hot, and he glanced down to find a red stain spreading out from where the hilt of a dagger protruded. A wave of nausea hit him and Kellan felt his knees buckle. Still, he retained enough of his wits to realize that had he not tripped moments before, the blade would have found his heart rather than shoulder.

"Amy?" he said, still not fully comprehending what was going on.

She stared down at him grimly. "Not Amy. Lamia, and I am sorry, but there is no other way. It's either you or them." With that, her face contorted in what seemed like pain and her lower body seemed to melt and pool about her, even as her eyes changed from their pale honey brown to a glowing dark red. In the span of two heartbeats she was on him. Her legs and torso had become serpentine and she wrapped around him, constricting, as she yanked the dagger free and made to drive it into his chest.

Kellan drew deeply from the river of power, eyes flashing to life, and felt his hair begin to stand on end as he channeled electrical energy, drawing from both environmental and bodily sources. He released the energy in a rush, blue sparks arcing all about his body and hurling Lamia across the room even as he was slammed backwards against the near wall. He saw her rise up on the thick coil that had now replaced her waist and legs. All the candles winked out.

Kellan staggered to his feet, holding a glowing ball of white hot flame in his left hand and screamed in pain as he willed a small tendril to leap towards his right shoulder. It buried itself into the knife wound, cauterizing it. He then hurled the fireball at Lamia while trying to make his way to the cottage door. The flame exploded on her, slamming her against the wall again, and showering the cottage with tongues of flame that quickly licked against the dry wood—bringing the cottage ablaze.

He grabbed for the door and fell down the stoop, sprawling on the grass, then rolled on his back in time to see her emerge from the cottage which was now fully engulfed in flame. The fire burned all around her. Her skin and scales seemed to glow from the intense heat, but she was not consumed.

Kellan began to scamper backwards on hands and feet, trying to regain a standing position, even as his mind assembled the recent facts, and demanded his attention.

Lamia, from the Greek. Queen of Libya, who, according to mythology, became a child-eating daemon. The ancient Athenian comic playwright, Aristophanes, believed her name to be derived from the Greek word for gullet, 'laimos', referring to her habit of devouring children. Known to take the form of a serpent in whole or in part. Immune to fire, thought to only be killed by decapitation.

"You're a fucking demon? What did I ever do to you?" he yelled as she loomed over him for a moment before a focused gust of wind struck her, lifting her up and hurling her back into the conflagration. Kellan regained his feet as she again emerged from the cottage, skin and scales glowing fiercely like embers in a forge.

"I'm sorry. I have no choice. I have to save them and this is the only way. He demands it."

"Yeah, well, the sexual mojo you shot at me was uncool, but then, who expects a demon to fight fair? Hands off my libido, bitch, and I'm giving you one chance to back off or I'm going to end you!"

Kellan saw her shake her head violently as she continued towards him. "Fine!" he yelled, "Have it your way." Then he raised both hands just above his shoulders, held them there a moment, and threw them forward until both were pointed directly at Lamia.

She paused, eyes widening in fear, locking on to his.

Nothing happened.

Kellan saw her relief and her face became a mask of determination as she raced toward him. For his part, Kellan didn't move, but continued to hold both hands towards her, brows knitted in concentration. She was only several paces away when the first projectile struck with a hiss, knocking her back, as the flying dagger sublimated from ice to steam when it struck her superheated body.

More followed in rapid succession as Kellan continued to channel heat from the nearby stream into the already burning cottage and directed a torrent of frozen projectiles toward the demon.

Dozens more struck her, again driving her back, but not surviving the heat long enough to do any real damage. She cried out in frustration as she strove to close the distance between them only to have another wave of ice daggers fly into her. This time, they were driving into flesh that was no longer hot enough to melt them.

She staggered and fell, blood pouring from dozens of wounds even as the last several ice daggers arced into the air above her and struck, pinning her to the ground where she struggled weakly against the frozen nails.

Kellan walked towards her as a glowing blue sword materialized in his outstretched hand. Her eyes were wild with fear as he stood over her sword raised.

"I'm sorry! I'm sorry, I'm sorry," she cried.

"Far too late for that," said Kellan, grim faced.

She laughed, blood coming to her lips, "Not you, Sentinel. I'm sorry for them—my babies."

"Well, confession is good for the soul which, I assume, you don't have, so not sure what you're hoping to accomplish by being sorry for all the children you've devoured over the years."

"Lies! Never!" She spat out the words, tears streaming from her eyes, then stared directly at Kellan. "Do it! It's what Sentinels do. They kill demons—so do it! Make Micah proud; you are just like him!"

Kellan felt his muscles tense as he began the downward swing just as she closed her eyes and whispered, "Then Asmodeus will kill my babies and we will be together."

The sword rang out as it struck the ground, cleaving cleanly through the large stone by Lamia's head. Kellan saw her wince and open her eyes as he knelt beside her in the grass.

"I was wrong," she said, "You are worse than Micah, to draw out my pain. He, at least, would have been quick."

Kellan ignored her, but stared deeply into her eyes, pondering what he saw there in the predawn light. "Who will Asmodeus kill?"

She spat at him, and Kellan felt it drip down his cheek. "Who will Asmodeus kill?" he asked again softly.

"I will tell you nothing. Great Sentinel Demon killer. Do what Micah taught you and end this!"

Kellan tilted his head slightly and stood, resting the flat of the sword on his shoulder. "Ok, I'll end it now." With that, he gestured and all the ice pinning Lamia to the ground vanished, turning to water in the blink of an eye. He watched as the wounds stopped bleeding and knitted up, then took several steps back—eyeing her warily. "Go. You are free."

Lamia stood, shakily at first, but rapidly regained her strength. Her lower extremities again took their human form. She narrowed her eyes. "What trick is this, Sentinel."

"No trick—go."

"Micah would never—"

Kellan interrupted her by lowering the sword from his shoulder and making her jump in alarm. "As I've been saying all too often, 'I am not he.'"

Lamia, clearly confused, turned toward the woods and Kellan saw her body tense, preparing to run.

"But," he began in a loud voice, causing her to turn back to him, fear returning to her face, "But, if you do go now, then you will never know if I could save your children from him. Your choice of course." Kellan smiled, turned his back on the demon, and began walking toward the stream. Moments later he heard the crunch of her feet on the grass as she followed slowly behind and knew his gambit was well played.

Kellan stripped off his shirt and tore a bit of fabric from where Lamia's dagger had entered. He dipped it in the cold stream water and dabbed at his shoulder while she watched him from a distance. Kellan winced more from cold than pain as the water slushed away dried blood to reveal a mostly healed wound. He slipped his shirt back on and leaned against Shannon's rock, staring at the demon expectantly. She said nothing.

Finally, Kellan glanced eastward at the brightening sky, "Sun's going to be up any minute."

"And what's that to me? I'm not a vampire."

Kellan shrugged. "Didn't know what the sun does to demons."

"It makes us warm when we lay in it," she replied sarcastically, then smiled and started walking toward Kellan. "But you know, this was really just a big misunderstanding and I'm terribly sorry."

Kellan felt the warmth begin to grow and butterflies begin to twirl about his stomach. He returned her smile even as several wickedly sharp ice daggers rose from the nearby stream, turned towards Lamia, and began to revolve menacingly. "Seduce me once, shame on you. Seduce me twice, shame on me. Let's not try that dance again, shall we?"

Lamia frowned and stopped moving towards him, eyes turning to the deadly ice, and held up a hand placatingly. There was a soft splash as they all returned to water falling back into the stream.

"I ask you three times, who—will— Asmodeus—kill?"

"I already told you," she replied, voice hard! "You didn't believe me."

"Your babies?"

She nodded.

"You have children?" he asked, a bit surprised.

Another nod. "Three. Two girls and a boy."

"How—" Kellan began...

"Do I really need to explain these things to you, mighty Sentinel? You seem old enough to know how and where babies come from."

Kellan flushed and she smiled wickedly, but he didn't feel her direct any effects towards him. Her smile faded and she continued, "Asmodeus killed their father, my husband, Taliesin, and stole them from me. He promised to return them unharmed if I served him for one thousand years and a day without fail. I was sent to kill you and if you still live when my time of service ends—my children will die."

"We'll see about that. How many years have you served him so far?"

"999 years, 342 days."

"Oh, wow, that totally sucks. You were less than a month from being done and he laid this one on you. Bad timing, Lamia."

She glared at him with undisguised hatred. "You would mock my pain, Sentinel?"

"What? No? I'm serious. Really bad timing—or really good timing on Asmodeus' part. Still, we have 23 days to figure this out. Do you know where he is holding your kids?"

"Why?"

"Well, maybe I can get them back for you."

"Why would you do that?" she asked with a sneer.

"Because stealing someone's kids and holding them for a 1000 year ransom is a serious dick move and I don't abide dick moves—that's all."

She laughed bitterly. "You can't help a demon, Kellan Thorne."

"Really, why not?"

Lamia seemed momentarily at a loss for words then answered, "Because, you are God's Sentinel. His unchecked hand upon the world. You kill demons. It's what you do."

"Well, maybe I'm just a kinder, gentler Sentinel who only kills the demons that need killing. The question then is: are you *that* kind of demon, Lamia?"

The two stared at each other for long moments and when she finally broke the silence, Kellan heard her voice crack, thick with emotion as she pressed both hands to her stomach and sank to the ground. "I just want my children."

Lamia looked up and her face was a mask of grief. This was not the recent loss of a friend or loved one. No, this was deeper, broader, and more engrained. As Kellan stared at her, he had flashes of insight come unbidden to his mind. Images, scents, and sounds—a cacophony of disparate information from which he gleaned a single, crystal clear insight. Every aspect of the being that now knelt before him radiated vast sadness and emotional trauma so powerful that Kellan felt himself stumble back at its all encompassing nature. She continued, "I fell with the other Angels and am forever damned I suppose. I don't even really know what being damned means, but I wanted no part of this endless war between Order and Chaos. However, those stronger than me held sway." Her eyes became wistful and she closed them, lowering her head, "I am a cliche'," she sighed, "The demon who sought to cause a man to fall and, instead, fell herself. I loved Taliesin, my beautiful bard for he could play the strings of my heart better than ever did he play those of a lute, and his skill with the lute brought beggars and kings to tears of joy. I bore him three beautiful children, two girls and a boy, each with a spirit as filled with light as my Tal. I loved him. I loved my children. I loved them all and someday I will have their stories told. But this story is not a fairy tale and its words are written on pages dark as pitch because Asmodeus found me and," she waved her hands, "this nightmare began." Her voice became hard and she rose to her feet, taking a step toward Kellan, eyes beginning to glow red. "Do you think I *want* to serve the Angel responsible for killing the man I loved, who stole my children, and who has used mythology to paint me as a monster who consumes the innocent? All this I suffer for the sin of simply wanting freewill and thus being cast down. All this for the freewill that is showered upon *you humans* and which is protected, *for you*, regardless of cost. So, judge me now, for that is what you Sentinels do; That is what Micah did. You judge and execute."

Kellan stood firm, stared into those flaming eyes without flinching, and spoke softly, voice filled with sadness and empathy. "I came to love Micah in a very short time, but I am not he. I will not judge you beyond knowing your pain is real and holds no glamor." Kellan shook his head slowly and continued, "No, Lamia, I do not think you wanted any of this at all." Instantly the heat went out of her and she slumped, staring back at him in disbelief.

"You—are an enigma, Sentinel Kellan."

"Yeah, I actually get that a lot from women. Nice to know it applies to female demons too. It's a gift."

She looked at him for a long moment, then laughed. It was a strong laugh—good, pure, and bright. It rang off trees, stone, and grass. Kellan saw its cathartic nature and found his laughter joining with hers. After long moments, her laughter and smiles faded into a contented sigh and she sobered. "You cannot save them. It's not like they are held captive in a cave or a tower waiting for a heroic, if delusional, Sentinel to come rescue them. Asmodeus is an Archangel, a fallen one to be sure, but an Archangel nonetheless. He holds them in a pocket universe of his own creation; they are bound there by his very life force. So long as he lives, they cannot escape and none can reach them unless he wills it."

Kellan hummed to himself. "Pocket universe? You mean like the workroom?"

Lamia started, eyes going wide. "*God's* workroom?"

"Yeah…" Kellan replied, curious at her response.

"You've been there?"

"Sure. Micah trained me there. I'm not particularly fond of it. No birds. I like birds."

She grabbed Kellan by both shoulders, staring up at him urgently, "Can you get back there?"

Wow she is so strikingly beautiful. I'd really like to—

"Hey!" Kellan yelled pushing, her back. "I thought we were past that. You just tried to whammy me again."

Lamia held up her hands. "No, no I didn't. Well, not intentionally. Sometimes it just leaks out when I'm excited."

Kellan narrowed his eyes. "Ok, but I'm watching you. To your question, yes, I can get back there easily. Why is that important?"

Lamia had begun pacing. "I can't believe this. This could actually be possible." She realized Kellan was just staring at her uncomprehendingly. "Asmodeus was not in God's workroom, Kellan. No fallen Angel can ever go there on their own. The last one to ever be there was Lucifer; that was right after the fall and only because God took him there. The pocket universe to which I referred is but a pale shadow of the workroom."

Kellan was nodding. "Ok, so I just need to go to his B-grade pocket universe, spring your kids, and bob's your uncle."

Lamia stared at him, then shook her head. "What? What are you saying? No, don't try to explain. You cannot go there. It's impossible. You're only hope is to collapse it which would cause my children to be freed."

Kellan shrugged, "Collapse it, enter it—whatever works. So how do I collapse it?"

Lamia's eyes grew large and she shook her head, speaking very slowly, "There's only one way to collapse it."

Kellan laughed, copying the cadence of her speech, "And that is? Out with it, demon."

She didn't smile, but rather leaned in closely and placed a soft kiss on Kellan's ear. His eyes grew wide as insight flashed into his mind.

"Holy shit! I've got to—"

Lamia placed a finger on his lips. "No. Never out loud." She stepped back again, looking dejected. "I know…it's impossible, reckless, and stupid."

Kellan closed the distance between them, took her face in his hands, and looked down. "Lamia, you are my favorite demon, and here's a secret you can take to the netherworld. I specialize in the impossible, reckless, and stupid— especially the stupid."

She raised her hands, wrapping them around his, tears flowing down her cheeks even as she gave a relieved half laugh. "I'm your *only* demon." Then she raised up on her toes, kissing his lips and lingering there for the span for three heartbeats. Kellan knew it was a more sincere and chaste kiss than any he'd received since those placed by his own mother long ago.

She settled back on the soles of her feet, still staring into his eyes. "Amy. Call me Amy. It's what Taliesin called me and the only name more precious to me is the one you are helping me to hear again." Her voice became a whisper nearly swallowed by the soft gurgling of the nearby stream, "Mama."

⌒ᐜ⌒

Kellan shot up, eyes blazing to life, as the icy water shocked him awake, sputtering even as dark clouds gathered overhead charged with electrical energy.

"Jesus, Shannon, what the hell!"

The young woman stood before him, face a thunderhead to match those above, one hand on hip and the other holding an earthen pitcher darkened by smoke and cracked by heat. Her flaming red hair had begun to rise slightly before Kellan became aware enough to dispel the lightning clouds he had caused to form.

"What," she began, eyes narrowed to mere slits, "do you think you were doing?"

Kellan had slid back down against the massive tree where he had found a soft, mossy spot between its roots to nap. He looked up at her exasperated. "You know, Shannon, this…" he waved at her, "is a good reason why I am not married." He felt power course through him in response to what seemed to be an almost reflexive reaction to the pitcher she hurled at his head. It shattered against a shimmering shield, shards of clay falling harmlessly to the ground.

"Like any sane woman would have you!" She pointed to his right and he turned to look at the smoking ruin of Micah's cottage.

Kellan sighed. "I had a rough night."

Shannon stared at him, sputtering, but no words came.

Kellan clapped. "You're speechless? Well, now that I know the trick to that, I just need to find a steady supply of houses to burn down."

"You idiot! You know nothing," she sobbed as she turned, running back toward the ruined cottage, leaving Kellan in bemused silence.

A few minutes later he had walked up the gentle hill to find Shannon silently poking through the charred remains, picking up the few recognizable things that had miraculously survived the fire, and placing them gently in a pile.

"I am an idiot," he said softly from behind her. She stiffened but didn't turn.

"He was like a second father to me, and this was all I had left of him."

"I know. I'm an—"

"Idiot. Yes, we've established that."

Kellan remained silent and she finally turned to him, eyes red with tears.

"It's not about the things really. It's about the place. We had so many good times here, my brothers and me. And then there's this," she said, holding out her hands which held a small blackened object.

"What is it?" Kellan asked softly.

Shannon sighed. "What was it you mean. Nothing important—just a box we made for Micah. All of us. The boys found the wood and carved it. I created the inlay and stained it. Then we each brought him little things from time to time. Treasures, he called them. They were all in this little box and now their gone, just like him."

Kellan felt sick. "I'm sorry Shannon. I really am."

She nodded. "I'm sorry too. I shouldn't have yelled at you or," she paused, "tried to kill you with a pitcher to the head. What happened?"

"C'mon. Walk with me and I'll tell you."

A few minutes later, the two found themselves down by the stream, Kellan having related the night's events, with some notable exceptions dealing with Asmodeus. She patted the large boulder. "So, it's Shannon's Rock now, is it?"

"It is, indeed."

"Well, every girl needs a big rock to sit on, I think," she said absently, picking up the charred remains of Micah's box that she had gently laid at the base of the stone. "I think I'm going to let the stream take this and then I can pretend that it's flowing to meet him somewhere." She smiled sadly, "I just wish I could go back in time and save it from the fire; I should have taken it home with me yesterday. It's really my fault that I didn't. Stupid really…I kind of wanted it to stay there as if he were coming home to look through it."

Shannon knelt down, reaching out to set the blackened wood adrift in the crystal clear water as it splashed past, but Kellan placed a hand on her arm.

"Just a moment—something you said. You just stay here and keep your rock company. I'm going to try something…"

"Stupid?" she asked, only half joking.

Kellan cocked his head, speaking slowing, "I…don't think so. At least not very stupid on the official Kellan scale of stupidity, but I suppose we'll find out shortly."

"Delightful. What exactly are you…" Shannon trailed off as she saw Kellan's eyes begin to glow brightly and he held up a hand. She took that to mean that he couldn't be disturbed.

A shimmering oval rotated into view in front of him and he leaped through, snapping it shut behind him, and leaving her alone by the stream.

Only a few minutes had past when the sound of feet crunching on dried leaves drew Shannon's attention and she saw Kellan walking toward her with a very self-satisfied look on his face.

"You look very pleased with yourself," she said warily. "What did you do, Kellan Thorne, and what are you are holding behind your back?"

Without a word, Kellan gave his best sweeping arm flourish with his free hand as he knelt before her, and held out his other hand, "For you Milady."

Shannon drew a quick breath as she saw what he held, eyes misting over as they took in the small, intricately inlayed oak box.

"How?"

"You wished to go back in time," Kellan smiled. "I made it so."

"But, I still have the ruined one," she said reaching for the small blackened object resting at her feet. As her fingers touched it, the ruined box wavered a moment and broke apart like motes of dust. "Magic," she whispered.

"Science," Kellan replied as she accepted the pristine box from him, "Well, science'ish. The ruined box represented a paradox so it couldn't exist for long since there can only be one reality, and I made that reality the one with," he pointed to her, "that box in it."

"Paradox?" she said, sounding out letters as if they were thick on her tongue.

"Yeah, like when I made that portal back to yesterday. I had to sneak past the two of us, get into the cottage, swipe the box and then hope you didn't notice it was missing." Kellan paused, thoughtful. "Hmmm, I wonder if the reason you didn't think to take the box with you last night was because I had already stolen, it and it wasn't there to remind you. And I guess I really needn't have tried to be so stealthy because surely if either one of us had caught sight of another "me" sneaking about we would remember it. So since we didn't remember it then I didn't get caught—which means I didn't even need to sneak."

Kellan smiled triumphantly. "See! Science—ish"

Shannon looked at him blankly. "Do you actually understand what you just said? It makes my head hurt."

Kellan waved her thought away. "Timey wimey, wiblly wobbly...don't worry about it; just enjoy your treasure box."

Shannon had it open and poked about with a finger, smiling to herself then looked up with moist eyes. "I will, Kellan. I really will." Then she closed the distance between them and kissed him on the cheek. "Thank you—so much!"

"Twern't nuthin but— listen, Shannon. Part of what happened last night made it pretty clear to me that," Kellan waved his hand around, "this time, was just a pit stop for me. I have to get back to my own timeline."

Shannon lowered her eyes. "Eight hundred years from now, when I'm long dead."

"Stop," Kellan said lifting, her chin with two fingers so he could look at her, and pointed toward her eyes with his other hand. "Don't forget those sparkly peepers you have, Miss McLeod. Micah said we'd be meeting again in my time and that guy, he's as straight an arrow as they come. Annoyingly so sometimes, but, point being, if he said we'll be meeting up it's because Raphael told him so and that Angel, while being twice as uptight as Micah, cannot even tell a lie if he wanted to."

"But when?" she asked, "What do I do now, and what if I need your help?"

Kellan finally saw the young part of this young woman. He put both hands around her shoulders, grasping them reassuringly. "Shannon, you are a true badass."

She pulled back slightly, frowning.

"No, no…it's a good thing," he continued, "It means you are tough and can handle anything life throws at you.

However," Kellan tapped his temple, "remember, we have this thing going on now, and I'm absolutely sure that if either of us needs the other, we'll find a way to get there. Have some faith—"

She laughed, "Says God's Sentinel with the seductive demon friend."

"I never said she was seductive."

Shannon looked at him flatly once again, assuming a posture older than her years. "Kellan, you didn't have to. It was obvious."

"Oh, really? Oh, well…that doesn't matter. As I told you, I'm not going to prejudge people, demons, or whatever. Once they prove themselves to be douche canoes, then I'll kill 'em. As for you and what you do now, well, you live your life. Have fun, take care of your family, grow up a bit and live a little. It's all stretched out before you, Shannon. Life is a giant adventure and you are just the gal to grab it by the horns and kick its ass"

She shook her head, smiling, "I know you told me you are really speaking a different language and I'm just hearing it in mine but, sometimes, it seems like you are still speaking gibberish."

"Pish posh. I don't even know if that's an accurate description of what's going on, but if I waited to fully understand the things I'm doing, I'd end up sitting in a corner drooling." Kellan raised both hands into fists, "Gotta grab it by the horns!"

"So, when?"

"When what?"

"Are you leaving?"

"Now."

She looked down again. Kellan struggled to find something to lighten the moment. "Hey, but you can see my future house as I go. That'll be cool, right?"

"Sure...cool," she replied without emotion.

"Ok, I've really got to concentrate because I'm having to make a portal to a place and time both very far from here, so don't distract me or I could end up on the moon or something."

She slapped his shoulder, "Yeah, like that. Don't do that."

"I won't. I want you safe."

She watched as Kellan's brow knitted in concentration and his eyes came alight moments before the portal resolved itself and he leaped through. He turned to look back at her—through the miles and centuries.

She stood there in the sunlight, hair ablaze, bright brown eyes staring into his as Kellan felt the power rushing from him in a torrent while he struggled to keep the portal open. He gestured around him. "

This is my home, Shannon. I can't wait for you to see it. I think you'll find this time very interesting. What do you think?"

He saw her pause for a moment, then straightened slightly, lifting her chin. All semblance of childhood evaporated like breath on a mirror. "I think, Kellan Thorne, that...I love you, and did even before we met."

She watched his eyes widen in surprise and a very self satisfied smile spread across her face as the portal winked out.

Chapter 9

REUNION

K ellan continued to stare, mouth agape, at the space in his living room where, moments before, he spoke to Shannon across both miles and centuries.

"You what?!" he said to open air, then grumbled as he turned towards the bedroom, sparing a glance backward over his shoulder, "Just a kid..."

Kellan dropped his iPhone onto the nightstand by his bed and plugged it in, but it merely acknowledged the event by showing a low battery image while refusing to power on. He sighed, stripped off his clothes, and threw them into the canvas hamper located in one corner of his closet while grabbing a fresh pair of faded jeans and a T-Shirt emblazoned with the image of Jeff Bridges along with one word: Abides.

Kellan stared at the shirt a moment. "I need a fucking drink and then I'll abide too, Dude." With the clothes still in his hands, Kellan heard his iPhone power up and begin to make all manner of customized tones to indicate a series of e-mails, text messages, and alerts had just been received. He walked over, threw his clothes on the bed, and glanced down at the now glowing device. He ignored the e-mail indicators and tapped the Messages app which indicated 12 new text messages: Three from Juliet, one from his mother, and 8 from James Clinton.

Mom: "Kellie…I told you I wasn't feeling well and you didn't call. I could be dead for all you care. I'm the only mother you have. Call me." Jewish on his mom's side and Catholic on his Dad's, Kellan was used to having a double dose of guilt and shame. He stood there admiring his mother's ability to wield maternal guilt like a finely honed sword. Still, she would have to wait to berate him until a bit later. He tapped the next name.

Juliet 1: "Kel. Where are you? I tried to track your phone and it's nowhere. I know you never turn it off. Where are you?"

Juliet 2: "Kellan! You are being a jerk. I've been running the store by myself for two days. Call me, right now!"

Juliet 3: "Kellan Thorne…you have me completely freaked out. It's been three days. WTF!"

"Shit!" Kellan said, as he bent down to tap on the iPhone.

"Juliet. Sorry, I'm an ass, and shitty time-traveler—must have screwed up my reentry. Just got back. Am ok—will see you soon."

Kellan stood back up, thought a moment, then tapped out a second message to Juliet. "Obviously, don't show this to anyone." He hit send, then plopped on the side of the bed, sliding his finger to James Clinton.

James 1: "Kel, brotha, you have got to see my new gadget. It kicks ass. Call me."

James 2: "Kel, dude, let's hook up tonight at Dark Horse Tavern. I'm dating someone new—need to fill you in."

James 3: "Ok, it's been two days. I'm not your bitch. Call me or I'm not texting you again."

James 4: "Fine. I guess I am your bitch. Dude…call me."

James 5: "Day 3 asshole. I'm going to make you pay."

James 6: "U R A Dick"

James 7: "W!"

James 8: "T!"

James 9: "F!"

Kellan smiled and looked at the charge on his iPhone—20%. He unplugged it and hit the FaceTime icon next to James' contact info. A few seconds later, James Clinton's face appeared on the screen. James was an empirically handsome guy with light chocolate colored skin and meticulous grooming habits. In years past, he had called himself a 'metrosexual' and while the term had died out, James' passion for a clean shaved face, head, and trimmed eyebrows had not.

"Hi handsome," Kellan said with a grin.

"Fuck you, asshole."

Kellan made to kiss his phone.

"Oh, please dude, you would turn a gay man straight with that shit, and as the straightest man in Atlanta, just imagine what that does to me."

"Ha! Straight," responded Kellan, "Methinks the lady doth protest too much."

"Yeah, whatever. Hey, where have you—wait, what are you wearing?"

"Huh, oh, I was just about to jump in the shower actually," said Kellan, grinning as he started to tilt the phone down.

"Stop!"

<Tilt>

"Stop! Dude, I mean it!"

<Tilt>

"I'm not looking!"

Kellan laughed and moved the phone back up to where it was squarely pointed at his face, then laughed even harder as he saw James peering out between the fingers of the hand he had been using to cover his eyes. James started laughing too.

"Seriously, dude, that kinda shit could detach a retina or something and, look at me, you don't want me having surgery that could alter this kinda perfection, do you?"

Kellan gave an exaggerated sigh and inwardly realized how much of the last week's tension had just unwound in the span of the past few minutes. "So," he began, "You said something about a girl, a gadget, and the Dark Horse."

James became animated. "Oh, yeah. So, I bought a coffee station. It's all stainless, imported from France, and it's actually built into my cabinets like a microwave, but, well, cooler, and for coffee. It's connected right up to the main water of my house so I never have to fill it. It grinds beans, makes expresso— the works. Did I mention it was from France?"

"Yeah, you mentioned that because, as we all know, the French are known for their fine appliance craftsmanship. What about the girl?"

"Oh, she's cool. But wait, I don't think you fully appreciate this coffee station. It grinds beans and makes cups of coffee, espresso, or a whole pot. You have to come over right now and see it."

"How do you clean it if it's built into the wall? What if it leaks?"

"How do you clean it? I don't know!" exclaimed James with exasperation. "Dude. You are missing the point. It's from——"

"France. Yeah, I get it. James, I ask you three times, what about the girl?"

James laughed, "Ok, Kvothe, I tell you three times, she's pretty, hot, smart, and hot."

"Smart, like Brandy was smart?"

James grimaced. "No dude, and that was like 10 years ago"

"Two," reminded Kellan

"At least five. And there was no way for me to know she had an active warrant. Are you ever going to let me live that down?"

"Nope."

"Well, fuck you then. Maybe I won't even let you meet Naomi. Ask me where she works, douche."

"Where does she work, douche?"

"The C...D...C," James said, slowly enunciating each letter in turn, "She's literally a scientist for the CDC. You know what that means?"

"That she might be able cure that raging case of herpes you got from Brandy?"

"Hardy fucking har. No dude. It means...if there are ever real Walkers, she'll know how to fix it. And I'll be right there, safe and sound, while you go out eating brains and looking like shit."

Kellan laughed despite himself. "So your argument for this gal isn't that she's obviously clever to both have earned a doctorate and a position at the world's preeminent public health institution. It's that she will be handy in case of the zombie apocalypse?"

"'Zactly."

"Ok," said Kellan seriously, "I can respect that."

"Guess what else?" asked James with a look that gave Kellan pause.

"What?"

"She looks like Zoey Deschanel."

"Bull. Shit!" Kellan had barely gotten the word out when his phone buzzed indicating a picture had been received. He tapped a few icons and groaned as he looked at what appeared to be a smiling Zoey Deschanel, arms draped around James' neck while the two posed for a picture. Kellan switched back to his FaceTime session to find James grinning like an idiot.

"So, she going to be at the Dark Horse?"

"Nah, she has to work tonight. Some kind of virus thing going on somewhere."

"Walker Virus?"

"Nope, I asked, Ebola I think. Hey, you think it's safe for us to, you know?"

Kellan narrowed his eyes at the image of his friend. "No, idiot, I don't think it's safe for you guys to, "you know," because there is a chance that it could result in your passing on your double helix and that gene pool needs to stop with you. What, do you think she sprays live ebola on herself like perfume?" Kellan held up a hand in front of the camera. "Don't answer that. I'm hungry. I need about 20 beers and I'm going to take a shower. I'll see you there in an hour."

"No no," said James frantically waving one hand. "Come by my place and we'll take Uber down. I want you to see that coffee station."

"Oh my God. Fine, I'll be at your place in 45."

Kellan didn't wait for a response before he disconnected the FaceTime, plugged his iPhone in, and padded over to the shower.

Kellan glanced at his phone as he pulled up to James' building—8:30. He was late, having taken longer in the shower than planned. But, Kellan reasoned, he had, quite literally, centuries of dirt to wash off. So James could just deal with it. The doorman, a twenty something with sandy brown hair, waved and walked around to Kellan's side of the car, running an appreciative hand along the hood and left fender.

"Hi Baby. You are looking fine as always," he said.

"Why thanks, Tommy, but you're gonna make me blush."

Tommy narrowed his eyes at Kellan. "Very funny, you know I was talking to the car. I don't suppose you want me to call up the valet?"

"Hells no!"

Tommy chuckled. "Yeah, don't blame ya, just pull over there," he said, pointing to what was supposed to be a second lane of the turnabout, but was, in reality, parking for folks who drove cars Tommy liked. Kellan raced the engine a moment before putting the car into gear and got an appreciative nod from the door man, as he made a sweeping gesture toward the offered parking spot. Kellan deftly slid the Impala in-between a Tesla P85D and a BMW 650 convertible, killed the engine, and hopped out.

"Thanks for the spot, Tommy. Baby's slumming a bit next to those two heaps, but it's better than her being lonely in some dark garage. Did you tell the idiot I was here?"

"Yep; he says you're late and that you should do something anatomically improbable," said the doorman with a grin. "By the way, be prepared, he just got a coffee station installed. I didn't even know what a coffee station was, but he has one, and it was made in—"

"France. Yeah, Tommy, I know all about the miraculous coffee contribution the French have made to world in general, and James' condo specifically. If anyone complains of screaming or of loud crashes coming from his place, pay it no mind."

Kellan paused and turned back. "Oh, we're going to take Uber down to Highlands and grab some beer and food at the Dark Horse, so I'm gonna leave Baby here till we get back—that cool?"

Tommy waved the question away. "No worries, Kel. I'm here till six. Hey you want to leave the keys with me? You know, just in case."

"No."

Kellan walked into the lobby and waved to the security officer, who waved back from behind the large, industrial, desk made of brushed steel and carbon fiber.

"I'll sign you in, Kel"

"Thanks Mike," said Kellan with a smile as he headed toward the bank of elevators, each of which depicted a slice of the Atlanta skyline, such that with all elevators closed, you had a pretty good view of what the city looked like by night. Kellan tapped the "up" button and the rightmost elevator slid open with a soft electronic chime. Once in, he quickly pressed the top button for floor 36 and a pleasant British woman spoke from the air, the voice affecting a slightly mechanical cadence.

"Secure floor access—prepare for retina scan." Kellan placed his eye near the scanner with a huff, annoyed at the fancy security measure for the umpteenth time. "Identity not confirmed," said the voice.

"What?" said Kellan.

"Identity not confirmed," repeated the voice.

"Do it again."

"Secure floor access—prepare for retina scan. Identity not confirmed."

Kellan ground his teeth and mumbled, "What did you do to my eyes, Raphael?" He reached to slide open a small panel in the elevator that covered what looked like a phone keypad, then said, "Manual identification."

"Secure floor access—enter access code now."

Kellan quickly tapped out the 12 character combination: STNGNCC1701D.

The door slid closed and the British woman spoke again with slight pauses as the system inserted custom responses James had previously programmed. "Identity confirmed. Welcome...Kellan Thorne. You are late for your appointment with Mr. Clinton. You, sir, are a douchebag. Enjoy your visit at Peachtree Executive Tower."

Kellan flipped off the security camera, just on the off chance that James was monitoring it. With his ears popping from the rapid ascent, Kellan left the elevator and turned right down the long hall that led to James' corner unit. He heard his shoes making soft squeaks as they moved along the gleamingly polished concrete; the interior of the hall was exposed brick while the exterior wall boasted long brushed steel panels that ran its length with intermittent carbon fiber accent lines.

As he approached the door emblazoned with the number 3604, Kellan heard the door lock click, having been informed of his arrival and paired to the bluetooth in his iPhone. The door opened on an expansive open floor plan that made up James' executive palace. The whole place made Kellan think that an Ikea designer had his head explode, with every jettisoned thought taking shape in the place. Everything was glass and steel with the only nod to anything organic being the gray washed bamboo flooring which, Kellan reminded himself, was a concession James had made after Kellan threatened to never set foot in the place were it left with acid etched concrete floors.

Kellan immediately saw James in the kitchen, his back to the front door, engrossed in doing one thing or another. Kellan walked over and leaned both forearms on the polished concrete breakfast bar.

"So, this you will actually use?" he began.

James turned, grinning at his friend. "Huh, I use this other stuff."

"Oh really?" replied Kellan, gesturing to the massive 60" Wolf range, "Turn that on."

"Well, I don't cook with it if that's what you mean."

"It's an oven, James."

"It's a display piece, Kellan. Look at those Hammersmith copper pots on it. If I used the oven to cook, it would get dirty and I imagine the copper would likewise; doesn't it turn green if you cook with it? Besides, do you have any idea what real copper pots cost? I'd never actually use them. And, Mr. Reclaimed Wood, which is another name for old rotted shit, the Sub-Zero is filled with beer, and Lisa filled the Miele," he pointed at the dishwasher, "with wine glasses just yesterday, so I use that too."

"Your maid uses it."

He waved a hand. "Same thing. And, look, let's not forget the microwave. I use that to warm up coffee," James paused. "Well, I used to, but this baby here will shoot out a perfect cup whenever I want, so maybe I'll swap that out for a Skybar." He shrugged. "We'll see. C'mon over, check this out."

"How about you check your privilege," Kellan said grinning. He noted the slightly crazed look in his friend's eyes. "Exactly how much coffee have you had this thing make for you?"

"Don't know—now shh, ok, so this," James waved in front of the appliance like a model on Price is Right, "is the Cafe Pristo CS24/S. It makes long or short coffees, espresso, cappuccino, late, or macchiato in seconds. It'll steam or froth milk for," James paused thinking, "for chai latte or even a kid's hot chocolate."

"James, you don't have any kids; you barely have a girlfriend, but I get it, the Cafe Pristo goes to Eleven."

The coffee station had been hissing and spitting during this exchange, but went quiet. James reached in to remove a cup. He took a sip, rolled his eyes, and handed it to Kellan.

"What? I don't want coffee. I want beer."

"Drink it, seriously. It's good."

Kellan took the cup and sighed. "If I drink it, can we leave?"

"Sure, sure. But," James raised a finger, "you need to drink all of it; can't be wasting good coffee."

Kellan growled softly, reached inward, channeled the smallest trickle of power, and felt the coffee cup cool dramatically, even as James' discarded cup began to boil slightly. "Fine, bottoms up," Kellan said and threw back the entire cup of, now, lukewarm coffee in a single gulp.

James' eyes widened in alarm. "Holy shit! You idiot—are you ok?"

Kellan simply smiled and put down the empty cup. "I'm fine. It was delicious, as only the French could make. Now let's go."

James looked dubious. "Maybe there's something wrong with the machine; maybe it's not coming out hot enough. Let me make another—"

"Dude. Stop. I already called Uber from the elevator; they are going to be here any second. Beer. Now."

James held up his hands in acquiescence and gave Kellan a frustrated nod towards the door, "Fine…go."

"Hi guys, I'm Seth. Where we off to tonight?" asked the Uber driver as Kellan closed the door to the Ford Fusion to find James glaring at him.

"We're heading to the Dark Horse Tavern—know where that is?" asked Kellan

"Nope, but I can find anything—no problem."

"It's in Virginia Highlands. 816 North Highland, if you know that part of town."

"Yeah, I know that area," said Seth, chuckling softly.

"What's funny?" asked James in a flat tone that earned him a punch in the leg from Kellan.

"Oh, nothing much, just the first time I was asked to go there, I thought it was going to be all Scottish. You know like little Italy is or Chinatown in New York. Either of you guys ever been to the real Highlands?"

"Yeah," responded Kellan, smiling to himself.

"What?" said James, "When were you in the Scottish Highlands?"

Kellan waved him off, "It was a long long time ago," then in a softer voice, "What is your problem? Why are you giving this guy attitude."

James leaned in. "When you said you got us an Uber, I assumed you meant a black car, or at least an UberSelect. This..." he rubbed his hand along the cloth seats, "this is just subpar, dude."

"Oh my God! You are so pretentious. I don't even know how you stand being around yourself. Ok, you get us home then."

"I will, and it will be in style mon frer."

"Oooo, French. Did your coffee maker teach you that?"

James made a cranking motion with his right hand, and slowly extended the middle finger of his left.

"So, you guys probably know the answer to this," began Seth, "Why do they call that area 'The Highlands,' since it has nothing to do with Scotland?"

"It's just the streets, Seth," answered Kellan, "There are two local roads that intersect there, one is called Virginia Avenue and the other is Highlands Avenue so, over time, the area around where those two meet has just been called Virgina-Highlands"

"Or 'VaHi'," offered James.

"No, Seth, don't listen to my friend. Only pretentious dorks call it VaHi."

"Noted," said Seth, and the three settled in to a comfortable silence while James used the time to show off several more pictures of his Zoey Deshcenal clone—then decided to text her for the remainder of their short drive to the bar.

"Thanks, Seth, have a great night," said Kellan after providing his 5 star review and closing out the app.

"You too. If you need a ride back home later hit me up and I'll come if I'm able."

Kellan waved amiably as the Fusion pulled back into traffic, even as he heard James say something about never getting in another Ford.

The Dark Horse was positioned right at the corner of Greenwood and North Highland Avenues. It was faced with classic red brick, sporting its name in large tavern font along with its iconic logo of a black horse being ridden by jockey number eight.

As the two walked into the dimly lit bar, James suddenly sprinted ahead, running along the length of the old double sided wooden bar, stopping at the end and shouldering his way into a seat that had just been vacated while propping his foot up on the neighboring stool.

"What luck is this?" he said as Kellan walked up beside him and took the second seat. "This is my favorite spot in the whole bar. I can see everyone who comes in the front door and the entire other side of the bar. This is absolutely the best seat in the house."

Kellan just shook his head as a young woman with short cropped hair streaked with blue and several piercings walked over, set down two coasters, and smiled his way, "Hi, I'm Kaylee, What'll ya have, boys?"

"You have any Innis & Gunn on draft?" asked Kellan

"Yep, we have the Scottish Ale and Regular on draft."

"Awesome. Is it a 16 oz pour?"

She frowned. "Sorry, it's a 10, but I could make it a pint. Would be extra though."

"Perfect," exclaimed Kellan, slapping the bar, "Please, make it a pint and price is no object. My handsome, if intellectually limited, friend here is paying."

"That true?" asked Kaylee turning to James.

"Which part?"

She laughed. "How about each part."

"Yes, I'm paying because I make a fortune compared to this guy. No, I'm not intellectually limited. And, as for being handsome," James spread out his hands, "Look at me. What do you think?"

Kaylee laughed again, "I think you are just the guy my mom warned me about, so what do you want besides my number—which you aren't going to get."

James feigned a frown then said, "I'd like a dirty martini—up with olives, super cold, and dry. I'm talking desert dry. Like, I want you to stare at a portrait of the inventor of vermouth and just whisper his name over the glass kinda dry."

"OooKayy, Vodka?"

"Kaylee, now you are just trying to hurt me. No. Gin—Tanqueray number Ten please."

She raised her eyebrows. "And what did you say you did for money?"

"I'm a partner in IBM's consulting practice. You rethinking my getting that number?"

"Not. at. all."

"That's good," interjected Kellan, "James here has a girlfriend who works with killer pathogens, so he needs to behave."

Kaylee gave Kellan a wink, left, and returned a few minutes later with their drinks.

"L'chaim," said Kellan

"Na Zdorovie," said James. They clinked their glasses then both took long pulls.

Many more drinks followed and the two friends relaxed, sharing stories both old and new. Kellan told his friend about "a book" he had recently read dealing with Angels, Demons, and Time traveling. James couldn't have been less interested, merely making a derogatory "nerd" comment before declaring that he had to piss like a racehorse—at which point he stumbled towards the back of the bar.

Kellan laughed as he watched his friend slowly weave his way towards the line for the men's room, when someone bumped his chair.

"Hey, sorry," Kellan began to the stranger, "My buddy just went to the restroom; he'll be right back."

The man didn't move but simply showed his teeth in a manner that Kellan found vaguely disconcerting. He was older than Kellan, maybe in his later forties or early fifties, had close cropped black hair and a Van Dyke beard. He wore an immaculately tailored navy blue suit that almost seemed to shimmer when he moved and a blood red shirt with onyx inlayed gold cufflinks.

"It's Kellan, isn't it? Kellan Thorne?" asked the man with an accent that Kellan couldn't quite place, but with precise, clipped diction.

"Uh, yeah, and you are?"

The man reached out to touch Kellan's hand even as the young Sentinel noticed the world around him slow. As their hands touched, Kellan felt heat come to his eyes unbidden and saw them flare to life in several of his reflections from nearby mirrors. He whipped his gaze back to the man beside him whose own eyes now glowed with a blazing red light even, as his smile remained."

"Allow me to introduce myself," and Kellan suddenly had The Rolling Stone's "Sympathy for the Devil," running through his head as the man continued, "My name—is Maurius."

Kellan stood staring out at the beautiful, but barren, landscape as Maurius continued, "I'm curious, why did you think I could not come to this place?"

Kellan turned to look at the man who Micah and Raphael had warned would seek his destruction even as Lamia's whispered words again ran across his mind, but which the young Sentinel kept well concealed. Instead, he simply smiled broadly, "Just another bad assumption, I suppose." He laughed in self-deprecation. Long before Kellan had taken up the mantel of a Sentinel, he had mastered the art of appearing smaller, less impressive, and even a bit middling. While it began as a blunt instrument used by his younger self as a means to fit in and dim the light of his eidetic mind, he later had refined it to razor sharpness. He could don his cloak of unexceptionalism with such accuracy as to ensure those with whom he interacted found him neither dull nor impressive. Now, as he let his chuckle subside, Kellan added just a dusting of confusion to ensure he maximized the desired effect and was rewarded by a familiar look on Maurius' face. It said simply, "This man is no threat. He is not my equal. What I want from him, I can have."

Maurius flashed his own smile, but Kellan noted how it did not touch his eyes. He dismissed it for the deception it was. "Oh, Kellan, I had so many of those bad assumptions, you have no idea. But tell me, why did you assume I couldn't come to the workroom?"

"Well..." Kellan drew out the word and then lied with all the conviction of a seasoned politician, "I assumed you had your own. You know the whole Lucifer - God thing. Order and Chaos. I figured it would be like matter and antimatter us both being here. So, you and Asmodeus can portal your way here whenever you like as well?"

Maurius barked an ingenuous laugh. "Of course we can, why wouldn't we be able to?"

Kellan gave his best sheepish look and shrugged while his mind captured micro changes in Maurius' facial expression, body positioning, and voice inflection. *He's lying. You see that don't you?*

Of course, I see that. Do you think I'm an idiot?

I am you and you are arguing with yourself.

Kellan frowned inwardly at his internal monologue. *Shut up—this is serious.*

You shut up—you realize this confirms what Lamia said about Asmodeus?

Kellan was about to answer himself when Maurius said, "Kellan? Are you alright? You have an odd look on your face?"

"Huh? Oh yeah, I'm fine just zoned out there for a sec; I do that sometimes when I forget my medicine." Kellan shrugged his shoulders and turned his hands, palms up, "Silly me—"

"Oh, that's fine. Don't give it a second thought. Why don't you sit?" asked Maurius, as he leaned back into the stone throne and gestured with a foot toward the bench nearby.

Kellan sat, rubbing his hand absently along the cool stone as Maurius continued to take his measure. "So, Kellan, what do you know of this place and, more broadly, what did Micah share with you about the dual nature of our roles?"

He told me you were hand picked by Satan's second in command to sow discord and chaos while Micah lived, and to do everything in your power to snuff me out before I knew what the fuck I was doing. Oh and thanks for the skin-walkers, asshole! Kellan dug his fingers at the stone until sharp pain radiated up his hand, silencing his internal monologue. He looked over to Maurius, "I know it's called the workroom and that we can do some pretty amazing things here. I know that Lucifer and God once met in this spot even as you and I are now meeting. As for Micah, we really didn't have much time together. He brought me here to teach me, but after only a few hours we went back to," Kellan raised his fingers making air quotes, "'the real world', because Micah said something was amiss there."

"Really?" said Maurius, "and what was amiss?"

Kellan shrugged. "Nothing that I could tell, but as soon as we got back, Micah slumped to the floor. He died, Maurius, and then Raphael took his body away."

Maurius looked crestfallen. "Yes, I felt when that happened, but had assumed you two were together for far longer than that. Micah always took too many pains to do what was right for others rather than himself. He should have stayed here until you two were finished rather than concerning himself with what might have been amiss. Still, I'm sure there was some time for you to get the basics." Maurius looked at Kellan pointedly with suspicion tugging at his eyes and mouth.

Danger...Danger, Will Robinson.

"Sure, there was time for more than just the basics. The first thing he told me was not to trust you, Maurius." The response to Kellan's words were immediate and exactly as he had hoped.

Maurius looked shocked, leaned forward, and pressed his hands to his chest in such a flagrant display that, for a moment, Kellan actually thought he was supposed to disbelieve the clearly feigned surprise and distress portrayed.

No, no, he thinks he's an amazing actor rather than an arrogant prick; and, he thinks you are a completely incompetent idiot; good job.

"Kellan," Maurius began, "I don't expect you to believe me, but please hear me out. My relationship with Micah was," he paused, "complicated, as any relationships would be given the circumstances around how we met and the length of time we knew each other. It's true that Raphael and Asmodeus chose us for our respective roles and it's equally true that those two Angels are pretty much bitter enemies, but that didn't mean Micah and I needed to be. More importantly, it doesn't mean you and I need to be. After all, we are both independent of God and Lucifer, right?"

Kellan looked at him blankly.

Maurius sighed like a patient parent and continued, "You were told that we each have a role to play, that I am tasked with Chaos while you are now responsible for ensuring Order. Of course, that just sounds ridiculous doesn't it? I mean, after all, what is Chaos? It's not as if I go around encouraging wanton violence and destruction, nor do I have to. You and I, Kellan, are more free to do as we wish than any other living creature. While those who gave us these abilities want us to behave a certain way, we are free to completely ignore their wishes without any consequence to us whatsoever."

"Really?" asked Kellan, his voice rising in surprise, "That's not the way Micah presented it. He said it was my responsibility to oppose you."

Maurius waved his hand, dismissing the notion, rose, and walked over to sit next to Kellan. "Micah was wrong in this, and I'm sorry for having threatened your friend in the bar. But needed you to come here. I needed you to give me the chance to explain myself. I'm not the villain of our story, Kellan. In fact, I'm more the hero. We both are. You just don't know it yet and I am here to try and help you understand. Promise me, Kellan. Promise me that you will at least give me the opportunity to state my case. You are obviously a strong and intelligent man; I can see that. It would be pointless for me to try and lie to you. You would see straight through any lie I could possibly weave."

He's piling it on a bit thick, don't you think?

Kellan looked at Maurius and said, "I am pretty good at picking out lies, but I also like to make my own decisions. So, yes, Maurius, I forgive you for how we got here and promise to listen to what you have to say."

Maurius smiled broadly and clapped Kellan on the shoulder. "Good. Good. I think Micah may have finally done something right in having you succeed him. I suppose even a blind squirrel finds a nut once in a while, eh?"

Oh, fuck you asshole!

"Ha! I love that saying and you sure are right about Micah. He wasn't around when these monsters came after me and then he went off and died without teaching me hardly anything. Say, Maurius, did you have monsters after you before you became a Sentinel?"

Maurius leaned in conspiratorially. "I did. They are called Skin-walkers, and they try to destroy every newly selected Sentinel before they can accept the power. In fact, they are the true sowers of discord. I couldn't hope to match them even if I wished to—which I don't."

"That's good. Micah said you sent them after me."

"I swear that is not the case," Maurius said, his eyes locking with Kellan's. "You believe me don't you?"

Fuck no—

"I do," said Kellan.

"Good," said Maurius, visibly relaxing.

"But," began Kellan, "Why would Micah lie to me?"

"Oh, I wouldn't say he was lying. He probably believed it, but he would also never have accepted the truth of our power—the truth I'm sharing with you now. No, Micah always believed what Raphael told him while I never believed either Raphael or Asmodeus. They are both liars and want to keep us in ignorance. We are the true powers, Kellan. You and me. Combined, our strength is that of God Himself and those Angels fear that more than anything else."

Holy shit! Did you see that? Kellan flinched imperceptibly as his inner dialogue took an unexpected turn. *He wasn't lying just then.*

"What do you mean? The truth about our powers?" Kellan asked.

Maurius got up and started pacing, clearly excited while Kellan tried to control his breathing. The abrupt change in their conversation left him extremely unsettled. He thought he understood this game and now the rules had clearly changed.

"The power within us is a fragment of the power of creation. You hold the power of Order and I the power of Chaos. With either half we can affect many aspects of creation. I, of course, can affect it greatly because I am so much stronger and more skilled than you. But, in time, you could learn to do some of the things I am able to do, if I showed you. Which, I assume you would want me to do?"

Ok, the lying asshole's back. I feel better.

"Thank you. I'd appreciate that," answered Kellan.

Maurius waved away the response. "It's nothing, happy to do it. But, as I said, separately we each can manipulate one half of creation, but neither of us can actually create. However, if we fuse the powers of Order and Chaos, then we can do far more than manipulate that which has already been created. With both aspects of creation within our control, we can become creative forces ourselves. We can become as God!"

Maurius paused, staring at Kellan and it took every scrap of the young Sentinel's will to control his external reaction.

He's completely off his rocker. We're talking a classic cartoon villain. All he needs is a handlebar mustache and a suit. No, wait, he already has the suit.

"I'm pretty sure that the real God wouldn't like that too much, Maurius, and the last time he dealt with an insurrection, it seemed to end pretty definitively. I'm equally sure that your friend, Asmodeus, wouldn't take too kindly to our ascension."

Maurius barked out a laugh. "Asmodeus and I are far from friends. I am a curiosity to him and a means of advancing his goals. A talking, hairless ape for his amusement." He paused. "Just as you are to Raphael."

"I certainly don't know Raphael well, but he and Micah seemed close."

Maurius waved a hand dismissively, "Illusion only. Trust me, Kellan, the entire war in Heaven started because of humans and no Angel will ever forget that let alone, forgive it. No, we alone stand apart from both humanity and the Angels. We two, Kellan, have the unique ability to wrest from God and His Angels, both fallen and in heaven, control of creation and our destinies."

Kellan shook his head and saw Maurius become tense with anxiety. "I just don't see how this is possible or even why we would want it to be so. I feel quite unprepared for the Sentinel's mantel I'm just now wearing. I have no interest in adding God-like responsibilities to my plate."

Maurius visibly relaxed and his cheshire grin returned, "Ahh, my young Sentinel, that is where I can help. I have spent nearly a millennia thinking this through so it is more than understandable why you would have doubts. If you will indulge me in just a few more moments, I think I can allay your concerns on both counts."

Kellan brightened. "You have a plan, then?"

"Of course. May I?"

"Yes, please."

No fucking way! He's totally going to monologue This dude really needs a 'Villains for Dummies" book. Don't smile. You almost smiled. Look interested and earnest, while slightly stupid and vacant. Perfect!

Maurius again took to his feet and walked silently to the edge of the precipice, looking for long moments into the distance. "Let me start with the easier of your two concerns. You won't have to worry too much about any specific responsibilities." Kellan purposely furrowed his brow slightly and opened his mouth, but Maurius held up both hands, "Not at first that is. Overtime, of course, you would need to become as comfortable with our new roles as I would be at the start. After all, the power can only work if combined so obviously its use should likewise be shared. I only bring this up so you can be at peace, not having to worry about too much, too soon."

"Very considerate," Kellan answered with an award winning amount of sincerity.

Maurius bowed slightly, "Think nothing of it. We are brothers of a sort are we not? Now, with that concern set aside for the moment, allow me to turn to the actual dilemma we face. The how's and why's of it all. Creation begins, endures, and ends all based on the combination of opposing forces. The asian philosophers really had a great deal right with their concept of Yin and Yang, or, for us, Order and Chaos."

"As I mentioned, all things begin, endure for a time, and then end at which point something else begins. Throughout that continuum there is always an aspect of both Order and Chaos. While it is not always true, generally speaking, there is more Order at the beginning of a creative act and more Chaos at the end. During time in-between, the two forces battle for dominance while keeping some semblance of balance."

"Like us," interrupted Kellan.

"Hmmm, oh, yes. Like us. We were set on paths where I command the power of Chaos and Micah, now you, control the power of Order. Although, I hope by now you no longer believe we must be adversaries or battle against one another except, perhaps, in the metaphorical sense." Maurius smiled. Kellan was quite sure that sharks looked less threatening.

"No, of course not. To be honest, I never liked the thought of having an eternal adversary. It all seemed very old-school biblical to me."

"Just-so, Kellan. Just so! I'm impressed at how quickly you take to these complexities. Micah never could grasp them. Now where was I?"

"Yin and Yang."

"Ah yes. Yin and Yang. Now, perhaps the easiest way to perceive all of creation is as if it rested on a massive wheel, like a mill wheel. How does that wheel turn? What force propels it?" Maurius paused and stared at Kellan pointedly.

"Oh. The force of Order."

"And?" asked Maurius.

"And Chaos."

"Exactly. Order may push on one side of the wheel, but a moment later Chaos pulls on the other side. As those two opposing forces work in unison, the wheel turns and, as the wheel turns, so continues creation."

Doctor Evil just described the plot to "Wheel of Time". Kellan bit down on the inside of his cheek to maintain his serious composure despite his continued inner conversation.

"Now, just as one hand cannot clap neither can one half of the power turn the wheel. This is why we cannot create, but only influence that which has already been created."

"So you are just suggesting that we work together rather than against each other. That sounds good and all but—"

"No, no," interrupted Maurius, "I am suggesting nothing of the sort. I am suggesting we fuse our powers together once and for all. We cease representing an aspect of creation and represent it as a whole. Let me explain. You have, no doubt, experienced the lake of power within you?"

"Lake?"

Maurius cocked his head. "Yes, you must have seen it or, at least felt it. A massive lava lake roiling with power from which you can draw. While the size of my lake, I'm sure, dwarfs yours as does my ability to draw from it, the principle should be the same. It might appear somewhat differently to you, perhaps green?"

Kellan made his face light up as if in sudden recognition. "Oh, yes, the green *lake* of energy. The color and size confused me. Mine is, indeed, green like liquid emerald, but quite different in size as you suspected. More like a small pond. Is the size significant?"

"Not at all," Maurius lied, "Remember, we are the epitome of balance, you and I. My red source may be larger than your green one, but our strength will be comparable. Were it not so, then one of us could prove a grave danger to the other, and that cannot be."

Oh, that can most certainly be.

"Of course not," said Kellan, "Thank you again for clearing that up, but, forgive me, I still do not understand how, apart from cooperation, we can affect one another."

Maurius walked back over to Kellan and rested his hand warmly on his should while looking down. "Nothing at all to forgive, my friend. The answer is simple in explanation, but somewhat difficult in practice. We simply must fuse our energy together and then each draw from the combined violet source."

"Violet?"

"Yes, the color of creation as it turns out." Maurius' eyes suddenly blazed to life, glowing a brilliant red. Kellan started in surprise, almost snapping a shield in place out of instinct. With no small amount of effort he allowed the alarm to play across his face but otherwise made no other reaction.

Maurius laughed but raised both hands in a placating gesture. "Peace, Kellan, I don't mean you any harm. I'm just trying to demonstrate. Now you. Draw on your power so I can illustrate."

Kellan silently applauded his masterful demonstration of ineptitude. He furrowed his brow. Nothing. He channeled enough power to cause a slight glow about his eyes, then released it. Finally, he channeled sufficient power for them to glow brightly but then released and took up the power in rapid succession to create an almost sparking effect. This latter demonstration made him the most proud because it brought on the patronizing response from Maurius.

"Perhaps if you cleared your mind a bit first. Take a breath, then grab hold of the power and force it inward. Do not be gentle. You must master it, not be mastered by it."

So he's half Doctor Evil and half Sith Lord. Kellan nodded to himself, his mind locking away the distinctly different method of channeling Chaotic energy from that of Order. Finally, feeling like he had fully demonstrated his complete lack of mastery, Kellan allowed himself to channel a steady stream of power.

"Good, now take my hand," said Maurius, but Kellan balked. "It's alright I need to show you this. Nothing will happen to you, I promise." Kellan had himself on full alert but did not want to end the charade just yet, so he cautiously reached out a hand and took hold of Maurius'.

Immediately he felt a jolt of energy, almost like an electrical shock and then pressure as Maurius pushed his power towards Kellan and into him. He could feel it entering him from his extremities and slowing making its way to his core—towards the emerald river of power.

"As our powers approach each other, you will feel resistance for they are not designed to merge. We will force them together and forge something new, but not yet. Right now, I am just trying to show you what it is and how it feels. Do you feel the pressure?"

"Yes, and it feels...wrong."

"Ignore that feeling, Kellan, it is the nature of things to resist change and these powers have been separate since the dawn of creation. There. Do you feel that? They are now close enough to act on each other." Kellan did feel it and, he had to admit, the feeling was intoxicating. Incredible power or at least the potential for it. He looked up noticing Maurius' eyes had grown a much deeper color of red. "Yes," he said, "Your eyes, too, are changing. I see the tint of purple in them now. If I were to but push hard and you not resist, they would touch and the merger might take place."

At his words Kellan immediately released his hold on the power, feeling it wink out and with it the sense of potential as well as Maurius' energy. The elder Sentinel rocked back as if slapped. He glared menacing at Kellan before regaining control of his features.

"I...I'm sorry," stuttered Kellan, "I've never been able to channel the power for very long and I lost concentration. Do you need me to be actively holding the power to try that again? If so, I might need a bit of a break to recover."

Maurius stared at Kellan intently, taking his measure as he had done several times before, then brightened. "Yes, you do. Without you actively holding the power there is no way for the two forces to meet. Certainly, you can rest. I can remember how tiring it was to gain control of our abilities."

"Thank you. It shouldn't take me too long, but I wonder…"

Maurius had retreated back to the stone throne and settled in it as he looked back again, wary. "Wondered about what?"

"Haven't you tried this with Micah? Surely he was far more adept than I?"

Maurius shifted his weight and threw one leg over the massive stone arm of the throne in what Kellan identified as an overcompensating gesture of relaxed unconcern. "We dabbled once or twice, but Micah had little interest in such things. He was very much a, what is the term I've heard used from your time? A Boy Scout. Yes, that's it. Micah was far too much the Boy Scout to have pursued this with much vigor. As you say, it certainly wouldn't endear us to either Angel or God."

"Speaking of that," began Kellan, "you never really answered me on that score. How do you think the real God will react to us if we're successful. He seems pretty emphatic about that whole 'no God before me,' thing. After all, it did make #1 of his top 10 list of things not to do."

"He will learn to adapt, Kellan, or we will make him learn. You fail to appreciate the amount of power to which I've referred. Once I posses the power of creation, He will need to deal with me as an equal. With only the power we now posses, we can be killed just as any other mortal, but with the full power of creation, we become one with it and thus only affected by similar unified power. If God chooses to get nasty, we can fight, but I've been fighting much more and much harder than He has of late. With us both wielding the full might of creation, He will find himself quickly on the losing end of utter destruction. I wonder sometimes what it will feel like to kill a God."

And that's the end game folks…smoke 'em if you got 'em. Kellan inhaled deeply, trying to calm his nerves at the revelation of his inner mind but outwardly, Kellan simply said, "We…"

"We? We what?" asked Maurius.

"You said once *you* possessed the full power of creation, God would have to deal with *you* as an equal. I assume you meant *we*. As in, once *we* possess the full power of creation."

Maurius shifted uneasily and showed his teeth. "Semantics. When I said "I," I was referring to us collectively, of course. As Sentinels."

"Of course," replied Kellan, "but indulge me a moment. How exactly will we share this power?"

"Don't worry yourself about it. There are complexities of balance and interchange that make it all very difficult to understand. Suffice it to say that once merged, we will both have access to the fused power and all its aspects."

"If you say so, but I have to tell you, without understanding the process more than I do, there is a very real chance I won't be able to channel the power very long at all. You see, my ability to channel it is directly related to how fully I understand the underlying cause and effect associated with what I'm trying to achieve."

Maurius straightened up and leaned forward. "I don't understand what you mean. Explain."

"Sure, as an example, one of the more impressive things I can do is start a cook fire. Well, I can almost always start one. Regardless, the reason for me being so successful with this use of the power is because I fully understand what I am trying to accomplish, how it should be accomplished, and why. This understanding allows me to channel the power much more effectively than I am able to do otherwise."

Maurius narrowed his eyes and shook his head slightly. "That doesn't make sense. I don't see why it would matter."

Kellan just shrugged his shoulders and spread his hands looking every inch the bewildered acolyte.

"Very well, let me try to put it in the simplest terms possible," began Maurius.

Kellen gave him a long blink as his inner thoughts raged about screaming. *Because I am an idiot who has no idea of your evil plan.*

Maurius continued. "As you felt before, there will be a sense of pressure as the two powers converge on each other. Eventually, that pressure will build to a breaking point where the two contrasting forces are juxtaposed with one another and only the slimmest barriers between them. It is at this point that you must will that the Chaotic power I possess be allowed past that barrier. In doing so, the barrier will drop and I will draw the power of Order into myself where they will fuse together into the violet power of Creation."

"So, all I need to do is drop the barrier that prevents your power from reaching mine?"

"Yes."

"Then you will be able to draw my power into yourself."

"Yes. Now you have it."

"I believe I do," said Kellan with his most innocent smile, "but, then where does that leave me once you have siphoned all of my power?"

"Hmm, what? Well, then we would just repeat the process and I would infuse you with one half the power, of course."

Kellan rose, stretching, "Ahh, I see. Yes that makes sense, but I have a bit of a wrinkle we could try."

"A wrinkle?" asked Maurius, looking wary and also rising.

"Sure. No big deal really. How about we do just as you suggest, but instead of me lowering the barrier, you do that part, and I'll draw your power into me?" Kellan grinned. "I like that approach a lot more."

Maurius closed the distance between them, his demeanor shifting dramatically. Kellan immediately saw the predator Micah had warned him about so many times. Still, the young Sentinel showed no outward alarm, even as he began to draw just enough power to heighten his senses, reflexes, and manifest the armor beneath his clothes, all unbeknownst to Maurius. "It won't work that way," said Maurius through slightly gritted teeth.

"Really? Why not?"

Maurius let out an exasperated breath. "I have neither the interest or time to explain everything to you. Suffice it to say that you do not have the control to manage such a delicate process. Now, are you rested enough to begin?"

"Yep, quite rested."

"Good. Then grasp—"

"But," interrupted Kellan, "I don't think now is a good time to try this. I think I'd like to learn a bit more about exactly what you are trying to do and what it would mean to me. Perhaps we should meet back here another day. Maybe Halloween? We could decorate and carve pumpkins."

Maurius stood dumbstruck for a moment and then the mask of geniality broke as he sneered at Kellan, eyes blazing red.

"You insufferable Idiot!"

Here we go. Kellan tensed as his inner warning bells all went off simultaneously.

"You have no idea with whom you are dealing. I am going to give you one more chance. Grasp my hand now and do as your told"

"Or?" asked Kellan.

"Or," continued Maurius, "I will use an alternative method to extract your power from you and that method will leave you dead rather than my partner in wielding the energy of creation."

Kellan casually wandered a few feet away while keeping watch on Maurius from the corner of his eye. "You know, color me cynical, but I just have a hard time believing you will ever share that creative power with me once you have it. I think it's much more likely you will vaporize me and then try to kick God's ass. But hey, that's me. What do I know?"

"You know, nothing—"

Jon Snow. Kellan winced at his own internal comment, biting his cheek to regain his concentration.

Maurius raised his voice. "Do you even know what this place is? Do you know what I can accomplish here? Power cannot be created or destroyed, Kellan. Did your would be trainer, Micah, ever tell you that? What do you think happens to the power of a Sentinel if the vessel in which that power resides is destroyed?"

"No idea, but I bet you are about to tell me."

"It seeks out another vessel!" yelled Maurius. "Do you see any other vessels around her here? Well? Do you? No, you do not, because only you and I are able to come here. So when I kill you, your power will seek its vessel and finding none available, I will claim it for myself."

Kellan smiled, trying to appear nonplussed. "Is this the part where you start to laugh maniacally at your master plan? I'm pretty sure it is."

Maurius started to visibly shake in anger, clenching his fists as his eyes glowed even brighter. "No, this is where Micah's lack of preparation and utter failure as a Sentinel reaches its final ignominious conclusion. Perhaps you should have had more than a few hours training."

Kellan saw the geyser of flame begin to erupt from the ground as if it were in stop motion, having already created a time bubble around himself as he leaped toward the throne while simultaneously snapping a shield around himself and summoning electrically charged clouds to form above them. A moment later the flames subsided and, to Maurius' eyes, Kellan had simply been consumed by the white hot flames, having moved too quickly within the time bent bubble to have been tracked. Too late, the elder Sentinel felt the hairs on the back of his neck rise up and turned to see Kellan standing behind the throne, eyes ablaze with glowing green runes running down both arms as they gestured in his direction.

Lightning streaked down burying, itself into the runes and then arcing out again through both outstretched hands. Maurius had only partially formed his shield when both bolts struck him square in the chest, hurling him into the air to land hard against the stone bench, smoke rising from where the energy had burned away his shirt and blistered the skin.

"How?" Maurius gasped, regaining his feet.

"Guess I had a bit more training than I let on, asshole," yelled Kellan as he willed plasma fire to ignite the air all around Maurius' body, engulfing him in a white hot conflagration.

It faded. Maurius stood unharmed and stepped deliberatively beyond the circle of scorched and slightly molten stone his shield rippling in a red aura against the wisps of smoke that brushed against it. Kellan looked inward to find a third of his power had been expended in this initial exchange and reminded himself that he was the novice here. Maurius' plan for obtaining the young Sentinel's power if killed certainly had the ring of truth to it. Not that he wanted to die under any circumstances, but under these circumstances, he really wanted to avoid it.

Kellan saw Maurius' eyes look past him and turned in time to see a barrage of stones hurtling towards him. Kellan fell to one knee, grunting with the exertion of channeling energy to his shield even as he angled it to cause some of the stones to skitter off rather than strike with their full force. "Telekinesis," Kellan thought, "I really need to learn that." But didn't have time to consider it further as Maurius strode toward him, a massive sword coalescing in his hand. Kellan raised his hand defensively as he felt the sword breach his shield and continue down until it struck with a shower of sparks, vibrating against his own which had materialized moments before the metal would have cleaved him in two. Slowly, Kellan rose, willing power into his legs as the two men glared at each other across their blades.

"I will kill you, Kellan Thorne!"

"Yeah, well, get in line, Red Ranger." Kellan felt Maurius' anger grow and could see him gathering energy in preparation of another strike. Kellan's sword vanished even as he pivoted to the left causing Maurius to stumble forward as the young Sentinel brought up his gleaming replica of Sting, glowing bright blue as he made to draw it across Maurius' neck. Off balance from his pivot, Kellan's blade missed its mark, leaving instead a deep gash along Maurius' cheek.

The elder Sentinel whirled on Kellan, raising his hand to his face and feeling the hot blood as it ran freely from the wound. He stared at Kellan in disbelief.

"Don't worry, chicks dig scars. By the way, I assume this whole kill the Sentinel in the workroom works both ways. Maybe I'll leave here a demigod instead of you?"

Maurius stood glaring at the younger man. "You have no idea the forces with which you mettle. You dare taunt me when you should be on your knees in worship? I have seen millennia pass by me and will see millennia more long after you are dust. You think you are my equal? You think you can learn in weeks what I have spent lifetimes mastering?"

He has a point. Shut up. Not helping. Kellan ground his teeth, dismissing his thoughts.

Maurius looked up and thrust both hands toward the sky which darkened at the gesture even as the sky split to reveal the black of space scattered with stars and a brightly glowing moon. Kellan ground his teeth and drew deep from his waning river of power calling up an elemental barrage the strongest he had ever summoned, and hurled them all at Maurius. Fire, Ice, and Lightning all struck the elder Sentinel, causing him to stagger back but his concentration never left the sky. Kellan sent wave after wave of projectiles only to see them shatter or dissipate against Maurius' shield, some few passing through to leave bloody gashes across his chest and legs. With the last of his energy, Kellan slumped against the bench as he saw the final flurry strike the shield, collapse it, and hurl

Maurius' body against the stone throne where he gasped. He smiled as blood dripped from his mouth.

Pain lanced though Kellan's shoulder and he saw a fountain of blood and flesh arc outward, pitching him against the stone. His right arm was a ruin with a fist sized hole, smoking black with cauterized blood. He rolled over just as a burning stone struck where his head had been moments before. The moon was gone or, more accurately, lay shattered with a full third of it missing. Above him, Kellan could see fiery trails all headed in his direction.

"Oh, fuck me," groaned Kellan, "He actually summoned a meteor storm." The blazing rocks seemed to be targeting him as he scrambled backward using his feet and one good arm. He had just reconstituted his shield when another meteorite struck, passing directly through as if no shield existed. Kellan howled in pain as he saw the rock pass through his calf, shattering the bone so badly that the lower part of his leg was held together by strings of tendons alone. He looked up at Maurius, who tried to laugh, but merely coughed, showering blood across his already ruined chest.

Kellan groaned. *It's going to be a race to see which of us dies first,*" He looked up to find a massive fire trail heading down directly to him. *No hiding from that one.* The young Sentinel frantically sought for some means of escape.

Kellan reached deep into himself and drained the last of the power leaving the riverbank dry and empty. He arched his back and pushed with all his remaining energy as he caused a gravity bubble to manifest around himself. The force of the push, hurled Kellan into the air and hundreds of feet in the opposite direction. He watched as the meteorite struck, leaving a long crack along the entire precipice and saw Maurius reach up a hand in his direction, even as the gravity bubble faded and Kellan began to fall.

The top of the precipice passed by in a blur and Kellan turned into the practiced stance he had learned many years ago when he agreed to skydive on a dare. He felt the air grip him and he stabilized. He reached inward seeking his power.

Nothing.

"No big deal," Kellan told himself, "This is the workroom. I can just keep falling here forever until my power regenerates. I'll just relax and—"

Kellan whipped his body to the side, barely avoiding a jagged outcropping that had appeared moments before. Maurius was changing the landscape from above. Kellan looked around and saw similar outcropping sprouting up at random. They appeared above, below, and to either side. Clearly the elder Sentinel did not know exactly where Kellan was, but sought to create enough obstacles to eventually crush him against one. Kellan knew it was just a matter of time until his luck ran out.

He closed his eyes and, again, reached inward. A tiny trickle had returned to the riverbed and Kellan greedily drew it in. He formed the power into what he needed most and opened his eyes to find a solid mass of earth rushing up to meet him.

Kellan screamed and threw up his hands as a shimmering portal rotated into view.

Kellan hit the bed hard. So hard in fact that the entire platform cracked, leaving him lying bloody on the foam mattress barely conscious. He opened one eye just to confirm he was, in fact, at his house and not dead. Both appeared to be true as Kellan cried out in pain, rolling over on his back

A detached and clinical part of his mind took stock of his injuries and current condition. That part of him decided he really should be dead from these injuries and was likely to go into shock at any minute. Kellan tried to slow his breathing and remain calm as he reached inward to find Nurisha standing with her back to him—ankle deep in the flowing emerald power. He sighed with relief as the pain of his corporeal self receded to memory.

"Nurisha?"

She turned and smiled. "You nearly killed us."

"Us? What happened to power not being created or destroyed?"

"Oh, my power would remain, but what makes me, me, would die with you. I like being me. Would you be more careful?"

Kellan felt ashamed. "Yeah, I really went off half cocked. Ended up bringing a knife to a gun fight and nearly broke the universe. Pretty stupid."

"Yes, pretty stupid," Nurisha agreed.

"Thanks for the support."

She smiled. "You are quite welcome. Look, Kellan, your vessel has grown again." She gestured to the distant riverbank. "Your capacity to hold and channel my power has increased by 20%. Being stupid does have some advantages."

Kellan felt himself smile. "Nurisha, did you just make a joke?"

She cocked her head, "Did I?" She smiled back at him. "I guess I did. That is delightful."

Kellan sobered. "The 20% you mentioned. Is that good?"

"It seems good."

"What I mean is, how does that compare to Maurius? How much can he hold and channel."

"I do not know, but I suspect much more. Even in the workroom, breaking apart celestial objects with the mass of a moon and then directing those fragments, while simultaneously managing a shield against a sustained barrage would require a substantial energy reserve."

Kellan sighed. "I really am an idiot."

"You are young and impulsive; that is not the same thing."

"Thanks, but right now my body is back there a bloody mess and I need to heal it. Any ideas on that front?"

"Yes, of course. Just hold me within you but do not channel and do not hold so much as to burn yourself out. Draw as much as you can comfortably hold without giving it form. The power will release itself into your body and seek to bring it back to the state it was in when you first accepted it. That is your body's natural state so the power will try to restore it. As the energy is expended, simply draw more to replenish it. Do not worry about how much you use for it will regenerate faster than you could possibly use for simple healing. Look, it already is nearly halfway up the banks now. Your advancement is quite impressive, Kellan. Micah took centuries to develop as much power as you can hold now."

Kellan sighed. "I'm sure that's because he wasn't as stupid and impulsive as I am."

Nurisha cocked her head again, "Yes, you are probably right about that."

"Wonderful, well, I'm going to go back to my broken body and scream in pain now."

Nurisha nodded and waved as the scene dissolved.

Kellan did, indeed, scream in pain as it stuck him like a thousand hot brands being driven into every point on his body. He drew in as much power as he dared and held it without form. Within moments he could feel it stretching throughout his body and the pain lessoned. He watched in awe as the ruined muscle and bone in his leg knitted together, followed by his shoulder. Kellan seemed to float halfway between sleep and consciousness as the power waxed and waned within him, healing the worst of his wounds. Finally, he had healed to the point where pain no longer provided enough to distract him from sleep and closed his eyes.

⌒⌒⌒

Kellan groaned and opened his eyes. It was dark, with only the odd electrical device to lighten the gloom. "Hey Siri, what time is it?" he croaked, mouth feeling dry.

Nothing. Kellan cleared his throat and tried again. "Hey Siri. Oh crap," he groaned as realization dawned, "that bastard meteored my bloody iPhone. Now I'm really pissed. Trying to kill me I can understand, but a man's phone should be off limits."

He swung his feet off the bed and grimaced as they touched the cool wood, then pushed himself up as a wave of pain and nausea washed over him. Clearly, he was far from healed, but as he padded around in a tight circle while windmilling his formerly broken arm, Kellan didn't feel the slightest need to complain. He found himself staring absently at his Kingsized foam bed that lay crumpled at an odd angle, the frame cracked in numerous places.

"That's going to be difficult to explain to USAA," he said to the empty room, then turned, slowly making his way into the bathroom and clicked on the light. Kellan sighed deeply as he took in the reflection. His face was bruised around both cheeks and his right eye was ringed in black with blood visible around the iris. He stripped off the bloody and torn clothes, dropped them in a pile, and whistled softly as he slowly turned in a circle. Like with his face, Kellan found himself covered with numerous bruises in varying stages of healing, but no actually open wounds. Apparently, his heightened healing abilities had their limits or perhaps he needed to actively help them along beyond a certain point. Kellan didn't know and didn't much care, as he spun up the shower and stepped inside once steam had begun to billow.

He stayed under the hot spray until the water began to cool, then reluctantly turned off the shower and gingerly made his way across the room to pull fresh clothes from the closet. After donning fresh boxers and jeans, Kellan flipped through a number of t-shirts, seeking inspiration.

"Don't Blink...Blink and You're Dead." *No, too close to home.*

"I'm a high functioning sociopath." *No, probably not even appropriate to ever wear again.*

"What the Frak?" Kellan set this one aside as having definite possibilities given his current mood, but as he pulled out the next shirt a smile broke across his face and he chuckled.

"Now, that's perfect," Kellan said as he slipped it on, but felt his smile vanish when he remembered that he'd left his car at James' condo. Kellan walked out of the bedroom and across the hall into the second room which served as his home office. A large corner desk took up much of the space with old wooden bookshelves lining each wall. The smell of leather filled his nose and, actually, seemed to make him feel a bit better. The desk was covered with several large pieces of matching, tobacco colored, full-grain leather—each stamped with cursive script which read, "Saddleback." Kellan ran his fingers across the leather, touching the brass rivets that reinforced each corner and snickered to himself as Saddleback's tagline of "They'll fight over it when you're dead" flashed across his mind.

Kellan plopped down hard onto the mesh that comprised his favorite Aeron chair and reached for the mouse. As he moved it, his iMac came to life and Kellan's eyes were immediately drawn to the red circle with the number 15 that appeared on the Messages icon. He groaned as he clicked it, expecting a torrent of profanity from James. He definitely got that, in spades, but also found the messages slowly devolve into a much more fearful tone and then saw an entirely different thread from Juliet, Meghan, and finally a thread from them both, combined.

Kellan glanced down at the calendar icon and his hand froze on the mouse. When he awoke, Kellan had assumed it was the same night he was out with James, but found himself shaking his head ruefully at the realization he had slept through an entire day and another night. Kellan quickly tapped out a series of messages to all three of his friends telling Meghan and Juliet he would head to the shop and James that he better take care of Baby, that he knew he was a douchebag, but that he had a good explanation. He shrugged, knowing there could be no good explanation. He decided to worry about that later. Instead Kellan spun his chair around, instinctively reaching for the small leather valet tray where he'd trained himself to rest keys and iPhone, then paused a moment, staring, as its emptiness seemed to mock him.

"Shit!" he exclaimed, pushing himself up with a mild grunt of pain and headed out the door.

Short minutes later Kellan turned quickly into the alley next to his shop and was reaching for the door when he was struck by an immense column of air that hurled him head over heels down the alley and against the brick wall at its far end. He had no time to properly form any protective barrier, but the partially manifested shielding he was able to erect absorbed enough of the force to prevent him from having his organs turned to jelly upon impact.

For a moment, Kellan lay pinned against the wall, then slid down as the force abated, while white hot pain flashed across his mind. He shook his head, trying to focus and saw Maurius standing at the mouth of the alley, looking none the worse for wear.

His immaculately groomed beard seemed to glow in the streetlight as if he'd just oiled it and his face bore none of the tell tale bruises that Kellan sported. More, as Maurius approached, he did so with a casual ease Kellan knew his sore muscles wouldn't allow. The finely tailored suite he'd worn to their last encounter was replaced with a long flowing black robe, intricate glyphs embroidered throughout with seemingly iridescent thread. As Kellan started to rise, he saw Maurius slip both hands into deep pockets on either side of the robe, withdrawing something and flashing both hands in Kellan's direction. Pain again blossomed as two wickedly sharp metal spikes ripped through both shoulders, slamming him back against the brick and pinning him there.

Kellan blinked away tears and forced his hands as close together as his pinned shoulders would allow, drawing deep from the river of his power. He formed a small sphere that looked for all the world like a miniature sun, then twisted both hands and hurled it towards his approaching adversary.

Maurius knelt down on one knee holding up both hands and Kellan saw the air warp and shimmer with red light just as his attack struck with the force of a small fusion reactor going critical. The elder Sentinel rocked back by the force but angled his own shielding to deflect much of the energy, even as Kellan directed bolts of electricity from four tiny cloud formations he'd manifested around Maurius. As the bolts struck, they flashed so brightly that Kellan was momentarily blinded and lowered his hands in exhaustion while squinting tightly to regain his sight. Before he could do so, two more piercing ribbons of pain radiated through his body, this time from each hand as, they too, were pinned against the wall.

Kellan cried out and tried to draw unformed power to heal himself but, while it served to sharpen his mind somewhat, a quick glance at the blood which continued to flow from all four wounds made clear what the young Sentinel already knew: he was in big trouble—again.

Maurius rose from his crouched position, hands still outstretched from his last attack, and smiled as he began to slowly walk toward Kellan. He made several gestures and the mouth of the alley became opaque, some sort of visual barrier cutting them off from potential passers by.

"I'll admit, you surprised me, Kellan. I haven't had a thrashing like that in, well, ever. Then you even managed to escape—very impressive. But, then, I've had a year or so to think about it and decided that our next encounter would need to be a bit less," he paused, glancing up at nothing then continued, "civil."

Kellan shook his head again mumbling mostly to himself, "More than a year, but—"

"—But it was just yesterday?" Maurius laughed again. "To you, it was yesterday my ignorant young friend." Then, Maurius' smile faded, his face growing hard. "I spent the last year, recovering and then making up to my benefactor,

Asmodeus for disappointing him. I assure you, that was not enjoyable. But, he's given me another opportunity which brings us to our pleasant meeting tonight." Maurius paused again, cocking his head as he watched Kellan struggling against spikes pinning him to the wall. "How do those feel? I imagine they hurt. You can't heal your way around them, if you are trying, and they will not react to any energy you direct at them. A tool from Asmodeus." Maurius' voice lowered menacingly, "Apparently he thought I needed some additional help, insurance against an insolent little pup. Do you have any idea how much that upsets me— that he would think I needed help to deal with *you*?"

Kellan's mouth was dry and his first attempt to speak came out as nothing more than a croak.

"You have something to add," asked Maurius, "Please, enlighten me with your perspective."

Kellan tried again. "As...Asmodeus shouldn't have blamed you. Not your fault."

Maurius took a step back and breathed deeply, "No. No he should not have."

Kellan continued to shake his head and repeated, "It's not your fault; finding good villains has always been tough. You guys really need some kind of Angie's List or something so he can check ratings."

Kellan's head smashed against the brick and he tasted blood from a blow he hadn't even seen struck. Now Maurius' face was a hair's breath from his and the young Sentinel noted, oddly, that he had very fresh, minty, breath.

"I am not," growled Maurius, "a source of amusement for you. I am going to kill you. I am going to kill everyone who you love. I am going to destroy every thing that you care about. You are going to die knowing that, and knowing what an abject failure you are." Then, he stepped back again, raising a hand to his chin in thought. "Perhaps, I won't kill two of them. Perhaps I will take the young one who you dote on so freely and that military whore you used to sleep with, and drop them both off in the workroom. They won't die there you know. They will just exist, forever. How does that sound?"

Kellan stared at Maurius silently as his mind clicked mechanically through thousands of options, each one dismissed as unworkable. Fear began to well up in him as he saw a smile spread across Maurius' face.

"Yes, that's it. That's what I wanted to see. No jokes now, are there? Then, I guess our time together has reached its end. Don't worry, you won't be completely dead until I get you back to the workroom."

Kellan saw a jeweled short sword appear in Maurius' hand, condensing from red mist which slipped off its gleaming blade like drops of blood. He drew it back, lips curling in a bizarre mix of excitement and hatred, then paused as he saw Kellan staring over his shoulder into the distance.

Maurius turned just as the portal winked out behind a shadowy figure that had leaped through head first, hands extended to break its fall and propel it in a curled ball to one corner of the alley where it seemed to vanish in the gloom. Kellan felt the power as Maurius' eyes blazed red and the air shimmered with his shielding. He gestured forcefully and air whipped down the length of the alley, stirring up debris and hurling it towards the open end but not revealing whomever had exited the portal.

"You cannot save him," yelled Maurius, "He's already dead. He just doesn't know it yet. It's not too late to save yourself. I have no interest in you. Leave now and—" Maurius broke off as Kellan saw a faint glint and heard the elder Sentinel curse, pivoting his body as if struck. There was a metallic clatter and Kellan looked down to see a small dagger lying on the pavement, its blade clean, having not pierced Maurius' shield.

Two more blades appeared in rapid succession, both striking Maurius square in the chest, or would have, were it not for the shimmering red aura that stopped each inches from his flesh. All three blades seemed to originate from behind a large green dumpster near the mouth of the alley. Kellan, again, felt energy being channeled and made to call out a warning when he saw a figure dart out from behind the cover in a flash of green and red. Moments later a gout of flame erupted from where the figure had been hiding, followed immediately by half a dozen jagged bolts of energy that seemed to chase it toward the opposite wall where it took several steps directly up and flipped backwards to the middle of the alley. There it stood, facing Maurius, who had summoned two glowing balls of flame which now spun menacingly in each hand.

Kellan's eyes widened as he struggled in pain against his bonds and stared past Maurius at the figure before him. Loose curls of flaming red hair framed a porcelain face with high cheekbones and a softly cleft chin. She was a tall, well muscled, woman, in her late 20s or early 30s, clad in what looked like a dark green wool tunic and brown leather pants, each looped with numerous daggers and other throwing weapons along with a short sword strapped to each hip. Lit by the flaming spheres Maurius held, her eyes seemed amber, but Kellan knew they would be light brown, like autumn wheat. Her face was flushed with exertion bringing color to cheeks while her full lips turned upward in a mischievous grin as she locked eyes with Kellan.

"Hello, Sweetie. A little bird told me you could use a hand."

"Shannon?"

She winked.

"Look out!" screamed Kellan and he desperately formed a shield around her as Maurius hurled the first ball of flame. It struck her and the shield shimmered, absorbing the blow, then Kellan felt it it falter and vanish. His head lulled to one side from the exertion and watched in horror as Maurius released the second flaming sphere while Shannon stood motionless, still wearing her small impish expression.

It struck her directly in the chest, flames engulfing her, while Kellan failed to stifle a strangled sob. With flames licking all about her, Kellan saw Shannon tilt her head back and reach up both arms as if seeking divine intervention. The flames began to falter, spinning about her more and more rapidly, changing from blood red to emerald green, whereupon they gave a final swirl and then seemed to be absorbed by her as a sponge does water. She lowered her chin, staring directly at Maurius, who took an involuntary step back from the flame haired woman whose eyes now glowed as if they were made of molten emeralds.

As she lowered her arms to unsheathe the swords from her hip, Maurius saw, for the barest of moments, an image on her wrist—a small dove.

"Impossible!" he yelled, "Impossible. I killed you. I watched you die."

In response, Shannon spun both blades menacingly and showed her teeth. "Actually, you evil bastard, you killed my mother, which is really bad news for you."

Growling in frustration, Maurius thrust out his hands and first billows of wind rushed past her, followed by a string of red bolts cascading from micro-clouds all about her. As each bolt struck it vanished, causing Shannon's eyes and the soft green aura surrounding her to brighten further.

She tensed and leaped to the right, foot stepping once on the top of the dumpster to propel her lengthwise to the other side of the alley where she again reversed direction and hurled herself downward toward Maurius, screaming with decades of pent up rage and anger.

Maurius' shield parted like silk meeting razor. Shannon's spinning blow sliced through his robe at chest and stomach, nearly slicing through the summoned armor beneath. She braced herself against the wall nearest Kellan, lifted up both feet, and kicked outward, striking Maurius full in the face and sending him sprawling toward the mouth of the alley. In a second motion, smooth as quick silver, she grasped the spikes holding Kellan and tugged. As each came free, he could see her eyes dim slightly with the effort She turned back to face Maurius while Kellan slumped to the alley floor.

"That all you got?" she taunted, thrusting both arms outward, hands each gripping her small curved swords. "No more fire and lightning for me? Come on! Burn me like you did her!"

Maurius stood silently, regarding Shannon as her eyes slowly reverted to their natural color, green aura fading. He shook his head and the wicked blade again formed in his hand. "No, child, I do not think I will feed you anymore this night. My powers cannot touch the soul-born as you well know, but my blade most certainly can. I'll finish what I started back in that flea bottom you called home."

The two hurled themselves at one another, their weapons meeting with sparks and the shriek of metal on metal. Shannon was a blur of motion, using every object within the alley as distraction, weapon, cover, or all three. Maurius brought down his gleaming blade time and time again, only to find it biting nothing but air.

Each time he overextended himself, Shannon would dart under his guard and land a lightning quick strike, first against Maurius' shield, and, later as he tired, against the summoned armor that remained his final defense. The two performed their deadly dance with neither able to gain advantage on the other until Shannon saw Maurius' powerful lateral attack provided a momentary opening and lashed out. Her mouth opened in surprise as her double bladed attack on his exposed torso was deflected with a spark of red glowing energy as a small shield manifested then vanished. Cursing herself for being taken in by his feint, Shannon tried to correct her balance, but Maurius swept his right leg outward, knocking her to the ground hard enough for the air to escape in a whoosh and her blades to clatter away.

Maurius screamed as he whirled his massive blade in an arc with two hands, driving it down while Shannon held up two crossed daggers in a feeble defense she knew could not save her.

"Fuck you, asshole," yelled Kellan with a deeply affected Austrian accent, and Maurius looked up just as a small flaming orb the size of marble weaved its way past Shannon's supine form and softly touched the elder Sentinels cheek.

The sword continued downward but paused, tip quivering above her nose for a moment then vanished to red mist while Maurius shrieked in pain, raising both hands to the ruin that was his face. He staggered toward the mouth of the alley and a glowing red portal rotated into view. He stepped through but before it could wink out, Kellan saw a glint of metal followed by a bloody dagger protruding from Maurius' back. The portal closed, leaving the alley in gloom as Kellan collapsed next to Shannon, who remained propped up on one arm. The other, which had released the dagger, still pointed where the portal had been.

"Goddamn it," she yelled.

"What? What is it?" cried Kellan.

"That dagger was my mother's, Kellan Thorne, and I want it back!"

Meghan glared at the younger woman. "I definitely heard something. Dammit, Juliet, I said get back in the store, now!"

Juliet pressed the side of Kellan's .45, catching the magazine in her left hand. A quick glance showed her its magazine was full. Juliet replaced it, pulled back the slide to chamber a round and looked cooly at Meghan. "Nope."

"You don't know what's out there," Meghan growled, "I spent last week killing werewolves."

"And I shot the Archangel Raphael with this very gun; I'm glad you are catching up," replied Juliet, the corners of her lips curling up smugly.

"Jerk," said Meghan.

"Bitch," answered Juliet.

They both smiled.

Meghan took a deep breath and narrowed her eyes at Juliet. "Ok, you turn the knob. I'll kick the door open. You crouch low. I'll aim high. Don't shoot anything unless I say so. Agreed?"

Juliet nodded.

"Ok—here we go. Turn it. 3…2…1"

Meghan braced herself on her back leg and slammed the military boot of her right foot hard against the door. It burst open, revealing the darkened alley as Juliet took a step onto the landing and crouched, sighting along her .45.

Kellan was on his back, with streaks of blood scattered around him. A woman lay partially over him, braced on forearms, loosely curled red hair cascading down, obscuring much of his face as she pressed hers close to him.

"Vampire!" yelled Juliet, and started to squeeze the trigger.

"Hold!" screamed Meghan.

The woman's head whipped up, eyes glowing a bright green. Her arm blurred. Juliet's hands flew to the side, losing her grip on the .45 and she watched, stunned, as it clattered to the alley floor along with a small dagger.

"Stop! Stop! Stop!" yelled Kellan, leaning up on his elbows. "Nobody, kill anybody!"

The alley seemed to crackle with tension. Meghan hadn't moved from her offensive sideways stance. Kellan could see her weapon trained directly at Shannon's head. For her part, Shannon had a wicked looking dagger in each hand and Kellan could see her arm muscles rippling in anticipation of a forceful release.

"Ladies…" Kellan said calmly, "Stand down ladies. We're all friends here."

"The vampire bitch glamor'ed him, Meghan. Shoot her in the face."

"Juliet, no! Meghan, no! She's not a vampire. Jesus, this is Shannon."

Meghan took in the lithe figure of the woman before her and saw the intensity in her eyes. That intensity reminded the Marine of the reflection she saw that morning. This woman knew conflict and horror, and had overcome both. Slowly, she lowered her weapon, sliding it in the holster under her left arm, and let out the breath she hadn't realized she'd been holding.

"Yeah, well, fuck, Kel. She doesn't look fourteen to me."

"She grew up?" Kellan offered, his voice sounding apologetic, then lapsed into coughing, with blood foaming on his lips. "I don't feel so good."

"Is that house yours?" demanded Shannon, "Is it safe?"

Both women nodded.

"Help me with him. He's lost a lot of blood. We need to get him inside and help him heal."

Kellan barely stirred as Meghan and Shannon lifted him from the alley floor. His eyes fluttered and head lulled to one side as they laid him on one of the large leather couches in the reading nook.

Shannon slipped out a dagger and made to cut free Kellan's shirt, when Juliet groaned softly causing the older woman to glance at her. "What?"

"Nothing. He just loves that shirt is all."

Shannon snorted. "Loves it enough that he'd rather us lift those ruined arms than cut it off him?"

"Definitely!" Meghan and Juliet answered in unison.

Shannon looked back at the bloody T-shirt, lips moving, "Saving people, hunting things. The family business."

"He got it at Dragon Con," offered Juliet by way of explanation.

"He's an idiot," replied Shannon, but started to roll the shirt up from his waist. Juliet rushed over to gently lift his back up while Meghan slowly raised his arms.

Kellan's eyes flew open and he cried out in pain as Shannon finally pulled the shirt free. He slumped back against the couch breathing rapidly. "Are you three trying to finish the job of killing me?"

Shannon glared at him, then gestured pointedly at Meghan and Juliet. "Those two said you didn't want this stupid shirt cut off you," she said, brandishing the blood soaked cloth.

Kellan tried to focus and recognition flashed across his face, "Good call. Got that at Dragon——" His head slumped back against the pillow and his breathing deepened.

Shannon leaned in and softly placed her lips on Kellan's, causing Meghan and Juliet to exchange a pointed glance. Kellan stirred and Shannon reached behind his head, pulling him more deeply into the kiss.

"Awkward," murmured Juliet, looking away.

"Uh, what the hell are you doing?" asked Meghan as she grabbed hold of the younger woman's shoulder, pulling her away and she turned to Meghan, eyes blazing green. Both Meghan and Juliet took a half step back. Shannon held up a hand.

"Just a moment. Where are the entrances to this building?" she asked.

"Why—" began Juliet, but Meghan interrupted.

"This way. Follow me."

Shannon did, and the three of them first approached the back door near Kellan's office where Shannon stopped, rubbed both her hands together, and then leaned forward—placing them on the door. Moments later a soft green glow could be seen emanating between her fingers and she stepped back.

"Wow, those look like the symbols on Kellan's arms," said Juliet.

"Enochian," said Shannon curtly, then added, "Next."

Twice more they repeated the process. After the third door, Shannon stumbled backwards and would have fallen were it not for Meghan supporting her.

"Thank you," she said, her eyes having returned to their natural brown, "That takes a lot out of me, but I'll be alright in a moment or two so long as I don't need to do it again."

"Yeah, what exactly is 'it'? " asked Juliet as the three returned to where Kellan lay sleeping.

Shannon knelt before him, shaking him gently, then looked back at the younger woman. "They are defensive runes and should prevent Maurius or any-one channeling Chaotic energies from entering this building?"

"Ok," began Juliet, "I understood pretty much none of that." She looked to Meghan, who also shook her head.

Shannon turned back to Kellan sighing, in frustration, "I don't have time to explain everything right now. It keeps bad things out."

She shook Kellan again—this time harder.

"Hey!" yelled Meghan.

Shannon glared at her. "Do you want him to die? He needs to heal or he's going to do just that. Now, stay out of my way."

"Kellan. Kellan!" the young Sentinel did not stir. Shannon took her thumb and pressed it hard into the wound in his left shoulder. He screamed in pain. She held his head in both hands as his eyes started to flutter closed.

"No! Look at me. Kellan! Look. At. Me. You are wounded. Badly. You have been pierced by demonic runed alloy and you need to focus. You need to seek Nurisha and channel all you can into healing. Do you understand?"

He stared at her, eyes half closed. "Shannon?"

"Yes. It's me."

"How are you here?"

"You told me to come; you showed me when and how."

Kellan looked confused. "No, I didn't."

"Yes you did, or you will. I mean future you will. Look, it doesn't matter now. Talk to Nurisha. You need to heal!"

"Shannon?"

"What?"

"You're pretty. Will you kiss me again? That will help."

Megan and Juliet groaned. Shannon drove her thumb into the wound in Kellan's other shoulder. "Nurisha, now!"

The three women watched as Kellan's eyes lost focus and his lips moved, speaking words they could not hear. His breathing became rapid and, suddenly, he arched has back so violently that all three stepped back. Three times he convulsed and on the third, his eyes blazed to life, brighter than any had seen before.

Shannon sighed heavily and folded her legs beneath her as she settled to the floor. Kellan had lain back against the couch, wounds already beginning to knit. She reached out, taking his hand in hers. Tears filled her eyes, then left streaks down her face. She looked back to Juliet and Meghan, "He'll be alright now. We just need to keep him safe and quiet for a few hours."

Shannon stood and attempted to brush some of the dirt and grime from her pants and tunic.

Meghan slowly reached up to take her hand, stopping her. "I see what you are doing. I understand," she said softly, then smiled, "I'm afraid your gear is pretty much a lost cause."

Shannon stared back uncomprehendingly.

"Look, you are in a bit of shock and I get it. Let me help."

"My clothes are fine."

"Shannon, they are covered in blood. And there are more holes than there are solid parts. Then there are those," she said, pointing generically toward the younger woman's chest.

Shannon looked down and saw her tunic had been torn so badly that mere wisps of thread seemed to be holding it together. She looked back to Meghan, who smiled gently.

"You want our boy there to be able to focus at all, we need to wrap those girls up. Besides, I've got stuff you are just gonna love. I'll hit up a buddy of mine and be back in an hour. What size are you?"

"Size?"

"Never mind, I have a sense of it." Meghan turned to Juliet. "You should order in some food."

"Yes!" Shannon exclaimed, "I'm famished."

"Ok," said Juliet, "What do you want?"

"You kids work that out. I'm outta here," said Megan and a moment later they heard the back door slam, its automatic lock reengaging as it closed again.

Juliet turned again to Shannon. "Food? What kind? Shannon? What are you doing?"

Shannon turned to Juliet, smiling as she clicked the light on and off for the third time, clearly amazed. "Hmm? Oh, I'm sorry. He told me about things here, but it was hard to fully grasp it. I don't know what kind of food can be easily prepared. Whatever is fine."

"Haggis?" offered Juliet.

Shannon wrinkled her nose. "If that is all you can find, I won't complain, but I don't enjoy it at all."

Juliet laughed. "I'm joking. You know, because your Scottish. I don't even know where in Atlanta I could find haggis if I wanted to. How about pizza?"

Shannon shrugged noncommittally.

"Pizza it is," said the younger woman as she pulled out her phone and began tapping on it.

Shannon's eyes widened. "Does that make food?"

Juliet glanced up. "Huh? Funny. It's my phone. I'm just ordering—oh. Umm, hold that thought. Let me get the food on its way then I'll give you a crash course on the 21st century while we wait."

45 minutes later, there was a knock from the front of the shop and Juliet hopped out of her chair. Shannon watched her scamper toward the door as her head swam with all that she'd been shown over the past hour. She had seen some truly magical things in her young life, but placed Juliet's iPhone and its ability to talk to "The Internet", as among the most magical. A talking oracle you could carry in your pocket. Shannon definitely wanted one.

"Here you go—Pizza! I got four different ones just in case." Juliet set the four thin, square, boxes on the low coffee table and lifted each one in turn "Cheese. Veggie, UberMeat, and Garbage."

Shannon breathed in deeply, her mouth watering at the delicious scents, but looked to Juliet questioningly: "Garbage?"

"Oh, it means both veggies and meat—lots of both."

"I want that!"

Juliet pulled a triangular slice from the box and handed it to Shannon, who placed her nose near it and smiled, peering over the food at Juliet. "It smells amazing!"

"It is amazing. Food of the gods."

"Really?"

"Well, not literally. Shannon take a bite."

She did and Juliet watched her eyes widen.

"That's what I'm talkin' about—Pizza!"

Shannon swallowed. "Juliet, this is the best thing I've ever eaten. Ever!"

"I know, right? And this isn't even great pizza. You need to try a Pizza from Fix, down the street. It's to kill for."

"I'd kill someone for this one," Shannon said around another mouthful.

The two settled into a comfortable silence as Shannon continued to try each of the Pizzas in turn, finally pronouncing that "Garbage" was the best followed by UberMeat with Veggie and Cheese declared as a waste of good pizza material.

"Juliet?" Shannon began.

"Hmm?"

"Is there water nearby? I don't mind fetching it, but the pizza and," she waved a hand dismissively, "the fighting, have left me quite thirsty."

Juliet slapped herself in the forehead. "I'm an idiot. Sorry. Sure, we have water. Kel, keeps a mini fridge in the back. I'll grab you one." She hopped up and disappeared into the back of the shop returning a moment later with three bottles. The first she set down next to where she'd been sitting, then she held the other two up for Shannon to see.

"This," Juliet said, "is plain ol' water."

Shannon reached for it saying, "It's so clear."

Juliet pulled it back from her and offered the second bottle. "And this… is Coca-Cola. Try this first." Then she twisted off the cap with a soft hiss and handed it to Shannon.

"It's cold."

"Of course it's cold. Drink it!"

"Why are you smiling at me like that?"

"Because you are like an alien who has never tasted Coke or Pizza and this is amazing."

Shannon snorted. "I'm glad I'm such a source of amusement." She placed her lips to the bottle and took a drink.

Juliet clapped softly at the reaction.

"I want to live here," said Shannon reverently as she stared at the bottle.

A moment later, there was a bang from the back of the shop and both women leaped to their feet.

Meghan walked in carrying a large duffel bag and stopped, taking in the scene. She barked a laugh, looking first to Juliet and then to Shannon, who stood poised with a dagger in one hand and a mostly empty bottle of Coke in the other. "Only one dagger?"

Shannon relaxed, but looked sheepish. "I didn't want to spill it."

Meghan shook her head. "Pizza and Coke, huh? Good choices. How's our boy?"

Shannon glanced over to the unconscious Kellan. "Still sleeping. Wounds are almost all closed up. He'll be waking soon."

"Good, then you come with me so I can get you all suited up before he does. I don't want him tearing something open by seeing you like," she waved up and down, "that."

Shannon slide her knife away and drained the rest of her Coke, then grinned mischievously at Meghan. "He's seen more than that."

Both Juliet and Meghan froze, then said together, "What?"

"That bastard," Meghan added, "You were what, 15 when he met you?"

"I think I'm gonna be sick," said Juliet.

Shannon looked confused. "I was 14 when we met," then held up her hands, waving them in negation. "No, wait. You don't understand. I'm talking about when he met me—later. I was much older. 25, I think."

"Future Kel?" asked Juliet

Shannon nodded.

"He's still a bastard, or he will be," grumbled Meghan looking confused.

"Timey Wimey," said Juliet.

"Wibbly Wobbly," finished Shannon brightly, "That's what Kellan always says. Oh, and to be clear, he was a perfect gentleman when future him came to see me. I seduced him. Tripped him right into my bed." said Shannon, lifting her chin.

"Oh," said Megan in surprise, "I suppose that makes him less of a bastard then."

Juliet just grimaced, "Gross, Shannon. Just gross."

Megan rolled her eyes at the younger woman and motioned to Shannon with the duffle. "C'mon. You—in the back. Now"

Even though Kellan had expanded the shop's bathroom when he first opened, it was still a tight squeeze with Megan directing, standing in the tub, and Shannon donning clothes in front of the mirror.

"What is this made of?" she asked, rubbing her fingers between the fabric.

"Ballistic nylon with a double kevlar weave. There are also thin ceramic plates that cover vital organs. That shit'll stop a bullet cold."

Shannon raised an eyebrow. "Knives?"

"It laughs at knives."

Shannon had been pulling her mane of red hair back into a tail, but turned to Meghan and grinned. "You are my new best friend."

～⁊⋀⟋⟍⟍

"Look who's awake," said Juliet with a flourish, gesturing in Kellan's direction as he sprawled lengthwise across the couch.

Shannon flashed a wide smile and folded herself next to him. She leaned in and gave Kellan a long, deep kiss.

"He looks surprised," whispered Juliet.

"He looked surprised," mumbled Meghan, "now he just looks like the teenage boy they all are in their heads. Hey. You two. Cut it out."

Shannon pulled back and stroked Kellan's cheek. "You had me worried there for a minute," she said.

He laughed nervously. "Yeah, well, you know me. I'm always the cause of worry."

"Oh shut up, you idiot," said Meghan, pulling Shannon out of the way and sitting down beside Kellan. "Don't pretend you have any idea what's going on or why she's acting like this."

"C'mon Meghan, I know exactly—"

"Kel?"

"—what's going..."

"Kel!"

"Ok, fine. I don't know what's going on!"

Meghan looked smug. "Better. Well, apparently, future you traveled back in time to see past her to warn you about present this."

Kellan looked to Shannon. "Huh? I did? I will? What did I tell you?"

She shook her head solemnly. "Can't say."

He furrowed his brow. "Why not?"

Shannon sighed. "You said you would say that and now I'm supposed to say—" she held up a finger to her lips, "Spoilers…"

"Oh My God," cried Juliet. "She's River, Kellan! She's River fucking Song. She's even got the hair! This is totally worth you almost getting killed."

Kellan stared at her with a flat expression. "Thanks, Juliet. Now, watch your language. You know your parents blame me for it. And Shannon, why are you dressed like Black Widow? I'm so confused."

"Ok, everyone shut up," said Meghan, holding up her hands. "I don't speak geek, or nerd, or whatever you idiots speak. First, she's not dressed like a spider. She's wearing combat battle armor, because being around you is bloody danger-ous. Second, despite her fighting prowess, she clearly has poor choice in men, having apparently gotten entangled with you at some point in her past—which somehow is also your future." Meghan stood and rounded on Shannon. "Now you, stop with the 'spoilers,' act and tell us what the hell is going on."

"No!" yelled Kellan and Juliet at the same time.

Meghan shook her head in disbelief, "What? You don't want to know what is going to happen? Are you insane?"

"That knowledge could corrupt the timeline," said Juliet in a matter of fact way, "You can't do that."

"Corrupt the…" sputtered Meghan, "Do you hear yourself? Based on what?"

Juliet looked down and murmured, "Doctor Who."

"What?"

The younger woman looked up again and put her hands on her hips. "Doctor Who, ok?"

"Jesus, Kellan, you are making your decision of what tactical knowledge you should accept based on a British television show?"

"Well, when you say it like that, Meghan, it sounds crazy," said Kellan, looking embarrassed.

"Stop," interjected Shannon. "I don't care what you three say. My Kellan was very clear about this and I trust him. I'm not saying anything. Well, accept, 'Spoilers.'"

Meghan grabbed the last slice of garbage pizza, knocked the box on the floor, and sat on the table. "I'm surrounded by idiots."

"Hey Shannon?" asked Juliet

"Hmm?"

"What's it mean if those glyphy things on the door start to turn red?"

Shannon spun around and saw Juliet pointing to the alley door where the last vestiges of a defensive enochian glyph changed from green to red, then vanished completely. As it did so, a massive portal rotated into existence, knocking tables and bookshelves as it materialized. Moments later a robed man standing well over seven feet stepped into the room and glared at the small assembly.

He spoke and his voice resonated like thunder against distant hills.

"Sometimes, one has to do a thing oneself to ensure it is completed."

Shannon stared in horror at her nightmare come to life. He stood tall and beautiful with smoldering deep red eyes, olive skin, and cheekbones sharply chiseled as if made of marble. She could feel the power coursing through him and saw red streamers begin to play all about his body, then turned to see her companions all staring in mute awe.

"Kellan!" she yelled, but her words were carried away by the crackling energy as she saw Asmodeus about to strike. Shannon grabbed Kellan's bare arm and he felt her nails dig deeply into his flesh. The connection made, she reached inward and drew deeply upon his power, more deeply than ever she had before. As always, Shannon felt it burn within her, seeking release as she struggled to give it form. She felt the heat in her eyes fade completely as the shield snapped around the four of them, even as violent crimson energy struck them all, hurling them against the far wall.

"Kellan. It's happening. It's happening now."

He stared at her a moment, then she saw his eyes focus and his jaw clench— all remnants of awestruck revelry gone. "Thanks, Shannon. I'm here. I've got this."

She nodded and touched his cheek, her eyes blazing back to life, then leaped to the right calling over her shoulder, "Protect them! I'll be fine."

Accepting while not fully understanding the connection between the two, Kellan nodded at Shannon and snapped shields around both Meghan and Juliet. Meghan was already moving, both Glocks out and barking angrily, causing Asmodeus to rock backwards.

"Juliet, stay down. Don't move." For once the young woman just nodded and huddled behind a half fallen bookshelf as Kellan turned to launch himself into the fray.

"Consider your next action with due care young Sentinel," said Asmodeus with a smile that did not touch his eyes. Kellan felt panic rise within him as he saw both Shannon and Meghan struggling as he gripped each by the neck, several feet from the floor.

Shannon's eyes glowed with a fierce determination and small clouds formed throughout the room. Bolts of energy lanced out from each and struck Asmodeus, who winced and shook her violently even as her eyes dimmed, having expended all the borrowed power.

"Stop!" yelled Kellan.

Asmodeus again turned his attention to the young Sentinel. "Of course, but then I will need something from you."

"Fine. What do you want? Take it and let them be."

"What I want," the Archdemon said casually, "cannot be taken. It can only be given as my servant tried to do with you earlier. Sadly, he failed. Twice. That will result in some unfortunate ramifications for him, but no need to worry about such things now."

"You are killing them."

"Hmm, oh. Apologies." Asmodeus lowered his arms so both women's feet rested on the ground and seemed to release his grip enough so they could breathe. "Better?"

Kellan said nothing, and Asmodeus continued.

"It is simple, Kellan Thorne. Release your power to me and I will leave your friends in peace. Refuse and I will kill them. Then I will kill the cowering young one behind you. Then I will kill everyone who ever met or loved you. Then I will wait until someone new draws close to you and will kill them too. Ad in finitem" He smiled again. "Certainly the other way is preferable."

"I'll do it—just let them go!"

Shannon struggled in Asmodeus' grip. "No, Kellan. You'll die. Raphael told us you cannot survive without the power once it has bonded to you."

Asmodeus continued mockingly, "Raphael. Such a child. Always obeying. I had almost hoped he would face me here but, of course, such intercession is not permitted. Heaven forbid he do anything of the kind."

The Archdemon continued in a serious and more thoughtful tone. "Still, the soul-born one is right. You will die when you release the power to me. I may be fallen but, like my heavenly brothers, I never lie." He smiled again. "Of course they do not lie because they cannot. I do not lie, because I do not need to lie."

Asmodeus sighed, seemingly bored with the entire exchange. "Enough. I have waited millennia. Now, Sentinel of Order. Release your power to me or they die."

"I already said I would, but I want to hear you swear by your one true name that they will be free once I do."

"This is not a negotiation. This is unconditional surrender. You do not get to make demands of me. You are an amusement. A talking ape that my father decided to gift with some semblance of thought."

Kellan ground his teeth. "Well, this talking ape has something you want and if you are not willing to swear by your name, then I cannot believe you. If I cannot believe you, then it doesn't matter what I do, because you will kill those I love regardless. So do it. Burn it all, Asmodeus. But know you will never, ever, gain the power I hold."

The two locked eyes for a long moment and then the Archdemon tilted his head back and laughed. "You certainly are not anything like Micah. Under different circumstances, I could have made use of you. Very well. I accede to your request."

He released Meghan. Kellan saw her tense as if to resume their efforts, but waved her down. The Archdemon turned his gaze to Shannon and with his free hand softly caressed her cheek.

"It would have been delightful to make use of you as well, but alas, I will settle for leaving you this gentle reminder of our brief time together." Shannon continued to struggle in his grasp as Kellan watched the skin seem to slough off Asmodeus' right hand to reveal dark brown scales. His fingers ended in long sharpened blood red nails that he now used to slowly trace circles around her left eye. Shannon froze and the Archdemon laughed. "No more struggling? What? Are you afraid I might slip and gouge out one of those beautiful eyes?" He turned back to Kellan. "What do you think *Sen-ti-nel of Order*." He spoke the words slowly and each syllable dripped with disdain. "Shall I blind her for you so she'll never look on another man once you are dust? I will do that for you—as a final mercy"

Kellan said nothing and lowered his gaze to the floor in apparent submission.

Asmodeus snorted derisively, "You are a worm. Not even worthy of that mercy, so I will leave her both eyes with which to gaze on a different symbol of remembrance." Before Kellan could react he had slid a razor sharp nail across Shannon's cheek and traced out an enochian symbol which began to run with her blood.

"Stop!" yelled Kellan, "Or you will have nothing from me. You agreed to leave them be."

"And so I will, *after* you have given me what was promised." The Archdemon released Shannon and she staggered, falling to one knee. She looked to Kellan imploringly as her hands reached for fresh daggers, but he gave her a definitive and curt shake of the head. She slumped, ignoring the blood that ran freely down her face and made no further moves. Asmodeus stepped forward and looked down at Kellan. "You wanted my name, well, there you have it. I carved it in her flesh so she can remember me."

"I'll hear it from your own lips, freely given," Kellan growled.

Asmodeus bent down, his face mere inches from Kellan's own. "You realize, I know what you are trying to do. You think if you know my true name it will provide some advantage, but I am not some human wizard, Kellan Thorne.

I am Asmodeus. Right hand of Lucifer himself. You cannot comprehend my name, let alone retain it. So be it though." Asmodeus spoke his true name, given to him at the dawn of creation. It seemed as if it would never end and, like with Raphael, Kellan saw all of the potential and love with which the name had been crafted. He felt tears come, unbidden, as Asmodeus finished. Tears born of all the love with which Angel had been created and of all the pride with which the demon had fallen.

Kellan gestured and a portal rotated into existence. Before Asmodeus could react, he stepped through and turned back around to face the portal. In the distance large statues stared sightlessly out to sea, silent sentinels themselves, now witnessing the culmination of an age old struggle.

"What is this?" the Archdemon asked across this distance.

"If I am to die, then I want do so far from my friends and in the place I first came to as a Sentinel."

Asmodeus shook his head slightly in amusement, but strode quickly forward and leaped towards the portal.

"Now!" Kellan said to himself as Lamia's long ago whispered words cascaded through his mind. His eyes blazed to life and Kellan layered a second portal onto the first, then leaped though with Asmodeus only half a step behind.

Chapter 10

A PRINCE OF CHAOS

K ellan emerged through the portal hitting the ground hard as he rolled to absorb the impact and looked backward in time to see Asmodeus leap through a moment later, eyes ablaze with streamers of red energy playing about him like crimson lightning. Immediately noticing that their destination had changed, his beautiful features contorted with a rage and hatred Kellan had never experienced as the fallen Archangel turned in time to see the portal silently wink out.

Kellan could feel the energy that Asmodeus had channeled reach a crescendo as he whipped back around, throwing both hands forward, causing a twisting rope of interlocking elemental forces to crash into the young Sentinel's hastily erected shield. Kellan felt it begin to buckle beneath the onslaught as his mind lifted Micah's words to the fore: "In this place, you can do the miraculous—if you only have the will."

Kellan ground his teeth as traditional prayers to Saint's Jude, Gregory, Philomena, and Rita, flashed unbidden and unwelcome across his mind. He closed his eyes, let the shield vanish, and felt the combined energies of Asmodeus' attack strike him. No longer distracted by maintaining his shield, Kellan felt his world narrow into one focused thought as he reached deep into the well of his power, draining it in a single act of will. Kellan did not think what he was trying to do would work—he knew it would. All doubts banished as the young Sentinel fundamentally altered the physical laws around him. The world warped outward like an expanding bubble with Kellan at its center and he watched as Asmodeus' massive energy current reversed course like an electrical switch with its polarity changed. The Archdemon's eyes widened in surprise, and he screamed in pain and frustration as the full force of his attack slammed into him, driving him upwards and off the precipice where he and Kellan had exited the portal.

Kellan panted, wiping blood from his face, and groaned as he struggled to stand, steadying himself by grabbing an arm of the massive stone throne. He let go, wobbled, and nearly fell into the throne itself but managed to maintain his footing, then slowly walked to the mountain top edge and peered over. Just as his line of sight cleared the edge, Kellan felt a rush of air strike him, causing him to fall back a step as something blurred in front of him. Kellan looked up and involuntarily sucked in air.

Massive black wings moved rhythmically as Asmodeus stared down with murder in his eyes. Gone was the beautiful guise of moments before. It had been replaced by what Kellan's mind confirmed to be a common description of the fallen archangel through the ages. His face was all hard angles from a heavy brow that caused his eyes to be deep hollows in which fiery coals could be seen, to a pointed chin that seemed to have three boney clefts. His skin was uniformly brown, with boney protrusions prominent from both his shoulders and forehead. Long black hair was parted in the middle and swept down behind each curving horn to cascade across his broad shoulders. From his chest downward, he looked much like a heavily muscled man, save for the additional spikes protruding from both knees and the complete absence of any sex organs.

"What trick did Raphael teach you?" Asmodeus spat as the hot air continued to strike at Kellan from his beating wings. "How did you turn my power back upon me? Answer, and I will grant you the mercy of a quick death."

Despite feeling so terrified that his bowels threatened to let loose, Kellan laughed. "Did you seriously just say that?" As he tried to continue, Kellan's laugh turned into a cough and he tasted blood. Something was definitely broken inside and was not in a hurry to heal itself. Kellan took another shallow breath. "You sound more like the villain from an Ed Wood movie than a prince of hell. I'm not going to tell you shit. In fact, you can just fuck off and—"

Without warning Asmodeus pitched in mid air, angling down toward Kellan as a massive scepter with a glowing red gem appeared in his right hand. He rushed Kellan, moving so fast his eyes couldn't track the Archdemon properly. The young Sentinel moved just by instinct, sword coalescing in his hand a split second before the scepter came down. There was a deafening clang as the two weapons glanced off one another in a shower of sparks. Asmodeus' inertia carried the blow forward and he struck the plain stone bench, causing it to crack in two even as Kellan spun completely around whipping his own sword at Asmodeus' now exposed back.

The tip of the sword raked against the exposed flesh, drawing a thin red line across the Archdemon's neck even as his forward motion diminished the depth of the cut. Drops of dark red blood spilled from the wound to strike the stoney ground, where it hissed and puffed away.

Asmodeus whirled on Kellan while reaching his free hand back along the wound. He stared at his blood covered fingers with a look that Kellan couldn't immediately place—until those dark red eyes again locked on his.

Hatred—to be sure. But he had seen that all along. No, there was something new now. Kellan's own eyes widened in recognition. Fear. Uncomprehending fear was the emotion Kellan now saw in the ancient face that had once warred against heaven itself.

With a primal yell, Asmodeus gestured and a portal opened between the two, just to Kellan's left but the young Sentinel was already moving, sword rotating in his right hand, even as the Archdemon tried to leap through. The portal puffed away into tiny motes of light just as Asmodeus crossed its threshold. He stumbled as Kellan drove his sword downward with all the force he could muster. Asmodeus bent his head back and howled in pain as Kellan's brightly glowing weapon cleaved both wings cleanly from his back. Like the blood before it, the black wings hissed as they struck the ground and puffed away.

Asmodeus summoned another portal but it, too, vanished at his touch and he turned on Kellan with an expression of complete disbelief.

"What is this place!"

Kellan paused and cocked his head. "I guess you've never been here. Maybe Lucifer should have warned you. This, my fine wingless demon, is the workroom of creation."

"Impossible! Impossible! I cannot be here. You cannot bring me here."

"I didn't bring you here, I just made a portal. You came of your own free will."

"I did no such thing! There are rules to creation, you insignificant whelp. There are consequences. Release me now from this accursed place."

Kellan leaned against the shattered bench as he felt his wounds knitting, and the river of his power begin to swell to a level higher than any he had felt before. A distant part of his mind pondered whether that was due to this place or the strain he had been putting on himself.

"Are you seriously trying to tell me you didn't run through that portal after me?"

"That portal," Asmodeus growled, "was simply to a grassy island; it was not to here!"

"Oh, quite true, but I made another one and fused it to the first. You actually went through two portals in rapid succession." Kellan beamed. "Pretty clever, huh, especially for a talking, hairless ape?" He watched as realization dawned on the fallen Angel.

"I. Will. Kill You!" he roared. Kellan felt a charge in the air and looked up as the dark clouds roiled above. A flash of bright blue lighting flew down and Kellan drew deep from the river of his power, eyes blazing and runes streaking down his arms as he lifted one hand to catch the lightning. In his mind's eye, Kellan pulled apart the the lighting at the atomic level, photon from electron. He channeled it down his right arm through his body and out his left where it coalesced as a gleaming ball of pure electrical energy that Kellan held between his two outstretched hands.

Again he reached inward and pulled forth power, but the river did not diminish. Rather, its banks grew higher even as the river's breadth increased. The ball of lighting fragmented to become dozens of rotating spheres of luminescent energy.

Asmodeus charged toward Kellan, hurling all manner of elemental attacks but as each came close, one white sphere detached itself and intercepted the projectile, causing the air to warp with heat that buffeted a glowing shield Kellan held about himself. No more than twenty feet separated Asmodeus from Kellan when the fallen Angel reached upward with both hands, forming words Kellan could not hear and thrust them toward the young Sentinel.

Nothing happened. Asmodeus gestured again. Nothing. He stared at Kellan dark eyes wild with anger and rising panic. A third time. Nothing.

Kellan stared at the two remaining white spheres as they rotated between his hands. He felt the anger well up within him as he stared at Asmodeus, recalling all that Lamia had told him. "This is the bosom of creation! You have no power here but what you brought with you and that is now gone. This is *my* place. My will rules here." Kellan whipped out his hands, causing the last two spheres to fly outward and strike Asmodeus in the chest with a blinding flash of light, throwing him fifty feet into the air, leaving him sprawled and dazed in the massive throne.

Kellan narrowed his eyes, teeth set, as he walked toward the Archdemon, sword again forming in his hand.

"Stop," Asmodeus said while trying to rise from the throne, only to collapse back. "You cannot do this. I am an Archangel."

"You are a demon who has killed legions and tempted legions upon legions more. You tried to kill me, which I could forgive. But you meant to kill those I love and those whom I protect—that I will not forgive."

"You cannot kill me. I am balance. I am necessary to God's plan."

Kellan had spanned the distance between them and glared down at the fallen Angel with sword upraised. "Then God's plan has a problem."

"Brothers!", screamed Asmodeus, "I invoke our pact. I summon you!"

Kellan had begun his downward swing when he heard a voice like a thunderclap. "STOP!"

Altering his blow at the last moment, Kellan cleaved a large piece from the Throne and looked toward the sound of the voice. Before him stood both Michael and Raphael. Raphael looked pained and worried while Michael, brandishing his massive flaming sword, looked only slightly less angry than did Asmodeus short moments ago.

"You may not harm him, Sentinel," boomed Michael.

Kellan lowered his sword, feeling its tip bite into the solid stone. "Who asked you, Michael? But, for my own edification, why the fuck not? Look at him. He's literally sitting in the throne made by Lucifer himself after *your* war, and you intercede on his behalf!"

"He is an Angelic Prince and cannot be destroyed by one such as you. It should not even be possible, but you have tricked him into coming to this place."

Kellan laughed mirthlessly. "Yeah, I tricked him into coming here to kill me so he wouldn't stay where we were and kill my friends." The young Sentinel turned to Raphael. "Are you buying into this shit, Raphael? This asshole set the whole thing into motion. He created Maurius. He's promised to kill everyone I've ever loved or who will ever love me."

Raphael looked pained. "They are both correct, Kellan. You may not kill Asmodeus. His power, the energy of chaos within him, is necessary for creation to exist even as the energy of order within us," he gestured to Michael, "is necessary."

Kellan glared at Raphael. "What are you going to do Raphael? Stop me?"

"If I must. And if I must, you will die to my unending sadness. We will harness your power in this place and instill it in another."

Kellan paused, considering. "Can you do that?"

"I do not know, Kellan Thorne. I beg you. Do not put it to the test."

"Yeah, well, I'm betting you and your big brother over there can't do shit about it." Kellan again raised his sword and made to strike.

Raphael leaped for the young Sentinel with arms reaching to block the blow, even as Michael hurled his massive sword directly at Kellan who, for his part, simply smiled and rested his sword on his shoulder, waiting. Michael's sword arrived first, coming within a foot of Kellan before veering off inexplicably at an acute angle to clatter against the stone. Raphael, too, came close but was then hurled backward, crashing into Michael as if propelled by an unseen force.

Kellan stared at them both, shaking his head slowly. "Freewill, bitches! You gave me this power of your own freewill and of my own freewill I took it up. I sit outside the sight and intersession of God Himself. Do you think you have the power to interfere with my free access of that power?"

By this point, Kellan's voice had risen to the point where, unbidden, the river of power coursing within him amplified it further.

Raphael had regained his feet with Michael's help and pleaded with Kellan, "Do not do this thing. The world cannot exist without the balance between these energies. You cannot destroy him and the energy he holds. Micah understood this. Micah would never act this rashly."

Kellan stared at his Angelic teacher with an expression devoid of all emotion. "Raphael, energy cannot *be* destroyed and, as for Micah, how many times must I say it?" His voice rose as he drew more power from the river than ever before causing his body, eyes, and sword to glow so brightly even the two Angels had to look away. "I. am. not. he!"

With that, Kellan spun tightly in a circle, and thrust his sword directly through Asmodeus' chest, pinning him to the throne. The fallen Angel arched his back and screamed as red energy played along the length of sword. He thrashed, but the Sentinel's sword held him fast to the throne as Kellan leaned down, still grasping its hilt, and stared into Asmodeus' panicked eyes. He yelled, "I bind you to this place by the power of your one true name. By that name, I destroy you utterly." And the words that were not words flowed from Kellan's lips as they had once done long ago, in this spot, at the time of creation, long and perfect. As the last syllable faded the young Sentinel leaned forward and whispered, "Don't feel bad, I hear oblivion is really nice this time of year." Kellan twisted the sword violently causing Asmodeus to shudder once. A piercing red beam of energy leaped from the dead Archangel's sightless eyes to burn its way into Kellan's own.

He heard a scream and, at first, thought it was his own, but when it came again, Kellan knew its source. Nurisha called him. She needed him. Dimly, Kellan felt himself release his grip on the sword as he sought the inner river where Nurisha had met him so many times before. Something was very wrong, and Kellan knew it was his fault.

Kellan felt his inner world fade in around him as he stood along the rocky banks in which raged the torrent of green energy that formed his power. He gasped, taking it in. The far bank seemed fully twice as distant as when he had first met Nurisha here those few weeks ago.

Guess I've been straining. Kellan quickly scanned the area for Nurisha's glowing form. He heard the scream again, filled with fear and pain, then started sprinting upstream in the direction from which it came. Within moments he saw her in the center of the river, heading towards him while angling toward the nearest bank. She flailed as if beset by angry biting insects or unseen creatures from the river's depths, both of which Kellan knew to be impossible in this place. He saw her try to elevate and run on the surface as she had done so many times before, but just as she raised herself to where this might be possible, Nurisha would writhe as if struck and sink back into the depths. Only moments had passed since Kellan first appeared. He leaped recklessly onto the churning water, forming his will into an iron determinant that he would not sink. His feet struck the surface and it curved with his weight but he did not fall though, nor even take notice as he raced towards Nurisha.

Kellan was close enough now to see that she appeared to suffer from numerous wounds across her glowing green skin that appeared for all the world like she'd been scourged. Bright red edges framed the wounds and from them dripped liquid green energy that fell to be lost in the rushing torrent. She turned, reaching for him, her face a mask of fear and pain just as Kellan saw a bright red tendril of liquid energy slide off the surface of the river and strike her in the face, leaving a long gash as she cried out and fell beneath the surface.

In a panic, Kellan launched himself at the point where she had submerged, willed the surface to part, and reached beneath. His hands quickly found her, holding her tight as she continued to thrash while in his embrace. She broke the surface and he stared into her eyes. They were wild with more than simple fear. Kellan shook her.

"Nurisha! Nurisha!" he yelled, "What is wrong with you? What is wrong with this place?"

"Chaos, Chaos, Chaos," she screamed, squeezing his face in her hands so tightly it brought tears to his eyes. She tried to wrench away but he held her fast. She pointed upstream, shrieking, "Chaos!"

Kellan looked and for a moment didn't see anything but the roiling green energy. Then, as he turned back to her, out the of corner of his eye, Kellan caught a glimpse of something bright red glinting among the omnipresent green. It slid along the the water's surface like a malevolent stain but seemed like it would harmlessly pass them by. As if in reaction to Kellan's thought, the red streak changed directions as it drew close, angling directly for the pair. Nurisha tensed in his arms.

"No no no! Chaos and Order…No!"

Kellan's blood ran cold. He knew what this was. He knew what had caused it. He knew what he had done and cursed himself a fool. Just as the red stain was about to strike Nurisha's exposed back, Kellan spun around and protected her body with his own. He braced himself for pain which did not come. As it passed through his clothes, Kellan felt its touch like if one were to place a finger in a live electrical socket. He shuddered at the curious buzzing sensation, but had expected far worse.

Nurisha looked up at him in horror and, for the first time, seemed to recognize him. "No! You cannot let it touch you. Let me…I will do this."

For his part, Kellan had been looking for more red streamers. He saw them coming—dozens, hundreds, all swirling and joining until the emerald river appeared to have a blazing red stripe running down its length, headed directly to them both. He turned to Nurisha, holding her face gently in his hands. "You told me that all energy needs a vessel. Asmodeus was such a vessel, wasn't he?"

Kellan could feel her tremble as she nodded and then spoke in words so soft that the slightest breeze would have carried them off, never to be heard, "and you broke it."

"And I broke it," Kellan repeated in agreement, then continued, "All energy needs a vessel so it came into me. How do I get rid of it?"

Her gaze was upstream where the glowing red stripe had seemed to slow in its approach while continuing to broaden, like a thickening red oil slick riding along the surface. Kellan shook her again and she turned. "Get rid of it?"

she asked perplexed, then spoke in her mantic staccato, "You cannot destroy it. Energy cannot be destroyed. Even God could not destroy it. It can only change forms. Only HE can do that!" Her eyes took on the same glaze of a moment before as she continued to rant, "Chaos and Order! Only He can channel them both. Chaos and Order are life. Only He can make life!"

"I'll stop it, Nurisha. I will. When it touched me, it barely hurt. If that entire streak of Chaotic energy hits you, it would be worse for you. It could kill you."

"Kill me?" she asked and then Kellan saw her countenance change, becoming calm and confident in blink of an eye. "Kill me." This time it was not a question. "Yes, it will kill me and in doing so, be itself destroyed." She caught herself. "Not destroyed—changed. We'll both be changed."

"What? Changed? I don't want you to be changed, Nurisha. I will deal with this. It is my mistake. I need to clean it up."

"No!" she said, her voice sounding like a whip, "It must be this way." Nurisha stared deeply into Kellan's eyes, her brows furrowed in worry. "That slight touch has already marked you; I see it in you even now. I will not allow the taint to increase by further contamination. Trust me, Sentinel, it will be better this—" She broke off as Kellan's eyes blazed to life and the liquid energy in which they stood began to swirl about him and into him. "What are you doing?" she asked.

Kellan tightened his grip on Nurisha's shoulders and placed a soft kiss on her forehead. "I'm sorry. I brought you into self awareness out of ignorance and narcissism. I will not allow you to be destroyed by the same." Kellan felt the power coursing through him as he heaved her far into the air while creating a gravity bubble around her. The two combined, causing her glowing form to be softly deposited on the far shore even as the wide ribbon of red energy struck Kellan. He shuddered at the shock.

He felt the energy course around him and through him. He felt it entering his mouth, eyes, and ears. There was something familiar about this new power—something that reminded him of the first time Micah had taught him to embrace the energy that fueled him. Yet, there was much different as well. This power was wild where his was structured. This power strained to rend and ruin, while his sought to mend and preserve.

Kellan doubled over in pain, letting out a primal scream as the two powers warred within him. In some distant corner of his mind, Kellan observed
himself dispassionately, assembling facts, looking for patterns, asking questions,
making hypotheses. It's what his mind did whether he was peacefully lying on a
beach or in what felt like the fight of his life. This small, seldom acknowledged,
piece of his mind is what first had made Kellan a person of interest to an Angel
who sought a successor. This was the essence of what it meant to be Kellan
Thorne. This quiet corner asserted itself now and, with deliberation, and he
felt his mind divide in two. As sometimes happens in dreams, Kellan pictured
himself looking down on the scene where he struggled waist deep in the raging
green torrent while red energy played about his body. Just in front him, stood
another Kellan, although somewhat stylized, with sharply angled ears. His other
self stood calmly atop the flowing energy, wearing a blue shirt, black pants, and
black boots. He held a small device which he pointed at Kellan and then looked
down, brow furrowed.

"You must stop the fighting," this other Kellan said.

"Who are you?" Kellan asked, and to his surprise the other Kellan glanced
upward to where Kellan seemed to be viewing the exchange, and arched one
eyebrow.

"Fascinating," said the other Kellan as it pointed its device into the air.

"It's not fucking fascinating. Who are you and why are you cosplaying Mr.
Spock?"

The other Kellan seemed to sigh. "I am the personification of your intellect
fueled, of course, by your rather prodigious eidetic gift. As for appearing as
Spock, I am as you made me, although I do believe the representation apt. All of
that is of little import. You must stop the fighting."

"What fighting? I'm not fighting anyone. I don't understand what you are
talking about," yelled Kellan with as much frustration as he could project.

Vulcan-Kellan sighed again, this time visibly, and tapped on what was now
obviously a vintage 1960s era Tricorder, then turned it so its small screen faced
where the other portion of Kellan's splintered mind was taking in the scene. On
it he saw two animated puppets attacking one another, each from their respective fortresses. The first had flaming red hair and threw endless balls of fire;

the other had hair made entirely of blue snow and met the attack with torrents of ice, which simply resulted in massive clouds of steam as the two forces met.

"Seriously?" asked Kellan of the vulcan, "A Rankin-Bass cartoon is how you choose to explain this to me? The Miser Brothers?"

Vulcan Kellan simply stared up, impassively. "I was trying to keep it simple for you. We don't have much time for you to figure out anything complex. You must stop them from fighting. The Chaotic and Order forces cannot coexist in their raw forms. You must change that form into something stable and you must do it." Vulcan Kellan paused, turning his tricorder back towards himself, tapping. "In about 30 seconds or the two forces will tear your body apart. You will die. This place will vanish. Nurisha will die. There is a seventy-five percent chance the resulting energy would destroy the place where your physical body currently stands. In that eventuality, both Michael and Raphael would also be destroyed. There is slightly less than a seven percent chance the unstructured release of all that unbalanced energy could create a universal atomic cascade at the sub quantum-quark level." The Vulcan seemed to catch himself. "Sorry, let me dumb that down for you. There would be a second Big Bang, destroying all life as you know it."

"Holy fuck!"

"Yes. Twenty seconds."

"Ok, you pointy-eared bastard," yelled Kellan, feeling his perspective shift so he was now staring directly at the Spock version of himself, "How do I make them stop fighting?"

"Channel them both. Energy cannot be destroyed. Those energies cannot exist together. You must force them to change form. Ten Seconds."

"How?!?"

"Isn't that obvious? You must create." With that, Vulcan Kellan unhooked a small device at his waist and Kellan heard it chirp as it was flipped open, "Kellan to Enterprise. One to beam up." A split second later as his form began to sparkle and fade, he raised one hand, fingers outspread. "Good Luck. Live Long and Prosper."

Kellan closed his eyes, opening himself to both energies, and feeling the familiar warmth as Order filled him. Chaos continued to rage, flashing and striking him like the sharpened end of a many tailed whip. He called to it, coaxed it, pleaded with it, but still the power ignored his will. Kellan felt the anger rising in him. He would not fail this way. "Obey me!" he screamed, stretching out his left hand, palm up. He felt the chaotic storm pause, then growled again, "Obey...me!" This time he felt all the energy flow out from him and gathered in his open palm like a blazing red sun, slowly rotating. As he moved to place his empty right hand palm up, Kellan felt the chaotic power begin to break apart. He glared at it.

"Remain!" It immediately subsided and silently rotated. Again Kellan lifted his right palm, and green energy flowed effortlessly up from the river, through him, and gathered as a rotating sphere.

Kellan stared at the two, as countless memories skittered across his consciousness gathered throughout his life from books, lectures, sermons, and conversations. He slowly brought his two hands together and felt the pressure like two opposing magnets. The respective energies fought his will to remain, but Kellan's will was inviolate. The young Sentinel spoke directly to the opposing forces of chaos and order he held in his hands. "Creation is order and chaos, preservation and ruin, life and death. It cannot exist without both and only with both can it be formed. By my will, I bring these forces together. By my will, I channel them!"

Kellan slammed both hands together and the two energies fused into a gleaming violet ball of sparkling energy. Then they exploded, ripping Kellan from his inner world to find both Raphael and Michael stepping backwards from him, hands up, shielding their eyes. Power flooded from the young Sentinel in waves as he held both hands outward toward the throne on which rested Asmodeus' corpse. Violet cords of power ripped through the body, shattered the throne, and buried themselves into the rocky ground. Kellan twisted his hands, placing them together as if making a bowl and lifted upward, arms shaking with the effort. Rocks shattered, flying upward as the ground split open to reveal a massive tree trunk sprouting from the hole. It thickened as it rose becoming so broad that ten men with arms outstreached could not embrace its trunk, and at least one hundred feet high. Michael and Raphael looked up in undisguised awe as foliage continued to appear and blossom, even as the energy ceased its flow and Kellan sank to his knees.

"I'm scared, Oren" came a small voice, causing Kellan to look up.

"Me too," came a second voice, "Where's mama?" The voices drifted down within the lowest branches of the massive tree Kellan had created.

Finally, a third voice joined the other two. "Nissa, Shaylee, I need you to be brave. I will find mama. Just let me get us down from here."

Kellan slowly stood and looked at the towering tree. Its dark brown bark seemed to gleam with interlacing scales that were almost iridescent. Graceful branches both thick and thin spread upward and out each covered with a multitude of leaves the like of which Kellan had never seen. They all were shaped like a five pointed star and shimmered purple in the even light of creation's workroom.

A young boy swung down from one of the lowest branches and landed on the ground with a thud. He started to brush himself off, then froze as he took in the sight of Kellan, Michael, and Raphael. The latter two had neither moved nor spoken. Kellan raised both hands and crouched down, trying to make the boy at ease.

"Hi Oren. I'm Kellan. Don't be scared. No one is going to hurt you. Are Nissa and Shaylee your sisters?"

Oren squinted at the three of them and brushed the dirt from his pants. He had sandy brown hair, high cheekbones, bright blue eyes, and seemed to be about eight years old. "I'm not scared of anything," he said, squaring his shoulders.

Kellan rose smiling. "Really? Well, you're certainly braver than me, because I'm pretty much terrified all the time lately. Maybe you can give me some lessons in courage."

Oren couldn't tell if he was being made fun of, but gave a shy smile back.

"How about we get your sisters down from there and then find your Mother?"

Oren brightened visibly. "You know my Mother? You know where she is?"

From within the leaves came two voices as one, "Can you bring mama here now?"

Kellan laughed and cupped his hands to mouth and yelled, "Hello there, tree faeries. Yes, I know you mother and will try and find her while my friends help you two down. You do want to come down, don't you?"

"Yes please," came the chorus.

"Well," said Kellan with mock impatience as he waved to Raphael and Michael, "Make yourselves useful. I need to find their mother."

Neither Angel moved.

"Go!" yelled Kellan, and Raphael flinched while Michael moved to grasp the hilt of is sword. Kellan looked at him. "Really, Michael?"

"You," began Michael, "You created and that—"

"Later. Please. Help those children. I have a promise to keep."

Kellan walked away from the tree and rested on the cracked stone bench. He closed his yes and concentrated, trying to secure his will to the image of the person he sought. He drew deep from the river of his power and felt his eyes warm as a portal rotated into view. Through it, Kellan could see the night sky and a dirt road with a lone traveler. She stood staring at him across distance, time, and realms. Kellan felt the smile spread across his face and tears blossomed in her eyes as she started running toward him. She leaped through the portal and Kellan caught her, keeping her steady on the rock strewn landscape.

His smile faded and eyes widened in alarm as he pushed the woman to the ground, lifting up his right hand, long sword forming instantly from green mist. The sound of metal on metal rang out loud as thunder as Michael's flaming sword struck Kellan's and their eyes locked: Kellan's filled with anger, Michael's with surprise.

"That is impossible. My sword was forged by God when creation was new. It cannot be stopped by a mortal blade."

"Try to keep up, Michael," said Kellan using his free hand to point at his brightly glowing eyes. "Not. Mortal. And where do you think I got this sword? The Magic Claw at the arcade with a lucky quarter? I'm guessing it came from the same guy that made yours, so," Kellan lowered his voice menacingly "back the fuck off. I've already killed one Archangel today."

Michael glared but sheathed his sword and took two steps back, staring down at the woman. He gave Kellan a patronizing look.

"You realize, she is a D——"

Kellan interrupted as he helped her up. "D...amsel in distress? Friend in need of help? Someone who gave me the insight I needed to drive a sword through Asmodeus in the one place in all of creation where he could be utterly destroyed? She has a name, and it's Amy."

"Mama!" came a chorus of yells as Raphael approached with Oren, Nissa, and Shaylee in tow. She opened her arms and all three ran into her embrace while Kellan turned to look again at Michael, speaking softly.

"Is your first instinct to just kill everything?"

For his part, Michael actually looked contrite as Raphael asked, "What did he do?"

"Oh, nothing much, just tried to kill Amy in front of her kids."

"Amy?" asked Raphael, "That's Lamia. She is a high demon of the first fall, Kellan."

Kellan sighed and pointed at them both. "You two. You two are racists or whatever the equivalent term is. I'll tell you one thing. AMY has been much nicer on the whole than the Terminator here. She's only tried to kill me once and that's because she didn't know any better."

Kellan felt something tug at his hip and turned to see a small girl of about six staring up at him while holding the hand of her younger sister. They looked like twins born two years apart, pale skin with freckles across nose and cheek. Bright blue eyes sparkled up at him and both had hair so blonde it almost appeared almost white.

Kellan crouched down so he was at eye level. "Are you Shaylee?"

"No, I'm Nissa." She lifted the hand gripping her sister's and gave it a little tug. "This is Shaylee. Mama says we are supposed to thank you for finding us. She says you kept your promise and keeping promises is really important."

Kellan smiled and stared at each girl in turn. "You are both quite welcome. Nissa, Shaylee, you remember what your mother said about promises because she is absolutely right."

Oren walked up and stuck out a hand. "I wanted to thank you too. I'm sure I could have gotten my sisters back home, but it was nice of you to help."

Kellan accepted the boys offered hand and gripped it warmly. "I'm sure you would have had them home safe and sound, Oren. We just maybe saved you a bit of time is all and you are most welcome."

Kellan looked up at Amy to find her smiling at him and then tilted her head in the direction of the tree. He turned to Raphael. "I'm going to have a quick chat with Amy before she leaves. Please make sure he doesn't kill anyone?"

"I do not kill children," growled Michael.

"Whatever," said Kellan, following Amy toward the tree, then over his shoulder, "Tell that to Pharaoh."

"That wasn't..." his voice was lost as Kellan caught up with Amy and she leaned against the tree looking up.

"Asmodeus?"

"Dead. You were right. In this place he had no means to stay connected to the source of his power. Once he had expended it, he became vulnerable."

She nodded contemplatively. "He held tremendous power. How did you manage to get him to expend that energy so recklessly?"

Kellan smiled. "That was the easy part. I just had to be myself and it made him want to kill me—like really want to kill me."

Amy ran her hand along the gleaming bark. "And this?"

"That's a longer story. The short version is: I created it."

Her eyes widened and she shook her head sadly, "What do Raphael and Michael have to say about that? They can't be happy."

"Well, Michael is never happy and he will probably think the best solution is to kill me because that's his solution to everything. Raphael just seems in shock, so we'll have to talk it out."

Amy stepped close, placed a hand on Kellan chest, and looked up at him. "I'm serious, Kellan. This magnificent tree is the first spontaneous creative act since, well, Creation. And you did it. No one can create but God. Well, no one is *supposed* to be able to create, but God. Just be careful, please."

"Amy, it's not like I can go around creating things willy nilly. I'm not God and I have no desire to be. All that power was expended to create a tree that none but us will ever see. The power is all gone."

"That kind of power is seldom all gone, Kellan," she cut off as Raphael approached.

The Angel nodded to Amy. "Lamia…" then turned to Kellan, "There are things we must discuss and Lamia's children seem anxious to depart as well."

"Ok, Raphael, we were just finishing up anyway." The three walked back to the broken bench to find Michael, his back to them, entertaining the children with minor acts of Angelic magic.

Kellan cleared his throat and Michael immediately stood and glared at the young Sentinel, who smiled broadly. "Too late, I saw you doing something nice."

Amy embraced Kellan tightly and he promised to visit them all at some point. Nissa and Shaylee each gave him hugs and kisses while Oren again offered another strong handshake and a nod. Moments later, the four had passed through a portal, leaving Kellan alone with the two grim faced Angels.

"You killed an Archangel," Raphael said again, "You cannot do that."

Kellan sighed. "Archdemon and, Raphael, I do not think that word means what you think it means. I did it, therefore, I can do it. Maybe you mean that 'I mayn't' do it or maybe that 'I shouldn't' do it."

"He means," began Michael, "that you should not have been able to do it at all and even if you could do it, yes, you should not have." Michael then turned to Raphael. "I told you he was not the right mortal for this role."

Raphael just shook his head. Kellan said, "I'm right here. Don't talk about me like I'm just some hairless ape that cannot understand what the brilliant Archangel has to say."

"Fine!" said Michael, standing and looking down on Kellan who did his best not to feel intimidated. "You killed an Archangel and could have ended all of creation. Does that sound like an endeavor you should have taken up?"

"Well, when you put it that way," said Kellan, "but look at it from my perspective. First, he was an asshole and I give you stealing Amy's kids and killing her husband as exhibit A. Second, he's the dude that recruited Maurius who, by the by, tried to kill me several times just this week. Third, he tried to kill me himself and nearly succeeded too. In fact, I think we should all chalk this up to good ol' self defense and call it a day."

Kellan thought he could almost hear the sound of Michael grinding his teeth in anger and could definitely feel heat coming off the Angel in waves as Raphael stood and placed a placating hand on his shoulder. Michael shoved it off and crouched down to be eye level with Kellan. "Asmodeus was the second most powerful Angel that fell. Can you guess how much Chaotic energy he held? Where is that energy now?"

Kellan shrugged. "I guess it's in that tree. I channeled it and the tree appeared."

"You *created*, Kellan Thorne. You killed an Archangel, and used that appropriated Chaotic power to channel with that of Order and *created*. Mortals do not create. Angels do not create. Demons do not create. We are the created, not the creator."

Raphael stepped in again. "Please, calm yourself. I do not believe that Kellan has any more creative acts planned—is not that correct?"

"Of course not and besides, I couldn't if I tried. After all that violet energy burned itself out, I went back to check on Nurisha and confirmed it was all gone. There is no more red energy and therefore you two have nothing to worry about. It's not like I'm going to try and gank a bunch of fallen Angels because I've developed a taste for creating trees. Besides, I'm not the mass demon killer here—seems that job is already taken."

Raphael turned to Michael. "Satisfied?"

The other Angel gave a snort of derision. "Hardly, but this is the best one could hope for. Let us pray his wisdom begins to grow faster than his capacity for folly." With that, Michael turned, gestured, and walked through a portal which winked closed behind him.

Raphael sighed and sat down beside Kellan on the broken bench. Kellan put his arm around the Angel and gave him a squeeze. "So, am I all that you hoped I would be?" he asked with a smile.

To his utter surprise, Raphael turned to him, grinning as Kellan had never seen him do before and said, "Oh yes, Kellan Thorne, you have most certainly surpassed even my most optimistic hopes. I cannot wait to tell Micah. He will float his lid."

Kellan laughed. "Flip his lid—not float his lid. Dork. Remember to pass him my message when you see him."

"Flip his lid," Raphael repeated somberly, "And yes, I will remember."

Chapter 11

EPILOGUE

"No, I'm tellin' ye, the werewolves ran along on all fours when they got to goin', and were far more beast than man. I don'na know where ye be gettin' yer lore from lassie but it's straight up wrong. Now let me explain something else to—"

Kellan lifted his glass and swirled it watching the amber liquid spin as the ice cubes made soft clinks that served to help drown out Hamish's Shannon-directed diatribe. He took a long pull from his glass and closed his eyes.

All things considered, it had been a pretty good few weeks. He hadn't been killed by netherworld shape-shifters, got granted super powers, met a super-hot redheaded Scotswoman who seemed really into him, and killed a prince of hell. A very solid month.

The shop door bell jangled as James ignored the "closed" sign and let himself in. He clapped both hands together and approached the small gathering of friends. "I'm here, so let's get this party started. Where we going for dinner?"

"Fickle Pickle!" shouted Juliet.

"Adel's," added Meghan.

"I don't much care," said Shannon, "as long as I can have pizza. I really—"

"love pizza," came a chorus from all those assembled.

"Well, I do," confirmed Shannon in her lilting accent.

"I want to go to Mac McGee's," said Hamish, slamming his hand on a table.

"Good, go there," said James, "This is a private gathering of friends to celebrate Meghan's new job. Just because you are always here, Hamish, doesn't mean you get to come. Go home or go to Mac McGee's, but just go somewhere."

Kellan finally opened his eyes and took in the scene. James stood at the far end of the reading nook wearing a crisp purple shirt and jeans, both of which were impeccably tailored to his athletic frame. Everyone else was sprawled in varying degrees of sloth poses in the deep leather chairs and sofas that comprised the reading nook. Juliet sat crosswise, sipping a Coke, leaning against one overstuffed armrest while the crooks of her knees rested on the other. Kellan was reasonably sure she had spiked her soda with some of the Jamaican rum he kept in his office. Megan and Shannon both occupied the love seat and had been laughing softly about something just before James arrived. From the guilty look on Meghan's face, Kellan assumed that Shannon had deftly pried yet another of his past transgressions out of his friend. His suspicions were confirmed by the flat expression Shannon wore as her eyes locked with his, and she gave him a subtly disapproving shake of the head.

"Who's buying dinner?" Kellan finally asked, "Because if I'm picking up the tab, we're going to McDonalds."

James walked over and picked up a clean glass from the small table next to Kellan, on which sat both a decanter of Scotch and an ice bucket. He dropped in a few cubes and poured three fingers.

"Stop," said Kellan as his friend was about to take a sip, "That's really old scotch and very expensive."

"I'm worth it," James replied with a grin and, again, lifted the glass to his lips again.

"Stoppp," Kellan said, "I'll make a deal with you."

James looked wary, but lowered the glass. "What kind of deal?"

"On your honor, if that's not the best scotch you've ever tasted, I'll buy everyone dinner at Adel's." Kellan raised a finger. "But, if it is the best tasting scotch you've ever tasted, you will buy us all dinner at Little Alley Steaks."

James made a quick count of the room. "That's like a thousand dollars, Kel, and that's assuming we don't let Hamish get sloppy drunk on expensive wine."

"Oh, so I am coming," said Hamish.

"Ok, I'll sweeten the pot," added Kellan with a smile, "I will also give you a full bottle of the scotch for you to take home. Again, you only will pay if it's the best you've ever tasted. Deal?"

James considered for a moment, staring at his glass. "And you trust me to answer honestly?"

"Of course. You are a gentleman and a friend. I trust you completely."

"Oh, shut up, Kel. Fine. I accept your deal." James took an exploratory sip form the glass and Kellan smiled as his friend's eyes widened. James took another, longer, pull from the glass and slowly shook his head. "Oh my god, Kellan, that is amazing. What is it and where the fuck did you get it? Oh, sorry Juliet."

Juliet just leaned her head back so she was viewing James upside down and waggled the fingers of her free hand to dismiss his profanity, grinning. *Definitely rum in that Coca Cola.* Kellan shook his head, clearing away the thought, and turned back to look at his friend.

"Well," Kellan began drawing out the word, "If you really want to know, I'll tell you, but it won't help you much."

"Yes, I really want to know."

"I have a cask of it. It's from a special clan Macallan batch, distilled in 1824 and aged until 1974."

James' mouth fell open. "That's 150 years."

"Your math skills continue to astound, mon frer."

James ignored him. "Dude, the 64 year old Macallan went for over 400k."

Kellan waved him off. "That was a charity auction and probably at least half of that price was because of the Lalique decanter in came in."

"La-What?"

"LaLique. It's a fine crystal that the Macallan 64 was—"

"Blah blah blah. Whatever. The point is you can't afford to buy us dinner, I don't see you kicking in for even a 100k bottle of scotch. Wait, what? You said you had a cask of this stuff. A whole bloody cask? That's like two hundred bottles."

"Two hundred fifty seven 70cl bottles to be exact."

James took another drink and poured a bit more in his glass. "Two hundred fifty seven?"

"Two hundred fifty seven, including the one you keep pouring from."

"Of this exact scotch?"

"Yes."

"And I can have a case if I buy dinner?"

"A bottle. And only if you admit it is the best you have ever tasted."

"Half a case and it is definitely the best I've ever tasted."

"Two bottles, and you go wait for our table to be ready."

"Deal," exclaimed James. He turned to leave, then paused, "How did you get a whole cask of one hundred fifty year old Macallan? That's insane dude."

Kellan smiled. "It was actually pretty easy. I traveled back in time to 1824 and went to Easter Ellochy House where The Macallan was founded. Delightful people. I gave them four hundred Francs. Ten, forty Franc Charles X gold coins to be exact and they agreed to distill and age a private cask until 1974 at which point they would bottle it and then have it shipped to this very store where it arrived safe and sound only yesterday."

James gave his friend a flat look, drained his glass, and set it on the table with an overly loud thud. "Fine, be a dick and don't tell me. I don't really care, but the deal is two bottles of this same stuff. I'll text you when the table's ready. C'mon, Hamish, you can wait with me since you've weaseled your way into a free meal."

Everyone stared silently as the two men left, James swaying ever so slightly, then all turned to Kellan.

"What? He asked," said Kellan innocently.

"You are an idiot, boss," said Juliet. Shannon and Meghan nodded their agreement.

"He's your best friend," added Meghan, "You should tell him the truth."

"I did tell him the truth," responded Kellan.

"You know what I mean."

Kellan sighed. "I do know what you mean, and I'm not telling him—at least not now." He paused before continuing, "I know it's selfish and wrong, but I need him to be my touchstone to normalcy. With James, I'm just a dude and we can drink beer and make jokes without any of this weird shit. I'm sorry, but I need that right now. Is that so wrong?"

"No, it's not wrong, Kel," said Meghan, "Trust me, I get it. Just be prepared for the day he does find out. He's gonna be hurt you didn't tell him."

Juliet nodded, and Shannon got up and walked over to Kellan. She folded herself into the chair with him, resting on his lap. She smiled at him and leaned in, whispering something softly in his ear.

Kellan pushed himself out of the chair, dumping Shannon unceremoniously to the floor in the process, and swept his gaze to the other women—both of whom wore amused expressions, "I'm going to shave in my office. Maybe you two can give the Highlander here a lesson in 21st century empathy." He turned back to Shannon, who had simply swiveled her legs to sit crosswise on the floor. She looked up, showing her teeth. "As for you," he continued, "No, they don't have pizza at Little Alley. It's a steak house. They have steak there—deal with it."

A moment later, all three heard the distant sound of a door slamming and the room dissolved into giggles.

Kellan rubbed his face again, fingers searching out any last traces of missed stubble. Finding none, he set his Braun razor in its cleaning station and pressed the glowing blue button, causing the little device to whir and gurgle.

The young Sentinel stared at his reflection and thought he looked older somehow, but couldn't immediately place it. Maybe the eyes. He leaned closer to the mirror and looked deeply into his own eyes.

"Uh oh, that's probably not good," Kellan said to himself. Around the light blue iris and encircling his entire pupil, lay a distinct thin ring of dark violet.

Kellan backed away and grinned at himself. "Oh well, a problem for another day. Tonight…steak!"

The end of Sentinels of Creation: A Power Renewed

AUTHOR'S BIO

Robert W. Ross has spent the last twenty five years spinning stories and user journeys into web, mobile, and social experiences for brands ranging from the obscure to the iconic.

He has both a passion for pop culture and a deep loathing to discuss himself in the third person. However, his wife convinced him that anyone who took the time to reach the last page of his book might want to know a little about the person who wrote it.

To that end, Robert's influences include authors such as Robert A. Heinlein, Phillip Jose Farmer, and Brandon Sanderson. He has a deep and abiding love for all things Star Trek, Doctor Who, and Sponge Bob. While Robert can often make obscure TV, Book, and Movie references, he sadly lacks Kellan's eidetic memory. He is quite sure the brain space taken up by all that trivia is directly responsible for his lacking any sense of direction.

Sentinels of Creation: A Power Renewed, is Robert's first published novel and he is already hard at work on the second book of the series. He lives in Atlanta with his wife of over twenty years, their kids, two Siberian Huskies, and about 11 different Apple products.

<<<<>>>>

Made in the USA
San Bernardino, CA
20 March 2016